SACRIFICIAL LAMB CLUB

Kim Cormack

Copyright © 2023 Kim Cormack
All rights reserved
Mythomedia Press 2754 10th Ave,
V9Y2N9, Port Alberni, BC
childrenofankh.com
kimcormack.com

Dedications

Souls must be broken to be built. Hardships make us stronger. We endure violence, grieve broken hearts and persevere. We're all survivors of something. The end of one story is only the beginning of another.

This book is for the ever-evolving survivours. You fight tragedies with laughter and resolve. You gain wisdom through adversity. It feels like life is a test and you're failing but it's kind of hilarious. Somehow you keep standing up every time you're knocked down. This is who you are. It's what you've become. This is what it means to be a Dragon.

Thank you to my spawn. Jace and Cam you mean everything to me. I set out to raise good humans. I wake each day and go to sleep every night knowing you are my greatest accomplishment.

To my Mom and Dad, you are my light in each day. Thank you for your love and support.

Thank you to my awesome editors, Haley and Leanne. You have supported this dream since the beginning. Thank you for all you do. To my universe

Arc Team. Thank you for jumping onboard. To those extra awesome readers who buy a book and follow through with reviews, thank you so much for diving down my rabbit hole, and supporting my field of dreams.

Happy Reading

A Memorial For A Shiny Thing

A few weeks before the release of Sacrificial Lamb Club, my ex-husband and youngest son's Dad passed away. We've been divorced since Cam was little. He just graduated from high school. It's been a long time. His Dad was going through a difficult time. After really no holds barred talking things out with him, a lot of healing was done on my end. We'd found a semblance of low-key friendship, for Cam's sake. I hoped he'd heal enough to do the same with everyone else. He was a shiny thing. Digging through memories today, I'm trying to focus on the good. 'Don't Want To Miss A Thing' by Aerosmith was our Vegas wedding song in 2003. There were sterling roses and the cheesiest wedding video. I got picked out of the lineup at Studio 54, and he got stuck in the line that night. I left him there for ten minutes because his ego needed a pat down. It was hilarious.

 We were magic for a heartbeat. Man, could he make me laugh. We were so beautiful and young. I haven't looked at these pictures since we split up. I had them put away for Cam. Perhaps there's just been enough distance and time to put the pain of it to rest. I wish healing for his current wife, his family and my son, who was getting to know his Dad. If you know someone struggling, reach out to them.

A MEMORIAL FOR A SHINY THING

You gave me Cam, and I will always be grateful for that. Rest easy, shiny thing.

Till we meet again, Jackson.

Fun Goa Series Quotes

She was a murderer, a psychopath and a victim. She was all three of those things.

Broken to fulfil an immortal destiny, she was granted a second chance as a hitman for a Clan of immortals. They needed to create a Dragon. Her sanity was collateral damage.

She was an unapologetically feral hit woman for a Clan of immortals and sometimes just a girl in love with a boy destined to be her Handler. The only thing standing between them was cannibalism and intimacy-induced amnesia. What could go wrong?

Endearing antiheroes, titillating dark fantasy warriors and a heartbreaking, magical tale of survival against insurmountable odds. This will be unlike anything you've ever read.

Procreation is illegal under immortal law. You've triggered a Correction. They are coming to erase your family line. If you impress the

FUN COA SERIES QUOTES

Guardians of the in-between with bravery during your demise, you may be granted a second chance as a sacrificial lamb for the greater good in Tri-Clan. In your eighteenth year, you will enter Immortal Testing. Like rats in a maze of nightmares, you must come out mentally intact after being murdered in thousands of creative ways.

Fun Tri-Clan Lingo

Correction: The scheduled assassination of partially immortal offspring and their genetic line.

First-Tier: Mortal.

Second-Tier: Half-Breed.

Third-Tier: Both parents are immortal.

Guardian: Three Guardians created each Clan of immortals. Beings from the in-between. They may grant you a second chance as a sacrificial lamb for the greater good. You must join Tri-Clan for protection.

Tri-Clan: Ankh, Trinity and Triad are the three Clans of Immortals on Earth. Your Clan will brand you, prohibiting entry to the hall of souls. Each time you die, you return to the clean slate desert of the in-between to await your resurrection.

FUN TRI-CLAN LINGO

Crypts: Homebase for each Clan, scattered all over the world.

Sealed: At eighteen, you become sealed to your Clan forever.

Attaching a Testing Group: All the newest members of each Clan train for Testing. After reaching the age of eighteen, they enter a hellscape challenge in another world. They may lose one to trauma if they haven't formed solid attachments, trapping everyone's souls in endless torment.

Immortal Testing: A floating Crypt the size of New York City, containing your worst nightmares where you must die thousands of times to prove your partially mortal brain can withstand the trials of immortality. Three Clans enter and race for the Amber room. Only the first two will be set free. The third remains lost in their worst nightmares.

Tombs: If you survive the Testing, you have earned your own healing tomb generated from your Clan's stone. For example, Clan Ankh is rose quartz, Triad is jade, and Trinity is sapphire.

Dragons: There are green scaly Dragons in this series, but in most cases, the word Dragon refers to the ability to turn off emotions. Lexy is the Dragon of Clan Ankh. A Dragon is used as an assassin.

Handler: A spiritual connection used to pull a Dragon out of the darkness

Dear Mortals & Second-Tier Spawn

The information within this universe is not intended for mere mortals. Reading this may inadvertently trigger your Correction. If you show bravery during your demise, the Guardians of the In-between may give you a second chance. You are still reading this, aren't you? You've got this.

Trigger Warnings

Everything. You must be broken to be built in this universe, and by broken, I mean rocking in a corner demolished. It's about evolving your soul. There are stages to becoming truly immortal.

All heroes are born out of the embers that linger after the fire of great tragedy.

Both series are in the same universe. There is an entire universe of books with these characters to keep you occupied until the next release. Watch trailers, see links to my social media, sign up for the newsletter, and find out what Clan you'd be in on the universe website childrenofankh.com.

I'd be releasing books much faster if I wasn't wearing so many hats. In a perfect world I'd just be lost in my fantasy world writing and handing it off to someone else. Please remember to review the universe and tell your friends. Help my field of dreams be discovered.

Happy Reading,
KD Cormack

TRIGGER WARNINGS

Retail wholesale Ingram
1-800-9378200
customerservice@ingrambook.com

1
Dragon Snacks

Torn between missing falling asleep in her Handler's arms and having the freedom to move on, Lexy stared at the ceiling. *She'd bedded her enemy right under everyone's noses. She wasn't sure how she felt about it. She'd believed it was a naughty dream until she saw what he'd left behind. She couldn't keep doing this. He'd crossed a line. He couldn't just show up in the middle of the night.* About to close her eyes, someone pounded on her hotel room door. Lexy leapt up, tugged on pants and peered through the peephole. *When their Oracle showed up this early it was time sensitive.* Letting go of the fantasy of a few hours' sleep, she opened the door.

Jenna announced, "Surprise job. Grab your things. I'll meet you in the lobby. To avoid sneak attack spoilers, Kayn needs to be taken out of the equation. Stop by their room and snap your sister's neck. Tell Frost to grab whatever he needs. We have no idea how long we'll be separated."

These were the days of our afterlives. Lexy sighed, "I have no idea where Grey is."

"Your Handler is waiting in the truck with the engine

running," Jenna affirmed, tossing Lexy a bracelet. "That should block your thoughts for the duration of the trip. For the record, teleportation booty calls with enemies are frowned upon."

Nobody snuck anything past their Oracle. Teleportation explained it. She'd been wondering how Tiberius showed up out of nowhere and vanished. "Guess I'll kill Kayn, collect Frost and meet you in the lobby," Lexy answered, walking away. *How did he solidify after teleporting? She vaguely recalled him mentioning Triad's Guardian, Seth. Her absentee bio dad.* Slipping on the thought blocking bracelet before reaching their door, she rhythmically knocked. Conveniently, Kayn answered. *Perfect.* Lexy snapped her neck. Her sister's shell flopped to the floor. *She really had to start looking through peepholes.*

Groggily getting up, Frost complained, "What in the hell?"

"We have a job. Kayn's compromised. Grab your things. Ask Jenna what happened when we get to the lobby," Lexy prompted, smiling at the state of the room. *They weren't getting a damage deposit back.*

Kneeling, Frost kissed Kayn's forehead, whispering, "Miss you already, Brighton.

They sprinted to the lobby. Marching over to Ankh's Oracle, Frost insisted, "Explain."

"Kevin was trying to convince Kayn to stop us from taking a girl he has a thing for," Jenna disclosed.

Confused, Frost probed, "When? We've been in bed for hours."

Walking towards the door, Jenna revealed, "While you were sleeping."

Frost stormed off, cursing. Lexy commented, "Working with him should be fun. What's the job?"

"You're stealing a Venom girl from Triad," Jenna declared. "How strong are your feelings? Are you compromised?"

"It's not like that," Lexy stated, irritated.

Passing her jacket, Jenna urged, "Keep it that way. He's Triad, you're Ankh. You can't trust him."

She wasn't discussing this. She was still pissed at herself. Zipping up her jacket, Lexy stepped out into the frigid Alaskan air. *So cold.* She glanced back when she noticed Jenna wasn't coming.

Jenna explained, "I have to keep Kayn down until your job is finished. We need a Venom in our group before Testing. Get the girl."

Nodding, Lexy rushed out to the truck with the engine idling and got in, avoiding her Handler's gaze. Markus' crew pulled out behind them. *The boss was coming.*

As they drove away, Lily fiddled with the music. Grey playfully swatted her hand, toying, "Driver's choice."

Frost was in the backseat fuming. He caught her looking and stated, "If Kevin's there, I'm kicking his ass."

Tiberius might be there. She'd despised him for so long, and now, he was a hedonistic addiction. Every time they crossed paths, it hurt her connection with her Handler. Grey was still ignoring her. It was a good thing their Oracle gave her an extra line of thought blocking defence with this bracelet. That illicit hook up was all she could think about.

Fantasizing while watching snow fall, hours passed in the blink of an eye. They pulled up at a seedy bar attached to a motel.

Glancing back, Grey cautioned, "You can't get sidetracked."

Meeting his eyes, Lexy responded, "I know." *It felt like he didn't trust her. She wasn't even sure she trusted herself.* Music blared in the parking lot as they got out.

Markus instructed, "Lexy, distract Tiberius while we search for the girl. Lily and Frost compel the mortals to leave. Grey, stay out of the way."

Trying to stop herself from grinning, Lexy strutted to the door.

At her side, Grey commented, "Funny."

Lily was lecturing Frost about his plans to kick Kevin's ass.

3

Luring Tiberius into a room to have her way with him, might be difficult with Grey as her wingman. She was excited to see him. This was crazy. They couldn't be anything.

Orin caught up, saying, "I'm with you guys."

Oh, perfect. Her Handler and her ex booty call. Way to go, Markus.

They walked into the seedy bar. Triad was dancing with locals. Lexy's eyes scanned the room. Tiberius was at a booth with a girl.

"Here we go," Grey mumbled.

She was an idiot. She'd romanticised their encounters. He was on a date. It hadn't even been twenty-four hours since he showed up in her room. Oh, she was going to kill him. She was going to rip every appendage off his body. It was on. Enraged, Lexy snatched a tray out of a server's hands, stormed over and smoked Tiberius in the face with it. The echoing clang caught Triad's attention.

"Guess a sneak attack's out," Orin remarked, grinning.

In a heartbeat, the bar erupted into a deep south no holds barred brawl. His fling fled. Enraged, Lexy cursed, "You pathetic piece of shit!"

Tiberius provoked, "I was bored," scrambling under the table to escape.

Chasing him through the drunken bar fight, Lexy dodged a flying chair. She tossed everyone who got in her way.

Swinging at Kevin of Triad, Frost shouted, "Who creeps into their ex's head while they're in bed with another guy?"

Manoeuvring out of his way, Kevin bantered, "You can't even begin to comprehend our friendship, you slutty sociopath."

Orin smoked Kevin with a chair. Frost leapt on Kevin before he regained his bearings, choking him out, yelling, "I'm not a sociopath, you little prick!"

Bulking up into a beastly Shifter, Stephanie of Triad came to his rescue. Frost soared into a flock of wasted patrons as Kevin scrambled away.

Lexy ducked as another chair came sailing her way and

smashed on the hardwood. Momentarily sidetracked, a Triad shanked her with a broken bottle, triggering her healing ability. Heat was all she felt battling her way through the immortal throw down. *She lost Tiberius in the fight. Where was he?* Scanning the crowd, she saw him flee through swinging doors. Forcing her way through scrapping immortals, Lexy burst into a kitchen and grabbed a butcher knife as Tiberius sprinted out. She chased him down a hallway. He dove into a room, slamming and locking the door. *Oh, he was a dead man.* Lexy booted the door open and ducked as a vase narrowly missed her. *Dick!*

Chuckling, Tiberius apologised, "Baby, I can explain."

Strutting over, Lexy coldly countered, "No need. I'm just going to tear you a new asshole and get on with my week."

"Shit," Tiberius laughed, tossing whatever he could find at her. He dove into the adjoining room. Pursuing him, serial killer casual, Lexy dodged everything he pitched to slow her down.

Her Handler blocked Tiberius from escaping out the door. Grey decked Triad's leader, saying, "I needed that." Grinning, he shut the door, leaving them alone.

Backing away, Tiberius flirtatiously provoked, "You're sexy as hell when you're angry. Lock the door, I need to be punished."

Her Handler was outside. Lexy taunted, "Thank you for making it easier to do my job."

"I've fantasized about this so many times. Baby, I knew you were coming. There's no need to murder me," Tiberius brazenly seduced like he stood a chance.

Lust smouldered in his eyes as she pinned him against the wall. Clutching a butcher knife, Lexy decreed, "Thank you for clarifying where we stand. This makes everything less complicated."

"Does it? You have feelings for me. You wouldn't care about any of this if you didn't," Tiberius pressed, gazing into her eyes.

"I guess you'll never know," she answered.

"Punish me," he seduced, staring at her chest. "You know how I feel about you. That was nothing."

Pressing the blade against his throat, Lexy whispered, "We're nothing. It's easier this way." With her lips a breath from his, she confessed, "I saw this night going in a different direction." *He was turned on. Damn it, so was she.*

"Fuck me or kill me. Make up your mind," he dared, groaning as Lexy pressed her body against his.

Caressing between his legs, she pushed him closer to the edge, vowing, "Oh, I'm going to kill you."

"Baby undo my pants," he moaned.

She slit his throat and left him gurgling, bleeding out on the floor.

"I didn't need to see that," her Handler commented.

Shit. Lexy turned to find Grey standing there, watching.

Disguising how turned on she was, Lexy tried to shove past, baiting, "Which part?"

Holding his ground, Grey confessed, "All of it. Everything. Are you insane?"

"Probably," she decreed, wanting to leave.

"Tell me it's over and I'll let it go," Grey asserted, blocking her route.

This was how it always was. Every time his feelings for her resurfaced, she moved heaven and earth for a night in his arms. He was spelt to forget. In the morning, she'd be friend zoned. She couldn't do this right now. She was turned on and confused. Lexy sighed, "I've had a shitty night, Greydon. Can we reschedule this lecture?"

"My night sucked too, Lex. I watched you do that. You can't have feelings for him," her Handler pressed.

"It's not an issue anymore," Lexy countered. "It's over, done. I killed him. Get out of my way. We have a job to finish."

Reaching for her, Grey persisted, "Even if I forget, you know I love you. Use me. Be with me."

They'd been playing this game for too many decades. Clutching the knife, Lexy warned, "Last chance. Get out of my way."

Firmly standing his ground like a dumbass, her Handler said, "You won't hurt me."

"I will," Lexy pledged, bubbling over with rage.

Gazing into her eyes, Grey whispered, "You won't."

Damn it, she couldn't. She could kill herself to make a point. She wasn't the only Healer on this job. Raising the knife to her own chest, she threatened, "Get out of my way. I swear, I'll do it." Shaking his head, Grey stepped out of her way. Lexy stormed out into the hall, heard multiple whooshes, and looked down at way too many arrows in her torso. *Shit. Trinity joined the party.* Looking back at Grey, her vision flickered as she went down.

Twitching her fingers in the warm silken sand of the in-between, Lexy grinned as she squinted in blinding light. *No Pina Colada for her, she had company.* Getting up, Lexy noticed she was the only deceased Ankh. *This was embarrassing.*

Attached to the multi-hued cerulean sky by luminescent light in a flowing ivory gown, Ankh's Guardian reprimanded, "You're usually the last one dead. Explain." Azariah motioned for her to follow.

She already knew. She could see it in her eyes. Lexy confessed, "Trinity sneak attack. I was distracted."

"Let's have a chat about why Handlers and Dragons shouldn't fornicate," Azariah teased as they strolled through the white sand desert.

There were lots of shells in the sand. If she picked one up it would quench her thirst for chaos. A wave would appear like a blinding wall of pain and wash her sins away. With her crimson locks shimmering in eternal sunshine, Lexy confessed, "It's like living in limbo. The love that connects us, tortures us. Every time I try to move on, Grey panics and pulls me back in. I love him too much to turn him away."

"You aren't the innocent party. You push buttons to bring him back. Your ability to supersede our rules may have something to do with your Guardian paternity. His memory wipe is supposed to last years," Azariah scolded. "You signed up for an eternity as a sacrificial lamb for the greater good. You have a job to do. Your relationship drama needs to be stifled. We don't care how you do it. Shift your romantic focus elsewhere or erase him. It's painful, but essential. This fling with Tiberius is causing damage to your Handler bond. Be more discreet or cut it off."

Walking in sandy womb like warmth, Lexy agreed, "Fine."

Ankh's Guardian clapped her hands, and they were on a cliff overlooking a clay ravine. *She loved training new Ankh here.* This was where they made newbies hold hands and jump. Everyone knew they couldn't stop while holding hands. They went splat in the ravine until someone let go. That's how they found the weakest link. When they went into Testing, they had to stay together, or they wouldn't be able to get out. She rather enjoyed creating bonds through trauma. Once the pregnant one had her baby, they'd begin training this new group of Ankh. Lexy peered over the edge. *Shit, they needed a Venom to put them to sleep. Trinity was there.* Lexy enquired, "We lost the girl to Trinity, didn't we?"

Strolling off the edge like there was an invisible bridge, Ankh's Guardian paused in mid-air, she turned and changed the subject, "Your presence has been requested in the Third-Tier Realm. Amar, from the other continent is your backup. He'll meet you there. It may be good to have a break from your Handler. The Aries group is transporting your shell. It'll be there when you come out. My brother uncorking your Guardian abilities early may work out in our favour. You're going to need them. It's a trap. The King of the Third-Tier Realm will try to capture you. You have an impressive grasp on pausing time. That's all you'll need to make your dominance clear."

"If we know it's a trap, why am I going? I've only stopped time by fluke," Lexy admitted.

"Knowing something is going to happen alters the odds of any situation. We have time to prepare. I can teach you everything you need to know about being Guardian in five seconds."

Well, now she was curious. "I'll bite," Lexy laughed. "Give me your five second wisdom."

"Intention," Azariah decreed like she'd given her a golden ticket.

Grinning, Lexy repeated, "Intention, that's it?"

"Test it out. Join me. Step off the cliff," Azariah prompted.

"Explain intention first," Lexy sparred.

Their Guardian stated, "Have faith you can do it."

"Why?" Lexy questioned, curious.

"Stopping a bullet to protect Grey was instinctual. I'll give you a visual. She waved her hand and a black, swirling vortex appeared. "That's where you need to go. Believe you can walk out here. You have the genetics for portal travel. Walk through it. Amar is waiting for you."

This was the training she needed to not be captured by a Third-Tier King? Just walk off a cliff and step into an ominous portal. This was super dumb.

"Keep thinking like that and you'll fall," Azariah teased.

She knew how to stop herself if she fell. Why not? Lexy stepped off the ledge and plummeted towards an unforgiving ravine floor. In a flash of light, she was on the cliff ledge.

"Faith isn't knowing what to do when something goes wrong. It's choosing something, believing there's no other outcome," Azariah lectured.

She was being held up by that ray of light.

"This may take a while," their Guardian laughed, strolling

back to solid ground. "Come, I'll explain this from another angle."

Lexy followed her away. *Yes, dumb it down. I spent my puberty in in a barn stall held captive by demons. High school was replaced by another form of torture.* Azariah swung her hand and they reappeared in the forest. Glowing sun descended, banishing day to embrace night as shadows reached for her like arms of an omniscient being. Ready to throw down with a shadow, the nocturnal serenade of wild creatures swelled her heart. *Grey would love this. Going anywhere without him was an interplanetary incident waiting to happen. Who would reign her in when the Dragon came out to play? He was best friend code choked about a fling. He'd freak out if she left the planet.* With the area around her lit by another's glow as per usual, Lexy whispered, "I can't go anywhere without Grey."

"Don't worry. We're sending your Handler a distraction to lighten the physical effects and nausea," the luminescent being soothed. "Just stand here with me. Relax your mind."

Handler separation side effects. Good to know. She was never going to leave him. He may drive her crazy, but at the end of the day, Greydon Riley was everything to her. His was the smile she needed in the morning. It was his eyes she longed for. His presence calmed her. He was her tether to Ankh. In truth, he was her connection to everything. He tamed the wild thing with his humour and light. Her fling with an enemy hurt their bond. She let an attraction get the best of her. A snake slithered across the path by her toes. A visual of hundreds squirming out of her palms in Immortal Testing slipped into her mind. *She wasn't afraid. Snakes squirming out of your palms would stick with anyone. When you were in the in-between your mind brought things with you.* Scrunching her nose, Lexy probed, "What lesson are you planning to teach me?"

"Sometimes it takes a fresh perspective. If a Mountain Lion attacked you right now, what would you do? Would you stand and fight or run?" Her magical relation asked.

"Fight. You know what I am. What does this have to do with intention?" Lexy answered, waiting for the punchline.

Their Guardian probed, "Why would you fight?"

"Instinct," Lexy declared, wondering why they were hanging out in the forest. *Walk off a cliff into a swirling portal. No, wait. Let me dumb this down for you, and now, they were hiking.*

Smiling, their glowing Guardian disclosed, "Intention is similar to instinct. Once you learn to harness your reaction, you'll see the connection. Besides your healing ability, what comes naturally?"

Watching the woods where light muted to darkness, becoming a void of hooting owls and crackling branches, Lexy responded, "You know, the usual depravities my Dragon self brings. I can block objects and stop myself from falling."

"Everything you used as an example required intention. If I called it instinct would that make a difference?" The Guardian toyed as a flash of tan caught her attention in the bushes.

"Maybe? Is it though? Instinct is something you feel, intention is something you do," Lexy answered.

"Okay, you're catching on. If I threw something at you, you'd block it and call it instinct. So why would walking off a cliff be any different when you know you're genetically capable? If you didn't believe you could block something coming at you, what would you do?"

"Kick it's ass or move out of the way," Lexy responded, as bushes to her left crackled. Scanning the darkened forest for a weapon, she picked up a stick. Clutching it, Lexy said, "You're going to make me fight a mountain lion, aren't you?"

"I'm not sure what's coming. Do you want to fight a mountain lion?" Azariah sparred, watching the crimson-haired Dragon of Clan Ankh prepare to brawl whatever showed up.

"I wouldn't mind," Lexy remarked as she thought of a blade.

It appeared in her grasp. Five cougars strode out of the bushes surrounding her. "You shouldn't have," she teased with a smirk. Stoked to throw down, Lexy cracked her neck and stretched.

"How do you know when you're in over your head?" Azariah commented, observing her excitement.

Cockily signalling them to her, Lexy stated, "I'll let you know. I'm a little insulted you put this simulation on the easy setting." Before her eyes, all five of her predatory foes morphed to triple the size as fangs elongated. *Now, it was a fight.* Unswayed, Lexy glanced at her Guardian relation, toying, "Are you sticking around for the bloodbath?"

"I'll watch from elsewhere. When you're done working out your aggression, hit pause," Azariah instructed, vanishing.

Snaggle-toothed monstrosities emerged from bushes. "What are you waiting for?" Lexy taunted, provoking the felines with a swing of her blade. *This was a no chance scenario. Azariah wanted her to freeze this fight.* Ego urged her to prove she didn't have to. Narrowly avoiding beastly claws, she took off with a flash of crimson hair, darting between trees as she sprinted through the forest. As salivating monstrosities closed in on her, Lexy swung her arms, launching them away with force of will. As the stunned struggled, Lexy killed them. Victorious for mere seconds, she sighed as more came bounding at her through greenery. *Enough.* She swung her arms, commanding, "Stop!" The in-between was motionless.

Doing a slow clap, Azariah appeared, saying, "Intention."

"I get it now. You want me to willingly walk into a trap and freeze time to freak The King out when he tries to capture us. How long does it freeze for?"

Placing a hand on her shoulder, Ankh's Guardian instructed, "Less than a minute. Use it wisely. Make it clear you have use of your Guardian abilities. Don't worry about playing nice. You're at the top of the immortal food chain. You've fought and prevailed in their Colosseum. The King fears you. You are Lexy Abrelle, the infamous Dragon of

Ankh. Follow Amar's lead. He knows who you can trust. He's been given a three-use safe word to calm you in Grey's absence."

She didn't want to go anywhere without her Handler, but it wasn't a choice. "Guess it's time to walk off a cliff," Lexy said, smiling.

Azariah teased, "Look up."

Lexy peered up. *Cool.* A black swirling vortex dropped from the sky like a tornado and sucked her up. It was like being inside a Rose Quartz Ankh Tomb. The sense of motion without sight, then everything stopped.

2
Interplanetary Guardian Adventures

*A*s her brain flickered, she was spat out of a swirling vortex above the Colosseum. Landing crouching in red sand to raucous applause, Lexy of Ankh rose in sparse gold attire with her crimson hair rippling like a victory flag in the wind.

A mauve guy, chuckled, "That's how you make an entrance."

He tossed her a knife. *Was she in the right place?* She scanned the stands as trumpets blared.

A voice announced, "Round one."

Guess this was happening. Lexy shrugged, and asked, "What are we fighting?"

"Who are you?" He laughed, clutching his weapon.

Watching the elaborate archway to see what they were up against, she said, "Lexy of Ankh."

"I'm Benji. Honoured to fight with you," the guy replied.

Oh, she had so many questions. Dropping her into a Colosseum with a purple guy named Benji was a good way to throw her off her game. He

SACRIFICIAL LAMB CLUB

looked human. Maybe it was makeup? Lexy glanced his way asking, "What did you do to end up entertainment for a colosseum of elitist Third-Tier immortals?"

"I volunteered," Benji chuckled. "I crashed in the desert. We need supplies."

This guy was going to die. "Are you immortal?" Lexy enquired.

"No. Why?" Benji answered as a massive terrifying beast with slick tar black scales, fangs and a scorpion tail emerged through the arches.

Damn it. She couldn't slip into a Dragon state and help this guy survive. Lexy instructed, "It's slow. It has no peripheral vision. This is your fight. If you don't have an active role in taking it out, they'll make you go again. Run around the colosseum. Stay close to the wall. Grab that axe by the archway. Chop off the tail. I'll keep it focused on me." The mortal was stunned. "Go," Lexy urged, shoving Benji. With blade in hand, Ankh's crimson-haired assassin casually strolled over, taunting, "I hope you brought back up." Pitchy wailing, the beast waddled towards her as the crowd roared. Lapping the colosseum, Benji grabbed the axe. As he snuck up behind the monstrosity, people yelled to warn the beast. It turned and saw Benji. Lexy leapt on it, yelling, "Run!"

Lumbering after Benji as he fled, it swatted her off with its tail. Lexy rolled away as it thumped crimson sand near missing her with its deadly tail. Benji sprinted at the salivating monster as it pounded sand, trying to squash her. Badass purple guy swung the axe, slicing off its tail. The beast shrieked as it spun to face the mortal. *Sacrificial lamb time.* Scrambling towards it, Lexy stabbed the tar demon's hind quarter. Yowling, it turned back, chomping razor teeth into her torso, shaking Lexy until her vision flickered as the crowd cheered. Blood rained as she hummed with rage. *She should have intended to make her flesh impermeable.* On the beast's back

Benji rage stabbed the monster, its jaw slackened, and it dropped her. *Ouch.* Rising from the sand as her stomach wound sealed, Lexy looked at Benji and said, "Well done."

He rushed to her, panicking, "How are you standing?"

"I have a healing ability," Lexy explained. "I'm fine." Royal guards surged through the arches encircling the colosseum.

Confused, Benji questioned, "What are they doing?"

Grinning, Lexy chuckled, "Don't worry. This isn't for you."

Benji stammered, "Good to know."

Waving at the royal seating, Lexy shouted, "You're only going to piss me off." *She wanted to turn it off, slip into her emotionless Dragon state and massacre everyone in this colosseum.* As guards raised their weapons, she yelled, "Get rid of the First-Tier if you want a real show!"

The King's voice came over an intercom, "Know your place, Dragon!"

"Know your place, Third-Tier!" Lexy cockily hollered back.

"Put the Dragon down!" The King commanded.

Oh, it was on. Rage bubbled within as palace guards rushed her. Intending to stop time, Lexy waved her hand. She sealed Benji in a blue orb. *Whoops.* With no idea what she'd done, she commenced taking out all who came for her as the orb protecting the mortal being bounced on the red sand unharmed. As visions of the dark farm flickered in her mind, emotion vanished. With each slash of her blade assailant's blood gushed and sprayed until all who dared challenge her were writhing in the crimson sand, pleading for their lives. *Dragons had no use for mercy.* The wild thing strode over to the incapacitated guards with an axe.

Over the loudspeaker, The King's voice decreed, "Enough!"

Unfazed by a lesser being's commands, Lexy chopped off fifty heads and pointed at The King.

IN THE ROYAL SEATING, AMAR COMMENTED, "SHE'S COMING UP here. I have the ability to stop it, but you've violated the Treaty. I'm going to need your word."

The King commanded, "I am the ruler of this realm. What you need is of no consequence to me. Stop the Guardian Spawn or be entombed."

The Princess rationed, "Entombing an Ambassador violates the Treaty. Clearly, she has use of Guardian power. Do you want everyone to catch onto her altered Tier status?"

Enjoying his brother's lesson in humility, Prince Amadeus coughed to cover up a chuckle as his Ankh friend rage-stabbed slaughtered corpses, shrieking.

Irritated, The King addressed Amar, "Fine. Shut this down. It's almost time for dinner. She will not be left unattended. You will stay by her side. Take her to be cleaned. I want her presentable. Can you do this?"

"That's the best you'll get," Amadeus whispered.

The Royals were ushered out. Immortals evacuated the stands as Amar jogged down the stone stairs against the flow of fleeing immortals, emerging on the interior of the archway. As the blood drenched Dragon of Ankh stormed through the arches too far gone for ration. He sliced his arm and held up his hand. The Ankh symbol on his palm strobed with white light. Squeezing his eyes shut, Amar used his safe word, "Oklahoma."

Emotion flickered in Lexy's eyes. He explained, "It's Amar. The fight is over. I need to get you cleaned up."

Coming out of a Dragon state was usually accompanied by the sight of Grey. *She didn't know Amar well.*

Showing her the Ankh brand on his palm, Amar said, "Please don't kill me, we're on the same side."

It took her a second. Lexy glanced back at the bodies and a guy inside a blue bubble, asking, "What's with the guy in the ball?"

Grinning, Amar reminded, "You dropped from the sky into a mortal being's battle. After you helped him win, The King tried to capture you. You put the guy in that orb... then decapitated fifty guards."

Seems legit. "I'd better try to get him out of the orb before we go anywhere," Lexy remarked, walking into the bloodbath.

Amar followed, chuckling, "They cleared the stands fast after you massacred these guards like it was nothing."

Reaching the guy in the bubble, Lexy glanced back at Amar, admitting, "I'm glad they left. I have no clue how I did this."

Intention. She'd saved him. That was the protective orb's purpose. She poked it. *Gross. It was squishy and warm.* She tried to cut him out and the orb reacted by bouncing away. *Wild.*

Amar ran after it. He caught up and held it steady, urging, "Try again. Quickly before someone sees you trying to figure it out."

Intention. She had to have faith she could do it. There was no other outcome. Lexy placed her hands against it and looked into the mortal's eyes, wanting him free. It vanished. He dropped into the crimson sand and remained where he was, scared shitless.

Amar held out a hand, explaining, "She's not feral anymore. No worries."

Awkwardly smiling, Lexy said, "I didn't want to hurt you."

"Besides the nausea from spinning in a ball, I'm good,"

Benji maintained as they wandered from the red sand colosseum, past livestock stalls onto the cool tile of an empty corridor.

"I guess nobody's coming to force me to bathe this time," Lexy whispered.

Grinning, as they wandered down a long white marble hallway barefoot, Amar reminded, "You just murdered fifty guards."

Lexy glanced down. *As per usual, she was covered in blood.*

Pulling aside a curtain, Amar ushered them into the bathing area. Scantily clad servants stood by the luxurious pools awaiting instruction. "I have no issues with being lathered up gorgeous strangers," Amar chuckled, removing his shirt.

In awe of the ornate marble pools covered in sweet-scented flower petals, Benji whispered, "Are they bathing us?"

She'd forgotten about her purple friend. Guess she'd get to find out if it was makeup in a minute.

"Enjoy being pampered. You're under our protection," Amar responded.

Wincing, Lexy began trying to figure out how to remove her mystery attire.

Smiling, Amar moved closer, whispering, "Get in. They'll take it off for you."

She didn't want anyone to touch her. After returning from a Dragon state, she required time to reboot her emotions before dealing with irritations. Amar didn't know. He was a temp with the use of magical words. She needed the boy who tamed a Dragon in the wild. Greydon Riley, with his dark blonde hair and beast enticing smile. If you overlooked the naughty time amnesia, he was perfect. Lexy looked for a weapon. *Nothing but green velvet curtains. She needed to stab herself and heel a few times to chill out. She couldn't do it here.* Her pulse raced as her lizard brain revved. *She wanted to scream. She had to get her shit together before anyone noticed.* Yearning for her Handler's presence, her eyes darted to Amar.

Catching her distress, Amar cupped her face, assuring, "I have two more safe words. Go ahead. Turn off your emotions."

That was a horrible idea. Maintaining eye contact, she whispered, "I'll kill everyone. Help me take this off."

Adjusting the shoulder of her sheath, Amar stopped himself from smiling as it slid down to her hips, exposing her chest. He provoked, "You're Guardian. You can do anything you want. You are an anomaly with magic these fools can't begin to comprehend. Own it."

Amar walked away bare assed. Benji followed him. She grinned at his mauve rear-view. *He really was purple. Her afterlife was strange.* Embracing her inner Guardian, Lexy stepped out of her sheath, kicked it aside and got into the steaming pool. Submerging under petals, she rose with the blood of her enemies washed away.

A woman she recognized directed, "Come with me."

Strolling over to another pool where Amar and Benji were being bathed, Lexy grinned. *They were purposely pushing her buttons.* Nude, she waded in like the queen of the universe and sunk beneath petals. As they began washing her, her eyes met with Amar's.

Amar's voice piped into her thoughts, '*Look at me.*'

Normally, prolonged eye contact would be out of the question but her attraction to the unfamiliar Ankh intrigued her. Gazing into Amar's sultry eyes as they bathed his toned torso, arousal flickered as sudsy hands slid over her ivory breasts. The desire to have her way with her co-conspirator, didn't give ration a speck of leeway as Amar inched closer. Concealed by petals, their hands touched beneath the water's surface. Their eyes locked. *She'd been hurt. She was primed to do something stupid.* Playing chicken with their morals, the servants left, closing the curtain. Fighting attraction, Lexy whispered, "You need to stab me."

Amar's eyes grew darker as he whispered, "Even the thought of stabbing you turns me on."

She felt his hand on her thigh. *This was a horrible idea.*

Benji commented, "I'm still here."

They moved away from each other. Amar apologized, "Sorry."

"I can leave if you need a minute," Benji taunted, smiling.

Relieved, Lexy assured, "It's just magic."

"He's attractive, and you have spots," Benji sparred. "There's no need to explain."

Spots? What spots? "You mean freckles?" Lexy laughed.

The curtains shifted as a lady in a tan sheath, came in saying, "Lexy of Ankh, I'm ready for you."

Without looking back at Amar, Lexy got out. Escaping the awkward situation, she vanished behind the curtains.

Leading her to a booth, her attendant introduced herself, "I'm Arielle, your stylist technician. We've upgraded the system. You'll find it faster than before."

Third-Tier use technology for strange things. Knowing the drill, Lexy stepped inside. Arielle closed the door. After a loud vibration, warm air dried her. She stepped out with ready to style hair. At the next booth, they gave her choices based on her last visit to the Third-Tier realm. Pointing at makeup similar to what she'd worn before on the screen, she opted for wavy hair and stepped inside.

A voice instructed, "Chin on the rest. Eyes and mouth closed."

It hummed while air brushing makeup on and tickled as it did her hair. She got out. Her stylist rolled out a teal gown and helped her put it on. There was no need to alter a thing. It fit perfectly.

"You look beautiful," Arielle declared. "See for yourself."

Wandering to the full-length mirror, Lexy took in the work of art. *She'd tried but never come close to copying the makeup she had last time she was here. Her face was a work of art.*

"I took the liberty of picking out your jewellery. I hope you don't mind," Arielle explained.

Lifting her hair as Arielle did up the exquisite emerald necklace, Lexy noticed the girl's brand of Ankh and enquired, "How did you end up here?"

Fixing her hair, Arielle answered, "I was in love with a Third-Tier. She was entombed for not welcoming The King's advances. I lost everything we'd built because Second-Tier aren't allowed to own property in this realm."

"That's horrible," Lexy replied, watching the Ankh in her reflection. "Were you with Amar's group?"

With chestnut hair and eyes that crinkled as she smiled, Arielle disclosed, "Amar's a good friend but I'm from ICCA settlement 5."

Curious, Lexy questioned, "Is that another planet?"

"It's here, in the southern hemisphere. My parents were Third-Tier. I have no abilities. It's a genetic glitch. Every Third-Tier born mortal is sent to settlement 5. They don't want us breeding with their pristine population. When I resurrected after an incident, I was transferred here because I'm dormant Second-Tier."

Scrunching her face, Lexy replied, "Did they bury you?"

"Unfortunately," Arielle laughed, motioning for her to follow.

Walking with her entertaining new friend, Lexy said, "I've been there."

"I'm one of Prince Amadeus' attendants. He wanted to make sure I was taken care of. Amar gave me the brand," the petite brunette with deep-set blue eyes revealed.

As they strolled under intricately carved ivory archways, Lexy disclosed, "I consider Prince Amadeus a friend."

Reaching the banquet hall, Arielle whispered, "He picked out your jewellery."

Smiling, Lexy thought of the Third-Tier Prince who'd always had her back. Knowing Amadeus was kind to everyone regardless of status, she touched the necklace he'd chosen as Arielle walked away. *She'd been on the edge. The conversation with a stranger calmed her.* When they opened the fancy double doors, announcing her, Lexy wasn't thinking about The King's capture attempt or her magical attraction to her temporary Handler. She was looking forward to spending time with Amadeus.

3
Guardian Spawn Issues

*A*ll eyes turned her way, sizing her up as she wandered to the table of royalty. Chandeliers hung from the ceiling with jewel toned tapestries decorating the walls. Amar got up and pulled out her chair. As she sat, Lexy whispered, "Where is our purple friend?"

"He's safe. We'll see him after we eat," Amar assured.

Her eyes darted to Prince Amadeus. *He'd backed up his age.* Their eyes met and the charming royal winked.

Leaning closer, Amar whispered, "You look gorgeous."

"Where's The King?" Lexy whispered, noticing the empty chair at head of the table.

Grinning, Amar whispered, "He has to be seated last. We were waiting for you."

Whoops. He was going to be bitchy. Sitting in the chair next to The King wasn't going to be good for her patience level. Noticing the goblet of wine in front of her, she picked it up and peered inside. *She wanted to drink, but after The King's lame attempt to assert his dominance, it might be poisoned.* Sensing eyes on her, she turned. Sinfully sexy in his tan attire, Amar was staring at her. "Do I have something in my teeth?" Lexy teased, grinning.

"This magical bond is making me think naughty things," Amar confessed, mesmerized by her.

Intrigued, Lexy locked eyes with him, provoking, "Like what?"

Everyone stood in silence as they announced The King and her stomach rumbled like a Grizzly bear's mating call. Half the table was silently, shaking laughing. *Guess she was hungry? Please don't growl again. Please don't.* Everyone sat down after The King. She did what everyone else did out of habit.

Amar noticed she hadn't touched her wine. He whispered, "It's good."

Hanging out with a smorgasbord of Third-Tier felt like juggling dynamite over a fire. Seductively crossing her legs, she sipped from her goblet, as a plate was placed before her with three chestnut sized things and sauce. *Bet hers was poisoned.* She watched everyone eating with their hands. *Yes, they have no cutlery here.* Scrutinizing her meal, hunger bickered with distrust. Amar's arm brushed hers, lighting up her libido. *Oh, my. She was a smidge off feral.*

"It's good," Amar urged, eating his.

The King baited, "I didn't poison it. I swear."

Award for worst timing ever goes to the douche wad with the pretentious jewelled crown. Smirking, Lexy took a sample bite, discovering it was fruit with something like brown sugar drizzled on it. *It wasn't bad.* The next course was meat and either soup or dip. Looking around the table, some Third-Tier were dipping, others were drinking from the bowl. She wrapped her meat in a tortilla thing and dipped it. *It was delicious.* Enjoying her meal, she listened to conversations about her marrying The King. *That wasn't happening. She'd rather be entombed.* Sensing the royal's gaze, their eyes met.

"We could rule everything together," The King seduced.

Squinting, Lexy replied, "You tried to rape my sister."

"I succeeded," The King decreed.

She couldn't allow him to think he had his way with a Guardian. Shaking her head, Lexy baited, "She was too intimidating. You were flaccid as dead Trout."

Concealing laughter by pretending to choke, Amar turned away.

"What's a Trout?" The King questioned.

He was trying to provoke her. Ironically, she was doing the same thing. Lexy sighed, "It doesn't matter. You couldn't get it up."

"Get what up?" He quizzed.

"Your wee willy. The dysfunctional brain between your legs," Lexy antagonized.

"You weren't there," he bantered.

"I was," Lexy disclosed, smirking.

"You lie," he stated.

Grinning, Lexy toyed, "You can't do anything about it."

Irate, The King stood up, commanding, "Seize The Guardian spawn!"

The guards looked at each other as they hesitantly inched towards her. After what she'd done earlier, they were terrified. Amar and Amadeus weren't the least bit concerned. *They believed in her. It was sweet.* The King started freaking out and a hoard of staff rushed her. She waved and time froze. She had a minute to make it count. Darting through the paused herd, she slit throats and pants The King, leaving him standing there with his wee winky dangling. Time started. Bodies fell in the crowd. The King was half naked. Everybody panicked and raced for the doors. "Everyone ran at the sight of you naked," Lexy teased, thoroughly entertained.

Switching personalities while pulling up his pants, The King opted out of his abduction attempt, saying, "You're a viable Guardian with abilities. I'll honour the Treaty. For now."

She really wanted to kill this idiot.

"The planetary migrator was paying for supplies by

offering to be our entertainment. We have a barter system. The one in need, chooses the direction of the barter. They opt to take or leave the request. If you want something, the price can be anything. Jewels are only pretty things and money is obsolete in this realm. You're an Ambassador. Guests in my kingdom don't ridicule my genitals. For safety reasons, we'll enter tombs and do a virtual gathering to discuss your debt to the crown."

Amar stepped in, "Agreed."

"When we're done with business, we can take different doors," The King decreed.

"I guess," Lexy answered, wondering how she was going to eat the cake they placed in front of her without cutlery.

"I had this Earth delicacy made for you," The King explained.

Swiping her finger through the icing, Lexy licked it off. *It tasted like vanilla.* Peering up, she noticed The King staring and confessed, "I have no idea how to eat icing covered cake without cutlery. It's good though."

Dipping his finger in his cake, The King offered it, "You can have some of mine. Lick it off."

"Hard no," Lexy stated, turning to look at Amar with wide eyes.

"Women yearn for me," The King proclaimed. "You won't be able to help yourself."

Mouthing, "Help me," to Amar, Lexy turned back to their delusional host as Third-Tier hesitantly sampled the messy Earth treat. Opting to make herself undesirable, she pushed The King's elitist buttons by picking up her icing covered slice and chomping into it like an ill-bred heathen. With bulging cheeks, and cake all over her face, she watched The King's intrigued expression. After devouring it all, Lexy wiped her face and hands on a silk napkin, grateful her makeup was a temporary tattoo. Grinning with cake in her teeth, she commented, "Not bad." A server passed her a tiny glass with liquid in it and an empty one. She sniffed it. *It didn't smell like anything.* Everyone was passed one. Confused, she looked at Amar.

Leaning closer, Amar whispered, "They do this instead of using toothbrushes. Gargle with the clear liquid. Spit it into the empty glass, then take a drink of water."

The King rose, announcing, "Be in the Crypts in fifteen minutes."

Amar took her arm as they followed the crowd, whispering, "I need to use the washroom."

"So do I," Lexy whispered as they detoured down the hall. "I sure hope they haven't upgraded anything."

Chuckling, Amar whispered, "We'll figure it out."

The door opened as they reached it, sliding into the wall. *They automated wacky things. It was just how she remembered it.* Soothing music was playing. There were dozens of sealed cubicles in each row, six rows deep. Black and white marble everywhere.

Amar went into a stall. He peered out, explaining, "The primary-coloured handprints on the wall are the same. Be straight with me, are you going to get trapped in the washroom? We only have fifteen minutes."

"I might" she taunted, closing the door. It locked and the hum of the music was gone. She sat on the toilet, and went, then felt for the button on the rim. She pressed it. A plastic wrap like bubble pressed against her bottom. The door slid and stopped close to her knees.

A deep voice prompted, "Choose your desired temperature by placing your hand on the wall."

There were yellow, red, green and blue handprints. Shit. She was drawing a blank. The voice kept repeating the command. *Quit pressuring me. Green felt like the safest choice.* She winced and placed her hand on green.

The voice announced, "You cannot choose the option for go until you have chosen your desired temperature."

Think Lexy, think. You've done this before. It's just an overcomplicated bidet, green means go. It started coming back to her. She pressed yellow. Nothing happened. *Whoops, she had to press, go.* Placing her hand on green, there was a spray of warmth followed by a burst of air. *Sitting with warm breeze blowing on her hoo ha was relaxing when it wasn't a surprise.*

"Press stop," the booth instructed.

Amar was waiting for her. Laughing, she pressed red.

The booth spoke in a monotone voice, "Repeat."

Lexy hissed, "Shit, no! Don't repeat! Stop! I want to stop!" *She made the same mistake last time.*

The air stopped blowing. A voice spoke, "Do you want to use the voice control option?"

Oh, good. "Yes," she declared.

The voice said, "What is your command?"

Exhaling, Lexy stated, "Stop!"

A gust of air sucked the film on her into the toilet and politely said, "Have a productive evening." The wall moved out.

Shaking her head at herself, Lexy escaped and closed the door, to avoid being doused with air freshener.

Leaning against the row of stalls, Amar chuckled, "I knew you'd figure it out."

"I was plotting to foil a virgin sacrifice the last time I used these bathrooms," Lexy disclosed, leaving Triad out of it. *Tiberius risked everything to help her save Kayn.*

Entertained by her unfiltered confession, Amar probed, "Why tell me? We barely know each other. What if I use that knowledge to get myself out of trouble?"

"They can't do anything to me now," Lexy replied, smiling as tension flickered in the air.

Caressing her crimson hair, his amber-flecked brown eyes penetrated hers as he flirtatiously toyed, "Try to get through the night without trying to assassinate The King again."

Exhaling as he ran his hand down her arm, Lexy

sparred, "No promises." *Amar was tempting. She had to stay on task.* Holding her hands under sanitizer, she enquired, "When you press the button on the rim of the toilet, what is that stuff?"

"Sanitizer with sensation enhancers," Amar answered as they strolled out together.

Grinning, Lexy revealed, "You can imagine the comedy that ensued after Grey puked in one of these toilets and pressed that button on the rim, thinking he was flushing it. He nearly suffocated."

"I heard about that," Amar whispered as they passed intricate tapestries and excited Third-Tier.

Playfully shoving her Ankh cohort, Lexy said, "Don't you dare say anything to Grey. He'll be so embarrassed."

Taking her arm, Amar whispered, "If you kill The King, you'll get me in trouble."

Chuckling, Lexy suggested, "If I were you, I'd keep him away from me tonight."

Grinning, Amar called her bluff, "You won't really do it."

"I'm supposed to make sure he knows I'm at the top of the food chain," Lexy countered.

"You've tried to kill him twice," Amar whispered, shaking his head as they manoeuvered the crowd.

Laughing, Lexy whispered, "If I was trying to kill him, he'd be dead."

As the crowd parted and went through separate doors, Amar led her into Ankh's Crypt, whispering, "We're going to have so much fun."

Coming at Amar as he walked in, Benji accused, "That asshole branded me!"

"You weren't making it off this planet alive. Now, you're under our protection. If you die, we can bring you back," Amar revealed, climbing into a large stone tomb lined with rose quartz. "Good news. You get to come to the party. Come on, you two. It's better if we go in the same one."

They couldn't just bring a purple guy back to Earth. She had so many questions.

Stubbornly, Benji declared, "I'm not getting in there until you tell me what it's for."

Touching his shoulder, Lexy explained, "We travel to the in-between in these."

Amar climbed in, prompting, "That brand is a get out of your next demise free card. Get in, kid."

The trio laid flat on their backs with Benji in the middle, the tomb closed automatically. A soothing voice instructed, "Place your hand in the symbol above if you agree to a discretionary short term memory wipe."

Chuckling, Amar directed, "Trust me. You want it."

She did trust him. This temporary connection was impressive. She put her hand in the print.

Benji questioned, "What are we doing?"

"I have no idea," Lexy confessed. Their mauve friend, put his hand in the print like a badass. *Benji was going to lose his shit.* The tomb began to vibrate. They squeezed their eyes closed as incapacitating light strobed. Lexy shouted, "Don't puke on me!"

"What?" Benji hollered back.

They were abruptly launched upwards with their new friend pitchy shrieking. After dozens of spins, they paused for just long enough to think it was over, then dropped, plummeting in a flat spin like a vomit-inducing carnival ride. Light flashed, and instead of free falling into the in-between, there was a smooth surface beneath their hands as the glare ceased. They opened their eyes.

As the waves of nausea subsided, Benji gasped, "That was horrible."

They were in a large circular room of vastly different doors. Helping him up, Lexy apologized, "Anything involving tombs is a wild ride. I've never been here before." Transparent immortals solidified each time she blinked until there was a crowd. Everyone was wearing Grecian attire. Torchlight flickered as Lexy took in the intricately engraved colourful doors encircling her. Third-Tier began entering rooms, releasing a burst of music or chatter that silenced each time a door closed. She turned to Amar. *He was right beside her a second ago.*

Glued to her side, Benji whispered, "Why does it feel like I could get lost in here?"

Self-preservation. Taking his hand, Lexy whispered, "Do you see Amar?"

Pointing at a crowd gathered by a teal door, Benji whispered, "He's over there, chatting with that ass who tricked me into fighting a monster for supplies."

Everyone vanished until the hall was nearly empty as they wandered over to the royalty. A scarlet-hued door was opened and closed, silencing hedonistic pleasure.

Greeting her with a wide smile, Amar teased, "Welcome to the Third-Tier playground."

Glancing her way, The King sparred, "It's the safest way to entertain heathens." Noticing her purple companion, he toyed, "Adopting an alien?"

Sensing the smart assed response on the tip of Benji's tongue, Lexy squeezed his hand, bantering, "If that's what it takes to protect him."

Entertained by the crimson-haired immortal's lack of respect for authority, The King decreed, "We can discuss payment for his safety in the red room."

"I wouldn't hold my breath," Lexy taunted, scowling.

Interrupting glare fest, The King's sister placed her hand on her brother's shoulder, saying, "If you require a visit to the red room, we'll entertain Earth's delegates until you return."

Irritated, The King accused, "So you can swoop in and steal her away?"

Wow. He was impressively delusional.

The Princess reprimanded, "Shut up, Ricard. Nobody wants your throne." The elegant royal with a feisty side greeted her, "We haven't been formerly introduced. I'm Sophia."

Shut up, Ricard. She was awesome.

As Lexy shook the princess' slender manicured hand, Sophia replied, "It's a pleasure. My brother speaks highly of you."

Grinning, Amadeus set the scene with a sweep of his hand, "This door leads to treasured memories. We won't know whose until we enter." He held open the door.

Walking into a pub, Lexy saw the shadow of a pinup girl on a mirrored wall and instantly knew where they were. She'd been to many Karaoke bars in her time with Ankh, but this place was a favourite. With burgundy pleather booths and chairs at tables around the area where patrons came to sing beloved off-key tunes. She recognised musical laughter. Her eyes were drawn to a table of partying Ankh. It was like watching a rerun of a movie as Grey was called up to sing. He walked past. *She had to go home. She needed to make things right with him. He'd be crazy worried by now.*

Still beside her, Amadeus explained, "They can't see you. It's just ambiance. Come sit. We have a booth."

Entranced by Greydon Riley as he got on his knees to serenade a girl, she watched his hologram shaking her head.

Nudging her, Amadeus ribbed, "Watch your slutty Handler seduce locals from our table with a drink."

Grinning, Lexy followed him to where the others were seated. *Drinking while watching the love of her afterlife flirting rarely went well.*

Entertained by Grey's musical seduction as he kissed a girl's hand and moved on, Amar chuckled, "I love that guy."

She did too. More than ration permitted. She'd never left him like this before. Sitting across the table from Amar, Lexy picked up a pinup girl coaster. *Everything was as she remembered it.* She grabbed a pencil contemplating putting a song in. Lily of

Ankh strutted by with silky black hair and a come hither everything. Everyone's gaze followed her.

King Ricard commented, "She's fun."

Wanting to stab the dickish leader, Lexy squeezed the pencil. Someone kicked her under the table. Amar shook his head. *Party pooper.* Her babysitter slid his fishbowl of long island iced tea over to her. She purposely drank all of it.

Stealing her pencil, Amar toyed, "You're a brat." He snapped it like he was making a power move.

"You're in way over your head," Lexy sparred, crossing her legs.

Leaning in, Amar whispered, "Behave."

Watching the exchange, Sophia slid her another pencil. Lexy replied, "Thanks, sweetie."

Her temporary Handler chuckled, "I'll spank you."

"For holding a pencil?" Lexy provoked. She tried to signal a server.

"They can't see you. In-between rules. Just think of what you want," Sophia explained with her gaze following their Siren like a firefly in the dark.

Staring at Lexy, The King flirted, "You are a magical creature."

Why was it speaking to her? She didn't like it.

Smiling, King Ricard disclosed, "Tiberius teaching you about healing pleasure with his blade while you were locked up during halftime at the colosseum was the hottest thing I've ever seen."

Her pulse raced as the titillating encounter entered her mind. She shut it down. *Oh, the irony. She had feelings for her enemy. She'd blown a job. She was a bloody Dragon.*

"I watch it on repeat for personal reasons," The King revealed.

Knowing they watched Tri-Clan through Oracles like a soap opera, didn't make it less creepy. Lexy tossed a pencil at Amar.

"On Earth it's frowned upon to admit you've been stalking," Amar pointed out, placing her pencil on the table.

"It's not stalking if you know you're being watched," The King taunted, sipping his drink.

"Being watched against your will is the definition of stalking," Amar confirmed.

With her chin in her palm and elbow on the table, Sophia confessed, "I'm a fan. Your storyline is my favourite. A surprise night with Amar would be a fun plot twist."

Her afterlife was already a train wreck. Entertaining the idea, Lexy fibbed, "My dance card's full."

"What does that mean?" The Princess probed, fascinated by earthling lingo.

"She's not into me. It's a metaphor," Amar interjected, calling her bluff with a wink.

A few weeks ago, Grey was her eternal soulmate and forgetful lover. She was trying to move away from the endless cycle. She'd just started something kind of amazing with Orin. The world was her oyster. She let a naughty flirtation get the best of her. She pulled the pin with Tiberius and blew up her Handler bond. Orin understood. He let her know, he was there if she needed him. His response clarified what she'd let go of.

Her attention was drawn back to Grey raking a hand through his sandy blonde hair with a mischievous twinkle in his eyes. *She'd broken his spirit for a booty call. She didn't want to dull her pain, she needed to wipe her hard drive.* Thinking of tequila, a bottle appeared. Amar, her partner in debauchery grinned as Lexy took a swig from the bottle. *She didn't want to think about the mess she'd made. Why couldn't she set her emotions aside and have flings like everyone else? She could turn it off for murder but not for a roll in the hay. A no strings hook up. Maybe that's what she needed?*

Princess Sophia questioned, "Is this the mid to late nineties?"

"Judging by the songs, clothes and overall vibe, it's the early two thousands. Right, Lex?" Amar interjected, playing footsies with her under the table.

Contemplating hooking up with her cohort, Lexy passed the tequila, baiting, "Want some?"

Their gazes locked as her sexy interim Handler took the tequila. She forgot anyone else was there as Amar pursed his lips and drank golden inhibition loosener from the bottle. He placed it on the table and slid it back like a dare. Her mind flashed her a visual of his naked ass walking away. She gapped out, fantasizing about what she'd wanted to do in the tub. Snapping out of it, Lexy chugged tequila as the royal siblings debated the year. Exhaling, she passed the bottle back to Amar. Their fingers touched, striking a hedonistic match between her thighs. *She was going to snap. She might have to tug him into the bathroom.* Her pulse raced. Trying to get her libido under control, she crossed her legs and looked for the hologram of her real Handler. Seeing Grey on the dance floor seducing a girl in white jeans, jogged her memory. Desperate to control her urges, Lexy threw her ego under the bus, "It's two thousand and two. We broke our Handler Dragon intimacy seal last night. His memories were wiped. He's magically deterred from seeing me in a romantic way. Grey's trying to pick up a girl. I'm at the bar boiling rabbits in my mind."

Everyone's eyes darted to Lexy's hologram as a drunk groped her. The crimson-haired Dragon smoked his head on the bar and stormed out of the pub. Grey left the girl and chased after her. They followed the action out into the parking lot.

Choked she'd wrecked another hook up, Grey pursued her, bitching about him having needs all the way to their room. Lexy unlocked the door, taunting, "Oh, you didn't get to take home a slutty girl from the bar. Poor Greydon Riley. Your life is so hard."

"Ouch Lex. You're being so mean," Grey chuckled, hugging her back.

Opening the door, Lexy strutted in, boldly stripping off her clothes, mumbling, "Just leave. I'm sure she's still there."

Standing in the doorway watching, he warned, "The door is wide open, Lex. You're wasted." Closing the door and blinds, he took off his T-shirt and tossed it at her. "Wear this. We have to sleep in the same bed."

"If cuddling me in my underwear repulses you, sleep on the floor," she slammed, climbing beneath the covers.

He crawled over and snuggled with her, offering, "Are you hungry?"

She knew every word by heart. Seeing enough, Lexy walked away. *A thousand breathtakingly beautiful nights followed by broken hearts. She'd tried to move past the cycle. Bedding her Handler's nemesis was a rebellious move. Their illicit encounters made her feel alive, but they could never be more. Overreacting and murdering him was a fitting end to their fling. Stomping Grey's heart was an unintended perk.* Guilt tightened her chest. *Everything was copied from her memories. From the fragrant rose bushes on a warm summer night, to the hum of the busy street. Clearly, she was doing this to herself.* Hearing footsteps, she winced. *Why did she bring witnesses?*

"I'd do you every day," the King flirted, catching up.

His comic timing was more depressing than watching herself be friend zoned.

Walking with her, King Ricard bartered, "I'll amend our Treaty and agree to your Tier adjustment, if you swear your allegiance to me."

Rolling her eyes, Lexy sighed, "Clearly, you don't understand your place in the immortal food chain, or the concept of a Treaty."

"I'll accept penance for your misdeeds in intimate favour," he continued, as they reached the door. "Final offer," the immortal decreed.

"If you stop speaking, I won't kill you tonight. Final offer," Lexy countered without looking his way. Amar glared at her. His spanking offer sprung to mind.

Opening the door to a nightclub with rock blaring, Amadeus enticed, "Welcome to the jungle."

As they walked in, their clothing altered. *She loved the late eighties.* There were multicoloured strobe lights and smoke rising from the dance floor. It was the ambiance of a less complicated time. Her sidekick lured the King away.

Dancing into the writhing crowd, they lost sight of Sophia in the smoke show. *This place felt familiar.*

Amadeus teased, "You wrecked Amar's night."

Someone shoved her into him. *There were lots of real people in here now.* Lacing her arms around his neck, Lexy announced, "Late eighties is a good look for you."

Embracing her, Amadeus whispered, "Finding out you were part Guardian had to blow your mind. I was hoping we'd have a chance for gossip before the shit hit the fan."

"I was too," she replied as music slowed. She rested her head on his shoulder as they swayed, and for a song, she was peaceful.

Busting into their touching moment like the Kool-Aid man as new music began, Sophie announced, "High heeled shoes hurt." She took them off and winged them into the crowd.

There's The Princess.

Dancing barefoot, Sophie quizzed, "Why are you smiling?"

Opting for honesty, Lexy said, "You tossed your shoes into a crowd of people."

"They're not all real," Sophie sparred as her brother howled. "Why would anyone wear those torture devices?"

"It's going to hurt when someone steps on your toes," Lexy cautioned, grinning. She saw Benji dancing and smiled. *What were they going to do with him?* Lexy slipped her heels off, explaining, "I don't want to be the one who does it."

They'd been partying with strangers for hours when she felt eyes on her. She noticed her sexy Ankh sidekick coming through the herd.

"We'll be right back," Amar explained, walking her into the hall by the washrooms for privacy. In a dark corner, he disclosed, "He's drunk enough to sway his interest. I told him you got in an argument with your Handler, and you're not in the right state to succumb to advances. I'm checking in. Do you have murderous impulses I need to address?"

Lexy provoked, "I really want to kill him."

Amar covered her mouth, whispering, "Filter." She bit him. He pinned her against the wall, cautioning, "Quit playing games with me, Lexy. I'm not Grey. I'll tear off your clothes and take you right here."

"What's stopping you?" Lexy provoked, titillated by his gutsy response.

Hovering his mouth a breath from hers, his hand grazed lacy material over her breast. He fought against magic induced primal urges, rationing, "Damn it. I'll be entombed. If you can think of a way to enforce your lack of interest without offending him, it would help me out. I have to go. There's a visual of you walking into that pool naked playing on repeat in my mind."

"I'll find a way to make it clear," Lexy replied restoring their PG-rating. As he turned, her gaze locked on his rear, confessing, "I'm having similar issues." Without turning back, Amar paused. He exhaled and walked away as she fought the instinct to lure him back with saucy banter.

As she strolled back onto the dance floor, Prince Amadeus was flirting with someone. *Good for him.*

Dancing over, Sophie shouted over the music, "You've been spicing things up! Your afterlife storyline is riveting!"

In the grand scheme of things, they were merely stars of a Third-Tier reality show. Benji danced over in rising smoke, grinding against everyone he passed. *Markus was going to shit himself when they showed up with a purple guy from another planet. They already had a pregnant girl and a kid who was purposely a dick.* Shutting down thoughts, Lexy danced her heart out, enjoying the sights and sounds of a time she adored until the hard partying foursome sashayed off the dance floor. Someone bumped into her. She teetered over.

Amadeus caught her, teasing, "Need another shot?"

"I'm going to be hung over," she chuckled, steadying herself.

Next to her, Prince Amadeus teased, "No hangovers after virtual gatherings."

Reminded she could do anything she wanted, and the slate would be wiped clean. Her eyes travelled to The King's booth. There were ladies all over the dreadful royal and her sidekick. *It was best to keep that attraction at arm's length. There was already way too much drama in her storyline.* Following the royal duo upstairs, Lexy commented, "This must be a popular decade. There are tons of people in here." They sat at a plush booth.

"It's one of my favourite times," Amadeus disclosed. Pointing to The King's table where he had a girl on his lap, and chuckled, "That could be you."

Lexy locked eyes with Amar. He tapped his wrist. *I guess avoiding him for hours wasn't going to make her lack of interest clear. She had an idea but needed to gather the guts to make that bold sweeps week soap opera move.*

Drawing her back to the conversation, Sophia questioned, "Astrid couldn't be more my type. Are her and Haley together?"

Passing her a whipped cream shot, Lexy replied, "They're both single. I'll introduce you someday."

Benji shimmied into their booth, chuckling, "It feels like I'm playing with fire staying down there."

Lexy introduced her mauve tinted friend, "Meet Benji."

"My brother's a vengeful shit when he doesn't get what he wants, sexy purple guy," Sophia remarked. "Stick with us. You'll be lower on his hit list."

The Princess was hilarious.

Downing her drink, the entertaining Princess declared, "That was delicious." Passing Benji a whipped cream topped shot, she noticed his brand of Ankh, and said, "You have to take him with you now."

Meeting her eyes, Lexy whispered, "I asked Amar to keep him safe. We're magically connected so he can be Grey's stand in. It's my fault."

Smiling, Sophia confessed, "Telling on you for bringing an alien back to Earth is the least of my problems. I'm next in line for a throne. Ricard's paranoia is off the hook. He knows I don't want it. I never have. He's entombed everyone loyal to me. I'd imagine, this is our last hurrah."

Our. Lexy looked at Amadeus.

"You'd think it'd come in handy to be illegitimate, but he's entombed my people too," her favourite royal mumbled.

Scootching closer, Lexy whispered, "Come back with me. Ankh would take you in a heartbeat."

"If anyone could lure me to another planet, it would be you," Amadeus whispered, placing his hand on hers.

She trusted him. He'd been her safe place in the Third-Tier world ever since she made it out of her Immortal Testing with Grey and Arrianna. She'd seen Sophia as the plain unassuming girl seen but not heard at the head table. Now, she understood why. When you're next in line for a throne behind a despicable King, it's best to fly under the radar. Lexy enquired, "Can I help?"

Leaning in, Amadeus whispered in her ear, "It wouldn't hurt our cause if you asserted your dominance, shut him down cold, and let it slip that there was a third Daughter of Prophecy on the horizon."

Their version of the evening sounded way more fun than playing nice. Amar was watching her. His ears were burning. He was going to be choked if she started shit and he had to spend the rest of his night fixing it. If she kept drinking, she could blame it on the tequila. Grinning, Lexy revealed, "Amar asked me to let him down easy without pissing him off." Thinking of another bottle of golden hellfire, one appeared. The Dragon cracked the seal, took a swig, and passed it to Sophia, disclosing, "I have an idea. I just need the guts to do it and an excuse."

Sophia took a drink and gagged, "This is terrible."

"To Silas," Amadeus saluted, loudly.

They raised their shots and drank. Lexy chugged tequila. *Ricard even entombed his prized fighter. He really was losing it.* A slow song by Def Leppard began. *Shit.* Lexy's heart sunk as her eyes darted to the dance floor. She was in Grey's arms. Time stood still as passion ignited a sizzling makeout session. Her hologram broke away and took off. He pursued her. *This night was one of her most treasured memories. They made love like it was the end of the world. She didn't need to look to know everyone saw. He was hurting right now, and she was a world away drinking tequila, plotting to piss off an evil King.* Her eyes darted over to Amar. *He might take the hit for this.* Guilt crept in. She silenced it with another swig of hellfire. Getting up, Lexy summoned the troops. "It's time to stir shit up. Shall we dance?"

Amadeus finished the bottle, commenting, "That is awful."

Nearly falling on the stairs, Lexy grabbed the railing, laughing. *An intellectual would have pretended to drink. She should cut herself off.* Safely at the bottom of the staircase, Lexy tugged Sophia to her, flirting, "Operation freak your brother out is a go." Caressing Sophia's auburn hair, Lexy kissed her petal soft lips in rising smoke. As they parted, fascination flickered in the Dragon's eyes. Her heart fluttered as she suggested, "You should hide."

Shaking his head at his sister, Amadeus sighed, "You know I like her. Be better than Ricard."

Fixing her hair, Sophia mumbled, "I didn't see it coming."

They weren't catching on. Lexy hinted, "How choked is The King on a scale of one to ten?"

They clued in. Leading Sophia away, Amadeus answered, "Eleven. We should go."

Waiting, Benji decreed, "I'm not leaving you behind."

"I'm not even close to done with Ricard. Stay with them. I'll find you when he snaps," Lexy replied, waving at her new friend. Benji hesitated, then went after the others.

Dancing over to The King's table, Lexy sat on her temporary Handler's lap, and sighed, "I'm bored. Entertain me." Noticing Ricard's irritation, she leaned closer with crimson waves concealing her cleavage, taunting, "It's not his fault, your lap was taken." Making herself comfortable, she thought up a bottle of tequila, suggesting, "Try this."

"Did you poison it?" He toyed, fascinated by her.

She should have. Cracking the seal, a new song began. Swaying to the music, she drank some, then placed it by the royal like a dare.

Intrigued, Ricard asked, "What is it?"

"Panty loosener," Amar disclosed.

The King took a swig. Coughing, he declared, "That burns in a good way."

Pretending she didn't know she was turning Amar on, Lexy rocked her hips, singing along to the music. Taking the tequila back, she flirtatiously gazed into The King's eyes as she had more.

Roughly grabbing Lexy's hips to stop her from squirming on his lap, Amar scolded, "Behave."

She didn't want to.

Doing a sexy squinty thing with his eyes while handing her the bottle, Ricard blatantly stared at her cleavage, provoking, "Have more."

He was hotter than earlier. She should stop drinking. Grinning, Lexy took it, pretending to drink this time.

"Spend the night with me," The King seduced, ignoring the girl on his lap.

Coyly, she flirted, "I'm not going to give myself to you when you've put no effort into wooing me."

He tossed the girl off, and said, "Sit with me."

Amar clenched her hips tightly. She spoke to him in her

mind, *I'm not as drunk as I look. I have a plan.* He loosened his hold.

Amar spoke to her with his thoughts, *'Planning to give a few lap dances and run away?'*

Dragons don't run away. Casually switching laps, Lexy pretended to drink. With big reveal plans, she enquired, "You must have a girlfriend?"

"A few," King Ricard confessed, touching her scarlet hair. "You're a magnificent creature. I bet you're a hellcat between the sheets."

With her skin crawling, Lexy played along, "You'll have to apologize to my sister."

"I'll go out of my way to make amends," Ricard vowed. "Be with me tonight."

"I'm thinking about it," Lexy baited, swaying to the music.

Groaning, The King said, "I'll do anything."

"Anything?" Lexy pushed, leaning against him.

He pledged, "Anything."

She got up. King Ricard grabbed her wrist, saying, "Don't take off, naughty thing."

"I wouldn't dare," Lexy seduced. Straddling him, he clutched her ass as she whispered in his ear, "You are tempting. What happens when your reign ends? Do they just entomb you? I'd hate to find out I gave myself to the wrong royal. I heard there's a third daughter of Seth. How much time do you have left?"

Amar spoke in her mind, *'Holy shit.'*

Pulling away to meet The King's shocked expression, Lexy leapt up, grabbed Amar's hand, and said, "I love this song. Dance with me." Without looking back, she towed her temp Handler into the crowd. Weaving their way through the dance floor hidden by the smoke show, they slipped out the first door they saw.

Back in the circle of doors, Amar yanked his hand away, accusing, "Do you have you any idea what you've done?"

Beaming, Lexy replied, "The good royals will explain. Which door do you think they chose?"

Motioning for her, Amar opened a door, revealing, "There's a meet up plan."

They walked through into desert landscape. Sweltering sun and hot sand underfoot gave it authenticity, making her feel a part of it. He whistled. A black stallion appeared, galloping towards them like a mirage, and solidifying.

Amar effortlessly leapt on the majestic horses' back, urging, "Jump on."

"Bareback?" She questioned, stroking the regal stallion's neck.

With a debonair smirk, Amar teased, "I wouldn't think you'd shy away from bareback after that performance."

He had to stop flirting. It was getting harder to control her urges. On a stallion with his dark features, mischievous grin and ripped abs, he looked like her next mistake.

Grinning, Amar chuckled, "Let's take the scenic route to your awkward situation."

Leaping on the stallion's back, she asked, "Why would it be awkward?"

"You kissed a Princess, and falsely dethroned a King during a lap dance," he reminded as the horse shimmied.

Visuals of Amar naked were messing with her ability to think up witty comebacks. They should skip meeting up and have kinky desert sex.

Looking back, Amar toyed, "How does Grey keep a straight face? I've never been one to turn down kinky desert sex. Let's save it for after we've checked on our friends."

Titillated by tension, Lexy wrapped her arms around his waist, sparring, "I'd expect someone your age to be unfazed by naughty inner dialogue."

Amar cautioned, "Hold on."

Soft, thudding hoofbeats stirred up a powder haze as the sun descended into sand and daylight bid adieu, swirling fuchsia and tangerine onto the eternal cerulean palate above.

She felt reckless and wild, galloping through the desert towards a miraculous horizon with crimson hair trailing behind her and arms wrapped around him. Holding on tighter as the stallion slowed to a trot, she noticed she'd forgotten her drama for a few minutes. *They weren't moving. She should let go.* Relaxing her arms, she leaned back.

Amar leapt off and said, "I'll catch you."

Were they back where they started? Lexy swung a leg over and slid off into his arms. Entranced by magic-induced lust, neither moved.

With a backdrop of darkening sunset, Amar whispered, "I bet Grey feels this way."

"This way?" Lexy probed, without budging.

Chuckling, Amar stepped back, teasing, "Turned on by your crazy shit."

What crazy shit? Cracking up, she looked back, and the stallion was gone. "I thought we couldn't interact with mirages?"

"We can't interact with our friends or ourselves in a memory. I thought up the horse. Do you see the door?"

Twirling with her arms out, she said, "Just endless miles of empty desert."

"You'd think a Dragon would be used to thinking outside the box?" he toyed, moving his hand through an area. The desert wavered. "Only Third-Tier need a visual like a door because they haven't had to use their imaginations in a millennium. Second-Tier don't need a physical representation. We're used to visiting the in-between. Think of where you want to be, and we'll go there."

She wanted Grey. Betrayed by her heart, she didn't respond.

Amar responded to her thoughts, "Grey's fine. Get your head in the game."

He wasn't. The trust that bound their connection was unravelling. Caring for their enemy had untucked the end of the string from the spool and rolled it across the floor.

"You can't change it. Own it and move on," Amar stated as they wandered the desert.

"It's not that simple," she whispered. The sky went pitch black for a heartbeat and exploded with glittering stars. *She might have to return feral and shake up his afterlife until he forgave her.*

"It is," Amar baited, tugging her through a hint of distorted desert into Amadeus' bedroom.

Everyone was lounging on the bed drinking wine. Amadeus announced, "Told you they'd find us."

It felt like they were really in his room. Reminiscing, Lexy touched the emerald velvet curtains, saying, "Mission accomplished." She poured herself a goblet of wine.

Joining the pair sprawled on the lavish bed, Amar snatched the likeable Prince's wine, mocking, "Come to another world. Be Lexy's temp Handler. What could go wrong?"

"What did you do?" Amadeus questioned, scootching over to make room for her.

Climbing onto the bed, Lexy regaled, "I sat on Ricard's lap, told him there was a third daughter of Seth, and asked how they were going to overthrow him."

"That ought to do it," Amadeus chuckled.

"Shhh. I'm enjoying my last five minutes," Sophia whispered with her eyes closed. "Why can't you do it, again?"

Amadeus responded, "Substandard pedigree."

Flamboyantly bursting in, an Oracle in a cape of royal jewel tones with flowing blonde hair, floated over like a super model on a runway. Perching on the bed by Sophia, he made eye contact with Lexy, baiting, "Busy night, Fledgling."

She'd heard fledgling before in reference to a recently discovered Dragon, but she was far from new. Her Dragon was seasoned, surly, and done with everyone's shit.

The Oracle touched the princess' leg, confirming, "It's begun. One week."

Colour drained from Sophia's face as she shook her head, whispering, "I'm not what you want."

"Until we've figured out where he sent the Crypt with his spawn, it's not a choice," the Oracle decreed. With a reassuring squeeze, he stated, "Stay in the simulation until you're summoned by the council." Looking at the rest, he clarified, "That goes for all of you."

The Princess took off into the adjoining room. Amadeus got up, explaining, "Sophie needs to scream into a pillow. Choose a door. I'll find you."

Alone, her temporary Handler's hand brushed against hers. Arousal twitched as their eyes met.

Amar raspily seduced, "What do you want to do?"

Grinning, Lexy grabbed a pillow and pummelled Amar as he cackled. They wrestled until she pinned him. Desire darkened his eyes. Hairs on her neck prickled as ration argued with libido. *Straddling his situation was too tempting. She had to go.* Rolling off, Lexy got up and went out onto the balcony. *Her feelings had been hurt. She was primed for stupidity. Dragons weren't supposed to have issues like this.* Starlight over a crimson sand desert for as far as the eye could see, took her breath away. *Grey would love this. Restrained by the devotion binding their souls, it never allowed her thoughts to move past him for long.* Immortal Testing hovered above the compound, casting a shadow, drawing her eyes to the place where pain was inevitable but never the end. She felt Amar behind her. *She'd toyed with thoughts of enjoying herself then ran from his touch like a coward, having fallen prey to the repercussions of lust too recently to trust any dalliance.* Her conscience kept replaying gut-wrenching visuals of the devastation in Grey's eyes as her feelings for his enemy sunk in. Staring at the purgatory that moulded them all, Lexy confessed, "It's not you. I overreacted and blew a job."

Leaning against the railing next to her, her hot middle eastern co-conspirator consoled, "It happens."

Grinning, she questioned, "Why did they send you with me?"

"They needed someone with close ties in the Third-Tier realm to accompany you. They're just killing two birds with one stone. They must know about Sami. I'm waiting for the you have illegal offspring punishment reveal. I've been trying to think of my entombment for procreation as a relaxing dream state afterlife hiatus," Amar responded.

Gazing into his eyes, she stated, "I won't let anyone entomb you."

"I know you're winging it," Amar bravely affirmed. "It's only twenty years. The naughty dream material you've given me should last at least ten." His expression softened, caressing her scarlet hair.

As they inched closer, Lexy vowed, "I won't leave you here." Footsteps snapped them out of it. They stepped away from each other.

An Oracle stormed out, swatted Amar, and scolded, "Did you brand that alien boy Ankh?"

Wincing, Amar was about to speak when Lexy took one for the team, "I ordered him to do it."

After a visual standoff, the Oracle maintained, "You can't just bring an alien back to Earth."

"I'm Guardian. I can't allow a Third-Tier King to flippantly kill any species of mortal," Lexy decreed, holding her ground.

The Oracle probed, "Are you planning to assimilate a mortal alien into to human society and bring him with the next group through Immortal Testing?"

"You're acting like it's never been done," Lexy saucily called his bluff.

His attention shifted to her sidekick, the Oracle grilled, "What shall we do about Amar violating procreation law?"

He was right. "Allowing Third-Tier to entomb someone with a magical connection to a Guardian would be unwise.

Let's find a suitable alternative," Lexy affirmed, dead eyed serious.

"I'll speak to the council about variations of punishment we'll deem acceptable," the Oracle declared, walking away.

Holy shit. She couldn't believe she pulled that off.

Amar whispered, "You wing it like a pro." Stepping away from the railing, he said, "I don't want to think about it until it's necessary."

She'd been obsessing about Grey when Amar had real issues.

Walking so fast she had to jog after him, he reached the door, suggesting, "Let's go somewhere quiet."

They walked out onto a beach at night wearing bathing suits with people gathered around a campfire. Taking her arm, Amar confessed, "I've never been on a date. Have you?"

Enjoying the peaceful ambiance, Lexy grinned.

Titillated, Amar probed, "Now, I'm curious. Who was it? How did it happen?"

"Orin asked me to watch a movie in his room. We were both trying to get over other people. We cracked open the mini bar and played truth or dare," Lexy revealed, sitting on driftwood.

Amar sat by her, enquiring, "How was it?"

"Awesome," she overshared with a tinge of guilt.

Intently listening, Amar asked, "Did it happen again?"

"A few more times," she responded. "It was supposed to be relief pitcher casual."

He repeated, "Supposed to be?"

"We had fun. Whenever I start to let go of Grey romantically, he's drawn back like we're karmically tortured magnets."

In the faint glow of the moon, he teased, "Is it over?"

"We haven't had a chance to talk since the Tiberius fiasco," she confessed as incoming tide washed over sand close to where they were. She leapt up, laughing, "We should move."

Jogging away from the water, he shouted, "Orin doesn't give up that easily."

A part of her hoped he hadn't. Chasing him up the beach, she called out, "It's your turn!"

Stopping on a dime, Amar flirted, "Right here?"

Kicking sand at him, she clarified, "I get to hear your secrets too."

"You'll be disappointed. I'm not exciting," Amar chuckled.

Enjoying their getting to know you side excursion, Lexy teased, "I showed you mine. You show me yours."

With a giant grin, Amar caved, "What do you want to know?"

"Were you in a relationship with Samid's mother or was it a one night stand?" she questioned, walking in cool sand.

Drifting away in thought, Amar confessed, "The Aries Group has a lab in my compound. Ryta was a scientist with mind blowing genius. She was classy pretty, with raging control issues. I have a type. I started making excuses to go to the lab. We became friends. Hanging out with her was easily the best part of my day. I'd shift something on the counter by a hair and watch as her spectacular brain prompted her to fix it. My day wasn't complete until she swatted me."

Enthralled by his story, she sensed where it was going. *Amar fell in love with a mortal. This was getting deep. What would Greydon Riley do?* She thought of a six pack of beer and tossed Amar one.

Grinning, he opened it and carried on with his story, "I knew she was in love with me too. Killian told me to compel our love away and get the Aries Group to switch her posting before we succumbed to our feelings, and it destroyed her career."

He was more evolved than she thought.

"For weeks, I couldn't bring myself to do it. When our eyes met, I couldn't breathe. No, seriously. When I opened my mouth to speak it was like someone was plugging my oxygen hose. One night she called me to the lab. When I walked in, Ryta dead-eyed tranqued me."

This was the best love story. #ROMANCE

"I woke up chained to a table, pleading for her to listen as she ran tests. With her background in biochemistry and genetics, she thought she had her bases covered when she experimented on herself. You can't recreate our conditions in a lab. We're not infected. It's not a curse on a genetic line triggered by killing someone. You need Second-Tier in your family line and brutal trauma to have a shot at surviving a brain expansion. She'd killed herself to be with me and I knew it. One minute I was lecturing her for breaking the rules, and the next, she'd uncuffed me and I was doing her on the counter. Our tryst was caught on camera. She was gone the next day. They told me they transferred her. I tried to find her, but she'd vanished."

Many months later, we were sent to do a Correction. It was a brain-dead pregnant woman in a coma. Easy in and out, we just had to unplug a machine. When I discovered it was Ryta, I broke every rule to save her baby. With forged paperwork, a friend from the Aries Group transferred her to our facility where they did a c-section."

"You did all of this without a DNA test?" Lexy asked, blown away.

Shaking his head, Amar admitted, "Even if he wasn't mine, I couldn't let anyone kill her unborn child."

He was an honourable guy.

Meeting her gaze, he confessed, "Once a Correction is sent, there's no stopping it. The Third-Tier Oracles needed to sense her elsewhere to cover our tracks, so we moved her away from the compound. Mortals love foolishly and make rash decisions. She was going to spend the rest of her days wasting away in a catatonic state and it was my fault. Before I had a chance to peacefully end her life, everyone at her facility was slaughtered."

Grey would love this story. It was a shame she'd agreed to a compli-

mentary memory wipe. *It wasn't complimentary, it was something else. She couldn't remember what she agreed too.*

He solemnly concluded, "My heart ached when I looked at Sami, so I didn't. I couldn't love someone else I was destined to lose. I wanted to put him up for adoption, but Killian wouldn't hear of it. He carried Sami around for a year in a baby Bjorn. Running Ankh on our continent, I was gone a lot. When I was home, I feared Third-Tier Oracles would find Sami through his connection to me. I should have given him the love I felt for his mother. I can't ever make up for it, but I'll have an eternity to try when he survives Testing."

If.

Prince Amadeus walked up, teasing, "I leave you guys alone, tell you to have fun, and you share traumatising stories."

Awestruck, Benji said, "This is incredible."

Lexy glanced back. *Benji had glowing eyes. Wild. Was his species nocturnal?* Curious, she enquired, "What it's like on your planet?"

"Show us. Think about home when you walk through the next door," Prince Amadeus suggested with a twinkle in his eye.

"What door?" Benji questioned, spinning in the dark.

Waving a hand through near perfect imagery, Amar directed, "Hold hands so we all go with him."

Holding hands, they stepped into the unknown.

4
Otherworldly Destinations

The air was sauna humid and four brilliant moons lit up the night sky. *This was cool.* For as far as the eye could see, there was nothing but barren lavender stone and not a hint of life. Lexy whispered, "Is this where you live?"

Holding a finger to his lips, Prince Amadeus whispered, "They live in cave systems. Nothing survives on the surface."

"Oh, fun," Amar whispered. "This place doesn't sound like a fantasy destination."

It was. Her fantasy. She needed a weapon. Grinning, as shadows of winged predators passed over glowing moons, Lexy chuckled with glee as she thought of a sword. It appeared in her clutches. With a practice swing, she cockily announced, "I've got this."

Nervously, Benji warned, "You do not have this. Run for that crevasse." Without waiting for a response, the kid took off and dove into a sliver of darkness between masses of stone.

Thunderous flaps echoed as winged monstrosities gathered above the trio. "Guess we're fighting predators," Amar sighed.

"I'm a predator too," she decreed, as frenzied pterodactyl

hyena lizards swarmed into a black twister muting the starry sky.

Double sided blades appeared in Amadeus' grasp as he said, "If Benji tries to run away, his mind may get trapped in here."

Her eyes darted to the crevasse the alien they were abducting fled into. With faith in her mauve buddy, Lexy replied, "He won't leave us."

"I would," Amar sparred with their demise spinning above like a mobile of terror.

What were they waiting for? Depravities massed into a category five creepy onyx twister of fangs and claws. *There were thousands. This was exciting.*

Grimacing, Amadeus met Lexy's eyes, warning, "Turn it off. We'll bring you out after. This is going to be unpleasant."

She wasn't afraid. The ravenous unforgiving swarm descended, Lexy pivoted barefoot, bravely thinning the herd with each skilled swing of her sword. Wounded flopped on lavender stone as she persevered, experiencing each slice of dagger sharp claws and searing bites until pain faded into nothing and the Dragon within came out to play. Heckling vile creatures feasted, as she tore gnawing jaws with razor fangs off her broiling skin, pummelling monstrosities with their kin while stomping on those unfortunate enough to linger underfoot. Void of trivial concerns, there were no unbeatable foes as sweltering healing ability rid her of flesh wounds.

Growing bored of playing games with lesser beings, jaws clamped on her neck. She tore it off and thwapped the pterodactyl hyena on rock until its jaw slackened. Enraged, Lexy staggered as her essence spurted from her neck. *If these assholes tore her throat out, she was going to be pissed.* Staggering as her brain grew foggier, she claimed her throne in the hierarchy. Raising her hands with the intention of siphoning energy, she primally shrieked, shrill enough to curl the devil's toes. Winged assailants rained from the sky as energy gathered in her chest. It shivered down her limbs, sealing her throat, healing imperfections. With her heart thudding like a kick drum, she noticed her skinless deceased friends. *Whoops. She forgot they were here.* They flickered and vanished. *Where did they go?* Her brain imploded. Clutching her head, Lexy dropped to the ground writhing until agony subsided. Gasping, as she regained her bearings, she peered up. *Lovely. It had been forty years since her last brain expansion. At least it happened after the fight.*

Amar solidified, frantically checking himself for wounds, he gasped, "I have skin again, that's a relief."

Out of nowhere, Amadeus appeared on all fours, coughing. He glanced up, mumbling, "No more letting Lexy pick the venue."

"I didn't pick this one," she decreed, thoroughly entertained by the visual reset. Not a winged creature in sight. *That was fun.*

Nervously, Amar probed, "You're perky for someone who just had their throat ripped out by a lizard hyena pterodactyl. Didn't you die?"

The predatory being twitched. More were enroute on the horizon. Her eyes sparkled with anticipation.

The Prince sighed, "Can we skip being skinned alive again?"

"It's too late. Round two," Amar declared, staring at the ghoulish tornado.

With excess energy from her hyena pterodactyl lizard snack, Lexy raised her hands preparing to stop time long enough for her friends to flee. A glaring light blinded the trio, switching her plans as monsters scattered.

Benji's voice shouted, "Run!"

They sprinted away and dove in without a second thought. Casually sauntering over, Lexy poked her head in, saying, "Thanks for coming back." *An escape chute. Brilliant. Where did the light come from?* Checking out Benji's handheld contraption, she questioned, "Something small created that much light?"

Grinning, Benji prompted, "Get down the chute before they come back, and I'll show you everything."

Not requiring an explanation, she vanished down the twisty chute and was spat out into water. Hovering in place as bubbles rose, she surfaced in a lake surrounded by a dark jungle. *What in the hell?*

Amar shouted, "Get out fast!"

Swimming for the rocky shore, something brushed against her. *Fun.* Benji was ahead of her. The largest snake she'd ever seen swayed straight for her new Ankh. Splashing, she lured it away as Benji scrambled ashore. *Maybe she could eat it?* Treading water as it bumped her again, she called out, "I'll just be a minute! I'm fine! I'll catch up!" *Impermeable flesh.* It tugged her under without breaking her skin. Proud of herself as shiny fish flashed by, she enjoyed the mystical scenery until her brain's insistence for oxygen, reminded her she couldn't breathe underwater. *She didn't think this out.* When wanting the ability to breathe underwater didn't work, she focused on where it had a hold of her, willing its energy into her. As her leg heated, it released her limply plummeting into darkness. Gasping, Lexy surfaced and swam to shore.

Reaching out his hand, Amar toyed, "Still have your legs?"

Did she? They were there. Good. Crawling out onto silky orange moss, Lexy stood up as she took in the breathtaking secret world of unfamiliar oddities. The massive fuchsia hued cavern went on for miles lit by large sunlight simulating contraptions embedded in a skyscraper high ceiling. *It was incredible.* With dark trees, and rich deep tones, it had a gothic wonderland vibe.

Beneath slick black branches of violet leaves, fragrant white blooms, and twittering creatures, Benji called out, "Coming?"

Jogging after their alien friend, she had so many questions

but didn't know where to start. Strolling through the otherworldly wilderness it felt like anything could happen.

Bushes rustled ahead, Amar probed, "Is anything else going to try to eat us?"

Petting the bush while strolling past, Benji replied, "They're harmless. They eat sunshine."

Bushes needed sunshine on Earth too, but she'd never thought of phrasing it that way. Hearing something behind her, Lexy turned back. The shrubbery was following them. *Plot twist, plants could move here.* Sensing the Prince's eyes, she glanced his way, smiling.

"The lake we fell into connects their settlements through cool underwater tunnels. That gigantic snake you dealt with is the only predatory species in the tunnel system. Those winged creatures we fought on the surface fear sunlight. I love coming here. Relax and take it all in."

"I guess you don't go swimming much here," Lexy mumbled, stroking a tree's outstretched branches as she passed by. *This was amazing.*

"There are failsafe sensors in the tunnel. Third-Tier genetics dose the pool with antagonising pheromones. We override it for visitors from other colonies. It didn't occur to me to rig it for a simulated visit." Picking a flower, roots extended from where it had been torn from soil, coiling around Benji's wrist to secure it's hold.

Awestruck, Lexy whispered, "Did it feel any pain when you picked it?"

"I've never heard complaints. Everything moves here. It's never in the same place you left it. Picking anything stimulates its reproductive cycle," he replied, placing it on the ground. "It's fun to watch."

Unwinding from his wrist, with reaching root legs it moved to a chosen spot. Burgundy petals opened, threadlike pale violet veiny strands, simulated rhythmic breathing. Fascinated as it solidified, expanded into a dome, and puffed seeds into the air, Lexy whispered, "Wow," as intoxicating fragrance filled her with glee. *It would be easy to lose yourself in this world of unusual beauty.*

Amar picked a berry, asking, "Can I eat this?"

"We make drinks with those," Benji responded, eating one.

Prince Amadeus did the same and tossed a berry to Lexy, saying, "You don't want to be the only sober one when we start doing crazy shit."

She trusted Amadeus and rather enjoyed doing crazy shit. Eating one, it was sweet but tart like a raspberry. She smiled as they wandered out into a meadow of thigh high lavender flowers. Shimmering bugs zoomed by, leaving trails of glitter in the air. Reaching for floating sparkles, they stuck to her hands. "Is it pollen?" Lexy questioned, spinning in the magical field with her arms outstretched and eyes closed.

Benji shouted, "Follow me!" He vanished into the flowers as music filled the air.

They wandered over. There was a lit tunnel slide with music and revelry coming from it. "Party in the chute," Amar laughed, diving down it headfirst.

Grinning, Lexy followed, landing on a pile of black feathers. Holograms of Benji's friends from a treasured memory were dancing and chatting. Amar tugged her out of the way. Amadeus missed her by a hair, and they sprawled on feathers, laughing.

She didn't want to move. Her hand brushed Amar's. Their gazes met as he intentionally caressed her palm making her tingle. With reckless thoughts flooding her mind, Lexy yanked her hand away and got up.

Witnessing the flirtation, Amadeus teased, "Adding another player to your game?"

"I'm already in enough trouble," Lexy sparred, glancing back. Amar was lying there chuckling.

Amadeus passed her a drink, provoking, "Loosen up. I won't tell anyone. These are consequence free shenanigans."

They clinked glasses, as Lexy saluted, "To consequence free shenanigans." She drank hers. *It tasted like grape juice.* Still thirsty, her glass refilled by itself. Grinning, she savoured the next, enjoying the catchy music.

Tucking a crimson tendril behind her ear, Amadeus tempted, "Have fun with me. It might be a year before we have a chance to hang out again."

Staring into his copper-flecked dark eyes, she enquired, "How come you're not in a relationship?"

Entertained by her line of questioning, Amadeus teased, "I'm waiting for this incredible girl who has me friend zoned."

Not catching on, Lexy replied, "You should just walk up and kiss her. You're hot and sweet. She might surprise you."

Grinning, Prince Amadeus answered, "Maybe."

Hours passed in a blink as they danced, enjoying bliss inducing berry juice. As light dimmed, she caught a glimpse of blonde hair walking away in the crowd. Pretty sure she was hallucinating Grey, she pursued him down a mossy path. He vanished. Walking in darkness, she came to the place where he disappeared. There was a hole. Lexy jumped in and landed on feathers. It was pitch black. *Calling out in darkness was always a bad idea.* Sensing someone else, she whispered, "Is that you?"

"Luring me into a private feather den isn't helping me behave, Lexy," Amar seduced, caressing her leg.

Ripples of pleasure shivered through her as he gently shoved her. On a bed of feathers, titillated. *Part of her wanted to deny she'd lured him here, but she wanted to see where this berry hallucination was going.* He kissed her calf. Shocked, she cautioned, "We can't do this."

"Why not?" He toyed, feathering kisses up to her leg.

Insanely turned on, Lexy rationed, "They're going to come looking for us."

"I'll stop if they show up. I'm testing a theory," he seduced, kissing her inner thigh.

This game was getting out of hand. He bit her inner thigh. Feverishly turned on, she grabbed his hair.

Chuckling, Amar teased, "Do you really want me to stop?"

She was about to answer when Benji hollered down the hole, "You guys down there?"

They scrambled out of the way. *She was going to kill him.*

Amar shouted, "We're down here!"

Oblivious, Benji jumped in and said, "I bet you guys couldn't figure out how to get out?"

Laughing, Amar said, "Sure."

They made room after for Amadeus to land as Benji clicked and went, "Did we interrupt something?"

Amar whispered, "As long as you don't call me out for hiding under the feathers, we're all good."

Turning on the light, Benji looked at Lexy and suggested, "There's a bale room back by the eatery."

She had no idea what that meant but she was going there to escape this awkward moment. She slipped behind a curtain, and it was a bathroom. *Sort of.* She was hoping for a mirror but judging by the hole in the floor and long tube of water with a nozzle, bathrooms were rustic here. *Could she drink this water?* She called out, "Can I drink the water in the tube?"

Peering behind the curtain, Benji explained, "That is just for washing up. There's filtered water in the eatery. You don't need to hide in here. Amar told us fighting with you turned him on."

Well done, Amar. Grinning, Lexy suggested, "Give me the tour."

"Not much to see. We sleep in whatever burrow we end up in," Benji admitted. We eat kelp, fish and berries. We go on trading missions to get anything else we need. This is mining colony."

Walking out, she asked, "What do you mine?"

"Baclavite," Benji answered. Those things you fought on the way in are Baclava. Their liquified excrement powers ships and equipment."

"I killed a bunch. I didn't know," Lexy commented.

Benji replied, "We could mine for ten thousand years and barely touch the surface of what we have here. It's in the stone. It's everywhere."

"How are you feeling about leaving?" Lexy enquired.

"If you told me a week ago, I was going to be branded and abducted by earthlings, I would have been terrified. You guys have the worst rep in intergalactic tourism," he responded, grinning.

Fair enough. "I've seen E.T," she answered.

"E.T isn't real," Amar pestered.

Rolling her eyes, she bantered, "You know what I meant."

"You seem tense," Amar provoked.

Dick. She pitched a bowl.

Her interim Handler ducked. It missed him by a hair and smashed on the floor. Shocked, Amar scolded, "You're an adult!" In a flash, she had him in a chokehold. He pled, "I'm being a dick. Oklahoma!"

She let him go. He dropped on the floor gagging. *He wasted a safe word.* Noticing Amadeus' entertained expression, Lexy politely said, "Carry on. I'm done proving my point."

Grinning, The Prince continued, "Primitive beings have a difficult time with change."

"Earth isn't primitive," Lexy defended her home planet.

Amadeus questioned, "Have you ever heard of intergalactic tourism?"

Intrigued by his saucy response, Lexy admitted, "No." Her eyes darted to Benji having the best time ever. She smiled at her alien friend. He offered her berries from a bowl. She ate a few and sweetly said, "Thanks Benji."

"So, our anatomies are the same?" Amar changed the subject.

Amadeus explained, "The sunlight generators and purple kelp tint their skin. He'll be passable on Earth after enough sunshine and transfusions. You'll have to hide him in Amar's compound until he's adjusted. The night vision is evolution. He'll need to wear contacts and sunglasses."

"I can turn it off," Benji replied.

Snooping in containers, Amar sniffed one, suggesting, "He may have brain function of a Second-Tier."

Stoked, Benji admitted, "I want to go with Lexy."

Nobody was going to believe they kidnapped an alien together.

Turning back to their chat, Amar explained, "They travel. My compound is Aries Group headquarters. You'll see each other."

Prince Amadeus flickered. He held up his hand watching it. He embraced Lexy and said, "We never have enough time together. Don't worry about Grey. He'll get over it. If he doesn't, I'll randomly show up and swat him."

"I'd pay to see that," Amar chuckled, hugging Amadeus.

The Prince pointed at Benji, suggesting, "Leave these two to work out their issues. You're going to love Earth. Amar's a good guy. He'll teach you everything you need to know." He vanished.

Walking over to the wall, Benji instructed, "The square opens up. That's where you climb out. I'll meet you back at the party later." He turned off the light, teasing, "Don't kill each other, or do. If that's what you're into."

Lexy waded through the feathers and turned on the light. "We don't need the light off. That ship has sailed."

"Has it?" Amar taunted, turning it off.

She turned it back on, cautioning, "You only have one safe word left."

His body pressed against her. Amar turned it off, whispering in her ear, "We can fight first if you want."

With nerve endings dancing, Lexy tempted, "If that's what you're into." Their chests heaved in unison. He slid her shoulder straps down. Every hair on her body rose as Amar inched her dress over her voluptuous hips, and it dropped at her ankles on the floor.

His warm breath seduced, "I'll be whoever you want me to be. You're murderously pent up. I'm irrationally turned on. It's just a dream. Why not?" Sliding a hand between her thighs, he caressed her until she whimpered. Amar groaned, "I'm so hard. Say yes."

Ready to snap, Lexy gasped, "Yes."

Feverishly aroused, their mouths lustily fused as they tumbled backwards onto feathers, fulfilling carnal desires in darkness. Groaning, Amar filled the torturous ache, and they were faceless hedonistic beings seeking pleasure until they loudly climaxed.

Sprawling next to her, Amar gasped, "That was so hot."

"So hot," she agreed, trembling. "I needed that."

Catching his breath, he laughed, "Whoever you thought of is who you need to be with."

"He's unworthy. He stays in my fantasies'," Lexy confessed, blissfully satisfied.

"I aspire to be in your fantasies," he enticed, turning to her.

Facing him, Lexy asked, "We're really not going to remember any of this?"

Tracing the curve of her hip with his finger, Amar coaxed, "Not a thing. Kiss me."

Inching closer, Lexy provoked, "Where?" Their mouths met as decadent tongues bewitched. Wanting more before they were forced back into reality, she mounted him, rocking her hips and they were lost in a gratuitous blur for hours.

5
Not The Mile High Club

Opening her eyes in a rose quartz tomb with a purple stranger on one side and Amar on the other, her memory scrolled back feeding her images of a fight in the colosseum. She recalled seeing both guys naked with no context. Lexy reached for Amar's hand to see if he was conscious, it flopped. She placed her palms on the inside of the lid to open the tomb. With familiar grinding of stone, it slowly opened. She peered out. *It was Ankh's Middle Eastern Crypt in Amar's compound.* Amar's eyes were wide open. *They were both dead. Awkward. Did she eat them? Amar's crew might be choked if she ate their leader. She needed Grey. She should wake them up.* Placing her hands on Amar's chest, she closed her eyes willing her energy into him. Heat gathered in her chest and travelled down her arms. The back of her neck tingled as Amar opened his eyes, gasping.

Amar asked, "What are we doing in a tomb together?" He sat up and noticed the deceased purple guy, "Who is that?"

Confused, Lexy confessed, "I was the only one awake. The last time I woke up with dead Ankh in my tomb, I'd drained everyone for the energy to get us home after accidentally killing the Healers operating the tombs. There are no Healers in here though."

"Why do we have a purple alien?" Amar quizzed.

Catching a glimpse of his hand, she checked out the Ankh symbol on his palm and said, "He's Ankh. Did we brand an alien? Can we do that?"

"I don't remember. We must have had our memory wiped. It takes a while to reboot events leading up to the erased portion of time. We have an alien with no backstory and the Aries Group has a lab in my compound."

"Where is Grey?" Lexy questioned, concerned. "What do you remember?"

"You fell from the sky into a colosseum in the Third-Tier world. That alien kid was fighting. I saw you naked. There was cake. That's all I've got," he recalled, grinning.

"Should I wake him up?"

"No, don't. He's going to panic. We need an explanation. Close the tomb. I'll store him until I have one," he suggested.

She placed her hands on the side of the tomb. It ground shut and hummed. Amar helped her up. Attraction tingled. She yanked her hand away, insisting, "I should contact my group. I've never gone anywhere without Grey."

"Relax, we'll figure it out," Amar assured.

Perched on the Ankh Tomb, a bar fight flickered in her mind. *Before she slit his throat, Tiberius called her out on having feelings for him, making it clear they'd slept together. Grey saw and heard everything.* Recalling the devastation on her Handler's face as it sunk in, her heart ached. *She was so furious. She wasn't paying attention and they were killed by Trinity. The lecture from Azariah in the in-between. She was summoned by the Third-Tier. Amar was her temporary Handler.* Shaking her head as tears filled her eyes, she blinked them away. *There was only one logical explanation for sending Amar. She'd destroyed her Handler bond.* The gravity of the situation settled in her heart.

Solemnly, Amar interjected, "I've been listening to your thoughts. I get why they opted out of sending Grey with his overdramatic history, but we barely know each other. I should be entombed for procreation. Sending me was a gamble." Willing the memories to return so they could fill in the blanks, their gazes met as Amar asked, "Do you care about Tiberius?"

"I can't," Lexy decreed.

Smiling, he sparred, "That look in your eyes, says you do."

"I have to get back to Grey to fix this," she whispered.

Amar replied, "You are part Guardian. You don't have to answer to anyone."

"I can't live this life without him," she whispered, as the distance between them vanished.

"You can," Amar assured, taking her hands.

It felt like they'd had this conversation. Their eyes locked. This time she didn't let go. Calmer as she looked at their joined hands, she whispered, "The hoodoo they used to give you a hold on me isn't gone."

Exhaling, he confirmed, "It sure isn't." Massaging, her palm, Amar soothed, "We'll find out where Ankh is, and I'll take you back. I'll leave the alien entombed until one of us remembers why we have him. I'll make sure you have a way to contact me."

A part of her needed to go back more than anything in the world. Holding Amar's hand, it felt like they knew each other. Images of freezing time, killing a bunch of Third-Tier at a banquet and pantsing a King whooshed through her mind. Without letting go, she silently snickered.

Intrigued, he said, "You remembered something."

Squeezing his hand, Lexy chuckled, "No biggie. I always kill people at banquets."

Tugging her up with him, he toyed, "Come on. Let's get you back to your group, troublemaker."

Fair enough. She was a troublemaker. As they reached the door,

Amar whispered, "Our memories were wiped. Stick with that until we know what happened."

"Yes boss," Lexy answered. Grinning, she retracted it, "Wait a minute. I'm your boss now. Playfully shoving Amar, she ordered, "Kneel."

Backing her against the door, he bit his lip, flirting, "They don't know we're back yet."

Wide eyed with flushed cheeks and her stomach in a knot, her reaction spoke volumes. *How close did they get?*

"Kidding," Amar laughed. "You should have seen your face." Messing her hair, he teased, "Let's go figure out where they are." He placed his hands on the print on stone. The door opened. They stepped into the hall, startling a group of Ankh.

A girl with lustrous raven hair, smoked Amar's arm, scolding, "Next time you take a side job, tell us what's happening. We were concerned." Turning to the crimson-haired Dragon, she said, "Sorry, that was rude. I'm Sarah."

"Hi, Sarah" Lexy replied, politely shaking her hand.

Walking down the passageway, Sarah divulged, "We've been in daily contact with your group. They're in Canada. We have transport awaiting your return."

"Fun. How many hours is this claustrophobic flight?" Lexy mumbled, wandering after the girl Amar left in charge.

Catching her comment, Amar offered, "You don't want to know. I'll go with you."

With a scathing look, Sarah commented, "Seriously?"

Touching her arm, Amar stated, "She's my responsibility. Save the pointless lecture our memories were wiped." Livid, Sarah stormed away cursing in French.

Nudging Amar, Lexy whispered, "Girlfriend?"

"It's casual," Amar replied. Sarah slammed a door.

Lexy whispered, "It doesn't look casual. Make up with her, I'll wait."

"I don't play games," Amar decreed. They wandered into

a cafeteria. Grabbing bottles of water, he suggested, "Hydrate and order something to eat. I'll finalize our plans."

Halfway through her second water, fragmented memories pieced together like a puzzle revealing a clear picture of what happened before entering the simulation. *She'd done an impressive amount of crazy shit. How did it all play out? They branded an alien and brought him to Earth. How were they planning to pass off a purple guy as human? She had so many questions. Did she get to hang out with Prince Amadeus? Why wasn't Amar entombed? She'd proved herself a viable Guardian before she agreed to the wipe. Maybe it was all fun and games after that?*

She was almost finished her meal when he came back. Visibly irritated, Amar snagged a premade sandwich from the display and ate it as they strolled down the corridor. "You don't have to come with me," she said, stepping out into sweltering heat. A black sedan was waiting with the engine running.

Amar opened the door, teasing, "They were adamant about not flying you anywhere without backup. You must have done something wild the last time you were with the Aries Group."

Getting in, she shimmied over, disclosing, "They can't sedate me."

Noticing tinted glass protecting the driver, as he got in, Amar whispered, "This is a long flight."

"They're all long unsedated in a tube," Lexy sparred, smiling. "Did you remember anything else?"

He whispered, "Not yet." Intrigued, he probed, "Did you?"

"Everything until the memory wipe," Lexy whispered. "It's not helpful. The answers we need happened in the simulation."

'They're recording this conversation,' he cautioned telepathically.

If they kill me, I can ask Azariah.

'All you'll do is freak them out if you heal too fast,' Amar replied via thought.

True. Glancing his way, she enquired, "Did you have a chat with Sarah?"

"I don't participate in head games," he decreed.

It would be nice if that worked on Grey.

'Shall I stick around to explain things or just drop you off?' Amar shot back telepathically.

I've never tried refusing to play his jealousy games. It's worth a try.

'Are you going to stay strong or fold like a cheap deck of cards?' Amar thought, smiling.

She was going to fold. She knew it. He was her weakness.

The vehicle stopped and the locks clicked. Amar opened the door, waited for her to get out and closed it behind her, thinking, *'How long are you down for when you die?'*

It used to be roughly twenty minutes. Sometimes I don't die now. I haven't had the opportunity to figure it out yet. I'm winging it. Their eyes met with a strange sense of déjà vu. Without a word aloud they followed a man up a ramp into the cargo hold. *Fun.* Pressing a remote control one tube opened, she glared at Amar saying, "Let me guess, you don't have to be in a pod?"

Amar laughed, "I'll travel in one so it's fair. I could use a nap." He nodded at a guy who opened a second pod and climbed in.

Must be nice.

A voice instructed, "Choose your method of sedation. Tranq, gas or dart?"

"All three," Lexy suggested. *You never know.*

'Stop messing with the new recruit,' Amar thought.

She heard him. He could have stayed awake to entertain her.

"If I give you all three, I'll kill you," the Aries Group Agent laughed.

Perfect. She wanted to wake up in the in-between. She had questions for Azariah. "Go for it. You can't kill me," Lexy dared.

Confined in a tube, Amar rolled his eyes, commenting, "I'll take the gas. Give it to her as well."

Gas hissed into her boring sterile pod. Grinning at the silence from Amar, Lexy knocked on the inside of her pod. The new recruit's head popped in. She sighed, "How many hours is this flight?"

"How are you conscious?" The agent grilled, amazed.

This guy might be fun. She dared, "I'm sure you've heard of me?"

"It's my first flight," he confessed. "My interview was over six months ago."

The Aries Group thinks you're expendable. She was going to entertain the shit out of this newb. "Aren't you the slightest bit curious about why you're gassing two people in a tube?"

"You are agents who need down time before their next job," he revealed what he'd been told.

This was going to be fun. Lexy quizzed, "Have you ever watched a superhero movie?"

"Why?" He probed, grinning in the glass.

She provoked, "Go ahead. Try to sedate me. You won't get in trouble. I'm sure they'd love to know how much it takes to knock me out."

"What if you're a captive and you're trying to get me to kill you before you can be questioned?" The new guy sparred.

Messing with the stranger's head, she baited, "Oh my, you're a mystery thriller guy too. Where have you been all my life?"

"How old are you?" He questioned, gazing through the glass.

Truth be told she wasn't sure anymore. Every time she tried to think about what year she was born, her brain switched lanes on the highway. Opting for honesty, Lexy replied, "I'm not sure."

"You're not sure?" He teased, smiling.

"Planning to ask me out?" She toyed, revelling in the fuchsia glow of his cheeks.

Grinning, he sparred, "Hitting on captives is frowned upon."

"I'm here willingly," the scarlet-haired Ankh revealed.

The young agent questioned, "What do you do for the Aries Group?"

"Assassin," Lexy volunteered, detached like she was reading off a menu. His eyes twitched with nervous energy and her dark trickster heart danced. "Is there anyone else onboard?"

Anxiously, he fibbed, "Twenty agents."

"For one person. Weird," Lexy baited as he looked down to his left. *He was thinking up a whopper. She should stop him before he embarrassed himself.* "What's your name?"

"Duke," he answered.

His parents were assholes. "Who saddled you with Duke? Was it your mom or dad?" Lexy enquired. *This guy hadn't gone through any training. Nothing.*

"It's my grandfather's name," he revealed.

Trying to see how much personal info she could get out of him, Lexy declared, "You're from the south like me. Texas or Kentucky?"

"Alabama," he replied, grinning.

She flirted, "I bet your last name is Lee."

"Edwin," he sparred with his elbows balanced on her tube.

Smiling, she chatted, "Cool. There's an Edwin family where I'm from. All of their first-born sons have the same middle name. What's yours?"

"Aaron," he divulged, innocently.

Duke Aaron Edwin from Alabama. This was far too entertaining. "I'm immortal, Duke," she slipped it out.

He said, "What?"

"That's adorable," Lexy corrected with a Cheshire Cat grin. "You should let me out, Duke Aaron Edwin from Alabama."

"You tricked me," he accused.

She confessed, "It wasn't hard."

"I don't have to talk to you," he stated.

"You shouldn't. I feel bad. Don't talk to assassins in pods, Duke," Lexy reprimanded. *They haven't told him anything.* "You got on a sketchy plane alone, to gas hitmen in pods with only a pilot. What if something went wrong?"

"It's good money," the new guy defended his choice. His eyes narrowed. "If they're recording this, you're going to get me fired."

Sending someone untrained was a red flag. She saw it floating in the breeze and tuned it out. Instinct nudged her. Were these pods waterproof? It was going to be inconvenient if they crashed and sunk into the ocean. Only behaving because Amar was with her, Lexy disclosed, "I won't tell anyone you gave me your name."

"Thanks," Duke replied. "I'd let you out if I was allowed to."

Grinning, she sparred, "I'd let myself out if Amar wouldn't get in trouble."

Her mind darted back to her age. *Why couldn't she remember? It was bothering her. She didn't even know the month of her birth.*

"I should sedate you before I give you my credit card info," he mumbled.

True. "Giving me all three may get you twenty minutes without me picking your brain," she toyed.

"Swear you're not playing me," he whispered, pointing at her through the glass.

He was far too sweet and innocent. He shouldn't be here. It was a shitty thing for the Aries Group to do. She'd never been in one of these pods for longer than four hours. She wasn't a fan of enclosed spaces. Calmly, Lexy tried pressing the issue, "Listen Duke, I can get out. I'm an assassin with an abnormal tolerance to sedation. If I were you, I'd take advantage of my offer to play with the dose and report your findings back to the Aries Group. If you find a way to knock me out, they'll be impressed."

"Swear it," he replied.

"Sure. I swear," she pledged.

He replaced the cartridge. It hissed filling the chamber. When the smoke cleared, she was fine. "Try something else," Lexy urged.

"I'm going to get in trouble for this," he mumbled as a dart sunk into her chest.

Humming a catchy tune as he tried again, the dart bounced off impermeable flesh. *Cool. She accidentally did that.* Lexy shook her head. *Nothing.* "The dart didn't break my skin," she disclosed.

"That's impossible," he stated, peering in at her.

His level of obtuse was making her sleepy. She had shit to do. She needed to die for a spell. "You're a science guy," Lexy hinted. He loaded another gas cartridge. It hissed into the pod. "How long is this flight?" She asked, growing impatient.

"Roughly thirteen hours to Vancouver. After we refuel, there's three more hours," he answered, unwrapping a chocolate bar.

Now, she wanted chocolate. Please kill me. She could take off her earring and cut herself? That would heal in five seconds. There were no other agents on this flight. She should get out and stretch her legs. She wasn't going to hurt anyone. Touching the inside panel, she shot a burst of energy. The pods opened. *Cool.* The plane lurched. *Uh, oh.* It nosedived. *Shit!* Leaping out, Lexy sprinted for the hatch and yanked on it. *It was locked. Dicks.* She broke it and ran for the slumped pilot. They were careening towards blue ocean. *Crap! Shit! Video games!* She pulled up with the force of descent shaking the plane bowing ocean as waves rippled away. *Holy shit.* Holding her breath as their elevation rose. *She almost crashed a plane.* With adrenaline racing, and no idea if they were going in the right direction, Lexy yelled, "Wake up, Amar!"

Freaking out, Duke plunged adrenaline into his chest.

Amar sat up, cursing, "What! The! Fuck!" The new guy fainted.

Holding the aircraft steady, Lexy shouted, "My bad!"

Bursting into the cockpit, Amar froze when he saw the unconscious pilot. Out of breath, he stammered, "I can't fly this! Tell me you didn't kill the pilot!"

Handing over the controls, she toyed, "Your guess is as good as mine. Handle this, temp."

Clutching controls, Amar muttered, "Bring him back from the dead if you must. I'll correct him after we've landed."

Placing her hands on the pilot's chest, heat gathered and tingled down her limbs. Startled, the pilot opened his eyes.

Shutting down the urge to throttle her, Amar softened his magical Siren gaze and locked on the pilot's eyes, probing, "How many recording devices on this plane and where are they located?" The pilot robotically listed them. "There was an unexpected wind shear. You saved us. We were in the cargo bay the whole time."

That was a lame excuse. Lexy snickered as he shoved her towards the hatch.

Frazzled to his core, Amar hissed, "What did you do? Explain before the new guy wakes up."

"I was bored. I wanted to see how easy it would be to open the pod," she whispered.

Wide eyed, Amar scolded, "Manipulating energy crashes planes. Do you understand why you need to stay in a pod now?"

Sheepishly, she whispered, "Of course, I see it now."

"If you fried the circuit board, we'll suffocate repeatedly for the next seventeen hours," he decreed. Checking the panel, he said, "Mine's fine."

Hers was fried. She shrugged and got in. *Whatever.*

Stopping her, Amar offered, "Trade me places. I'll stay dead. You won't."

"It might be fun," Lexy replied. "Shut it. I'm good."

Shaking his head, he chuckled, "You might be insane."

Might? Grinning, Lexy apologized, "Sorry for almost killing the pilot."

"Never speak of this, you maniac," Amar teased. "Want me to overdose you so it's faster?"

Shrugging, she answered, "I tried to get Duke Aaron Edwin from Alabama to tranq me with everything. I even told him I was a hitman who could get out. He was hesitant. When he told me how long the flight was, I didn't want to stay in the pod."

"Good thing I came with you," Amar sighed, grinning. "You need to hug your damn Handler and beg his forgiveness."

Laughing, she teased, "I thought you were on my side."

"Not anymore, Hannibal," he baited, shaking his head.

She didn't eat anyone. Grinning at the impromptu nickname, she sighed, "Let's find out what it takes to put me down."

"You fried the circuit board, so gas is out. Let's see what Duke has in his bag." Reading vials, he chuckled, "Want to drink this?"

Why not? He passed it to her. Downing it, she reviewed it, "It tastes like peroxide."

"I'm not going to ask how you know what peroxide tastes like," Amar muttered. Playing large animal tranq roulette, he handed her another clear vial.

"Bottoms up," she saluted, drinking it. *Nothing.* She held out her hand, prompting, "Just give me the bag." Duke stirred. Intending to put their mortal cohort down for a few more minutes, Lexy reached for him.

Amar swatted her hand, reprimanding, "What part of almost crashing into the ocean did you miss? You can't manipulate energy on a plane."

"Are we just going to let Duke wake up?" Lexy questioned, opening and downing random vials.

Reaching into the circuit board of Lexy's pod, Amar tore

the wires out. Pocketing tell-tale evidence, he directed, "Play along."

Sitting up, the guy groggily mumbled, "What happened?"

"Don't panic," Amar said, gazing into his eyes.

Wide eyed, the guy bartered, "Don't kill me."

"We have no reason to hurt you. I woke up. I don't need to be in a pod, so you let me out. We were going to crash. I tore the wires out of Lexy's pod. The pilot regained control of the plane and saved us. You were terrified. I vetoed Lexy being put in my pod if she voluntarily took tranquilizers." The mortal nodded mindlessly.

Taking another vial out, Lexy drank it like a shot. *Yucky.*

Nervous, the mortal said, "Did you just drink an entire vial of large animal tranquilizer?"

Cross legged on the floor, she showed him the pile of empty vials on her lap, saying, "It's fine. I took these ones and I'm not even buzzed."

"My god, you're going to die," he gasped.

Amar's hypnotic eyes met with the mortals. He tweaked his recollection of events, "Lexy offered to see how much she could take so the Aries Group could get the dosage right next time." Noticing the deck of cards, he added, "Nothing worked. We played cards. She's nice."

Liar.

'If they knew you almost crashed a plane because you were bored, you'd be banned from flying with Aries Group Air,' Amar answered via thought. *'Be nice to this guy.'*

I'll try. Bet I can trick him into telling me his sibling's names too. "Feel like playing crazy eights?" Lexy suggested, shuffling the deck.

"Whatever kills time," the mortal said, passing the cards to Amar.

6

We Abducted an Alien

*A*fter a thorough sweep for recording devices camouflaged as curiosity, and far too many hands of cards, they reached their destination in northern BC where they were given jackets and boots. Wandering out of the plane, the pilot apologized for what happened earlier. With game faces on, they high fived the pilot for his bravery. Amar told the agents he'd be back by morning. They dashed to their idling rental vehicle in a downpour and drove away in the wee morning hours with not a car on the road. As soothing rhythmic rain pelted the windshield, her eyelids grew heavier until she was fighting to keep them open. Lexy suggested, "We need coffee."

Amar turned on music, replying, "I'll stop at the first open gas station we see, but we're in the middle of nowhere, and it's two AM."

Glancing over at the guy who'd been all but a stranger with the same brand before they'd been partnered up, Lexy probed, "What do you think we did in the simulation?"

"Usually, I hardcore party and do naughty things. I went

into this job knowing I might not be granted permission to leave. I'd imagine that knowledge tainted my carefree state of mind. Your multiple murder sprees before even entering it, may have kept me locked to your side so I'd be willing to bet we didn't go anywhere near the fun room," her exhausted immortal babysitter teased, grinning.

Having her memory erased wasn't a foreign scenario. When she awoke from a Dragon state, her dastardly deeds from jobs were foggy at best. As scenery muted by darkness passed, Lexy enquired, "How will our Clan's know what deals we've made?"

"The Third-Tier Oracles will feed information to Azariah, and she'll pass it on to ours. Our Oracles will read our minds to fill in the missing pieces of the story." Pulling over at a lighted gas station with cars parked outside, he chuckled, "I don't miss this weather."

It was see your breath biting cold as they got out and sprinted into the station. *Amar's compound's heat gave you a wimpy temperature gage jumping climates. Bet he was freezing. Coming back to crisp, cool weather made her feel alive.* As they fixed themselves a coffee, she passed him flavoured creamer.

"I'm used to my coffee black," Amar disclosed.

Grinning, Lexy held it out, teasing, "Why have bitter coffee?" Attraction flickered as their hands touched.

Amar poured in french vanilla, whispering, "For you."

As he paid, she observed. Before this excursion with Amar, she'd known who he was but never seen past his status. *She hadn't noticed how attractive he was.* Their unspoken intimacy with no context intrigued her. *Had something happened between them or was this just a side effect of a magical bond?* Walking back to the vehicle, Lexy questioned, "Does your group ever go to cold places?"

"Europe is full of cold places," Amar teased, unlocking the doors as they approached.

Getting in, she put her coffee in the holder, saying, "In

forty years we've only had one Testing group make it out. Why would you send your son in with us?"

"You," Amar confessed, pulling away.

Shaking her head while fiddling with the station, she called his bluff, "Liar! You barely knew me."

Grinning, Amar reminded, "Your group came to our banquet to see if Dragons stomping out the egos of our Testing Group in the in-between made a difference. It didn't. Sami leaving with you, was their only chance. It wasn't that long ago."

Her priorities had been all over the place for six months. Blushing as the rendezvous in a dark hallway with Tiberius entered her mind, Lexy replied, "Middle of the night gapped. My bad."

Past coy games, he revealed, "I can hear your thoughts. I saw the footage from the hallway. I knew you were naughty before this job."

Tangible tension drew her eyes to his. Opting for distraction, Lexy offered him a bite of her Snickers bar.

Chewing it, Amar commented, "I'm bringing a box of these home."

She took a bite after him without thinking about it. *Weird. Her germ phobia issues usually got in the way of sharing food.* Steering the conversation, she teased, "Give her a Snickers bar. She'll forgive you."

Beaming, Amar chuckled, "I'm not sharing." Turning off the highway, down the gravel road past cabins into the woods, he forewarned, "I have to be honest with Markus."

She knew he did. Unconcerned, Lexy questioned, "Do they know we're coming?"

"I'm sure they know you made it back. Other than that, your guess is as good as mine," Amar answered, cruising slowly into darkness with crackling tires on gravel.

Finding their RV's next to a cabin, they parked. *It looked like everyone was asleep. She owed Amar an apology.*

Taking her hand, Amar asked, "Do you need help smoothing things over with Grey?"

"That's going to take longer than you have. You told the pilot you'd be back by morning," Lexy countered. "Thanks for having my back."

Kissing her hand, Amar flirted, "It's been an adventure. See you at our next banquet."

The cabin door opened as Lexy got out. Arrianna dashed to the car. The blonde with a messy bun and a heart of gold, embraced her, whispering, "Grey's been a mess."

Coming out, Markus strolled over with a welcoming smile. Leaning into the car, their leader offered, "We have plenty of room. Spend the night."

"Wish I could. There's a flight waiting. I should take off," Amar replied. Pointing at Lexy, he directed, "Contact me if you remember anything about our new friend."

Nodding, Lexy left Markus chatting with Amar. As the girls walked to the cabin, Arrianna whispered, "What new friend?"

Giving truth a shot, Lexy whispered, "We abducted an alien."

Shoving her, Arrianna laughed, "Sure you did."

From the couch, Orin mumbled, "I'm going to pass out now."

Checking out the rustic cabin. Her eyes were drawn to Orin snuggled under blankets on the dated mustard yellow couch. A toilet flushed. *Grey must be in the bathroom.*

With a welcoming dimpled grin, Ankh's Oracle came out of the washroom. Yanking an elastic out of her chestnut hair, Jenna announced, "We've been waiting up for you."

Grey wasn't here.

"Azariah linked to Amar before he left. His version of events was fed directly to me. Your memories will fill in the blanks," Jenna explained. "Do you mind?"

"Go for it," Lexy answered, shutting down the sting of her

Handler's absence. Following their Oracle, she sat beside her on the bed.

Touching her temples, their Oracle concentrated. Relaxing her hold, Jenna probed, "I bet you can't remember anything from the simulation?"

"Nothing," Lexy confirmed. Her eyes darted to the door. *Grey should be here.*

"It's a clean memory wipe but I'll find it," Ankh's Oracle affirmed. Only the whites of her eyes were visible as she searched for information.

As the Oracle dived deep into her subconscious, Lexy's eyes grew heavier until she passed out.

THE DOOR OPENED. MARKUS LEFT AN EMPTY BAG OF SALT ON the floor as their Oracle's eyes returned to normal. Getting up, Jenna walked over to their leader, revealing, "That was an impressively thorough memory wipe. Accessing sealed information fatigued her brain. Those two did a list of crazy shit nobody will believe."

Arrianna wandered over, enquiring, "Abduct an alien crazy?"

"Neither remembers why they did it," Markus confirmed. "Speak freely. I've circled the cabin with salt. Amar filled me in. They came to in his Crypt with a branded purple alien."

"That's hilarious" Arrianna commented, beaming.

Flinging a blanket off, Orin got up, laughing, "I'm up now. I've got to know the story behind the alien abduction."

With his arm around Arrianna, Markus explained, "I wasn't allowed to tell you anything past Lexy was summoned by Third-Tier. If our thoughts were read by their Oracles, the gamble we took would have blown up in our faces. Going into this, we knew it was a trap. The Daughters of Seth Prophecy signifies the end of King Ricard's reign. Lexy was told to make sure The King understood his place in the immortal hierarchy. Amar was sent as her temporary Handler, assuming it was a one-way trip. Azariah foresaw a way to stop his entombment for procreation, but everything had to play out perfectly."

Scowling, Arrianna whispered, "I can't believe you kept this a secret."

Hugging her, Markus gazed into her eyes, whispering, "I had too. You were in Lexy's Testing Group. They would have tried to read her closest connections first." Tenderly kissing her lips, he said, "Stay for the recap of their adventures." Looking at Jenna, their leader prompted, "Go ahead."

Taking a seat by Orin on the couch, Jenna regaled the highlights, "Lexy dropped from a swirling black vortex in the sky into the colosseum during an alien's battle. After the fight, The King came over the loudspeaker, scolding, know your place, Dragon. She shouted, know your place, Third-Tier! He tried to capture her. Lexy went Dragon feral. He evacuated the colosseum. Amar told The King he was given the ability to stop her, but he'd violated our Treaty, so he needed his word. Ricard told Amar to keep her under control at the banquet."

Struggling to maintain a serious demeanour, Orin whispered, "Has she ever not killed someone at a banquet?"

Markus shook his head. Jenna disclosed, "Amar was given a magical safe word."

"What was the safe word?" Orin probed, enthralled by the tale.

Jenna revealed, "Oklahoma." Everyone cracked up laughing. When they pulled themselves together, she continued, "She'd chopped off fifty of his guards' heads before Amar got close enough to use it."

"How did they end up with the alien?" Arrianna questioned.

Their Oracle whispered, "Amar branded him, so he'd be

safe in the Ankh Crypt while they attended the banquet. The King decided marrying Lexy was his next logical move."

"Oh, no," Orin gasped, on the edge of his seat, enthralled.

"When it didn't go as planned, he tried to capture her again, so she froze time, pantsed The King, and killed a bunch of his men. He conceded because she used a Guardian ability. They opted to do the rest of the evening virtually for safety reasons. I'm not allowed to discuss much about the simulation. I can say, when they came for Amar, Lexy told their Oracle, she couldn't allow them to entomb anyone with a connection to a Guardian and suggested they find an alternative punishment."

"What is his punishment?" Markus asked, needing the missing piece of the puzzle.

Jenna answered, "When they give me the information, you'll be the first to know."

Taking control of the narrative, their leader disclosed, "Our priority is reconnecting Lexy and Grey. On the way home, she busted out of a pod because she was bored and nearly took down a plane."

Wide eyed, Orin said, "What?"

Upset, Arrianna grilled, "Where was Amar?"

"He was gassed," Markus answered. Looking at their Oracle, their leader probed, "Do you have her version of events?"

Composing herself, Jenna revealed, "They were in a nose-dive heading for the ocean with an unconscious pilot. She managed to pull up in time and level out the plane. The pod attendant woke Amar. Lexy revived the pilot and Amar compelled him to believe it was wind shear. They destroyed the evidence and concocted a barely believable story."

"Wait. How did he wake up Amar?" Orin asked.

Markus revealed, "An EpiPen in the heart."

Shaking his head, Orin mumbled, "Grey should be here." He got up and put on his jacket. "If we're having a sleepless night worried about her taking down a plane, her bloody Handler can too." He stormed out, slamming the door.

Intrigued by Orin's outrage, Jenna declared, "Her methods are sketchy, but she gets the job done."

Markus replied, "Always."

The door opened. Orin came in, muttering, "He didn't come back with the newbies. He took off with a girl at the bar."

"That boy could get laid at a nunnery," Arrianna commented. "He'll show up in the morning."

Opening the door for his adorable, witty better half, Markus stepped aside so she could walk by, teasing, "Still making excuses for your ex?"

Glancing back as she sauntered back to their RV, Arrianna toyed, "Come to bed when you're done being jealous."

Leaning in, their leader suggested, "Get some rest before Drama Fest." He closed the door.

Laying on the couch, Orin tugged up his blanket, mumbling, "I can't wait."

7
Blowing Up Your Afterlife

*T*raitorous dreams kept circling back to illicit encounters with Tiberius. Dangling above the precipice of self-destruction by just her fingertips, Lexy reset each steamy visual with beautiful memories of Grey until the alluring aroma of fresh brewed coffee, sizzling bacon and easy conversation woke her. With the weight of remorse on her chest, Lexy opened her eyes. *Her Handler wasn't here. She didn't have to look. She felt his absence. A fling with an enemy tanked her afterlife. She thought she was too intelligent to be fooled by obvious shit.* Shoving down the onset of a pointless conscience, Lexy forced a smile as she got up, raspily saying, "Breakfast smells great."

Dancing with earbuds in as she wiped the counters, Jenna answered loudly, "Have a shower. Orin brought your bag over."

It hadn't gone unnoticed that Orin was here awaiting her return when her Handler wasn't.

After a shower, Lexy towel dried her hair, contemplating the merits of shutting her emotions off and letting the chips fall where they may. *She might as well look good while dealing with*

SACRIFICIAL LAMB CLUB

Grey. Putting on makeup with a coat of cherry red lipstick, she gazed at her reflection. *Everyone would know what she'd done.* Ready to face the day, she wandered out.

Passing her a coffee, Jenna asked, "Did you enjoy hanging out with Amar?"

Inhaling java, she took a sip, revealing, "Amar's a good guy. I'm missing a lot of time." *Their Oracle was grinning.* She probed, "Something tells me you know everything."

"I do," Jenna confessed. "Azariah set up a direct psychic feed to Amar. With your recollection, everything makes sense. I'll tell you anything you want to know."

Placing her coffee on the counter, Lexy said, "If it can wait, I need to talk to Grey."

"It can wait," Jenna affirmed.

Stepping outside, everything was damp. The overcast dark sky hinted foreboding. Nobody was under the awning at the picnic table. If she tore off the band aid, they'd get past it faster, but her legs wouldn't budge. *If Grey spent their time apart packing for a guilt trip, she didn't have to join him.*

Peering out the door, Astrid shouted, "You're back! Get in here!"

"My coffee is getting cold," Lexy backtracked, wishing she hadn't come out.

Shutting the door, Astrid came out, and embraced her, whispering, "We took the newbies out last night. He's not back yet. He knows he's wrong. Come inside and say hi. I'll talk to Haley. We'll trade driving partners for this next leg if he hasn't pulled his head out of his ass."

"Does everyone know what I did?" Lexy whispered.

"It's just Haley, me and the newbies. They are too hung over to care," Astrid answered.

Lexy followed her inside. *The four untested Ankh were at the table, looking rough.*

Frying eggs in a skillet with a friendly smile and fluorescent pink hair, Haley explained, "Orin went to pick up Grey. They should be back soon."

Staring into his coffee cup, the new Ankh Dean glanced up, mumbling, "Good morning, gorgeous."

When a guy with no interest in girls called her gorgeous, she believed it.

Looking too young to be hungover, with dark hair in an impressively wild birdy, Molly waved. Not involved in drunken shenanigans because she was pregnant, Emma smiled. Her eyes were drawn to Amar's son. Sami didn't acknowledge her. Lexy gave bonding a shot, "Your Dad says hi."

"What Dad?" Sami dared her to come to Amar's defence.

Entertained by the teen's candour, Lexy saw the resemblance to Amar. *Those almond shaped brown eyes must have come from his mother.* Deliberately pushing his buttons, she baited, "You have Amar's jawline and nose."

Wide eyed like she was working his last nerve, Sami poured himself more coffee from the carafe on the table.

She was looking forward to training him. Addressing the elephant in the room, no inner dialogue pun intended, Lexy looked at Emma, asking, "How are you feeling, hun?"

"Like a beached whale," Emma chuckled, spreading peanut butter on toast.

"Stop eating if it concerns you," Sami mumbled, buttering a bagel.

Scowling, Dean said, "Fat shaming a pregnant friend. Wow."

"I don't have friends," Sami taunted, smirking.

"Kick him," Dean decreed.

"Ouch," Sami complained. He tattled, "Molly kicked me."

"This shit is getting tedious," Haley sighed, bringing over a plate.

It was going to take so much work to attach this Testing group. They were still at ground zero with Sami.

Walking back with her to the other cabin, Astrid said, "If they were going into Testing without Sami, they'd make it."

"They'll attach through shared trauma," Lexy affirmed, aware it was an uphill battle. *Breaking Amar's kid was doable.*

Opening the door, Arrianna rushed, "We've been waiting for you."

Walking into the cabin, Astrid announced, "Grey isn't back."

Hooking up with a stranger was more important.

Jenna placed a plate on the table. Glancing over at Astrid, she invited her to stay, "I made extra."

Lexy refilled her coffee and fixed herself a plate. Jenna began scolding her for taking down an Aries Group flight. *She deserved this lecture. Knowing she was wrong didn't mean she intended to admit it.* Lexy responded, "I was going to be wide awake in a pod for over 18 hours. I'm not getting in one again."

"We'll avoid putting you on long flights," Jenna bargained. "These were extenuating circumstances. Other than the misstep in our world, you achieved everything you were sent to do. Well done."

Tires crackled over gravel. Astrid leapt up. Peering out the window, she said, "Grey's back."

Staring into her mug, Lexy didn't budge.

Getting up, Jenna announced, "Stay here until I'm done chewing him out."

She had no intention of going to him now.

With the hum of Grey's reprimanding as back noise, Astrid whispered, "He's been fixated on you being gone. I didn't even see him take off last night."

Weight settled on her heart, as guilt regained its hold. *Seeking pleasure to avoid pain was a predictable Greydon Riley move.* Lexy whispered, "Amar was there to blur my focus. I'm guessing he wasn't left with a surrogate Dragon."

"Jenna said his necklace for nausea and panic heightened his fear of losing you," Arrianna explained.

"Don't pussyfoot around the unhinged jealousy bullshit," Astrid mumbled, wide eyed.

Jealousy was warranted with how they left things.

"He's been obsessively bringing Emma orange juice. Folic acid for the baby, three times per day like clockwork. I keep expecting her to snap. The girl has the patience of a saint," Astrid changed the subject, grinning.

He found a wounded bird to focus on.

Refilling their coffee, Arrianna went with it, "Poor thing has to sit sideways on a bench seat."

"Another viable psychic would be an afterlife changing thing for Jenna," Astrid commented, snagging a piece of bacon.

If she survives Testing. It was quiet outside. Lexy shifted the curtain and peered out. Her Handler was sobbing in Jenna's embrace. *She had to go out there.*

Astrid blocked her path to the door, asserting, "No. Don't you dare. He took off."

"I'll go," Arrianna offered, standing up.

Standing against the door, Astrid decreed, "Sit your ass down co enabler. You went into Testing together. Grey suckers you two in like he's dangling a baited hook in the water. I'm tired of buckling up for his emotional rollercoaster. Lexy is a grown ass woman who deserves to get her freak on without a guilt trip chaser."

They cracked up. *Their situation was more complicated than that, but she appreciated the solidarity.*

The door opened. They froze as Jenna marched in, explaining, "Your raucous laughter postponed his apology tour. He's having a nap first."

And… that's how Karma works.

"We'll pack up the cabin. Lexy, go stow your bags under the bunks. If Grey's smart, he'll use the opportunity to fix things," Jenna suggested, smiling.

After everyone gathered their stuff, Lexy carried her bags

back to their R.V. The newbies were playing cards as she walked by. Pulling back the curtain, she shoved her bags under the bunks. *He was pretending to be asleep.* Being near her Handler was like inhaling soul reviving oxygen after being submerged underwater. *She'd missed him too much to continue playing games.* Waiting for him to acknowledge her, she sat on the bunk. *Loving him was sublime self-torture. His silence made her heart ache.*

Without opening his eyes, Grey pinched off her oxygen supply, whispering, "Not now. I need more time."

She couldn't breathe. Lexy rushed past the others. It was raining as she fled into the forest to grieve their connection without witnesses. *Not now. I need more time.* Her vision wavered. The trail grew brighter. Droplets of rain trickled through branches loudly splashing to the ground. Rays of sunshine filtered through with blinding intensity as her senses amplified until her brain exploded with agony. Clutching her head, she dropped to her knees, shrieking.

EVERYONE'S SYMBOLS STROBED AS THEY RACED INTO THE woods led by instinct. Ankh gathered as Lexy writhed on dirt and pine needles. Markus ordered, "Get the newbies out of here."

Holding their new Ankh back, Haley assured, "Everything is fine. Come on. Let's go back to the R.V." Understandably freaked out by the Dragon of Ankh, pitchy screaming, they hesitated. "I'll explain when we get inside," Haley urged, leading them away.

Watching her squirming on the forest floor, Grey confessed, "I said, not now. I need more time. I was so tired. I didn't want to say anything I'd regret."

Furious, Jenna scolded, "This is where the bullshit ends. This is an Enlightening. Lexy's gaining Guardian abilities.

Without your connection, Ankh won't have any control over what she does."

"I know," Grey whispered. "I promise, I'll do better."

Their Oracle countered, "A promise means nothing until you live up to it. I've been talking you down since she left the planet. At least you kept the necklace for nausea on. She's back now. The jealousy issues are a Dragon bond glitch. Being her Handler is your job. Fix this before we lose her."

Markus addressed Ankh's evolution onlookers, "Now, we have to explain brain expansion to our newbies. We have Amar's son and a pregnant viable psychic. Odds are slim for this group. Seeing this shit isn't helping." Meeting Grey's eyes, Markus commanded, "You'll stay with our newbie's protection detail until you've fixed your bond. Lexy nearly took down an Aries Group flight yesterday." Shaking his head, their leader marched away, muttering, "Do your job."

Stunned, Grey stayed by her side, witnessing her expansion as everyone else walked away.

8
Dismembering Dragons

*P*ine needles and tree sap overwhelmed her senses. Lexy fingers twitched on damp soil. The world shifted but she knew she was safe. Cradled in Grey's arms with her limbs dangling, she was carried into warmth. Unconscious for the remainder of the day as her savaged brain recovered, she dreamt of beautiful things.

With her skin crawling, Lexy opened her eyes on her usual bunk. *She was so itchy. Holy crap, was she rolling in poison oak?* Scratching her back with a vengeance, the irritation moved too her scalp. Ravenous with echoing whooshing in her ears, she noticed someone sleeping on the bunk across the hall. Watching their breathing, she tossed her comforter off and slid off her bunk.

Rolling to face her, Emma whispered, "You're awake."

Oh, no. She had to get out of here.

"It looks like you're having an issue." Emma calmly said, "I'll get Grey."

Rushing away, Lexy shut herself in the washroom and locked the door. Clutching the sink, she talked herself down.

Be calm. Be mellow. She checked her reflection. There were golden flecks in her eyes. *What in the hell?* Blinking, she leaned closer. *What is it?* It felt like ants were crawling all over her. Angrily clawing at her skin until her arms were red, didn't help. She peered down her top. There were crimson veins on her chest. *This can't be good.* Her heart was palpitating. *What did she need?* She drank from the tap. *Not that.* She splashed water on her face. *Think Lexy, think.* Itching her scalp, she racked her brain. *This wasn't a healing ability issue. That was easy. She felt murdery when she had too little or too much energy. With no idea what Guardian ability was trying to rear its head, she had no idea what to do. She needed something. She was sure of it.* Itching everywhere again, her eyes darted around the tiny washroom. She rifled through cosmetic bags. A straight razor. *She'd switch lanes in her brain.* She tried to slice her palm. *Shit. Not even a cut. She had to shut this off. Shut it off.* Visualizing the dark farm that gave birth to the Dragon, her emotions plummeted into the well of children lost, splashing in the sludge of submerged corpses, she sunk into nothing.

Grey's voice pulled her back, "Can we talk?"

No.

"Please open the door, Lex," Grey urged from the other side.

Placing her hand against it, Lexy didn't respond. *She didn't want to. No.*

"I screwed up. I should have been here when you came home. I'm a mess without you," her Handler bartered. "Forgive me? Let's start over."

Waiting for him to leave, she didn't say a word. *Go away.*

Sensing he'd missed his shot at an easy reconciliation, Grey backed off, saying, "I'll wait out here until you're ready to talk."

With the overwhelming urge to escape, Lexy climbed out the bathroom window, leapt to the ground, and ran to an idling car. She got into the backseat next to Jenna.

Gazing in the rear-view their leader enquired, "Where is your Handler?"

She didn't want to answer.

Sensing her post Enlightening feral, Jenna suggested, "Bring her. She needs to burn off energy. She may come in handy."

Glancing back, Orin sweetly greeted her, "Hi Lex."

Enticed by his Healer glow, Lexy poked his shoulder.

Zapped by energy, Orin smoked his face on the dash. "Ouch, Lex. Be nice," he reprimanded, putting on his seatbelt.

Lexy scrutinized her sparkling fingertips. *This was new.*

Grabbing a tissue to wipe his bloody nose, Orin said, "I got my first bloody nose of the week out of the way."

Grey rushed out looking for her. *No.* "Not now," Lexy firmly decreed.

"Drive," Jenna prompted, waving at Grey.

Markus coasted away, saying, "You're sure taking her without him is the right move?"

"This job is a clean up after a Correction. Guardian feed on immortal energy. If Abaddon hasn't left, a snack may help with this post Enlightening murdery vibe," Jenna assured.

A snack sounded lovely.

Gravel crackled beneath their tires as Jenna revealed, "Safe words work until they're removed from the subconscious."

Orin interjected, "Healers adapt to override spells."

"She'll stay with us," Jenna confirmed.

Turning onto a paved main road, Markus said, "Where are we going? We've lost our Wi-Fi."

"Not far. Right turn at the Hovine Peak bed and breakfast sign," Jenna instructed.

Her skin was crawling again. She should have fed on her Handler and strutted out the door. Her fingertips tingled. The sensation amped until it felt like someone was jabbing needles into her fingers. Pain was to her knuckles with her hands extended. With no control, her fists balled then straightened. *Her hands were sparkling. What was this shit?* Clenching her fists, it vanished. Her stomach growled. Everyone looked her way. *She was starving. With a Dragon alter ego, the urge to eat her friends wasn't an anomaly. It was better to avoid waving a red flag when you've got a white one handy. Surrender to silence. Give your feral brain a second to make good choices. She should talk to a Guardian about this intensified desire. She'd always been a carnivore with a Handler. Her devouring 'your teammates will cause drama' filter, wasn't here.*

Orin met Jenna's gaze, asserting, "Take the edge off before she gets bitey."

Yes. She did want to bite someone.

Grinning, Jenna approved, "I love this for you."

"She's not that into me," Orin commented. He pointed out, "There's the sign."

Slowing, Markus clarified, "Bovine Peak bed and breakfast. Did you get it wrong or is it down further?"

"This is it," Jenna confirmed as they turned onto a narrow road into dense forest.

She was going to be pissed if there wasn't an all you can eat demon buffet at this job. With her luck, she was going to be left wanting… Needing something she couldn't have. Lexy balled her fists and opened them. Her hands were glittering. *Awesome. She instinctively knew how to create it but didn't know what it did.* Keeping her hands open, she viewed the low key trippy light display.

Watching Lexy's sparking palms in the mirror, Markus sparred, "Are we allowing her to play with electricity?"

"Take allowing out of your vocabulary, she's part Guardian," Jenna suggested, intrigued by what she was doing.

Looking in the rearview, Markus advised, "Calm her down."

Jenna touched her, stifling tumultuous emotions. With a clear mind, her eyes were drawn to Orin's warm aura. He emitted the glow of midday sun, filled with pale hued firelight slow dancing with swirling shapes and a golden sheen. *Easy to see salvation. His road led to happiness she wasn't ready to accept.*

Removing her hand, Jenna decreed, "If she is going to touch anyone it'll be Orin. She's attracted to his shiny Healer aura."

Glancing back, Orin met her gaze, baiting, "I prefer touching to biting, if there's a choice."

She wasn't going to eat anyone in the car.

Watching the road, Markus chuckled, "Keep her distracted. We're almost there."

"Still with us, Lex?" Orin probed with his eye-catching aura.

"Fifty, fifty," Lexy teased, smiling.

Stunned she'd responded, Orin said, "Hi."

"Hi," Lexy replied, grinning. They didn't need a GPS to say they'd reached their destination. Their demon warning system made it clear as nausea twisted everyone's insides.

"Game on," Jenna decreed as her eyes scanned the forest on either side of the winding road.

They drove around a bend into a wall of pea soup thick fog. Slowing to a coast, Markus said, "This is creepy."

Jenna shouted, "Stop!"

A hysterical girl in blood spattered clothing leapt onto the hood of their car, pleading, "Stop! Help me! He's killing us! Help me!"

Orin asked, "Are we early?"

"She's mortal. It's a trap," Jenna declared with certainty.

Irritated, Markus decreed, "Abaddon lured us into another training exercise, didn't they? The blades are under your seat."

"We shouldn't kill their Testing group," Orin rationed as the panicking girl unfortunate enough to be caught in a game of immortal chicken banged on the window.

Ankh's leader stated, "Look at her forehead. The mortal's marked Abaddon. We have to Correct her. Are you sure you want to give them a pass?"

Unable to ignore the girl's pleas, Orin took a knife out of the glove compartment. He sliced his finger. Blood seeped from his wound as he opened the door. The terrified girl rushed into his arms. Marking her forehead with his blood, Orin stroked her hair. soothing, "We're here to help. What's your name? How old are you?"

"Amy. I'm almost eighteen. I want my mom. Please, take me home," the teen with chestnut brown hair pled, trembling.

Stricken by the resemblance to his daughter, Orin solemnly asked, "When is your birthday?"

"Tomorrow," Amy sobbed. "I want to go home. Take me home."

It was 11:55 pm. If they didn't send her through the hall of souls within five minutes, her soul would belong to Abaddon.

Enveloping her in sedating warmth, Orin questioned, "In life are your intentions good?"

"I try to be good," Amy pledged, as fear dissipated.

Stroking the teen's hair, tears filled Orin's eyes as her pulse slowed. He spoke the words granting her passage through the hall of souls, "From this life unto the next." Squeezing his eyes closed, he snapped her neck. Orin changed his vote, "Fuck it. Dance with our Dragon."

"Shit will hit the fan when they realise we're taking out their Testing Group." Unlocking Lexy's door, Markus instructed, "Watch our backs."

Orin tossed her a demon blade. *Fun.* Doing a practice swing in creepy fog, she wasn't concerned. *This job was a walk in the park.*

"We're not far from the campsite. I just warned the others to circle the RVs with salt." Orin pitched one at Markus.

Catching the weapon, their leader teased, "When have we ever done a job this close to camp without circling the RVs? You stepped over a thick line of salt, Orin."

Jenna's eyes rolled back. As her pupils normalized, their Oracle declared, "I'm not queasy anymore but I caught a flash of incapacitating smoke. They're blocking me with an aura filter. They have at least one demon."

Markus popped the trunk. Handing out water bottles, he instructed, "Let's avoid becoming a tar lizard demon entrée." Wetting each other, they doused themselves with salt.

Lexy passed on precautionary measures. *She was hungry. Let the darkest entities come.*

Grinning, Markus said, "Give the smoke another option. Stay with Lexy."

She was a predatory species. She needed this. Her spine tingled. *They were coming.* Cracking branches made her grin. *They weren't sneaky.*

With a teenage war cry, fighting commenced. Laughing, Orin avoided each swing of the young Abaddon's weapon, teasing, "You're on the wrong team, kid."

A teenager with short brown hair fiercely sparred, "I wasn't given a choice."

Manoeuvring clear of his blade, Orin taunted, "You always have a choice." Slicing his arm, the boy dissipated into smoke and vanished into the forest floor. He called out, "One!"

As an under qualified aggressor turned into a dark cloud, Jenna booted the next one at Lexy, yelling, "Two!"

Blankly slitting a throat, blood gushed over her hands, Lexy didn't play along. An Abaddon slumped, evaporating into black smoke. Breathing it in, power surged through her.

Ankh's Oracle shouted, "Don't eat the children!"

Spoil sport. Opting to leave inept teens to softer hearts, Lexy crouched in the fog. Lying in wait for worthy prey, more ran by.

Dodging a well-trained newbie, Orin provoked, "Untested Abaddon against three, thousand-year-old immortals and …"

Without flinching as an opponent's blade grazed his flesh, Markus cautioned, "Filter."

"Guardian half breed," an out of breath teenage girl

finished Orin's sentence. "We've taken her once. We'll do it again."

Orin manoeuvred away from her weapon, baiting, "Ankh sacrificed themselves, taking out Abaddon. We'll do it next time too. Sacrificial Lambs and all."

"Run!" Jenna screamed as incapacitating onyx fog descended on the battle. Leaving their opponents in the dust, the trio of Ankh sprinted away.

Blocking the demonic entity's path to Ankh, Lexy siphoned a hazardous amount of euphoria-inducing darkness. Being knifed in the back interrupted her snack. Snatching an Abaddon, she drained energy and launched her faceless assailant into a grey haze. Healed before the body thudded, she knew where there was smoke; there was an enormous beast with razor teeth and brute strength coming to feast on the sedating fog's rewards. "I've got the tar lizard demon!" Lexy declared, running into the fog.

"Don't lose her!" Markus shouted.

Manoeuvring obstacles with Ankh in pursuit, she leapt over a creek where instinct prompted and ran into a clearing. The fog remained in the woods. Spinning in a circle, she grinned as Ankh joined her. Shadows of Abaddon in foggy forest encircled the meadow. *Fun. They were surrounded.* Grasping her blade, hair prickled as onyx smoke snaked out of the forest. *Yum.*

Using telepathy, their Oracle piped into her inner dialogue, *'Lexy, take care of the smoke.'*

Already running to detour swirling vapour, Lexy sucked it in through her pores. Power lit her being.

Jenna hollered, "Ten and two o'clock!"

Too far away, Lexy motioned, trapping Orin in a womb-like bubble. Weaponised Abaddon fog veered towards Markus. With a half-second leeway, she blocked it, sucking both streams into her, screaming. *Shit. That did not go well.* The demon wasted Guardian spawn staggered. *Damn, that was excruciating.* Her vision wavered. *She couldn't think.*

Their Oracle's voice echoed, "Get rid of it!"

Motioning to the forest, an orb rolled out of the woods with Demons trapped inside, bouncing away with Abaddon chasing it. *Whoops.*

"Purge!" Jenna shouted.

Squeezing her fist, palms filled with light. She pitched it, and it soared over the meadow into the bushes. An explosion of luminescence lit up the tree line. *Cool.* Tiny white orbs shot up into the heavens. *Uh, oh. She sent a shitload of demons through the hall of souls.*

"You didn't," Jenna sighed, looking up.

Their Ankh symbols heated. Everyone turned to Orin in the orb. *Awkward, he suffocated. My bad.*

Seeing the size of the fight as a massive hoard came out of the forest, Markus asked, "Why aren't they running at us?"

"They're waiting for something," their Oracle said, spinning as her eyes scanned the circle of Abaddon.

Most were holograms or ghosts with scattered Abaddon. *This might be fun.*

"It's a confusing visual. We need Healing backup," Markus prompted.

Closing her eyes, Jenna repeated, "Emery," three times.

Lexy teased, "Who is she, Beetlejuice?"

"Bloody Mary, she's killing everyone when she shows up" their Oracle decreed.

Now, she was interested in knowing her.

Resurrected by his Healing ability, Orin began suffocating again. *That was fast.* Placing a hand on the orb, she willed oxygen into his bubble. Breathing, he gave her a thumbs up. Lexy mouthed, "Sure you want out?"

Reading her lips, Orin looked and saw what they were up against. Laughing, he motioned, no.

Grinning, Markus said, "Get him out."

Willing him free, the womblike bubble burst. Dripping with goo, he took his place beside the three as the hoard parted like an ocean of the damned. A girl in jeans and an oversized hoodie strolled out.

No way. It was the girl who unlocked all the doors in that asylum with her mind. Her name was Owen. "You hooked up with the bad guys," Lexy taunted, boldly walking towards her.

"Limited options lowered expectations. You know how the afterlife goes," the teen said, sauntering over without a care in the world.

"Why would you bring ghosts to an immortal fight?" Lexy questioned. *The asylum was only a few weeks ago, maybe a month. How was she in charge of a group this size? This didn't make sense.*

"The afterlife is more about the lesson from the beating than the revere," Owen sparred, looking like a teen she'd pass on the street.

There was a hint of yellow in her aura. Overruling Fate's design, Lexy offered, "Let me send you through the hall of souls. There's still light in you."

"I have a crescent birthmark behind the wrong ear. You'd try to kill me. My dead army would torture you. Camaraderie would be difficult to maintain long-term," Owen countered as her flock gathered into a thick wall of dead.

Holy shit. She was a Necromancer. "Let me try to help you. If you send Spector after us, I have to kill you," Lexy bargained.

With a mischievous smile, the dark-eyed brunette decreed, "You'll never get close enough." As her ghost army walked through her, the teen vanished into a mass, apologising, "We're on different sides. You understand."

Abaddon attacked with weapons raised and mouths twisted open mid-battle cries. Waving, Lexy froze everything. Sprinting through frigid Poltergeists, she captured the Necromancer.

In a choke hold, Owen reanimated, urging, "Do it!"

Intuition screamed to check behind her ear. *They lied. There was no mark of Abaddon. She couldn't hold this many beings.* Letting Owen go, Lexy shouted, "Run! It's not permanent until you're eighteen! I'll find you!"

The teen vanished into the hoard as time commenced. Blasted backwards through icy air, Lexy scrambled up, and swung her demon blade, turning Poltergeists to ash. Barely thinning the herd as enhanced Spectors pummelled her, she fought to stay on her feet with sweltering healing energy revving her engine as blades sliced flesh. Something thumped her against the ground like a dusty blanket until she was as limp as a rag doll. Struggling to get up, it stomped on her spine. *Shit.* Blood sputtered from her lips. *Impervious flesh.* Nothing happened as ribs splintered. *She couldn't breathe.* Her arms and legs were snapped like twigs. *She used her energy reserves to hold time. That was dumb.* With her brain dying from lack of oxygen, will to live faltered. She ceased writhing in the dirt and let go. *She had nothing left. Pina Colada time in the in-between.*

Markus' voice echoed through clashing swords, "Ankh!"

"Ankh," Orin repeated with rumbling back noise.

Ankh was still in the fight. Ghosts were energy. Remembering what she was, Lexy used intention to draw phantom energy into her pores, healing her vessel. Breathing with freshly repaired lungs, she toppled underfoot as fragmented bones healed in order of importance. Remaining an afterthought until her spine tingled, she caught a glint of silver in the grass and reached for her blade. She leapt up and went sailing through the air. Regaining her bearings mid-flight, Lexy nailed her landing. Understandably pissed, she commenced slicing her way through entities. *Some of these ghosts had clout. She should have killed Owen. This girl was going to be a pain in the ass.* Sprinting into the herd, she heard humming. *Chainsaws. Seriously?* Her symbol heated, strobing beneath her fingerless glove, telling her another Ankh went down. *She needed to be able to distinguish the living from the dead.* Her spine tingled. Heat signatures outlined living in the crowd of semi-translucent assailants. *Perfect.* She pivoted out of a chainsaw-wielding Abaddon's path, slashing with the demon blade as they passed. They turned to ash as she forced her way through tortured souls and burst out of the confusion into the crushing jaws of a gigantic tar lizard demon. *Shit.* Blood sprayed as it shook her. *She forgot they were here.* She sliced it. Wailing, it dropped her in wet grass, turning from embers and charcoal to ash. Crawling away, another hideous black-scaled beast snatched her ankles and dragged her off as she clawed soil. *No.* Struggling to reach back and slash it with her knife, she dropped it. *Damn it.* With rage bubbling over, Lexy hissed, "Die!" Meat splattered. Scrambling forward through innards and ash, she glanced back. *It looked like she pulled the pin on a grenade.* Getting up, she staggered, sputtering blood. *Shit. Her intestines were dangling. This was not her night.* Before she could think, a giant tar lizard monstrosity ran her down like a linebacker, stomping her while she was trying to crawl away. *Ankh was dead. Her symbol had ceased strobing.* Lexy dug her hands into dirt, screaming, "Die!" Meat splatted everywhere. Crawling through steaming entrails, the lights went out.

The scent of pennies filled her with irritation. Lexy twitched her fingers in damp, sticky goo. *Nooo. How was she still alive?*

"You're Guardian. Stand up," a voice commanded without a speck of empathy.

Who was that?

"Turn it off," the voice ordered. "Nobody survives. Finish it."

Releasing the burden of humanity like a snake sheds skin, concern dissipated as the Dragon emerged for vengeance. Covered in the entrails of her enemies, she willed all who harmed her dead. A baptismal mist of ash rained down on her as someone fled into the woods. Enjoying games in the shadows, she slinked through the forest hunting prey, subduing each Abaddon foe, feeding until all that remained was an empty mortal shell. When the chaos in her soul was quenched, and every foe was laid to rest, the Dragon curled up for a nap in the grass near the roots of a tree.

As Ankh's healing backup arrived in the aftermath, Grey and Arrianna wandered out of the trampled brush into a clearing with a macabre display of splattered meat and appendages. Accustomed to cleanup, they began sorting body parts.

Arrianna knelt by a severed male arm with an Ankh symbol on its hand, enquiring, "Markus or Orin?"

"Make piles of limbs. We'll use my tomb," Grey offered. Wandering to a semi-clear area, he tossed his rounded rose quartz stone on the ash-strewn grass. A hologram of an ancient tomb flickered and solidified. "Sort by skin tone. If we resurrect Orin first, he can help. Lexy isn't here. My bond is urging me back to the woods." Sifting through ashes and goo, Grey tossed Arrianna another male arm, asking, "Does it match?"

"It's shorter. It's Markus," Arrianna divulged, starting a pile. She commented, "It looks like a bomb went off."

Finding a female Ankh branded hand, Grey chucked it to her, answering, "That's Jenna's."

They matched as much as they could. Placing a palm on the handprint on the side of Grey's tomb, it scraped open, revealing the rose quartz healing chamber. They lugged Orin's parts over and pieced their friend together, encased in pink stone. Arrianna positioned her hand in the print.

Watching it close, Grey confessed, "Lexy climbed out the bathroom window and got into their car to get away from me tonight."

"You didn't really expect her to follow along with what you wanted after pushing her away? You triggered an Enlightening," Arrianna replied. Focused on duties, she closed her eyes as Healing energy gathered in her chest and travelled down her arms. The tomb hummed with vibration at paced intervals. Keeping her hands in place, her vision flickered. She mumbled, "Find Emery," crumpling on the grass.

On his knees, Grey stroked her honey hair, chuckling, "You can't pass out, Arri. If Orin wakes up with just his torso and head, I'll never hear the end of it."

Appearing out of nowhere, Emery teased, "Be more aware of your surroundings."

"I just pieced together three dismembered friends like jigsaw puzzles. My autopilot turns on when I'm dealing with ghoulish shit," Grey countered.

Emery touched the unconscious Ankh. Opening her eyes, Arrianna got up, admitting, "That didn't work."

Laying her hands on the tomb, Emery praised, "Getting this far into the process is impressive. Lexy is five minutes west."

Messing with her, Grey clarified, "Five minutes west as the crow flies?"

Emery scolded, "This one needs a spanking."

"More often than not," Grey flirted. Avoiding a rear swat, he chuckled, kicking a pile of ash.

They touched the tomb for a minute, and Emery opened it. Dishevelled but intact, Orin groaned, "That sucked so bad."

Emery instructed, "Go find Lexy. We'll catch up."

After a few minutes of trekking through the bushes, they came across Lexy snoozing by a tree. Arrianna whispered, "She's tuckered out."

"Murder sprees are lots of cardio," Grey whispered back. Sensing it was safe to approach, he knelt by her. Shifting blood-matted hair off her forehead, concern knit his brow. He whispered, "She's broiling hot."

Arrianna probed, "What's in her shirt?"

Lifting her bloody top as transparent flesh tightened, sucking intestines back into her stomach, altering thickness and hue to pristine flesh, Grey whispered, "Do you heal like this?"

"Not that fast," Arrianna affirmed, touching her sweltering forehead. "Check for big ticket injuries."

Peering under her, they saw her missing arm and watched in awe as bone extended with thin green and purple veins moving like baby snakes as it stretched. Fleshy ligament and muscle formed, thickening around it. Bones of the wrist and hands. Each finger was followed by veins and meat, then transparent flesh altered shades to a replica of her hand down to freckle placement.

Crackling branches announced company. Walking over, with dishevelled chestnut hair and a dimpled smile, Jenna checked in, "Just making sure everything is alright before we go. Markus is waiting in the car." Silenced by awe, neither answered.

Joining her, the Siren Emery probed, "Is there a reason she can't heal elsewhere?"

"She sucked in her own intestines and grew back a missing limb," Arrianna answered, looking up.

"How wonderful," Emery chimed in, clapping her hands.

Arrianna confessed, "I've never seen a Healer grow back a limb without a tomb."

Jenna asked, "How long did it take?"

Brushing herself off, Arrianna got up, answering, "Superficial wounds heal at the pace she reconstructed a limb."

"We need to go," Jenna prompted, nudging Lexy's Handler.

Grey scooped the Dragon into his arms, and they began the trek through the woods.

"A millennium ago, Healers resurrected with missing limbs and sucked it up," Emery jabbed, walking back.

With his soulmate cradled in his arms as their footsteps crunched over twigs, Grey sparred, "Sure they did."

Glancing his way as they forced through thick brush with flashes of moonlight streaming through branches, Jenna confirmed, "It's true."

"Did Markus go with Orin?" Arrianna questioned, pausing mid stride.

"Orin ran ahead to start the car," Emery answered. "There's another job. You need to stay with us. You're the only one with the patience to deal with Grey."

Carrying Lexy, Grey shook his head, saying, "I'm right here."

"You are hot but dense," Emery responded with no filter.

With ten comebacks on the tip of his tongue, Grey laughed. Jenna swatted Emery as they approached the cars.

Orin and Markus were waiting with the engine idling. Waving to Markus as she walked by, Arrianna opened the door for Grey. With tears in his eyes, he gently placed Lexy in the backseat and sat beside her.

Strolling around to sit on the other side of the recovering Dragon, she found it strange Markus didn't kiss her goodbye, but brushed off the feeling and got in. She buckled Lexy.

Looking out the window to hide his tears, Grey said, "You could have gone over there. Jenna and Emery are taking their time."

Picking a disgusting red hunk out of Lexy's matted crimson hair, she changed the subject, "It's a good thing she has red hair."

Grey wiped his eyes and turned her way. Scrunching his nose as Arrianna opened the door to toss it out, he confessed, "I miss her so much, but I can't even touch her without having flashes of her with Tiberius. I'm just so hurt."

"I'm sure it's never been easy watching you with someone else," Arrianna rationed, meeting his gaze.

"Not screwing the asshole who tortured me for a week isn't a huge friendship ask," Grey whispered, looking away.

Arrianna whispered, "Destroying your Handler bond to make a point is ridiculous."

Tugging on his rose quartz healing bracelet, Grey said, "I've devoted my afterlife to her. I'm allowed to be pissed when she breaks my heart."

"You push her away, she has an Enlightening. You try to apologize, and she climbs out a window to avoid you. Now, you come with us to clean up after a job wanting to make up and decided you can't follow through. Pick a lane and stay in it, Grey," Arrianna responded.

"Don't tell her I was here," Grey whispered, looking away.

Leaning out the front passenger side window of the other vehicle, Orin rushed, "Hurry up, and say goodbye to your girlfriend, Jenna."

Kissing Emery, Jenna apologized, "I've explained it's casual a few times."

The sultry Siren from Amar's crew confessed, "I'm not opposed to the concept. I just can't do the fidelity part."

"You don't need to explain anything to me. I know who you are. I'm fine with casual. Thanks for sticking around to help. Don't cause too much trouble," Jenna teased.

Shooing her, Emery vowed, "I'll help her. Go! Have fun!"

9
Big Sexy Vikings

*S*tretching as she opened her eyes, Lexy noticed an enormous form cooing like a kitten on the bunk across the hall. *Who was that? This wasn't her bedding. She was in the other RV. Good. She didn't want a forced reconciliation. Her safe place was now the storm she was sailing through. She had to erase him, but succumbing to passion to be forgotten was the equivalent of submerging one's feet in wet cement and permitting themselves to be hurled overboard. While sinking into a merciless sea, there was plenty of time for regrets as their love rotted on the ocean floor. They were a precautionary tale for future Handlers and Dragons. Never violate the intimacy clause. Only one gets punished. The other floats through their afterlife, blissfully unaware.*

The giant guy responded to her thoughts, "It's Killian from Amar's crew. That was deep. How much demon energy did you suck back?"

Deep wasn't her factory setting. It must have been glorious. "What are you doing here?" Lexy enquired, swinging her legs off the bunk.

The muscular adonis revealed, "Amar sent me to help with Sami. Emery's here to help with ability training."

Why was she thinking of a baby Björn? Standing up, Lexy glanced down at her huge t-shirt, saying, "Tell Amar I vetoed his entombment." Without waiting for a response, she wandered to the washroom. *She looked like she'd been killing shit. She was wearing a stranger's t-shirt. Awkward.* Contemplating storming back out there to smack a giant Viking, she talked herself down. *Amar knows Killian. You trust Amar. She needed clothes. Damn it. Her stuff was in the other R.V.* A knock on the door startled her.

Killian's voice said, "We're at the table having coffee."

She liked his accent. We're at the table. Who was we? Clearly, she'd been cleaned up. Grey must be here. Shutting down the urge to flee out the window, Lexy splashed water on her face and walked out. Killian and a beautiful girl were at the table. *They'd met before.*

Extending a manicured hand, the stunning immortal greeted her, "I'm Emery."

Another Siren in their midst. "We met at your continent's banquet," Lexy replied, shaking Emery's flawless, dark hand with her pale, freckled one. Her eyes darted to the door. *Time to face her Handler.*

"Grab your bag. Stay with us until you work things out," Killian suggested.

She opened the door. *She didn't even know what day it was.* Wishing she had pants on, Lexy dashed to the other RV. Mentally preparing as she walked in, Grey was on the phone.

He handed it to her, explaining, "Kayn woke up under a truck. Everyone's gone, and she's supposed to kill a demon who is trying to get thirty people to sacrifice themselves to resurrect his girlfriend. Here's your sister."

The scenario was familiar. Her mind settled on a demon they'd dealt with far too many times. Lexy questioned, "How in the hell were you drugged?"

"No idea," Kayn answered. "I didn't even know it was happening until it was too late."

"This demon isn't the sharpest tool in the shed. Call their phones and ask where they are," Lexy advised, glad to hear her voice.

Kayn responded, "They'd really be stupid enough to keep their phones?"

Reminded of how new her sister was, Lexy checked the time, explaining, "The window for opening demonic portals during a lunar event starts at eight pm and closes at two seventeen am. He'll kill time torturing Ankh. It's eight pm here, but we could be in a different time zone. What time did you pass out?"

"I have no idea," Kayn disclosed nervously.

She knew the feeling. The Ankh symbol on Lexy's palm heated. Her eyes darted to Grey. "We felt it too, Dragon up. Let us know how it works out," Lexy directed, hanging up. Tossing the phone back to Grey. He called Markus. *Nothing was a big deal when you were immortal. Torture was inconvenient.*

Unmistakable pink hair on a pillow mumbled, "Everything okay?"

Grinning at Haley, Lexy explained, "Kayn woke up in a parking lot alone. We know who has them. Our symbols will be going off all night if they're being tortured." Feeling eyes on her, she turned to find newbies gathered in the hall. *Awkward.* "We're immortal. We can be healed. If you can't ignore your symbols let me know. I'll snap your neck. Go back to your movie." They vanished into the backroom. Astrid came out of the washroom laughing.

Her Handler wandered into the bunk area, saying, "Markus, Jenna and Orin are on their way. Did anyone explain this to the newbies?"

Astrid chuckled. Glaring at Lexy, Grey grilled, "What did she do?"

He wasn't going to speak to her when she was three feet away. Without a word, Lexy grabbed her bag and left.

For days rejection stung each time her Handler brushed by

without speaking. Pretending her calcified heart wasn't aching for reconciliation as he flitted away like they were nothing, she decided to stop leaving her heart where it could be stomped on. Avoiding Grey gave her peace. She remained in the other RV, getting to know Amar's friends, pre-emptively dealing with overload issues by stabbing herself to dispel energy as they travelled. Gossip about Markus drifted back. While on route to represent Tri-Clan in Vegas, their leader was telling the other half of their crew he was single. The problem being, there was no break up. Of course, Arrianna had questions about how he was acting on the last job, but with her emotions at room temp, all she recalled were jumbled macabre images. *Grey was focused on their friend's heartbreak to avoid her, but Arrianna was in their Testing trio. If he was helping her, she couldn't take him away.*

    Switching off driving, Killian entertained her with tales of his continent's Ankh. Envisioning Amar's smile while hearing of their escapades got her through the days, but each night when her head hit the pillow, she longed for Grey's embrace. *Was he thinking about her? No. He wasn't. She'd always loved him more. This was just a sad fact on her list of unfortunate truths. When this fight was over, she'd erase his memories as she always had, then walk away as she should have the first time. She'd never allow herself to sleep in his arms or feel his breath on her hair. They'd be co-workers and nothing more. He'd still know she slept with Tiberius. She'd screwed their friendship either way. It didn't matter how she pivoted this tale, the ending was always, she loved him like oxygen to breathe and he loved her like a soft place to land. One sustains life, the other cushions your fall. Unfortunately, her welcoming leaves raised with spikes, and she morphed into a prickle bush from hell when she was pissed off.*

    Laughing, Killian whispered, "Your inner dialogue is way too entertaining."

    "Dear alpha school of flirting, I'm bad at this. Sincerely, Killian of Ankh," Lexy teased, grinning.

    Killian chuckled, "Asshole."

With an urge to speak to Amar, Lexy suggested, "Let's send your boss dirty texts from an unknown number."

"I'll leave my phone here," he teased, going to the washroom.

He meant sneak his number, not text dirty things from his phone. He didn't clarify that.

She texted Amar,

> "I can't stop thinking about doing you."

Amar texted back,

> "How did you get Killian's phone?"

He knew it was her. Why not?* She texted Amar her number. Minutes passed with no response. *Nothing. Awkward. Maybe she misread this? His flirtation needs changed after she almost crashed a plane because she was bored. Oh, shit.

Wishing she could erase her number, she texted him,

> "Murder you soon. You owe me one."

> "For what?"

Amar texted back

He'd had the time to think about how crazy she was.

She replied,

> "I'd opt out if our roles were reversed."

> "Out of what?"

He replied with a pirate flag emoji.
Lexy texted,

> "Grey's not talking to me yet."

>> "Killian told me he begged you to forgive him and you climbed out a window,"

Amar answered.
Smiling, she texted,

> "I forgot I did that." His reaction makes sense now.

>> "Say you're sorry. Grey will fold like a cheap deck of cards,"

Amar urged.

> "It doesn't matter what I do. We'll never be the same,"

Lexy messaged, knowing it was the truth. After a lengthy pause, Amar texted back,

>> "He wants to fold. He just doesn't want to give you the win."

Lexy texted back,

> "Killian's telling you everything."

>> "No. I'm Grey's unwilling therapist. Consider it repayment for getting me out of entombment,"

Amar confessed.

> "Fun plot twist, Azariah. This guy doesn't even remember we're friends. Way to give screwing me over your all,"

Lexy replied.
Amar messaged,

> "Lol. You screwed yourself."

That was saucy.

> "True,"

she texted back.

> "It's the middle of the night where you are,"

he responded.
Enjoying their chat, she texted back,

> "It is."

He texted,

> "You're in bed texting me, aren't you?"

> "I am,"

she texted
Her pulse raced as he tempted,

> "What do you really want?"

Lexy boldly baited,

"Having fantasies about kinky depraved things. It can wait."

Her phone started ringing. Oh no. He was calling. That was aggressive. Grinning, she answered, "Hi."

Amar flirted, "You had me at kinky depraved things."

"I had you at murder you soon," she provoked.

He seduced, "You did. I've been having kinky thoughts about you too."

Now, she couldn't help it. "Have you?" She toyed as her libido lured restraint away.

"Do you want me too? Say yes," he enticed.

Titillated, she played along, "Yes."

He raspily whispered, "Are you touching yourself?"

Flames ignited between her thighs as she obeyed impressively naughty prompts until she whimpered and muffled herself with a pillow. Killian opened the bathroom door. Halfway through Amar's throaty groan, she hung up. Lexy texted, "Not alone."

Her cell vibrated with his response, "Murder you later."

DID THAT JUST HAPPEN? CLOSING HER EYES, SHE PRETENDED TO be asleep as her racing heart slowed to a steady trot. She drifted off feeling desired.

Her alarm buzzed. *Shit.* Smacking her blanket in search of her cell, Lexy kept her eyes closed. *She'd been dreaming of Tiberius. She had to find a way to divert the deviant replays etched in her brain. She'd damaged their bond for a trip to nowhere with someone who didn't value her. Delete attraction. Come on, Lexy. Pace yourself. One humiliating jealousy-induced bar brawl per year.*

"Good morning," Emery toyed as she walked by.

After freshening up, she made her way upfront. Walking past as her friend yawned, Lexy teased, "Go to sleep."

"We're stopping for breakfast in a few minutes," Arrianna explained, stretching.

Lexy slid into the passenger seat, just in time to watch a stunning sunrise creeping up in the horizon. *Three hours of sleep didn't do much but she was rather zen. She needed that. It was fun, but she couldn't add another complication.*

"Have a good nap?" Killian asked with his eyes on the road.

Stretching, Lexy mumbled, "Sure. Yeah."

Nodding, Killian exclaimed, "Amar chilled you out. If Grey's not going to do it, why not?"

Had he overheard? Trying not to grin, she shifted the direction of their conversation, "They've been talking. Grey's waiting for me to apologise."

"I could have told you that," Killian teased as a spectacular dawn brightened the horizon.

Grinning, she volunteered, "I forgot I climbed out a window while he was apologising." *Watching the sunrise was one of Grey's favourite things.* She whispered, "He knows what happens when I shut my emotions down. It's his job to bring me back."

"Code for the ball's in his court," Killian chuckled, turning into a roadside diner.

She was starving. The other RV was there. Contemplating the merits of skipping breakfast to avoid him as Arrianna and Emery went in, Lexy bartered, "Bring me breakfast?"

Messing her hair, Killian provoked, "Come on, kid. You can't avoid him forever."

Walking out into a gravel parking lot, she smiled. *It had been a long time since anyone called her kid.* Bells announced their entrance as they walked in. Lexy muttered, "I must be over sixty."

"Still a kid for an immortal," Killian jabbed, pointing at long tables.

The only seats left were across from Grey. Without looking at him as she sat, Lexy picked up her menu. *What did she want to eat?*

"You look refreshed this morning," Emery baited, winking.

Shit. Siren naughty time radar. Peering over her menu, Grey was staring at her. *Awesome. He caught that. She'd just hide behind her menu for a minute.* Listening to the newbie's arguing about what horror movie was the most terrifying, she felt a twinge of guilt. *They didn't stand a chance with Sami in the group. They'd known it upfront but didn't have the heart to turn down Amar. There had to be a way to change their odds.*

Naturally pretty with short, light brown hair, it looked like Emma was smuggling a large beachball under a baggy T-shirt as she argued, "Nightmare On Elm Street. Imagine being hunted by a murderer while in a dream state. That marionette vein scene was brutal."

With no makeup, doe eyes and long dark hair in a ponytail, Molly disagreed, "Final Destination. That stuff could happen."

It really could. She should be taking notes for training in the in-between.

Gorgeous with his dark flawless complexion, and twinkling copper-hued eyes, Dean said, "You get laid or say I'll be right back, you die." Referring to their shared preference, the likable teen met Sami's eyes, teasing, "Bet their planning on offing us in the first round."

Squinting, Sami coldly shut him down, "I read."

Shaking his head, Dean sighed, "I tried."

The kid despised everyone. She use to. She hid in the bushes for years. Sami was a hard sell but she was a feral monster that lived in the woods. If her Testing group gave her behaviour a hard no, she wouldn't be here with this troop of loveable deviants. Everything felt normal when she didn't overthink it. Laughter and witty commentary at a quirky roadside diner with pleather décor was an afterlife staple. Sipping a coffee, Lexy tuned into a conversation about Frost setting up a crash course in Siren duties for Kayn. *She was out of the loop.* Eavesdropping as they discussed what the other half of Ankh had been up to, she couldn't help but wonder why they'd risk provoking her sister with this timing.

Refilling his coffee with a carafe, Grey stated, "Let's piss off a Conduit with unstable Guardian abilities and point out the sketchy fidelity of her relationship. Frost doesn't think."

Irritated by everything Grey said, Lexy baited, "It's piss off a new Guardian week here too."

Topping up her coffee, Killian whispered, "Shhh. Happy place."

He shushed her. He liked to live dangerously. Before Grey had an opening for a comeback, their orders arrived. A ham and cheese omelette was placed before her.

Sliding the hot sauce over, Killian flirted, "Fuel for the fire."

Dumping it on, Lexy felt her Handler's gaze, but didn't look. *She didn't know how to fix it. Maybe they were too far gone?*

A cell rang. Everyone scrambled for their phones. She caught Arrianna's disappointment when it wasn't hers. *She wanted to kick Markus' ass.*

While chatting on her cell, Astrid nodded, saying, "Okay. I'll tell them." She hung up. Everyone was staring at her waiting for news on how the banquet went. Grinning, she looked up and announced, "Kayn went missing in Vegas after eating everyone at the banquet."

Seems legit. She wasn't concerned. They were immortal. Everyone's phones started buzzing. Avoiding eye contact with Grey, Lexy asked, "Where was her Handler?"

With blonde hair in a messy bun and grace untainted by her boyfriend's mistreatment, Arrianna read the text she'd received aloud, "Frost says, they're still piecing together the details. They had a surprise job with inconvenient timing. That annoying Demon from one of their last jobs was in Vegas. Lucien offered his crew as backup. He triggered Kayn, and left thinking Zach had her back. Long story short, she was shot in the head and kidnapped. Lucien was unconscious when they got there."

"How do they know she was shot in the head?" Dean asked, pausing with a forkful of waffle at his lips.

"Brain matter is black," Grey responded, wiping his mouth with a napkin.

Using it as a teaching opportunity, Arrianna explained, "It was spattered all over the entrance to her room. She opened the door without checking through the peephole. She does that."

Twice this month.

Disturbed, Dean lowered his fork, clarifying, "We come back from a headshot?"

"A shot in the head is a lengthy timeout in the in-between," Grey replied like they were discussing the weather. Enjoying the newbie's raised brows, he continued oversharing, "Odds are she's having a shitty day. The last time we were kidnapped by Abaddon, Kayn and I woke up tied to posts in a barn. She lit herself on fire to avoid putting light into a blade. We woke up crispy fried in the trunk of a Triad's car."

Eating a mouthful, Lexy recalled waking tied up in a potato sack as they buried Kayn's Handler alive. *That demise was Zach's worst fear. Mirroring the kidnapping before her five years of torture at a demon farm was a wee bit of a trigger for her as well. Once you gave your Dragon the wheel, nothing mattered. Her sister was fine.*

Receiving another message, Arrianna filled in more time, "After leaving the banquet, Kayn ate a bunch of Lampir at a Vegas nightclub. Triad brought her back to the hotel to feed Lucien, per our usual agreement."

"Eat up! We have a job. Want to eat some Poltergeists later driving buddy?" Killian sparred, nudging her.

"I could eat a Poltergeist," Lexy bantered, smiling.

Grey whispered, "Planning to screw Killian too?"

Where did that come from? Meeting her Handler's gaze, Lexy provoked, "Do I need to decide right now?"

"Perfect. Do everyone we know," Grey whispered, shaking his head.

Irritated, Lexy said, "I'll leave that to you." He stormed away.

Glaring at Lexy, Arrianna sighed, "Was that necessary?"

"Yes," Lexy replied. *Why would he bring Killian into this?*

Crossing killer legs, Emery backed her up, "Agreed. Grey's not doing his job. Arrianna's problems are much worse. Surely, he sees that. Pass the sugar."

Handing the clueless immortal sweetener, Arrianna got up, offering, "I'll go talk down Grey."

As Arrianna left, everyone glared at Emery. Confused, the bewitching immortal said, "Social cues aren't my thing. Everyone seems upset. Dumb it down for me."

Enjoying her filterless logic, Astrid explained, "Markus told everyone they broke up but he hasn't done it yet. We're avoiding the subject."

"Ohhh," Emery caught on.

Emma hadn't touched the orange juice Grey ordered for her. *She had to be close to due.* Dean took her juice and drank it. Smiling at the new guy, it clicked. *Killian was the only other straight guy.* Done eating, Lexy decided to make nice for Killian's sake. Walking through the parking lot, she ran into Arrianna."

"He's flirting with Haley," Arrianna revealed. "Good luck."

Of course, he was. Killian had a crush on her. Her Handler's revenge tactics were predictable. Reaching for the RV, her phone buzzed. She ignored it and went in. Sure enough, he was hitting on their pink haired friend at the table. Lexy warned, "That's a mistake."

"You're the expert," Grey slammed.

She sat on the other side. Blocking Grey between them, Lexy said, "Flirting with the girl Killian likes to punish him for an imagined offence isn't going to get you Karma points."

Haley swatted her player Handler, scolding, "I knew this was too random. Thanks for the heads up." She shimmied out of the bench seat. When Grey tried to follow her out, Haley threatened, "I'm blocking the door. Work it out."

Grey took off past the bunks to the washroom, slamming the door a half second before she reached it. The lock clicked. Lexy warned, "Fine. I'll kick it in." She started the countdown, "Four, three, two…" He unlocked the door and backed up. She came in and shut it. They stared at each other. "We can't keep doing this."

He countered, "You couldn't have given me five minutes to get over it before sleeping with someone else."

Rolling her eyes, Lexy sighed, "Oh, the irony. Every time your memory is wiped, you same day hook up with someone. I have to choke it back." Gazing into each other's eyes, the pull of their bond calmed her as she clarified, "Killian's a friend, nothing else. You owe me an apology."

"You owe me one too," Grey whispered, inching closer even though he didn't intend to.

Backing down, she confessed, "I shouldn't have climbed out the window while you were apologizing. You weren't there when I got back. It hurt. I shut down. Bringing me back is your job."

Shaking his head, he whispered, "I'm sorry for not being here when you got back but we both know what this is really about. When this flirtation with Tiberius started, I told you I wouldn't be able to handle it. I begged you not to do it. The way you were looking at him gutted me."

"I slit his throat," Lexy decreed.

"Say you don't care for him, and I'll never bring it up again," he implored.

Her phone buzzed. *She couldn't. It didn't matter.* Dulling her emotions, Lexy asserted, "I'm not playing games with either of you."

Patiently, he rationed, "Can we discuss this like adults?"

Fine. Blankly meeting his gaze, Lexy confessed, "Yes, it hurt. No, I didn't intend to care. It's humiliating. I blew a job. Can we move on now?"

Staring into her eyes, Grey conceded, "I can't lose you, Lexy. There's nothing I'm more afraid of." Toying with a silky crimson strand of her hair, he confessed, "I'm an idiot."

"I took down a plane," she revealed to lighten the mood.

Tenderly kissing her forehead, he teased, "I know."

Her prickly exterior turned to mush as the stars aligned. *Their argument was silly.* Lexy whispered, "I don't want to fight with you anymore."

So close warm breath tickled her ear, Grey whispered, "Who gave you this recently satisfied glow?"

"I thought the king of the half hour shower would catch on faster," Lexy taunted. Someone banged on the door. He stepped away.

"Just making sure you didn't kill each other," Arrianna's voice teased.

With their gazes in a self-destructive tango, Grey answered, "We're talking."

Their mutual bestie asked, "Can you drive together?"

Lexy's phone buzzed. She looked at it. *Amar.*

Grey asked, "Who keeps texting?"

"It's just Amar," she showed him without thinking.

Recoiling from their bond, he answered their friend, "Maybe tomorrow."

Lexy moved out of his way. Closing her eyes so she didn't see him leave, she whispered, "Maybe."

Opening the door, Grey said, "I'm sure your side Handler's got this." He took off.

Amar was a sore spot. What was going to piss him off next? Her social skills were not refined enough to do this. She was going to need empath backup to manoeuvre this situation. Not wanting to get stuck in the same RV, Lexy stepped down into the parking lot as a rig pulled in. She choked on a face full of dust. *She felt his gaze. This time, she didn't glance back even though every fibre of her being yearned too. Leaving him destroyed her less than loving him now.*

Entering their RV, the engine hummed as she leaned into the cab, offering, "I'll refill your coffee."

Leaning back, Killan said, "I was hoping you'd work it out."

She was too. Quickly filling their travel mugs, Lexy passed his back and put hers down, dodging the topic, "Quick washroom break."

As she passed the bunks, Emery offered, "I'll drive with Killian if you need a minute."

Renewing her resolve, Lexy assured, "I'm fine." Continuing down the hall, she checked her frazzled reflection, and peeked at Amar's text.

"Chin up, you're a Dragon."

Only one message was from Amar. The others were about her sister. They didn't have her perspective. Dragons were resilient. Abducting a monster was an unfortunate mistake. Road surfing to her seat, she sat beside her mountainous companion. He took her mind off her issues talking about Haley. *His crush on their pink haired friend was entertaining.* Still able to count romantic exploits with one hand, she didn't have any magical words of wisdom.

Leaning over Killian's seat, Emery complained, "Everyone got mad at me for being insensitive at breakfast. Why are we not talking about Markus' behaviour?"

"Either he morphed into an asshole, or she misinterpreted a breakup speech. I'm reserving judgement until he gets back," Killian explained with his eyes on the road.

"I'm snapping his neck before he has a chance to explain," Lexy announced, without flinching.

Playing with his hair, Emery asked, "Markus didn't say anything?"

Catching her inquisitive gaze over her cup, Lexy decreed, "I'm not chatty when I'm feral."

Unable to keep a straight face, Killian started laughing.

She had flashes of memories, but nothing made sense yet.

"You slaughtered Abaddon's Testing group," she disclosed.

Her lack of candour was refreshing. "That didn't even make my highlights reel," Lexy confessed, sipping coffee.

While braiding Viking locks, raven-haired Emery probed, "What concerns you most? The Necromancer you let slip through your fingers or the thirty demons you sent through the hall of souls?"

"I don't know why or how I did anything, or care about the repercussions," Lexy responded. "I assumed I had a lecture coming though."

"Everyone with enough seniority to scold you is in Vegas," Emery countered, securing his braided bun. "Magic doesn't come with instructions. There's a learning curve."

Checking out his hair in the rearview, Killian chuckled, "I'm not a douche."

"Have I ever steered you wrong? I'll drive. Go shave and use deodorant," Emery suggested.

Shaking his head, Killian pulled over and walked away. *It was kind of cute that he obeyed.*

Slipping into the driver's seat, Emery pulled out, explaining, "That one has a golden heart, but he needs to be taken care of. Tell Haley he's hung like a stallion."

Grinning, Lexy whispered, "I'd never use those words."

"How would you say it?" Emery asked like she really wanted to know.

"I wouldn't bring size up," Lexy explained.

"Why?" Emery enquired.

Intrigued she'd found someone with less social knowledge, she said, "I'd say, I like Killian. I don't like many people so that's high praise."

"I like you, so I won't sleep with Grey again," Emery replied. "He's fun so that's a sacrifice."

She didn't need to know that. It wouldn't sting if she'd let herself move on decades ago. Doing her best to evolve past a reaction, Lexy changed the subject, "What's it like working with Amar?"

"He's fun too," Emery disclosed.

That wasn't what she meant.

Reappearing, Killian pointed out, "Has she been driving this whole time without touching the steering wheel?"

She didn't notice. "We're bonding. Emery assured me she wasn't going to sleep with Grey again," Lexy said, meeting his gaze.

Catching on, he said, "I'm sure it was years ago. She doesn't think to reference time. Emery's seeing Jenna."

Wait. What? How did she miss this?

"She's in Vegas. Orin's tempting. I don't like it, but they needed me here," Emery confessed.

"I've never seen you jealous before," Killian teased. "You do have feelings."

"No, I don't," Emery protested, pulling into a gas station with a convenience store.

Rubbing Lexy's shoulders, Killian offered, "Sit this round out. We'll go in."

Grey wandered by with the newbies as a song came on that reminded her of them. Their eyes met. Instead of going after him, she changed the station. *Baby steps.*

10
Guardian Snackccidents

As they drove South, she resumed driving with Grey using Arrianna as a buffer. They filled her in on what she'd missed. After hearing about Thorne's arrow in the heart for Mel, and Kayn's surprise Pyrokinesis, her stunts slipped into the narrative with a modicum of normalcy. When each shift was over, his attention returned to the pregnant newbie.

They were left behind to guard the new Ankh while the rest did jobs. Grey embraced his defence status, but the Dragon was hungry as hell and ready to snap. Usually, he'd sense it and talk her down. After an irritating amount of, get your temp Handler to do it barbs, it sunk in. *Knowing they'd replaced him was as hurtful as her fling. He took away the connection she was dependent on. His hand was there, but he didn't place it on hers. The eyes she longed for looked away. These insignificant acts were nothing by themselves but essential to maintaining her sanity. Why go through the trouble of domesticating a monster if you don't intend to keep it? He should have left her a Wild Thing in the woods.*

On a bunk across the way, he was pretending to be asleep. Missing his embrace, the narrow hall was a mile high impassable wall. *In the past, they fell into bed. When bestie mode reset, she'd promise herself it was the last time. The night of ecstasy came with a chaser of ego neutering betrayal. He'd take off with whomever caught his eye with no clue he was unspooling her intestines. Nothing more than co-workers was how it had to be.*

Sick of pretending, Lexy flung her legs out of bed, and groggily wandered upfront. *She needed a blunt narrative to follow but her champion of cold hard truths was sound asleep at the wheel.* Accustomed to Emery's magical shenanigans, she sat in the co-pilot seat, starring at the yellow line in the headlights. *Her powers were impressive.* The steering wheel shifted with each hint of turn like the RV was a living entity. *It was cool. She'd mentioned she could help her with her abilities before their driving shifts were altered by Arrianna's attempt to fix their bond.* She watched the yellow line until the road ceased to matter.

"You're drooling," Arrianna whispered, waking her.

Fantastic. Lexy wiped her mouth and focused. *They were parked at a campground. The driver's seat was empty. How long did she sleep?* Rubbing her eyes, she got up.

With a smile, Arrianna said, "Today's Correction requires your expertise, Lex."

Aware of eavesdropping newbies, Lexy teased, "You can say murder skills. They get me."

Eating a spoonful of cereal, Molly choked. Emma patted her back.

Scrutinizing the assortment of sugary crap, Lexy questioned, "Who bought this cereal?"

Handing Emma a glass of orange juice, Grey said, "I did."

Messing with her food was crossing a line. Go ahead, give the pregnant girl a weird amount of orange juice. She wasn't going to stop him from making a fool out of himself. Looking out the window, Lexy asked, "Where's Emery?"

"She's in the back," Arrianna responded, stirring her coffee.

Sitting at the table with the newbies, Lexy said, "What's the job?"

"A Lycan pack has been eating tourists. Lampir turned them in. One of us has to comply," Arrianna replied, placing a coffee in front of her.

She didn't like the word comply. "Reword that and I'll volunteer," Lexy teased, smiling. *She was hungry.*

"Only elitist dicks use the word comply, Lex. Dismembering a hive is a public relations nightmare. I'll go," Grey offered, meeting her eyes.

Locked into his gaze, Lexy quietly sparred, "Great idea. Let's light them on fire."

"Do we have to argue about everything?" Grey whispered, touching her arm.

Missing his touch more with every breath, she whispered, "You can't touch me if you don't mean it." He let go.

Staring at his revenge cereal, Grey whispered, "Why should I care if you don't?"

Idiot. She kicked him under the table. He swatted her. *Asshole.* She swatted him back.

Arrianna hissed, "Cut it out."

With juice balanced on her belly, Emma tried to change the subject, "Vampires and Werewolves. Cool." Everyone laughed

"You can't play with us until after you've had your baby," Arrianna teased.

The baby kicked. Her drink flew off. With speedy reflexes, Lexy caught the cup. The visual of the babies movements filled her with a confusing mixture of awe and dread. *This wasn't a safe place for a baby. Salt wouldn't deter Lycan.*

Killian walked in, saying, "It's a full moon. Four pm wake up call. Off to bed. Lexy, you're coming. Get ready. They're picking us up to discuss terms," the Adonis confirmed, rifling through the cupboard.

This was exciting.

"She's not going anywhere without me," Grey argued.

"We need you here. We can't leave two Ankh to defend four newbies on a full moon," Emery rationed, walking in.

"Not an issue," Astrid decreed, leaning against the counter with debonair swagger.

Fondling Astrid's short hair, Emery seduced, "Love your vibe. So cocky."

Inching by the flirtatious duo with her bag, Lexy ducked into the washroom. Changing into bloodstain friendly attire, she overheard Emery bickering with Grey. *He was choked she was going somewhere without him again. This wasn't going to help simmer down the ask your temp Handler barbs.* Tussling crimson locks, she emerged in black pants and a burgundy tank top. Avoiding eye contact with Grey, she walked outside as a limo rolled up, and said, "I'm underdressed."

Wearing shorts and a t-shirt, Killian whispered, "With you."

"How fancy," Emery declared as the driver got out and opened the door. She got in, toying, "Hello human driver."

Killian got in, explaining, "She's watching too much Sci-Fi."

After Lexy got in, the driver sparred, "There's no such thing as too much Sci-Fi."

She liked this guy.

"There's chilled champagne," the driver announced.

"Delightful. What's your name?" Emery probed crossing her silky mocha thighs. Killian passed her a flute of bubbly golden liquid.

"Paul," he answered, as they drove away.

"Are they going to try to drug us, Paul?" Emery probed, scrutinizing floaties in the champagne.

"Probably," he answered. Confused by what he said, the driver recanted, "No. Of course not."

"No way to scroll that back, Paul," Killian chuckled,

passing one to Lexy. "This one has a high tolerance to everything but bullshit. Thanks for being honest."

Unconcerned, Lexy and Emery drank champagne without flinching. Ankh's Adonis opted out, grinning. Before they'd finished their first glass, they pulled down a long dusty driveway and parked at a Mediterranean style mansion with an elaborate empty fountain and statutes of nude women on either side of large red double doors.

Opening the door, Paul said, "I'll be out here waiting to drive you back. Go down the hall and press the intercom."

Emery took the driver's hand. Gazing into his eyes, she said, "It was an uneventful drive. We didn't even talk. We drank the champagne. See you soon, Paul."

Wandering past the fountain with change scattered on the bottom, Killian said, "Wonder whose wishes they stole when they took this mansion?" He ushered them in.

Walking past, Lexy said, "This red door triggers me."

"Flags, doors, it's all the same," Killian assured, as they strolled down a hallway of peculiar gothic paintings.

"At least they're making it obvious," Emery said, grinning. She pressed the intercom.

They stood there in silence for a minute before a woman's voice prompted, "Come in. Close the door behind you."

Stepping into what appeared to be an elevator, Killian tried to text. "There's no service. I can't tell anyone our location."

Telepathically, Emery's voice cautioned, *'Quick warning, if Lexy triggers an Enlightening, we have to vanish a Lampir hive.'*

Noted. I have no control over that, Lexy responded via thought.

'That's why I'm here. I need time to wade through this cess pool of powers. I've known a few Guardian in my time. They are what they eat. If you sense a loss of control, expel it,' Emery telepathically cautioned.

The intercom voice piped into the elevator, "It won't move until you close the door."

Grinning, Killian, shut it, apologizing, "Sorry."

A metal panel slid in front. Humming, it descended. It opened to music and chaos with glowing stripes on stone walls. *A cave of rowdy partying Lampir wasn't what she expected.* "They threw me off with the elevator. I was expecting more James Bond, less Joe Dirt," Lexy confessed.

Gnashing teeth, Lampir rushed the trio, Emery waved her arm with the effort it took to shoo flies. They splatted on the cave walls. The other Lampir cowered.

Lexy touched the glowing paint. *It was what they used as the middle line on roads.*

Lampir shuffled out of the way creating a path for an elegant woman with strawberry blonde hair wearing a white satin cocktail dress. She greeted the Tri-Clan, "Welcome Ankh, I'm Eden. My apologizes, riffraff are security dogs for imperials. Follow me."

Strolling past salivating starving yearlings, Killian disclosed, "We train our new Ankh."

"These are strays with no bloodline," Eden decreed, pressing a button, a passageway opened through stone.

Grey was right. They were elitist dicks. She was a stray who knew the agony of starvation. Weight on her heart triggered the urge to shut down emotions.

Emery's voice piped into her mind, *'Suck it up, or I'll take you out before the job starts.'*

I can take you, Lexy sparred via thought, unconcerned.

'I was sent to control and train two Guardian offspring. Try me,' the ebony-haired seductress telepathically provoked.

Killian's laughter echoed. Something closed, submerging the trio in darkness. Eden opened the door to a dimly lit area, urging, "Come inside. You'll find our feeding chambers more elegant than most."

They followed her into a room with two cubicles. In each was a plastic-covered couch. *This was her idea of elegance.*

Strolling over to a candle-lit table, the Lampir urged,

"Come. Sit. Drink and eat. Enjoy. They'll wake shortly. Until then, let's get to know each other. The crimson-haired Dragon of Ankh needs no introduction. Your Handler's description was a bit off the mark. I didn't picture Grey this tall."

Pouring himself a glass of wine, Killian did his best Greydon impression, "I can get on my knees if that's what you're into."

Lexy kicked him, apologizing, "He was shot in the head too many times last month. His game's off but he's a trier."

"Your mom had no complaints," Killian taunted, sipping his wine.

"You didn't know her," Lexy played along, plucking off a branch of grapes.

After a silence, Emery said, "I knew her. She was a trier."

Bravo. A slam dunk for Emery.

Winking at Eden, he toyed, "The offer's open ended."

"Have we met?" Eden inquired, staring at Killian.

Hovering his glass by his lips, he responded, "We have our memories wiped a lot. It's possible."

'Jenna would be pissed if I let that happen,' Emery thought. She said, "We have to be back early. Let's work this out."

"I'm sure we can agree on terms," Eden prompted. "Can we have all three of you?"

Emery seductively bartered, "Are we pretending you aren't aware our Dragon Healer is part Guardian?"

"I was going to try," the Lampir confessed.

"New Guardian are unpredictable. I need full disclosure of your Hives abilities. I know what she needs to avoid. To be clear, if you overfeed, she will lose control and eat you. The big guy remains untouched. He may need to subdue her."

"Agreed," Eden responded. "We have heightened senses, along with fast healing, strength, speed and compulsion. Most of us do alright in the sun."

"I'd go into it anticipating a nap," Emery replied, aware Lexy required immortal energy.

A door opened. A Lampir wandered over to the table, saying, "I've heard about you."

It was talking to her. "You have?" Lexy bantered, sipping wine.

"We haven't had cause to summon Lucien in a decade," The Lampir with an air of authority revealed. "A few months ago, a Lycan turned in our tavern. We compelled the locals who witnessed it and set it free in the morning with a bruised ego. Lycanthrope retaliated by turning our donors. Campers have gone missing in this area. The Treaty has our hands tied."

"We'll handle it," Emery assured.

The Lampir motioned towards the private rooms. *She could eat.*

As they got up, Emery instructed, "You have to want it to happen."

Got it. Intention. Following the Lampir into the chamber, she lounged on the plastic covered couch, teasing, "Are we not even exchanging names?"

"It's more titillating if we don't," he confessed, sitting next to her. "I prefer the thigh. Is that an issue?"

"Whatever you want," she agreed, inching up her shorts.

"Higher," he seduced, baring pearly white fangs.

She was so going to eat this guy. Tugging down her shorts, her eyes darted to the plexiglass barrier. *She wasn't comfortable with Killian watching. Feeding Lampir put her libido on overdrive.* "Look away," Lexy mouthed. Respectfully, Killian turned with his back against the glass. As fangs sunk into her gossamer inner thigh, Lexy gasped arching her back. Pleasure filled her senses as he suckled. Every hair stood on end as euphoria shivered through her. She bit her lip. Killian stepped out of the way as two more Lampir entered the cubicle. A female straddled her, sinking fangs into her throat, seductively moving. Razor sharp teeth sunk into her wrist. Lost in the hedonistic blur, the flagship of her darkest desires walked in. *Tiberius.*

Unbuttoning his shirt, her kinky nemesis seduced, "You need me, Baby?" He unzipped his pants.

Without looking, Killian banged on the cubicle, shouting, "My hand flashed."

She snapped out of her kinky Triad Leader fantasy. *They were still suckling. Oh, yeah. She was lightheaded. Those stinkers.* Regaining control, Lexy drew their life force into her until they crumpled on the cubicle floor. Doing up her shorts, Lexy said, "You can turn around."

"Are you sure? It was getting hot out here and you're encased in plexiglass." Seeing unconscious Lampir, Killian probed, "Can you can get through a job without killing someone?"

"They got carried away, so I had a snack," Lexy announced, strolling out the door.

"A snaccident," Killian sparred following her to Emery's enclosure. "I'm using that excuse for something this week."

Leaving her barely conscience fan club, Emery got up, and wandered over, saying, "You look sparkly."

Killian whispered, "There was a snaccident."

"It's not their first trip to the Healer rodeo. They overfed after being warned," the Siren decreed. "How are you feeling, Fledgling?"

She didn't like that word.

Walking down the riffraff free corridor, Emery whispered, "Five minutes, not fifteen. Unless you're making a weekend out of it."

Making a weekend out of it. There's a thought. Where were the starving Lampir?

As they stepped into the elevator, and rode up with hollow warbling, her ability Obe Wan whispered, "There's way less drama if you stop short of eating a hive."

Probably. Returned to the hall, they made their way to the door and sauntered out into the courtyard as a dimming sun sunk in the tangerine sky. *It might be faster to run back.* They got into the limo.

BACK AT THE CAMPSITE

After a long nap, they were midway through an intense game of scrabble their brands heated. Standing at the stove, Arrianna assured, "Ignore it. We're trading blood for information."

Peering up from the game, Molly questioned, "What time do Werewolves turn?"

Smiling, Arrianna corrected, "Lycanthrope."

Too agitated to focus, Grey got up and went outside.

Watching him leave, Sami mumbled, "Why is Killian doing his job?"

"It's complicated," the blonde with a messy bun and sweet smile assured.

"When did you know you were a Healer?" Emma asked, with a hand resting on her stomach.

Arrianna shared part of her story, "I heard my family being killed and hid under the covers. I was stabbed but managed to escape out a window. One of those miracle I survived stories. Ankh had me for like five minutes before I was stolen by Trinity. I was with Trinity for a year before ending up in Ankh."

"What does Grey do besides forcing pregnant teenagers to drink orange juice?" Emma teased, smiling.

"Pyrokinesis," Arrianna answered. "He's not himself right now. He's fixated on giving you juice so he doesn't have to deal with his feelings."

Moving tiles to make a word, Dean grinned, saying, "I think we can all identify with avoiding feelings. Is there a plan or are we just hanging out playing scrabble waiting for Werewolves?"

"Lycanthrope," Arrianna reminded. "Best to be certain we haven't been fed shotty intel. When they come to kill campers, we have irrefutable cause for a Correction."

"We're bait," Dean confirmed with laughter dancing in his brown orbs of mischief.

Arrianna smiled, and said, "Yes."

"How old are you?" Molly questioned, getting to know her.

"I was in Testing with Grey and Lexy," Arrianna answered. "Fifty or sixty-ish."

Intrigued by her vague response, Dean probed, "What year were you born?"

Drawing a blank, Arrianna gave wisdom a shot, "Age ceases to matter when you have no expiration date."

Grinning, Dean said, "So, we get to live forever with low grade amnesia?"

Why lie? Arrianna confirmed, "Having your memory wiped on a regular basis is in the fine print of your contract."

"Ahhh, the greater good clause," Sami joked. "I never made a choice. I was branded Ankh when I turned sixteen. Someone snapped my neck. I woke up in the desert, thinking, what in the hell? A voice said, tell your dad he owes me one. I turned to sand, blew away and woke up to Killian apologizing, sorry kid. Breaking your neck was the most humane way."

Guess it worked but it didn't sound right.

Fixing her ponytail, Molly shared, "I was in a car crash. I thought my chat with Azariah was a hallucination. Nobody came for me for months. I was waitressing at a restaurant, then I woke up locked in the bathroom of this RV. I beat up Zach with a plunger. Kayn branded me and snapped my neck."

"That's sweet. I bet you were her first brand, "Arrianna said, smiling.

"Yeah. So magical," Molly bantered.

"I'm psychic. I was stuck in the plot of final destination, trying to head off my family's demise. Eventually, I failed and everyone died. They burned down my house. I had nowhere to go. I tried to evade what was coming by keeping my routine random. I couch surfed. Sometimes, I hid in the school and slept there. Eventually, I opted to give in to fate and thought, whatever. If I die, I die. That's when I found out I was pregnant and it ceased to be about me."

Pointing at her friend's belly, Molly teased, "Only virgins survive horror movies." Dean burst out laughing.

Grinning, Arrianna got up. Motioning for them to follow, she said, "When we start really training for Testing, you'll wish it was a horror movie." When they reached the closet, she pointed, saying, "You know this stuff. Salt deters ghosts and demons. Wood for Lampir. Lycan and Demons use silver. Grab a silver weapon. We'll go outside and practice. Choose your own adventure."

Dean grabbed a slingshot, enquiring, "Can you pierce the heart with a slingshot?"

"Silver anywhere weakens a Lycan. A Beta will shift back," Arrianna explained. "Orin loves this weapon."

"Orin is so hot," Molly sighed, dreamily.

"Seduce millennium old immortals after Testing," Arrianna teased, smiling. Snatching the slingshot off Dean, she shoved silver projectiles into her pocket, saying, "Come on. We've got time to play with it." They went outside. They gathered around as, she rigged it with a silver bead, and pulled it back.

"Don't even think about it," their witty friend with pink hair teased coming out of the bushes exactly where she was about to shoot.

"Get over here and shoot me then. I'm demonstrating a distance weapon. We'll be guarding the exterior. Lycanthrope aren't getting near the RV," Arrianna decreed, passing her a handful of silver marbles.

Holding it, Haley whispered, "Why aren't we shooting at a target?"

"They need a moving one. It's near dusk. A lesson couldn't hurt," Arrianna jogged backwards.

Raising the sling shot as their blonde friend sprinted into the woods, Haley said, "Pass me that bottle cap. I'm not good at this. No point in shooting things we need into the woods." She focused on her running target and shot.

"Not even close!" Arrianna shouted, dancing around.

Glancing back at the new Ankh, Haley chuckled, "I should have let her shoot me. I'm not even a year out of Testing. She's going to have me practicing this for weeks when she figures out, I'm bad at it."

Beaming, Dean said, "We're going to be best friends."

She gave it another try and missed. "Shit," Haley laughed.

Sami commentated, "We're being trained by morons."

Haley spun around. Squinting with her slingshot aimed at Sami, she prompted, "Run!" Panicked, her sassy commentator took off into the woods. Tugging it back, she pegged Sami off at thirty feet. Their symbols heated. Haley chuckled, "Guess, I just needed motivation."

Sprinting back with Grey and Astrid at her side, Arrianna scolded, "What in the hell, Haley? Don't shoot the children. It's dusk. I don't have excess energy to heal him before a fight."

"I've got it," Haley passed the weapon to Dean. "Have at it."

Stoked, Dean squinted as he positioned a bottle cap and stretched the slingshot back aiming at Arrianna. Releasing it, he winged Grey.

Cursing up a storm, Grey chased the newbie around the picnic tables until he was laughing too hard to maintain his murderous vibe. "Good shot," he praised. Removing his shirt, Grey pointed out, "A left torso shot does more damage."

Pushing her way through bushes, Arrianna said, "A bottle cap will only piss a Lycan off. Anywhere with silver for a Beta." She touched Grey's wound. Concentrating as her healing ability worked it's magic, she teased, "Put your shirt back on before Molly changes her crush."

Noticing Molly's gaze, Grey winked as he put it on.

Arrianna swatted him, scolding, "Don't even think about it."

"Switching back to me now?" Grey provoked. She sacked him and stormed off.

Patting his back, Astrid whispered, "Arrianna is having a shit week. You were a dick. Fix it."

"I'm not even sure why I went there. I'll talk to her," Grey vowed.

Walking up, Sami sparred, "How will I bond with untrained strangers, if you shoot me every time I open my mouth?"

Catching his glee, Astrid bantered, "It smiles."

Sami whispered, "It finds joy knowing you morons might be dismembered by wolves tonight."

"Why are you such a dick?" Astrid enquired.

"Inbreeding," their surly newbie jousted.

Chuckling, Grey declared, "Get Emma into the bathroom. Sprinkle mountain ash in the hall. Sami won that round. He's coming with me."

As they strolled into dimming forest, Sami pointed out, "I'm not helpful to anyone dead."

Handing the newbie a blade, Grey sparred, "You volunteered by being an ass."

"Great job protecting me," Sami bantered following him.

"I also enjoy watching morons getting eaten by wolves," Grey countered, grinning.

"Shit," Sami mumbled as the full moon appeared through the trees.

Wandering over to Arrianna, Grey apologised, "I'm sorry, Arri. I don't know why I said that."

"You always lash out," she whispered as shadows loomed. Crackling branches and glowing eyes surrounded the trio.

Clutching his knife, Grey met the kid's eyes, whispering, "Let it pin you. Stab the left armpit."

Salivating gigantic Lycanthrope burst through foliage and the battle commenced. Panicking, Sami took off through the trees. Allowing one to take him down, Grey stabbed it. Pinned beneath it, he couldn't breathe. It changed back to it's mortal state. Shoving it off, he leapt up swinging his blade, ending up back to back with Arrianna as they held them off.

"They're all underage," Arianna shouted, as she put down another.

Knocked down, Grey lost his blade.

IN THE CAR DRIVING BACK THEIR SYMBOLS HEATED. *GREY WAS in trouble.* Lexy leapt out of the limo and sprinted into the woods. Instinctually knowing his location, she ran for her Handler as the others put down each Lycanthrope they passed and burst out of the bushes. Grey was holding off snapping jaws. She stabbed it in the back and shoved it off. Their eyes met. Arrianna was being towed away through the dirt. Lexy ran after her, leapt on the beast and drove her blade into it's back. Grey scrambled for his weapon. The trio fought with a rhythm only those trained as one reached until others joined the fight and every Lycan in their vicinity was returned to mortal form.

Walking back in darkness with only what light persevered

through the veil of trees, Lexy noticed her Handler limping and said, "You're wounded," reaching for him.

Grey moved out of the way, saying, "I'm fine."

"You're not," Lexy insisted, keeping pace.

"Don't worry about it," Grey said, avoiding her.

She let him go. Lagging behind, she watched as Grey knelt to close a deceased teenage girl's eyes.

Spotting a wounded Lycan crawling away, Emery strode over, pinned it with a foot, and grilled, "Where is your leader?" The injured creature responded with a variation of deep tones. Crouching, Emery sniffed it's fur. "You're free to go," she offered, releasing the beast. It vanished into the woods.

They began the cleanup routine. Arrianna ordered, "Gather the bodies. Don't miss anyone."

Touching Lexy's shoulder, Emery suggested, "Let's follow the scent and cut off the head of this snake."

"Sure," Lexy responded, glancing back. She busted Grey watching her. He looked away.

Trudging into overgrown brush, Emery said, "He shouldn't get to pick and choose when he accepts your help."

"I know," Lexy replied, picking up the scent. Without a word, she sprinted over dark terrain. Losing the trail at a swamp, the urge to blink away emotion and succumb to autopilot rose. *A Dragon without a Handler was a feral beast with no recourse. If she let go of her humanity, who would bring it back? Maybe it didn't matter anymore? Why abide by rules of decorum set to maintain a floundering connection with a Handler who only wanted to be one under his terms? She should shut her emotions down and eat everything. Everyone.*

Wading into the murky shallows, Emery drew her back to her duties by sassily barbing "I'm stronger. Keep that in mind. Watch for gators."

Whatever. "If you say so," Lexy mumbled, knee-deep in sludge. *She couldn't see shit.* Losing a shoe, she cursed. With a hand in mud digging for it, jaws chomped into her calf. *Frigging insect.* She tore a small gator off and tossed it.

"If I can smell blood, everything else does," her partner cautioned.

Leaving her shoe, Lexy strode out. *Lycan were flesh and bone. Seeing heat signatures would speed this up.*

Eavesdropping on her thoughts, Emery advised, "Fill your lungs. Hold it for a three count and vocalize haaa as you exhale."

Copying her, Lexy exhaled, "Haaaaaa." Red and orange haze lit up her cohort. *I'll be damned.* Scanning her surroundings, she said, "Just yours." Closing her eyes, she submerged her mind in darkness to focus on the fragrance filling her senses. *Damp fur and dead things.* She took a few steps, then returned to the same spot. She opened her eyes, saying, "Right here." On all fours, she sniffed the grass. *Underground.* Feeling the area, there was a patch of trimmed grass over hard surface. Searching for the rim, she pried it open. Pungent scent wafted out. *This was the way.*

Descending a ladder first into a bomb shelter, Emery said, "I always forget how many people have these." She felt the walls until she found a switch. The place hummed as lighting turned on.

It was rancid. There were canned preserves and alcohol stacked on metal shelving with a door. *The bodies were in there.* Emery opened the door, revealing rotting piles of corpses and carcasses. Manoeuvring grossness, there was uneven stone with an opening to a cave.

Emery picked up a tuft of fur, saying, "This way."

Not wanting to admit to the preference to avoid enclosed spaces, she crawled into the crevasse until it narrowed, then squirmed like a limbless reptile. Submerged in darkness, something squeaked. *Rodents didn't bother her.* Grinning, as the tunnel separated into two routes, intuition led her into the left one. Wiggling for a few more minutes, the Dragon torture ended.

She waved her hand and felt nothing. *It could be a cliff.* Telepathically, she cautioned, *there's an opening. Cutting myself to see where we are may go badly if something is waiting for us.*

Emery answered via thought, *'Something is crawling up my leg.'*

Lexy sliced her hand. A visual strobed. *Thirty feet headfirst onto rock was iffy.* She heard something. Cutting her hand, she pointed her glowing symbol at a ceiling carpeted in bats. *Shit.* Light vanished as she healed.

'That cave spider on your back is the size of a cat,' Emery fed to her mind.

Eight furry legs danced shiver-worthy morse code up her spine. *Nope. Stay calm.* A bat flew at her face. Adrenaline rushed while swatting it. The aggravated arachnid reared as it soared by Emery, vanishing into the darkness. Her brand lit, as the spider bit, summoning a swarm of bats. *Shit.* Forcing through a hoard of projectiles, she thwapped against stone and landed on her back. Her Ankh symbol strobed a bat runway. Rustling wings descended. Cackling, she flipped to her stomach. As they feasted on exposed skin, Lexy turned the tables, absorbing their essence through her flesh. Flutters became quiet thuds on stone. Ready to rumble, Lexy sat up and cracked her neck as she healed to pristine condition.

Elegantly landing, Emery handed her a knife, saying, "You dropped this. I'm right behind you."

Knives were fun. She sprinted into the cave. Hairs on her neck prickled. *She wasn't alone.* Foul moist breath huffed. She cut herself. Her symbol flashed as a salivating grizzly roared in her face and spittle rained. *Ahhh. Gross.* Her golden eyes lit up the dark and she was able to see details. She roared back, and as it cowered, her stomach growled. *She wanted to eat it.* Footsteps announced her hunting partner's arrival.

"You will not eat it," Emery responded to her inner dialogue.

Party pooper.

Her tone shifted to soothing Siren, "I have questions to ask. Follow the fresh air out. I'll catch up."

Questions for a bear? Whatever. Faint breeze lured her to the mouth of a cave. She walked towards a glimmering campfire through the trees, and a mortal on a lawn chair drinking a beer, foiled her murderous plans. *She wasn't allowed to eat it.*

"Wandering in the woods at night is dangerous," the guy flirted, grinning.

As sky tinted warm amber, Lexy took in his aura. *There was nothing clear about this one's destination.* Unsure of how to decipher the muted hues, she stalled, "It's morning. Pass me a beer."

Handing her one from the cooler, as luminescence lit the horizon, he baited, "What brings you to my woods?"

There it was. My woods. Yup. Territorial bullshit made her bitey. She chugged the beer as rustling grass signalled Emery's arrival.

With gossamer raven hair in sunlight, her partner toyed, "Your woods?"

Grinning, he confidently decreed "My territory."

"You're too young to be causing this much trouble." Emery said, eyeing him up.

"What trouble?" He coyly asked.

"Where is your Alpha?" Emery said, slicing her palm.

Already bored, Lexy followed her lead. They held up their hands with Ankh symbols strobing in unison.

"Cool glowing tattoos," the teenager commented without flinching.

"We're Clan Ankh. These brands prohibit our entry to the hall of souls," Emery explained.

"You sound important. I should have offered you Sherry," he instigated with a smile.

She didn't get it. "Who is Sherry?" Lexy enquired, squinting.

"It's fancier than beer." Standing up, he simplified, "What an honour."

Was that sarcasm?

Emery tossed the filter, "We're here to kill the moron who turned half of the teenagers from the local high school."

He laughed, "You're joking."

They looked at each other. *He didn't understand who they were. That was unfortunate.*

"You break the Treaty, you die," Emery decreed, dead-eyed.

"I didn't even know there was a Treaty. That's not fair," he countered.

This guy was funny. Fair?

"We die at least ten times a week. Nothing fair about that either, but here we are," Emery sparred, winking at her. "Suck it up. Most of you just shoot through the hall of souls into another life."

Suck it up. It was taking everything she had to not laugh.

"I've only turned people accidentally though bite or scratch or if they've chosen it," he defended himself.

Intrigued by his response, Emery rationed, "If you were just allowed to make Lycan everyone would be one. Mortals romanticize this shit, and nobody mistakenly turns over a dozen teenagers."

"Some window lurking asshole bit me. I was at a party in the woods with friends when I turned for the first time. Most of my pack was bitten that night," he rationalized.

"A moonlight enhanced species jump isn't an excuse to hulk out and eat people," Emery reprimanded.

It kind of was. "I ate a bunch of people tonight," Lexy shit disturbed.

"You ate Lampir," Emery sparred, smiling.

"They were a pain in the ass." He mimicked, "You can't just turn in a bar. Don't eat hitchhikers. They do the same thing. They compel people to be donors."

It was the wording. Donors sounds way less murdery. We can't kill this kid and not the Lampir.

'*We can't kill that Hive,*' her partner mentally sparred.

Why?

'Conflict of interest.' Emery explained the difference, "Lampir discreetly feed on people and wipe it from the hard drive like catch and release fishing. You are eating campers. One is inconvenient and the other is permanent."

Catch and release fishing. Funny. She'd never heard it described that way.

"We're hungry. The Lampir kicked us out of town. They cleared the forest of huntable wildlife. I'm sure our full moon selves would love to eat deer, but they've limited our options," the teen responded.

She'd done impressively macabre Treaty violations while starving.

Rolling her eyes, Emery sighed, "Grab your stuff. I know an Alpha of a pack a hundred miles from here."

"So, the Lampir get to stay?" The teen confirmed.

Holy shit, kid. Take the win.

Smiling at his lack of survival instinct, Emery clarified, "Relocate to avoid conflict or we have to put you down. The choice is yours."

They weren't allowed to do this. She liked Emery.

"We have to contact our parents," he bartered.

"No, you'll trigger their Correction. If I find you a place in this other pack, I don't want to hear about you challenging the leader. You are Beta. This is your punishment."

Puffing up his chest, he got in Emery's face, "Who put you in charge? You come to my forest. You are dinner. That's how I run this pack."

That was dumb.

Tired of playing nice, Emery stared the insolent teen down. He dropped to his knees screaming with blood pooling from his eyes and ears. His friends came running. As he flopped in the dirt dead, they froze. With otherworldly authority, the powerful immortal offered, "Stand down and you may have the same choice." They submitted by kneeling. Telepathically, she shoved Lexy into her role. *'Nobody stands up to a*

Guardian and lives to tell the tale. You aren't just Ankh. Explain what we are and where we're taking them. I'll check the tents.'

Um, okay. Diplomacy wasn't her thing. Her partner vanished behind the tents. Lexy addressed the cowering teens, "We're Clan Ankh. Tri-Clan are Second-Tier who triggered a Correction with our abilities, died and were sent back by the Guardian's of the in-between to maintain the balance on Earth. There is a Treaty all immortal beings adhere to. Your Alpha was offered amnesty. He turned it down. Now, you know, altering a mortal life path triggers your Correction. If you tell anyone what you are, it triggers their Correction. It would be wise to take us seriously."

One raised their hand. Smiling, Lexy said, "You may speak."

The girl cautiously spoke, "We didn't know any of this. Did everyone else really die?"

Softening her eyes, Lexy responded, "Yes. We knew if we camped here, you'd come to us."

A hand darted up again. Lexy prompted, "Yes?"

"They didn't know either," one of the teens said.

"You came to kill us. You knew it was wrong. There were options to taking lives. You'd been starved out locally but you could have hunted further away. I know you were hoping there was a way back to your family. There isn't one. I'm sorry this happened to you. Relocating to a pack with a viable Alpha is your only option. Go. Gather your things. I hope there's an easier way out of here."

Once they had their bags, they arranged a pick up for the new Lycanthrope and rode dirt bikes back to the main road where they met up with Ankh. Covered in mud with a yucky shoe in her hand, Lexy walked towards the RV.

Grinning, her Handler teased, "Fun night?"

Scowling, Lexy threw her muddy shoe at him and went to the washroom to wash up. She felt the motion of the RV and knew they were driving. Coming out, she expected to see the teens sitting with everyone else, but they weren't. Peering into the backroom, she saw Emery watching the Lycan teens riding dirt bikes on the road behind them. Wandering over to the window, Lexy whispered, "Guess they might need their bikes."

"That's what I was thinking," Emery whispered.

Staring out the rear window, Lexy whispered, "We adjusted a Correction."

Emery whispered, "I know."

"Are we going to get in trouble?" Lexy quietly questioned.

"No," Emery whispered. "We had fun."

Smiling, Lexy whispered, "They led us on a wild goose chase through a gross swamp and murder bomb shelter into a bat cave. We ran into a bear."

"Do you have another pair of shoes?" Emery whispered.

"That was the last pair that fit me," Lexy whispered, as one of the newbies sleeping on the floor stirred.

Measuring their feet side by side, Emery, said, "Our feet are the same size. I have a pair you can use until you have a chance to go shopping."

Glancing over at her, Lexy whispered, "What did you do to the bear?"

Scowling, Emery whispered, "Nothing. There was no bear. I'm not discussing it."

Alrighty then. Lexy asked, "Where are we off to next?"

"The possibilities are endless," Emery whispered.

11
Plausible Deniability

oliage grew sparse as lush forest turned to sandstone and tumbleweed as they settled into a routine without camaraderie. *She'd never let it go this far.* Close enough to brush against him, she didn't. Done caving on lingering looks or meeting his gaze when a song they loved came on, she harmonized in the chorus with everyone. Faking peace for Arrianna's sake until Grey decided he was done punishing her for wanting someone wicked and vile. Pretending a crucial aspect of her afterlife wasn't missing, Lexy watched the road ahead knowing there was no point in looking back. *What she'd done was dust on the highway and they had nothing but time.*

When she went to sleep, Lexy dreamt of Triad's roguish leader. Their kind of tempestuous lust was meant to stay hidden in the shadows of hallways and dark stairwells. A titillating secret to fantasize about with plausible deniability. *She didn't mean to care for him.* Each selfless risk lured her closer. Protecting everyone involved with the virgin sacrifice fiasco meant not telling Grey the one thing that would help him understand. *She was mad but didn't want Tiberius entombed when his questionable acts were for her. Seeing good in him, even in a minute way lured her into falling just enough for the loss of the thrill to sting.* Consciously altering thoughts from lust to disgust to appease Grey wasn't going to stop her from ditching her panties in a dark hallway. The repercussions were tedious, but her nemesis gyrated a tingle to a scream so intense it shattered all moral clout. Her phone vibrated.

Her heart cracked an eye as she read a message from Amar.

> "Did he get his head out of his ass yet?"

> "Still shoulder deep."

She chuckled, pressing send.
After a lengthy pause, there was another message.

> "Bendy. Duty calls. Chat later."

Shoving the phone in her pocket smiling, she felt Grey's gaze. *Bet his ears were burning?* Their eyes met.

He predictably baited, "How's your temp Handler?"

He wanted to fight. "I'm going to shove this phone up your ass," she stated.

"Do it," Grey called her bluff.

"You're driving," Arrianna rationed.

Tipping in her seat as he swerved to pull over, Lexy started laughing. *Crazy shit impressed her.*

Haley shouted from the table, "What in the hell?"

Leaving the engine idling, Grey opened the door, and leapt out, saying, "Come on, Lex. Do your worst."

Staying put, Arrianna cautioned, "I'm not letting you out."

Lexy shimmied over into the driver's seat, closed the door,

stomped on the gas and peeled away, leaving Grey in a blur of dust on the side of the highway. *Ankh's other RV will pick him up.*

Glaring, Arrianna urged, "Go back, Lex."

She'd taken this ego duel too far. She made a U-turn. Cruising up to her grinning Handler, Lexy unrolled the window.

"Having fun?" Grey teased with laughter crinkled eyes.

There he was. Resentment was lost in his grin. She offered, "Have a nap. I'll drive your shift." The door opened and one liners about poking Dragons commenced. He took it without shifting blame as Lexy squinted in the sunshine, pulling out.

Getting up, Arrianna sighed, "You are your worst enemy, Lex."

Fair enough. It wasn't like she didn't know it. The sun was irritating. Digging in the console, there was nothing but gum, CDs and napkins. *She needed sunglasses.*

Glancing back, her friend was too far away to hear over the whirling tires. *She could wait until she came back.* Concentrating on the road, adrenaline shivered. She checked out her reflection. Flecks of amber glinted in her emerald eyes. *Cool.* Her stomach growled. *Ahhh, she was hungry.* Flashes of light skewed her sense of time.

ARRIANNA SAT ON GREY'S BUNK, TEASING, "SHE LEFT YOU BY the side of the highway."

Face down in his pillow, he mumbled, "No lectures. I'm trying to find my way through this."

"Are you, though?" She whispered, "From everyone else's vantage point, you're being a judgemental prick who leaves your duties dangling in the wind."

Grey whispered, "Every night in my dreams I confess my love for her and wake with my ribs pried open to expose my heart. I have no armour. I'm grieving while she's spreading her wings to fly away. Knowing they replaced me with Amar is triggering. It would be helpful if he stopped texting."

"I bet he's checking on her because you're still making her pay for Tiberius," she pointed out.

"I was trying to pretend it didn't happen," he commented.

"Get your ass up there and tell her everything you just told me," Arrianna urged, shaking her head.

"We've already talked about it," he answered.

She asked, "When?"

"That morning, you interrupted us in the bathroom. Amar texted and I overreacted," he explained.

Clutching his shoulders, her eyes narrowed as she clarified, "You kept this argument going for no reason?"

"He keeps texting," Grey defended.

THE YELLOW LINE BLURRED. BLINKING TO FOCUS, LEXY'S whooshing heart grew louder until it muffled out conversation at the table. *Not now.* Rock-strewn landscape flickered. *Pull over.* Squealing in her ears made her coast off the road. *Get out.* She leapt out onto the gravel and staggered away to a dinging door. The light was overwhelming. It flashed like snapping pictures until it was too much. She crawled under the RV to hide from the sun.

PRIVACY CURTAINS RUSTLED. ASTRID POKED HER HEAD IN, AND said, "Lexy took off."

Confused, they rushed to the door where everyone was gathered. Sensing her distress, Grey assured, "I've got this.

Stay inside." Walking around the RV, the driver's door was dinging.

With intuition tuned to pick up Grey's slack, Arrianna leaned out, saying, "I can sense her distress. Where is she?"

There was nothing but sandstone and muted tones for as far as the eyes could see. He peered under the RV. Looking up, he prompted, "It's an Enlightening. Roll up the window and keep everyone distracted."

"Let me know if you need me," Arrianna said, closing the window.

Laying on his stomach in the gravel watching her writhing in agony, guilt crept in. Tempering the urge to reach for her, Grey soothed, "I'm here with you. I love you, Lex." Watching her agony as her eyes rolled back, the knowledge that some brain expansions were too much to endure, heightened the urgency to touch her so she'd know he was there. She ceased seizing. His Ankh symbol heated as her emerald eyes cleared, staring off into eternity. He inched closer. Caressing her crimson hair, Grey whispered, "I don't know who I am without you. I'm a dumbass, but I'm yours. Always."

Everyone's symbols went off inside. Unable to take it, Arrianna and Haley sprinted outside leaving Astrid to deal with explaining it to the new Ankh. As they appeared, the other RV pulled up. Standing there as Emery and Killian rushed over. Arrianna glanced back, saying, "The Enlightening killed her."

As everyone peered under the RV, Emery cautioned, "Get back. I'll move this out of the way." She held up her hands and the RV shifted with the force of her mind, revealing a deceased Lexy. "She'll be fine. Put her in the passenger seat so you're the first thing she sees when she rises."

Cradling her in his arms, Grey carried her to the side door. He asked, "Is this normal?"

Walking him there, Emery met his eyes, saying, "A Second-Tier brain expansion is taxing enough without adding

Guardian to the mix. She'll be extra feral for a day or two. I'd avoid being lippy."

"She'll be herself again, though. Right?" He pressed while putting her into the RV.

Grinning as he got in after her, Emery said, "If you love her, you'll let her grow." Before Grey had a chance to respond she closed the door and walked away.

Hearing spinning tires, she opened her eyes. *She must have dozed off.* She saw her Handler haloed in sunshine.

"You had an Enlightening so powerful, you died," Grey filled in the blanks.

She didn't care. Her mind flickered back to squinting in sunshine, excruciating agony and the knowledge that she was alone. Titillating snippets of stairwells and dark hallways on mute replayed. Rage broiled like a festering wound, and as they drove, plucking off Tiberius' arms like the wings of a bothersome fly became her go to illicit thought diversion tactic. *He'd screwed her over and left her in a lack lustre sitcom of the afterlife with a reoccurring role as a heartbreaker. She'd wrecked an impressive amount of banquets, but demolishing her Handler with a scandalous hookup and tanking their unbreakable bond was self-destruction at its finest. She was drawn to turmoil. There was no way to stop it. She'd plucked the pin out of a grenade and blown up nirvana because that's what she was. It was who she'd always been. She was a frigging Dragon. Fucking up her afterlife wasn't a shocking turn of events.* After her scathing inner dialogue rant, she felt the thaw as Grey started laughing.

Her sister had been missing for nearly a week when they detoured to help search. Heading for Nevada, the climate warmed. Big Sexy manoeuvred his way into their RV this morning. They were singing upfront with everyone at the table as backup when they saw a girl by a broken down vehicle on the side of the road. *Holy shit.* Pointing, Lexy said, "Is that her?"

As they coasted up to Kayn, Grey leaned out the window, teasing "Problem?"

"I woke up in the trunk again and accidentally murdered my kidnappers," her blonde wild haired sibling announced, walking towards the RV, grinning.

This felt way too easy. They got out of the RV and wandered over to the car. Peering through the window, there were two deceased mortals with blood oozing out of their noses, eyes and ears. *This was 'I just fled from a research facility' sketchy.* Pretending she didn't already know the details, Lexy probed, "Where did they kidnap you from?"

"Someone knocked on my door and I woke up in the trunk," Kayn disclosed.

Entertained by her siblings matter of fact response, Lexy teased, "You really need to start looking through peepholes." Grey reached for the door. She swatted her Handler taunting, "Do you feel like being lit on fire today?"

Catching on as he noticed the passengers, Grey chuckled, "I'll pass."

Joining them on the deserted road, Killian toyed, "Enjoying the sunshine? Nice outfit. Way to keep it casual."

"The alternative was nothing," Kayn sparred, grinning.

"You would have got a ride faster," Killian chuckled. Seeing what she'd done to the mortals in the car, he commented, "Impressively brutal. How did you do this?"

"No idea. It must have been someone I ate last night," Kayn admitted, smiling.

"Last night?" Killian questioned, looking at her curiously.

Her sister was missing time. Lexy suggested, "We'll drive these two off a cliff so the fire burns up whatever this is. There's a ravine back the way we came."

"I'll turn the RV around," Killian offered.

Already running over there, Grey shouted, "I can do it!"

They watched as Grey turned and began inching the RV back and forth. *Shit. This was going to take all day.* Struggling to keep a straight face, Lexy called out, "You sure you don't need help?"

Grey hollered back, "I've got it!"

"No, he doesn't," Lexy mumbled, watching her Handler cautiously inching forward and backing up. With scarlet hair shining in sunshine, she sighed, "It's going to take a while."

Beaming, Killian declared, "He's impressively stubborn." Checking out the trunk, the burly immortal started howling.

Strolling over to see what he was laughing about, Lexy viewed the trunk's contents, saying, "They were so going to bury you in the desert."

Joining them, Kayn said, "Waking up in a trunk wrapped in plastic is a red flag."

She'd been there.

"Unfortunate run-ins with nefarious intentions is part of the package," Killian decreed checking out the collection of murder cover-up memorabilia. "An axe, a shovel and Lyme. There are bullet holes in the plastic and lots of blood in this trunk. Being shot three or four times point-blank in the head would put any Healer down."

Without reacting to the knowledge that she'd been shot in the head repeatedly, Kayn explained, "While I was trying to signal for help, I couldn't break my skin. It sure would be handy to know how these abilities worked."

She barely flinched. She was so proud.

Glancing at Grey trying to turn, Killian muttered, "It might be faster to just go with you guys and take the decontamination fun that follows."

Already feeling better about the direction of her day, Lexy grinned. *The Dragon needed to come out to play. Lighting herself on fire and healing would help with the murdery vibe she'd been shoving down for days.* The door slammed on the RV. Dean hopped out to see what they were doing.

Lexy yelled, "If you come over here, we'll have to light you on fire!" Saying nothing, Dean returned to the RV.

"They may not even know I'm missing with the spiritual blocker the Aries Group had at the ball," Kayn explained.

Oh, she had no clue how long she'd been gone. Exchanging a look with Killian, Lexy switched the subject, "We'll chat while we dispose of these bodies. I'll ride with you."

"I'll follow you in the car. We can chat afterwards. It's not necessary to light yourself on fire to have a conversation with me," Kayn teased, looking at her.

"Are you certain these men weren't magically compelled to dispose of your body, and infected with this virus to tie up loose ends? Maybe it wasn't you?" Lexy enquired, digging through the trunk's contents.

"I woke up in the trunk, smashed lights out and zapped the wires with a surge of energy to see if I could unlock it. The car slowed, I got out and these two were dying," Kayn answered.

Killian sighed, "There's no way of knowing for sure. I guess Grey's lighting us all on fire."

"That'll be fun for him," Lexy said, slamming the trunk.

Leaning out the window, Grey yelled, "Get in."

Waving the RV away, Lexy shouted back, "We need to be decontaminated after touching stuff in the trunk. We'll meet you there!"

They lifted out the driver and sat him in the back. Killian volunteered, "You two chat. I'll drive."

It was sweltering in the car as Kayn disclosed, "Bad time to mention this, but the car stalled."

Chuckling, Lexy watched the RV vanish in the distance.

"That would have been great to know before Grey drove away," Killian taunted. "Cross your fingers." He turned the key, the engine hummed, and they took off.

As they enjoyed the scenery on the way to their next demise, Kayn questioned, "We're not just outside of Vegas, are we?"

Glancing her way, Lexy asked, "How long do you think

you were missing?"

"I'm usually only dead for twenty minutes. I never have much time in the in-between," Kayn replied.

She was about to die in an unpleasant way. She might as well tell her, "That ball in Vegas was nearly a week ago. You've been missing for five days. They've been frantically searching." *Her sister wasn't buying it.* "We were on our way there to help. You really have no idea where you were?" Lexy enquired, unrolling the back window.

"I was just there," Kayn mumbled. "I answered the door, woke up in the in-between. I wasn't there for long."

"When your slate is wiped clean, it's usually a blessing," Lexy assured, knowing it to be truth.

Meeting her gaze, Kayn asked, "Is Frost's number in your phone?"

Nodding, her phone started ringing. Looking at the number printing up, Lexy grinned, and said, "Speak of the devil. If I talk first, you'll have less explaining to do." She gave Frost the short version and handed her sister the phone.

Nervous, Kayn reverted to humour, "Heard I got kidnapped in Vegas."

That was cute. Tuning out the conversation, Lexy smiled as Killian grinned at her in the rearview.

Leaning closer, her sister whispered, "Where are we? They're going to come to us."

Lexy answered, "Tell him to call Grey."

"Why? Where are we?" Kayn grilled without attempting to be stealth.

"Pass me the phone," Lexy instructed with her hand out. With her ear to the cell, she said, "Let's give her time to absorb the situation. I'll get Grey to call after we drive these guys off a cliff."

Frost clarified, "You haven't told her where you are yet?"

Lexy answered, "No."

"Have fun lighting yourself on fire, Lex. If I can get

someone to snap my neck, I'll meet you for a Pina Colada in the in-between in twenty minutes," Frost chuckled. "See you soon. Hand the phone back so I can hear her voice. It's been a long five days."

Lexy passed the phone. Kayn started grilling Frost about how she was taken without anyone knowing. *Frost would have snuffed out this spat between her and Grey on day one.*

"Earth to, Brighton." Killian announced as he pulled over, "Your love life is adorable and all, but we need to move a body and light ourselves on fire. I'd like to be healed before everyone else shows up and I need to compete for Haley's attention."

Getting out, Lexy teased, "She doesn't like him, it's sad to watch."

"Give it time. I grow on people," Killian chuckled as he got out, leaving the car running.

It was true. Unfazed by dead bodies, she carried the mortal back to the driver's seat with Killian.

"How are we doing this?" Her sister asked, watching.

Eight Ankh were a distance away as they propped the body up and did up his seatbelt, so he didn't slump. "We can do this ourselves," Lexy decreed, turning on the radio. *She loved this song.* Dancing to a catchy tune, she tossed Killian a lighter. With mid-eighties music video over accentuated sexy, the hot oversized Adonis strutted around the car waving a lighter singing along. Leaning in, he lit the driver's shirt on fire. Lexy sashayed over, doing the same thing to the other guy. He grabbed her hand and twirled her. Amused by the show, Kayn laughed.

Wandering over, Grey instructed, "Get in the backseat and buckle up. We'll push this car over the edge and retrieve what's left of you."

No way. She wasn't letting Grey have the satisfaction of lighting her on fire. "Get back!" Lexy cautioned. "We'll do it ourselves."

Her Handler reasoned, "Lex, that is needlessly slow."

She didn't care. Grinning at Grey, she lit herself on fire with no reaction as her flesh bubbled. Agony gave way too deviant bliss. Engulfed in flames, she dropped.

Light flickered as she twitched her hands in the warm inviting sand of the in-between and raised her head. *She was alone. Guess Frost couldn't find anyone to break his neck?* She sat up thinking, *I could use a Pina Colada.* The slushy drink materialized in her hands with a yellow umbrella. *This was delightful.* Her first sip didn't make it up the straw before she disintegrated into fine granules of sand and floated away on a breeze.

In a flash of white light, her consciousness returned to the land of the living. Wheezing as her singed lungs filled with air, her chest rose and fell, gaining momentum with each laboured breath. Charcoaled flesh rapidly healed becoming red, then pink. Freckling, it paled to match her original immortal canvas. Aware she was in her Handler's arms, faint warbley echoes of newbie awe over how quickly she healed became audible. Squinting in desert sun, she saw the love of her afterlife's sunshine hallowed face.

Smiling, Grey whispered, "That was silly."

He was right but she wasn't going to admit it. Leaping up like a certifiable superhero, Lexy complained, "I heal too fast. I wanted to drink that Pina Colada."

Grey stripped off his shirt revealing his bronzed torso and tossed it to her, baiting, "You should have gone over the cliff. It sounded fun."

Without allowing her gaze to linger on his libido enticing abs, she turned away while he put on his shirt. She peered over the edge to check out the flaming wreckage. *It looked fun.*

Swaggering over in a baggy top, mid-thigh length shorts with short blonde hair, Astrid flirted, "Nice butt, Lex."

"Love the cologne," Lexy toyed. Glancing back, she noticed the second RV, and Ankh gathered like she was an attraction at a carnival as her hair grew back.

Astrid gave her shorts, saying, "You need to shower."

All she could smell was campfire. Lexy asked, "How long was I dead?"

"Not long. We pulled up as Grey pushed those guys over the cliff. You were still burning," Astrid explained.

Lighting herself on fire to win an argument might have been excessive.

Checking out the action, Astrid said, "They're climbing back up now."

As she looked, her sister lost her footing, dangling one-handed. Lexy hollered, "You all good?"

Grasping another rock to pull herself up, Kayn shouted, "I'm fine! I just need a snack!"

She needed one too. Sensing Grey at her side where he belonged, she didn't say anything.

Killian made it to the top and helped Kayn. They collapsed on their backs. The big guy started laughing.

Kayn looked his way and said, "What?"

"Thanks for not eating me mid-climb," Killian chuckled.

"Damn inner dialogue," Kayn commented, staring up at a cloudless sky.

Grey rushed, "Let's go."

Wandering back to the RV it felt like the chess pieces of her afterlife were moving back into place. Light breeze rustled her hair as Grey held open the door. Thirsty after lighting herself on fire, Lexy grabbed two drinks from the fridge, and gave him one. She chugged hers and fled the crowded table area for a nap.

12
Dragon Bonding

All she could smell was campfire.

"You'll have to clean up here. The bathroom is full. We're stopping to eat," Killian said, tossing her a package of wet wipes.

Oh, yeah. She lit herself on fire. Sprawled on her bunk, Lexy raised her head. *Cleaning her up after a job while she was asleep was always beyond Grey's call of duty. He hadn't done that sweet gesture in a while.* Swinging her legs over the side of the bunk, she wondered where he was. *She didn't even have a mirror.* She blindly wiped her face and arms.

Coming back to grab his wallet, Killian smiled. Pointing at her chin, he said, "You missed a spot."

Lexy asked, "Who is in the bathroom?"

"Kayn wouldn't let us feed her, so Arrianna did. She's been in the washroom for hours." Wiping her chin and creases of her nose, he teased, "You lit yourself on fire."

"I've done it a few times this month," she chuckled, sliding off the bunk.

As they walked out into the sweltering parking lot, Killian handed her his phone.

She read the text from Amar.

> "Did she just do something sketchy?"

Grey looked up as they went in, then carried on chatting with the waitress. Sitting in an empty seat, she texted back,

> "Define sketchy, Temp?"

He messaged back,

> "Don't you have your own phone?"

Grinning, she answered,

> "It was in my pocket when I lit myself on fire."

> "That explains my migraine,"

he responded.
Enjoying herself, she texted,

> "What are you doing right now?"

> "It's the middle of the night. I'm in bed. What are you doing?"

> "Sitting in a diner getting ready to have lunch. Maybe dinner. I had a nap. I have no clue what time it is."

He teased,

> "Isn't the time on the phone?"

> "You want to be spanked,"

she taunted, grinning. He dared,

> "Always."

> "Same,"

she replied. Her phone vibrated.

> "I'll get on a plane if you keep messing with me."

She bit her lip, hovering her finger. Sensing eyes on her, Lexy looked up. Killian held out his hand for his phone. She passed it back. He read her chat with Amar, grinning.

Arrianna suggested, "Kayn's coming. She's stressing about eating everyone at a banquet in Vegas. Maybe you could bond with your sister through a shared experience?"

She didn't get it. "I didn't eat anyone in Vegas?" Lexy stated as Grey sat down. The door bells jingled.

Shimmying into the seat beside her, Kayn picked up a menu, flipping through it.

Giving bonding a shot, Lexy said, "You made yourself a target by going postal at a ball. It happens. I get it."

"Markus ordered me to do that," Kayn asserted, perusing the specials.

"There's no way Markus ordered you to break every rule we have," Killian debated, from across the table.

Meeting disbelief, Kayn put her menu down, explaining, "They found Leonard in Vegas. Markus ordered me to graze so the Aries Group would have an excuse to shut the ball down early. Afterwards, I was supposed to wait for Lucien in my room."

That sounded fun.

"So, what actually happened?" Astrid prompted, knowing there's no way it played out as planned.

Serial killer casual, her sibling overshared, "I ate everyone at the ball. They got up and came after me, so I used a new trick I'm not supposed to discuss to get away. I stole a couple's cab and ended up at a club where I ate a hive of Lampir. Triad was sent to collect me. I compelled Tiberius and Stephanie to sleep to shut them up, then Kevin ushered me back to my room so I could feed Lucien."

"Where was your Handler?" Grey questioned, upset.

Oh, the irony.

Blankly, Kayn shared, "Markus sent the rest of the Clan away and told them they had the night off. I was alone."

"He did what?" Processing his actions, Arrianna said, "I knew something was wrong, but nobody would listen."

"Where was Jenna during all of this?" Grey probed.

"We were all dancing at the beginning of the night. I have no idea where she ended up," Kayn explained.

"Not a word about this conversation. I'll feel the situation out," Arrianna said as their server showed up to take their order.

Lexy sweetly put her off, "We're going to need a minute."

After a drawn-out silence, Samid declared, "Who in the fuck is Leonard?"

"Language!" Killian reprimanded, scowling at the newbie like he was serious.

Kayn giggled behind her menu.

Cracking a shit disturbing grin, Big Sexy chuckled, "I don't give a shit. Only Markus thinks it's crass."

Their server reappeared, Lexy ordered a chicken burger

with hot sauce, fries, water and a beer. Her sister ordered the same.

A chocolate milk was placed in front of Molly. Dean gave her a side hug, whispering, "I'd give you my beer, but the waitress keeps looking over here."

"I won't be seventeen forever," Molly mumbled, stirring her chocolate milk."

In solidarity, Grey asked for chocolate milk.

Their server teased, "Whipped Cream?"

Grey naughtily flirted, "If you think I need some."

"Definitely," she agreed with a sexy smile, heading back to the kitchen.

Grey leapt up and took off after her. Catching up by the counter, he leaned against it, whispering in her ear. Killian commented, "That boy has the morals of an alley cat."

Sipping her beer, Lexy choked laughing.

Arrianna mumbled, "Alley cats have higher standards."

Watching the server over-spraying whipped cream on his chocolate milk at the counter, Emma defended him, "Maybe he just loves whipping cream?"

Grinning, Killian whispered, "Young Emma, you are far too knocked up to be having impure thoughts about much older men."

"Gross," Emma mumbled, pouring tea with a smile.

Returning to the table with a cream moustache, Grey sat, announcing, "Angel will be right out with our orders."

Shaking his head, Killian toyed, "Will you be taking off later with Angel?"

"We'll see what time everyone else shows up," Grey replied, looking at the number she'd written on his hand.

Their waitress placed food in front of Emma, enquiring, "When are you due?"

Looking at Grey, Emma innocently asked, "It's two weeks, isn't it, honey?"

Covering his face, Killian teared up. Angel coldly plunked Grey's plate on the table and left to get the next platter.

Amused by his expectant slanderer, Grey teased, "I thought you were on my team?"

Poised to eat a fry, Emma patted her belly, replying, "It was too funny to pass up."

Sipping his beer, Killian teased, "At least she said it after you got your food." Their server came back with trays, put plates down and left without saying anything.

Happily dumping hot sauce on her meal, she caught Grey watching Emma. *The idea of her Handler having a short-term romance with this girl didn't trigger animosity. That was a first.* "Earth to Kayn," Lexy prompted, passing her hot sauce. Devouring her meal with sauce dripping down her chin like a maniac, she noticed Killian taking a picture. Enjoying her meal too much to care, she listened to conversations and people watched patrons while taking in the earthy ambiance. *It looked like someone bought out yard sales for everything in here.* The tables and chairs were mismatched even the particle board panelled walls were varying shades. Their waitress slammed a beer in front of Grey. "I wouldn't drink that," Lexy said, entertained.

As the hostess stormed away, Arrianna warned, "She spit in that for sure."

He raised it to his lips. Everyone turned away. Grey laughed, "I was going to swap spit with her anyway."

Gross. Nope. She couldn't even watch.

"I'll buy you a case of beer if you can walk it back," Astrid dared, casually drinking coffee.

Glancing at the pregnant teen, Grey taunted, "Guess beer isn't a motivator when you're nine months pregnant?"

"Not so much," Emma said, squinting. Looking directly at Lexy, she asked, "Are we just letting Kayn drown in hot sauce?"

What? Lexy turned to look. Her sibling was face down on her plate. Everyone scrambled into cover up mode. Haley went to pay as she cleaned her sibling's sauce-stained face and Grey stalled their server with an apology.

Everyone's gazes turned as Astrid opened the dinging door. Carrying their unconscious friend with dangling limbs, Killian loudly explained, "Narcolepsy." Everyone took off into the parking lot, holding it in until they were inside the RV, they laughed and cracked jokes for hours.

13
Reconciliation

*A*waiting the rest of Ankh's arrival at a campsite surrounded by gently rolling desert hills, Arrianna's wellbeing was her primary focus. Relaxing by a campfire roasting a wiener, Lexy glanced her way. Evolved enough to know she should say something, she gave empathy a shot, "Are you okay?"

"Not really," Arrianna answered with wispy blonde tendrils framing her face in dancing firelight. Pretty without a stitch of makeup, she blinked away the moisture forming in her eyes.

She deserved more than the secondhand knowledge that she'd been dumped. Wishing there was something she could do, Lexy watched her rotating a golden marshmallow above the flames. Through the haze flickering firelight and pirouetting smoke, she noticed Grey at the table preparing buns. *It had been decades since she'd put her own condiments on a hotdog bun. She missed him automatically doing things for her. They weren't arguing anymore. Maybe she should take the win?* Opting to eat it without a bun as she had since their strained bond ceased beyond the call of duty devotion, she stared up at the dark canvas of twinkling stars. Pretending he wasn't making a point with every squirt of mustard, dry desert air called her thoughts back to her electric tension induced choice outside of Tiberius' hotel room in Mexico. *He whispered, don't go... Stay. She'd wanted him despite all of the reasons she shouldn't. She still did. Damn it. She couldn't think about this. No good would come from ever allowing herself to be alone with him again.*

Arrianna responded to her thoughts, "It's time to stop beating yourself up. We all have weaknesses. You're allowed to have one or two. Do you need me to make you a bun?"

"I can do it," Lexy answered aloud.

"But, you're not going to," Arrianna teased, smiling.

"No," she confirmed. *She knew her so well.*

Removing the golden crust of her treat, Arrianna popped it into her mouth, saying, "Switch to marshmallows."

Grey passed a prepared hotdog bun to Emma, saying, "So you don't have to get up."

She felt silly. He was helping someone ready to deliver a baby. She was overthinking everything. They'd work it out if she could avoid thoughts of the person capable of destroying their painfully slow-moving reconciliation. Kayn wandered out. All eyes turned to her. Smiling, Lexy began roasting another wiener.

Seeing her there, Grey prompted, "Grab a stick. Hotdogs are on the picnic table."

Kayn sat by the fire. Meeting Arrianna's gaze through a wall of flickering flames, her sister asked, "When will they be here?"

"A flat tire altered their schedule by a few hours. That was a long nap," Arrianna commented, with firelight reflecting in her shiny hair.

Smiling, Kayn confessed, "I've lost track of how many times I've died this week."

Air high fiving her across the fire, Lexy declared, "I lost

my sense of time decades ago." Her eyes were drawn to the pregnant newbie. *The lawn chair was hurting Emma's back.*

Waving, Grey suggested, "Drag a chair over here, Emma. I'll massage your back."

For once they were on the same page.

Killian scowled at Grey, reprimanding, "Do you have no shame?"

With a dirty look, Grey sighed, "Why would you go there? She's cramping. I'm trying to help."

As they bickered back and forth like grumpy old men with sexy accents, Lexy ate another plain wiener. *Their personalities were too similar. That was the issue. Before Frost got into a relationship with her sister, he was their show pony. When the part as player extraordinaire was open, Grey took on the role. He'd always been slutty. He was just obvious about it now. He was hooking up with Mel on the sly for a year and nobody knew but her. With Orin coming back after a twenty-year sabbatical, it was no harm no foul before the reality that he was Mel's father sunk in.* Tuning into Bitch Fest, Lexy grinned. *So dramatic.*

Towing Emma's chair over to Grey, Kayn interrupted their tiff, "I'm going for a jog. Do you have this now or do you need a few more minutes to get your shit together?"

Snapping out of it, Grey chuckled, "I've got this. Take a newbie with you. Campers may tick you off."

Nice that he cared about backing up Kayn's absent Handler.

Scanning the horizon, Kayn laughed, "What campers?"

"Rolling hills hide indiscretions," Dean announced. "I'd love to go for a jog with you."

Downing what remained in her water bottle, Kayn took an elastic off her wrist, and put her hair up, baiting, "Keep up." Leaving Dean in her dust as she sprinted away.

"Wait, cardio beast!" Dean hollered, pursuing her.

Killing campers sounded fun. Hot damn her libido was hiked. Damn it. Sex or murder? It was hard to tell the difference between the two urges.

Catching her thoughts, Arrianna whispered, "You make me smile."

She should text Amar.

"Use my phone. I bet he's waiting for your call," Grey tossed it on her lap, making it clear, he'd also heard her inner commentary. He went inside with the new Ankh to watch a movie.

Well, her Handler's dirty thought radar was working.

They went inside. With Grey's phone in hand, she parked her butt at the table. *It was super dumb to be an ass, then give her his phone.*

Grinning, Killian warned, "Don't text Amar with Grey's phone."

Scrolling through Grey's assortment of messages. Cute. He's keeping his options open. Oh, it was on. She typed,

"Hi Sexy. What you wearing?"

Chuckling, she sent the flirty message to a bunch of numbers on his phone.

Arrianna's phone buzzed. She texted back,

"Sure you want to play this game?"

Meeting her eyes, Lexy filled her in, "I'm texting what are you wearing? When they text back, I'm responding with who dis? We'll figure out who it is based on their reaction." Grey's phone started buzzing.

Killian's phone buzzed. "That's so evil," he whispered, smiling.

Reading the responses, Lexy laughed, "Okay. Who said, we'll be there less than an hour, you freak?"

"That's Frost," they answered in unison.

Agreed. **Cackling, Lexy reported,**

> "One number keeps texting back, who dis?"

She texted back,

> "Who dis?"

The phone buzzed with another,

> "Who dis?"

This was Mel.

"Who dis on repeat is Mel," Arrianna decreed.

His phone buzzed. She laughed, "Who answered, you're so obsessed with me?"

"That's Lily," Killian said, entertained by the game.

"Wrong equipment," Lexy read aloud.

Arrianna whispered, "That's Astrid. She's in the backroom with Grey. The jig is up."

Busted.

They pressed their lips together trying not to laugh as Grey stormed out and snatched his phone. Glaring at Lexy, he shoved it in his pocket, shaking his head. Without uttering a syllable, he left.

That was fun. She felt better now.

Kayn and Dean wandered in at the end of their first hand of Crazy Eights. Raucously laughing, Killian announced, "Last card!"

With a killer hand, Lexy peered up, saying, "Back already?"

"We found the showers," Kayn explained, walking by.

"One second," Lexy placed her cards down and jogged to her bunk. She gave her a bag, urging, "Keep using my stuff."

Grey walked past without a word. She rolled her eyes and wandered back to the table. Resuming the game, Lexy stared at her hand, saying, "In retrospect, may not have been a good idea to poke the bear."

"Fun and great ideas rarely go hand in hand," Killian sparred, dealing the next hand.

It wasn't fair. Nothing was though. Lexy suggested, "Let's play outside."

Collecting the deck, they wandered out and sat at the picnic table.

Dealing cards again, Killian said, "Wonder how far away they are now?"

Fanning out her hand, Lexy's symbol warmed and lit up the night sky. *Shit!*

Leaping up, Killian ran inside to stop the newbies as Lexy and Arrianna sprinted into the desert. Skidding to a stop when they saw him at the bottom of a hill, Lexy smiled. *Awe. He must have broken something.*

"Damn it, Greydon. We thought it was serious," Arrianna razzed as they shimmied down.

Deciding this was as good a time as any, Lexy announced, "This is a perfect opportunity to have an inescapable chat with my Handler. We'll catch up."

Glowering, Grey declared, "If you let her play this game with me, I'm going to be pissed at all of you!"

"Go. He's being overdramatic. It's far past time we talked our shit out," Lexy said, shooing them away.

As they left, Grey shouted, "You guys are giant assholes!"

Squatting beside him, Lexy toyed, "Are you done being a dick?"

"Not even close," he decreed, furious.

Sitting on the ground next to him, she sighed, "What do you need from me to end this argument?"

Shaking his head, he said, "You know."

"Every time we start moving past it, something triggers

you. Explain it to me," She whispered, staring into his blue eyes.

Forced to answer, he said, "I can't."

"You can," she asserted.

His eyes softened as he answered, "I'm tuned into your thoughts, Lex. How can I move past it when he's all you think about?"

She stuck to the only version of the story she wanted him to hear, "I'm thinking about killing him."

"To stop yourself from wanting him," Grey deciphered.

"He hurt me. It's done," she confirmed.

"Plotting his death isn't fooling anyone. Understanding how many times I've hurt you, hasn't made me stop wanting you. I'm irrationally jealous. I can't control it. I wish we could go back to how we were, but we can't."

She ripped off the band aid, "I understand. Are you done being my Handler then?"

"It's not a choice. Is it?" Grey whispered with their eyes locked.

She inched closer, asking, "If it was, would you be done?"

As the force of their connection lured his lips to hers, he confessed, "I hate this. You're trying to stop wanting me. How could it not hurt?"

She offered him all of her, "I can erase this for you."

"You can't," he whispered with lips a breath away. "I've stopped myself from pushing past friends so many times. Wanting more is inevitable."

It was true. She sparred, "I've always wanted you more."

"Debatable," he teased, tucking a lose wavy strand of crimson hair behind her ear.

Bowing her head, she whispered, "What are we going to do?"

"I need to focus on someone else until we figure this out. Can you handle that?" He probed, caressing her cheek.

"I'll try," she whispered. Raising her eyes to meet his, she stayed the course, "I have to do the same. Can you handle it?"

Beaming, he teased, "We've already established, I can't."

He really couldn't. Neither could she though. Pretending their friend zone was going to work, Lexy suggested, "Maybe if both of us try to move on at the same time?"

"Maybe," he whispered. "My leg is killing me."

"Shit. Sorry. I forgot," she laughed. Laying her hands on his broken limb, healing energy warmed her torso, mending his bone.

Staring into her eyes, he asked, "Did you sleep with Amar?"

This was never going to work. Opting to satisfy his curiosity, she replied, "Honestly, I have no idea what I did in the simulation."

"I don't care what you did in a dream state," he fibbed, smiling.

"We've already established you do," she sparred, helping him up.

He tenderly kissed her forehead. Grey flirted, "I'll behave now." Music turned on at the campsite. Lacing his fingers with hers, they strolled back under glittering desert stars and joined the others at the campfire for a night of comical camaraderie.

Kayn and Frost's desert reunion kept setting off a chorus of wolves. It turned into a drinking game, so nobody slept. After hours of pissing themselves laughing, they went for a drunken stroll with a blanket. After finding the perfect spot, they lay staring at desert sky.

Drunk enough to ask questions he feared answers to, Grey reached for her hand, and asked, "How do I rationalise waking up next to you naked?"

Why get into it? She let him off the hook, "You assume you got into bed naked and apologize."

"It feels like that's the nice version," he teased, caressing her palm.

"We just made up," she hinted, smiling.

Grey whispered, "Let's talk expectations before we get into another spat about something stupid."

Looking his way, Lexy whispered, "What do you mean?"

Grinning, he asked, "Is there anyone you'd prefer I stay away from?"

Everyone. Lexy confessed, "I don't ever want you to be with anyone else, but that's not realistic."

"I have a list," Grey teased, squeezing her hand.

Laughing, she played along, "We've established Killian is a hard no."

"Frost is a hard no," he added, grinning.

Curious, Lexy asked, "What bothers you so much about Killian?"

Grey mumbled, "The guy annoys me. All giant and buffed."

"He intimidates you," Lexy provoked, staring his way.

"Being replaced by Amar stung," he switched topics, gazing at her.

This list wasn't fair. Smiling, Lexy said, "Basically, you'd like me to stay away from every straight guy in Ankh?" *He didn't mention Orin.* "Fine. I don't want you to go near, Lily, Haley, Jenna, Mel, Emma, Molly and definitely not Kayn. I don't think this game is going to work," she sighed.

"Clearly," he chuckled. "You have to give me someone."

"I'm semi okay with Emma," Lexy baited, with her crimson hair on the blanket under the stars.

"The girl is nine months pregnant," Grey sparred, poking her.

"That's why she's on the list," Lexy teased, beaming. "New idea. Use discretion and stay out of each other's love lives," she suggested, gazing into his eyes.

"If you hook up with Tiberius, I'm throat punching the guy," Grey warned. "Keep it a secret."

"I plan to stay away from him," Lexy conceded.

"I always plan to steer clear of Lily, but Siren pheromones," he confessed.

"Oh, yes. Emery's not going to sleep with you again because she likes me. So, take her off the list," Lexy sparred, wondering what he'd say.

"That was a long time ago." With his mesmerizing blue eyes, Grey inched closer, whispering, "Getting drunk and coming out here alone was a bad idea."

Lexy got up, prompting, "Friend zone pact. Come on. Let's go back to the RV where everyone else is."

Caressing her ankle, he seduced, "I'll watch you touch yourself."

Holy shit, Greydon. Stepping out of reach, Lexy sighed, "That's not helpful."

He gazed up at her, confessing, "I'm not going to be able to stop myself from thinking about it now." He jumped up.

"Don't," she reprimanded. *He wasn't going to make this easy. He never did.*

Wrapping his arms around her waist, Grey flirted, "Too late. It's in the naughty thought vault now." He whispered in her ear, "The things I would do to you if we were allowed." He caressed her.

Her libido was cranked 'until you blow the speakers' high. Squirming out of his embrace, she directed, "Carrying the blanket will keep your hands busy." *If this was her Guardian afterlife setting, she might have to hike up her weekly body count to chill herself out.*

They snuck into the RV and crept to the bunks. He whispered, "We should have slept in the desert."

Climbing into bed with her clothes on, she glanced back as he took off his shirt, and whispered, "Don't you dare."

"I never sleep with my shirt on," Grey quietly toyed, smiling.

They forgot something. She shushed him. *Damn it. They went for a walk and left Arrianna here. They were assholes. They'd been so wrapped up in their apology tour they forgot Markus didn't come back with the others. He was at a hotel with Jenna. That would never happen. She'd be willing to lay her soul on the line to claim it as the truth.* Coming to their friend's aid with comedy, Grey sat on their bunk singing, "Tomorrow we're all killing Markus. Markus... Markus. Tomorrow we're all killing Markus and pooping in his shoe."

Chuckling Lexy teased, "Pooping in his shoe? Come on, happiness Guru. Get your zen worthy shit together."

"I'm drunk," Grey whispered, flopping backwards on the mattress, laughing. He gave his lullaby another shot, "Tomorrow we're all killing Markus, Markus, Markus. Tomorrow we're all killing Markus because he deserves it."

"That ending didn't even rhyme," Lexy commented.

Grey bantered, "Maybe it was a haiku? Think on your toes."

"We're singing songs not writing haikus," Lexy chuckled, sprawled beside him where she belonged.

He mumbled, "It's my art. I can do whatever I want."

Cracking up on her bunk, Arrianna sang, "Tomorrow we're all killing Markus because it's the right thing to do."

"That was gold," Grey commented.

From the bunk above Arrianna, Killian's voice piped in, "I'm in."

Grey hissed like a cat. Lexy swatted her Handler, whispering, "You're an adult."

"Debatable," Grey sparred, touching noses with her.

Without budging an inch, Lexy conceded, "That's true."

From the bunk above theirs, Lily sang, "Can we plot my father's death in the morning, I'm trying to get some sleep."

Everyone cracked up. *Astrid was up there too.* They grinned at each other.

Grey sang, "Good night, Astrid."

Astrid hung over the side of the bunk, singing, "Good night, Greydon."

Hopeful, Lexy drifted off to sleep in his arms.

Waking in her Handler's embrace, everything felt right in her world. Smiling, Lexy heard everyone shuffling around getting ready for the day.

Cuddling her, Grey nuzzled her neck. Kissing her ear, he whispered, "This is my favourite way to wake up. I've missed this so much, Lex."

Recalling their drunken murder plot, empathy fizzled away surface level joy. Longing to stay wrapped in his arms forever, she knew they had to be outside when Markus returned. Unable to help it, Lexy whispered, "I love you."

"I love you more," Grey whispered, kissing her shoulder.

"Debatable," she baited, smiling.

Smelling her hair, he whispered, "Shhh."

"We have to be out there for Arrianna," Lexy whispered.

Hugging her, he groaned, "Five more minutes."

Lexy quietly teased, "Your morning wood is giving me impure thoughts."

Groaning, Grey rolled onto his back making a tent. "I woke up thinking about it."

"You need a cold shower," she announced. "Kayn has my bag. I have to breakup their reunion to have a shower."

Sprawled on his back with his arms behind his head, Grey made no attempt to hide his blanket tent as newbies shimmied by. He toyed, "Morning."

Far too pregnant to be impressed by blatant flirtation, Emma dragged wide eyed Molly away as Dean laughed.

Rolling her eyes, Lexy said, "Not the newbies, Romeo."

"We could save water and shower together," Grey flirted, concealing his situation with his backpack.

He talked a good let's be friends' game, but she was going to end up sleeping with him and erasing all of this if he didn't stop tempting her.

Cooking pancakes and bacon with gossamer midnight hair and show stopping smile, Lily said, "Shower quickly. Everyone is hungover and in dire need of pancakes and bacon."

Stopping her, Mel said, "She'll be right out, Grey. We need to chat."

"Five minutes and I'm showering without you," Grey toyed. The door swung shut behind him.

Leaning against the counter with her coffee, Mel chuckled, "He can't help himself."

Flipping pancakes, Lily remarked, "He needs a distraction."

"Are you volunteering?" Mel teased.

Grinning, Lily stated, "No."

"Is there something happening, Grey shouldn't know about?" Lexy teased. *That bacon smelled amazing.*

Apprehensively Mel disclosed, "I'm wondering if it's wise to rock the boat. I heard you just made up last night."

"You can't leave that open ended now. You might as well just tell me," Lexy sparred, trying to swipe a piece of bacon.

Lily swatted her hand, "No!"

Grinning, Mel explained, "At the Banquet, Tiberius picked a fight with Orin. Jenna finished it. I tripped him. We talked. He cares about you. It wasn't a game. Even if this information is only ever used as a band aid for your ego."

Her heart fluttered. *Damn it.* Lexy whispered, "It doesn't matter. I can't be with him again."

"I just thought you should know," Mel responded.

"That's all?" Lexy probed, smiling.

"Yeah. That's it," Mel replied.

Wanting to smile, Lexy held it back until she walked outside. *It didn't matter.* Wiping the grin off her face as she wandered over to Grey, she concentrated on their renewed bond. *They were good now. She couldn't even think about it.*

Killian came along on the trek to the showers. As they reached the top of the hill before the washrooms, they found their friends.

Covering his junk with a red t-shirt as Kayn scrambled to

get dressed behind him. Frost waved, shouting, "Good morning!"

They were so in love.

"He deserves a fist bump for his stamina," Grey whispered.

As they came down the hill, Kayn waved and sang, "Good morning." Frost was dressing behind her.

Snatching her backpack, Lexy teased, "We figured we'd stumble upon wolf instigators on our way to the showers."

Discreetly passing her sister sandy panties, Killian leaned in, whispering, "I'm assuming these are yours."

Ten shades of burgundy, Kayn mumbled, "Thanks."

Actually, they were hers. As she walked to the showers with her sister, Lexy harassed, "You left my underwear in the desert." She turned on the hot water, stepped under the spray, and soaped herself up.

Beneath the next nozzle, Kayn apologised, "Sorry." Wetting her hair, she confessed, "I love him."

They were in that blindly in love stage. She longed to know what day two would be like. A week into a relationship, a month, a year. Under soothing spray, Lexy smiled, responding, "I know."

Keeping their sister bonding flowing, Kayn asked, "Did you work things out with Grey?"

"As long as I stay away from Tiberius," she divulged, rinsing her hair. *He told Mel he had feelings for her. Why would he do that?*

Her sister probed, "Are you going to?"

Under the spray, Lexy revealed, "I spent all night talking with Grey. We've worked everything out. I'll always love him more than anything. We can't be together physically without him forgetting, so we've set ground rules. He has people he doesn't want me to be with. I have a few on my list. It was all dealt with, but this morning, Mel told me Tiberius has feelings for me. He's a horrible idea. I should honour our agreement and stay away."

"I recall you saying, Frost was a horrible idea before the Testing," Kayn answered. "Look at us now?"

Laughing, Lexy countered, "I haven't altered my opinion, Frost's a horrible idea. Surviving Immortal Testing changed you. Now, you're also a bad idea so it works."

Impressed, Kayn commented, "That comeback was epic. Well done."

Walking to the sink, Lexy said, "Our comic timing may be priceless, but I still want to strangle our seed sowing sperm donor. I won't be going out of my way to thank him." Tossing Kayn undergarments, shorts and a tank top, they dressed in front of the mirror.

Curious, Kayn asked, "Is Orin on Grey's hard no list?"

Brushing her crimson locks, Lexy smiled and said, "He's all good with Orin, but I'm fairly certain, I've wrecked that." She passed the brush.

Smiling, Kayn tussled her damp curls, saying, "Maybe that's why Grey left him on your to-do list?"

Packing her bag, Lexy said, "Odds are slim he still wants to hook his caboose to my train wreck."

"I'm surprised Frost hooked his caboose to mine," Kayn ribbed, about to put blush on.

Snatching the rouge away, Lexy teased, "You won't need blush. You two set off a choir of wolves all night. For future reference, screams echo here."

Pressing her lips together mortified, Kayn asked, "Was it really that loud?"

Grinning, Lexy harassed, "We used it as a drinking game and did a shot each time the wolves joined you. Everyone at our campsite is dead on their feet hungover."

"You're joking," Kayn said, embarrassed.

"Nope," Lexy replied, shaking her head. "Most of us were impressed if that helps."

They walked out. Frost, Grey and Killian were pitching rocks like bored kids. As they made their way back to the campsite, everyone began disclosing hilarious things. Kayn revealed, "After the banquet, I compelled Tiberius and Stephanie to sleep when they were being lippy in a limo and left without undoing it."

Walking beside her, Grey said, "Nice."

Her heart fluttered at the mention of Tiberius. Shutting it down, Lexy looped her arm through Grey's, saying, "Come on. I'm starving." Frost and Kayn lagged behind. They kept walking, giving them privacy.

Kissing her damp hair, Grey ogled her cleavage, whispering, "It's going to be impossible to honour this friend zone pact if you don't start wearing bras that fit."

Chuckling, Killian changed the subject, "We need to replenish the clothing supply. I need a new bag of socks."

Grey offered, "I have some you can use."

"My laundry was mixed up with Mel's or Astrid's," Lexy said, smiling.

Peering down her tank top, Grey teased, "I thought it looked familiar."

Knowing Astrid wasn't interested, Killian deduced, "Mel's not in a place to be trifled with."

Grey pledged, "I know she took an arrow in the heart from Thorne. For the record, Mel's not easily played."

She should have offered to kill Thorne. Frost and Kayn raced up behind them, laughing. Frost walked ahead with the others. Taking the opportunity to be with her surprise sibling, they strolled the rolling hills with sandy gravel shifting underfoot. *Kayn was stressing about her feelings for Frost. Love was a weakness she understood all too well.* Lexy responded to her thoughts, "Fear is normal. It's terrifying to have something to lose."

Everyone was drinking coffee at picnic tables as they approached. Jogging over, Zach hugged Kayn apologising, "I'm the worst Handler."

They hadn't seen each other since Kayn went missing either. Lexy sat with her Handler.

SACRIFICIAL LAMB CLUB

Handing her a coffee, Grey whispered, "I'll massage your feet if you behave."

Code for don't murder Markus. Lexy sipped coffee. Closing her eyes as sunshine danced upon her skin, she heard Grey's musical laughter. *Her heart was home.*

Touching Arrianna's shoulder, Grey assured, "He won't be able to escape a conversation with you forever."

Damn it, Greydon. Whacking her Handler, Lexy whispered, "Rethink that sentence."

Clicking in, Grey backtracked, "I meant, he'll be here today to set us up with our next job. We're all in the same place." Looking, he asked, "Where are my newbies?"

Coming out of the RV with a mountain of waffles on a plate in one hand, and syrup in the other, Astrid teased, "The newbies are behind you," pointing at another picnic table. "Emma is a zillion months pregnant, and it's hot, so she's napping." Placing a plate on each table, she teased, "How hungover are you?" Smiling at Arrianna, Astrid advised, "Tequila is not your friend. Eat a waffle."

Grimacing, Arrianna picked up a dry waffle, mumbling, "No promises it's staying down."

"I'll hold your hair if you end up praying to the porcelain god," Grey assured, eating his waffle dry in solidarity.

Naturally pretty with sleek blonde hair and a golden tan, Arrianna mumbled, "I may need you."

Nearly due, Emma waddled out of the RV. The new Ankh shifted to make room for her at their table. Grey got up, poured her a glass of orange juice and placed it in front of her, saying, "Folic acid for the baby."

"Thank you," Emma replied, smiling.

With her Handler's attention elsewhere, Lexy offered, "I'll deck him. Everyone else got to hit a leader this week."

Meeting Lexy's eyes, Kayn provoked, "I double-dog dare you to do it."

"Stop egging her on. Neither of you is hitting Markus," Grey reprimanded, returning to his seat, pointing at Kayn.

Touching her chest, feigning shock, Kayn baited, "Well, I wasn't even thinking about doing it myself."

Tossing a waffle at Kayn's Handler, Grey scolded, "Pay attention!"

Scowling, Zach said, "What did you do?"

Innocently, Kayn answered, "One of us should hit him."

She missed her sister.

Shaking his head, Zach pled, "Give me an hour before you start shit, Brighton. I'm so hungover, I can barely see. How do you have energy for anything?"

Laughter erupted as the picnic table of newbie Ankh began howling like wolves. *She knew they weren't going to let that slide.*

From the top of the immortal food chain, Kayn reprimanded, "By all means, keep digging your graves. I'll have an opportunity to work out my aggression after Emma gives birth while chasing the lot of you around the in-between with an axe for a couple of weeks." In the snap of a finger, it was quiet enough to hear a pin drop.

Grinning, Lexy said, "Nice. That made my day."

"We should hunt them down and kill them like we're in a slasher movie. Have you ever thought up a chainsaw as a weapon in the in-between?" Kayn suggested like they were making plans to go to the beach.

"Um, no, but we're so doing that," Lexy decreed, winking at Dean, who'd paused mid waffle bite, listening.

Grinning, they Dragon sister high-fived. Their Handlers shook their heads. Frost was holding his forehead with his elbow balanced on the table like he had a headache.

Unaffected by lippy shenanigans, Zach remarked, "Done torturing the children, Brighton?"

"For now," Kayn saucily replied, snatching a golden waffle off the plate.

Smiling at Arrianna, Lexy instigated, "Do you want me to hit Markus? I'll do it."

"No. He looked past me like I wasn't even there and drove away last night," Arrianna explained. "If leaving me with an ounce of dignity was a stretch, why give him the time of day?"

"That's the spirit, gorgeous. Only an idiot would cheat on you," Killian declared, raising his coffee, winking at Grey.

Grey was Arrianna's last boyfriend. He cheated on her with Lily. Who told Killian?

Instead of being pissed at Killian for calling him out on misdeeds, Grey turned to Arrianna, and admitted, "I'll always regret hurting you. Markus will too."

Lily emerged from the RV like a gorgeous ray of Arabian princess sunshine with a plate of bacon for each table, urging, "Eat up." Shimmying onto the bench by Killian, she met Frost's gaze, asking, "Have you eaten?"

"What do you need me to do?" Frost enquired, finishing his coffee.

"Please wake up, Orin. He's still sleeping," Lily answered, fixing herself a plate.

Grabbing bacon as he got up, Frost sauntered over to the other crew's RV and went in. Crackling gravel summoned Lexy's eyes away from the plate of bacon. *Markus better have one hell of an explanation.*

Getting up, Arrianna volunteered, "I'll go clean up."

Cutting waffles, as her father's rental car approached, Lily said, "I can't believe they broke up. They seemed so happy."

"He left on a job like everything was perfect and ghosted her. There was no argument," Kayn filled her in.

With blind trust, Lily defended him, "He wouldn't do that."

Something wasn't right.

"Are you sure?" Kayn asked, watching the vehicle pull up and park. Jenna got out, slammed the door, and stormed into the RV without speaking to anyone.

Swaggering over, Markus snatched a handful of bacon and ignorantly decreed, "Jenna's a handful."

Confusion filled Lily's eyes as she clarified, "How so?"

"She showed up at my hotel room in the middle of the night and came onto me," Markus gossiped, smirking as he reached for the empty syrup. "Is there more?"

Smiling blankly, Lily replied, "I'll be right back... Dad. I need to use the washroom." She got up and went after Jenna.

That wasn't Markus.

Moments Earlier

When Frost came in, Orin looked up, stating, "Sorry, I'm not going out there."

"Lexy?" Frost probed as he sat across the table.

Chuckling, Orin shook his head, saying, "No."

"Spit it out then," Frost baited, smiling.

Stalling, Orin switched subjects, "Judging by the all-night wolves' serenade, your reunion with Kayn went well."

"Quit wasting my time. Tell me why you're hiding in here eating Corn Pops," Frost asserted, smiling.

"We're testing a theory. Jenna will be back soon," Orin replied, eating a spoonful of cereal.

Sipping lukewarm java, Frost asked, "Is that coffee fresh?"

Enraged, Jenna stormed in, slammed the door, muffled her face with a dishtowel and screamed. Massaging bruised wrists, she calmed enough to speak, "That's not Markus. He tried luring me to his room, then threatened me. There's no way."

Rushing over, Orin checked her wrists, declaring, "I'm going to kill him." He reached for the door.

Grabbing his arm, Jenna commanded, "Stop. I've pieced

together my visions. He can't know we've figured it out. He's outside with the others. Nobody can react."

They froze as someone came in. Closing the door quietly, Lily said, "That's not my father. What do you know?"

Peering out the window, Frost whispered, "He's going into the other RV. Tell us everything."

Defeated, Jenna sat at the table, saying, "Somehow, he's been switched or cloned, maybe possessed? Where's Emery? I can't explain why, but we need her."

"She was with the other group. She should be here," Lily whispered, tearing up.

Taking Lily in his arms, Frost consoled, "We'll find him."

"Until we've had a chance to speak privately to everyone full Ankh, do everything Bad Markus says no matter what," Jenna asserted. "He can't suspect anything. If this is a Clone or a Shapeshifter, good Markus is being held somewhere. He needs our help. If this version of him vanishes, we'll have nothing to barter with. No proof."

"If we don't want anyone to call him out, we have to make sure everyone understands why they can't. Bad Markus is with Arrianna right now," Orin explained, watching out the window.

Their Oracle Jenna urged, "Arrianna's intuition is strong. She'll be useful. Quietly, take everyone with enough seniority to question his motives for a walk."

Mel wandered out of the bunk area, groggily saying, "I'm way too hungover for this shit."

"Sorry, I forgot you were back there," Orin apologised, peeking out the window. "Emery just came out of the other RV. She's coming over."

The door opened as Emery walked in. Everyone went silent. She walked over, planted a kiss on Jenna's lips and addressed the room, "I'm guessing everyone knows that's not Markus trying to sleep with Arrianna?"

"Nope," Mel commented. "Not doing this today." She

spun on a dime and took off to the washroom, muttering, "I've suspected it for days. I'll let you guys catch up. Let me know when you figure out a plan."

Watching Orin's lippy hungover offspring stagger away, Emery chuckled, "I like her."

"What do you think? Is he possessed or cloned?" Jenna enquired, looking at Emery.

Pouring a coffee, Emery decreed, "You can't possess or clone immortals who belong to Tri-Clan. In theory, another immortal being can bounce a soul out into Crypt storage and temporarily highjack a body if they are the same tier soul. It won't hold longer than two, maybe three weeks."

"Weird information to know," Frost toyed, suspiciously.

With a grin, Emery divulged, "I have special friendships with Third-Tier who have loose lips after a few drinks. The Crypt containing the soul belonging to the inhabited body is usually close by."

"How close?" Jenna probed. "A Crypt can't be difficult to find."

Smiling, Emery revealed, "Not a full-size Crypt. It could be the size of a pendant on a necklace. Small enough to be on one's person. Arrianna might be able to find it. In my experience, Third-Tier rarely say no to being propositioned by a pretty anything."

Letting it sink in, Frost announced, "Orin, take a group and get the newbies out of here for the day. I'll go stop it."

FROST WALKED PAST EVERYONE AT THE PICNIC TABLES WITHOUT looking and went into the RV. "Something's going on," Lexy whispered.

"Definitely," Grey answered.

Their Oracle opened the door and motioned them over.

They got up and went inside. After suspicions were shared, Lexy mumbled, "I knew something was off. Arrianna is in there with him." At the door in a flash, she was blocked by Emery. "You should move," Lexy suggested boiling rabbits in her mind.

"Calm down," Emery directed.

She was going to smack her.

Emery responded telepathically, *'Try it. I dare you.'*

She was cocky.

Grey touched Lexy, saying, "Let's hear the plan."

"Frost went over there to stop it. She'll be here in a minute," Jenna explained.

Irate, Lexy grilled, "When did someone switch out Markus? How did nobody notice?"

Jenna answered, "It must have happened right after we left. Between the aura blockers and Oracle fatigue, I'm missing big things."

"I'll stay here. We'll fix this together. This isn't your fault. Nobody is meant to spend a thousand years as the only Oracle," Emery rationed, gazing into her eyes.

Emma had to survive Immortal Testing. The door opened. Grey and Lexy embraced Arrianna before she had a chance to speak.

Blinking away signs of weakness, Arrianna addressed the group, "Explain."

They gave her a rundown of how they'd concluded, Markus was inhabited by a Third-Tier soul.

Their Oracle, Jenna stepped in, "This version of Markus has been setting us up for failure. He's doing something to stifle my ability. Everyone should have caught on when he ordered Kayn to take out high ranking immortal community members in front of the Aries Group, but we were all drunk and stupid. There's nobody to blame but ourselves. His soul must be contained in a pendant or jewellery close to the inhabited body. You need to steal it."

A mix of relief and fear washed over Arrianna. Cupping her face, Lexy prompted, "There's no time to breakdown. You have to do this. Does he have any jewellery he always wears?"

With tears in her eyes, Arrianna disclosed, "He doesn't wear rings or a necklace, but he has piercings, one nipple and his..."

Unfazed, Jenna probed, "You'll get him drunk. It's still his body, can you do this?"

"Back that up... What?" Grey blurted out, shocked.

Grasping what she needed to do, Arrianna confessed, "I don't know how I'm going to get those off. I need a gift."

Intrigued, Emery declared, "For what?"

As resolve set in, Arrianna explained, "Frost interrupted us saying, Jenna found his birthday gift."

They scrambled around the RV looking for something gift worthy. Passing her weird things until Arrianna asserted, "Come on people. I need a reason for coming over here."

Strutting out of the back, Emery tossed Arrianna lingerie and decreed, "This will do. Change over there."

Clutching her shoulders, Jenna coached, "It's his body. Find where his soul is being stored and get it to us. We'll be waiting."

Passing bottles of alcohol, Emery gave her a quick pep talk, "Third-Tier have a high tolerance, take these. Now, get back over there and get him drunk enough to pass out so you can get that piercing off his Tally Whacker."

Scrunching her face, Lily complained, "I'm traumatised."

Tossing her a bracelet, Jenna said, "You'll need to hide your thoughts."

AS THE DOOR CLOSED BEHIND ARRIANNA, THEY SUCCUMBED TO silence, knowing what they'd asked her to do. *It felt wrong. It* was, but they needed to outwit a Third-Tier. Go seduce the being who stole your boyfriend's body.

"It feels wrong asking her to do this," Grey stated. "Can't we just tie him up and beat it out of him?"

"I second that," Lexy backed him up.

Visibly pissed, Emery asserted, "Do I need to repeat the Tri-Clan job description? Sacrificial Lambs. Whatever it takes."

"We have to find his soul. Nobody was expecting this to happen. Everything is going to be okay," Lily talked herself into believing it.

Staring at her, Frost vowed, "It will be."

They all knew it wasn't that simple. Bodies were expendable. Pushing the limits of love may lead to a catastrophe but trauma was a crossbreed's cross to bear.

Pacing, Jenna struggled to figure it out, "I know a Coven capable of removing and trapping a soul. Only a high-level soul can operate our brains. Abaddon has been a step ahead of us for a while. If there's technology blocking my abilities, they may have slipped a tracking device on us too. We should check both RV's."

Peering out the window, Frost rationed, "We'll figure this out. I sent the newbies away with Killian, Orin and five Ankh. Arrianna will get anything that can store a soul to us."

Reversing their roles, Lexy sat next to Grey. Taking his hand, she whispered, "You'd do the same."

Unable to help it, a smile crept across his cheeks. He teased, "Sleep with Markus?"

Swatting him, Lexy clarified, "Seduce someone who stole my body to help find me."

Grey kissed her hand, confessing, "In a heartbeat."

"Toxic and beautiful," Emery announced, pointing at the Handler, Dragon duo. Everyone's' head turned. "I'm trying to understand feelings. Did I get it right?"

Shaking her head, Jenna whispered, "Filter. We'll talk later."

It was true. Staring out the window at the other RV, all she could think about is the wrath someone would face for high jacking her Handler's body. *She'd tear the thieving soul displacer apart. Bendy morals were an afterlife prerequisite. Nobody made it out of Immortal Testing without them.*

Arrianna frantically waved out the door "I'll go," Grey offered, dashing out of the RV before anyone could stop him.

SEEING HER LINGERIE AND FLUSHED CHEEKS AS HE CAME IN, Grey toyed, "Hi Arrianna."

"I took enough energy to knock him out. I don't know how long I have. There's nothing out of the ordinary," she quietly explained as he followed her down the hall.

Taking in the kinky majesty of their leader blindfolded, naked, and bound with piercings, Grey whispered, "Did you check his ass?"

"No," Arrianna asserted, "You do it."

Scowling, Grey whispered, "You're his girlfriend."

She'd barely grazed his rear when blindfolded Markus stirred, mumbling, "That's nice. Do that."

Shit! She put her hands on his chest, drained more, and he went limp. Looking up at Grey, she implored, "What am I supposed to do?"

"I'd wash my hands," Grey chuckled, following her to the washroom. He pressed the pump soap, saying, "I've got your back."

Shaking her head, she mumbled, "I barely touched him."

"I was joking. I can't believe you tried to check," Grey chuckled, evading a swat.

Shooting him a dirty look, she whispered, "Why did they send you over?"

"I lost rock, paper, scissors," Grey confessed, grinning. "Also, I've seen you naked before." He waved his hands in her direction. Pointing to the backroom, he admitted, "That shit is going to haunt me for decades."

"Be serious, Grey. What are we going to do?" Arrianna whispered.

"Quick, take out his piercings before he wakes up. I'll give them to Jenna. Tell him we need the bunks. Get a room, and see what he takes with him," Grey whispered. "Make sure he's out. Do it now. I'll wait."

With her hands on his chest, Arrianna drained his energy. Bad Markus slumped over on the pillows as she searched his pockets. "I can't lose him," she whispered, placing piercings into the Kleenex in Grey's hand.

Wrapping it up, Grey quietly answered, "You won't. Keep him with us. Use whatever means necessary. Emery offered to do it if you can't."

No, Emery wasn't touching her boyfriend's body. "Can't we just force him to tell us where Markus is?" Arrianna whispered at the door.

"We don't know how high up it goes. You'll get a room and keep him distracted while they search through personal items. We'll figure it out," Grey whispered, squeezing her shoulder. He went to leave, turned back, and repeated, "You don't have to do this. Emery will take your place. I'd take your place if I could."

Smiling, Arrianna replied, "I've got this. Get out of here."

Knowing she was capable of doing whatever she had to do, didn't stop the surge of guilt as he dashed back to the other RV where everyone was awaiting news. He walked in and passed Frost a Kleenex, announcing, "That shit is going to haunt me for decades. She has him tied up. This Third-Tier is freaky. She knocked him out by siphoning Healing energy so she could take the piercings off. Maybe he put it down somewhere? She's going to take him back to the hotel under the premise of another job and uninterrupted alone time."

"We have to separate. Lily, Jenna and I will go stay at the hotel. We can check their room when they go out to eat. We'll tear these RVs apart and make sure he hasn't placed tracking devices. Don't let the newbies come back until he's gone."

14
The List

Watching the pregnant girl drinking a shake balanced on her tummy. Orin switched the subject, "When are you due, Emma?"

"Honestly, I don't even know what day of the week it is," Emma mumbled, stirring her shake.

Astrid's cell rang. She walked away from the table to talk. Watching Astrid pacing outside the front door running a hand through her short blonde hair, it was obviously bad news. Playing with her straw as Astrid came back, Kayn looked up and said, "We're taking off, aren't we?"

"After they're done searching the RV," Astrid replied, visibly concerned.

"How bad is it?" Killian probed.

"We'll talk about it in the car. Pack up your food," Astrid instructed.

Giving her a half hug, Zach teased, "It won't be forever. You'll be able to sleep tonight."

Samid chuckled, "So will the wolves."

Smacking the back of his head, Killian scolded, "Don't be a dick, Sami. She's going to miss her friend with benefits."

Finishing the remnants of her shake with a noisy slurp, Haley clarified, "Boyfriend."

"That blows my mind," Killian chuckled, putting wrappers on the tray.

As he put their trash in the garbage, Astrid whispered, "Ignore him. He's missing his trolling buddy."

They drove back to the campground listening to the newbie's debating random situations.

With dancing chestnut eyes, Molly bantered, "If someone gets rid of a ghost and it comes back is that repossession?"

"In theory," Zach laughed, enjoying being back with the newbies.

Curious, Dean flirted, "Hey, sexy Viking guy. Can you get repossessed?"

Grinning, Killian answered, "If you're stupid."

"How so?" Dean bantered.

"Avoid people who only have pupils," Killian chuckled.

Molly laughed, "That's in every horror movie. Are you telling me that's real?"

"It is," Emma confirmed, gazing out the window.

Playfully poking her, Molly badgered, "How would you know?"

Emma responded, "I'm Clairvoyant and Psychic. Having visions of future events comes with afterlife spoilers."

Testing her, Samid pestered, "Are you having a boy or a girl?"

Emma stated as fact, "A girl."

Samid pressed, "What are you going to name her?"

"Don't," Killian reprimanded, giving him a look.

"I'm not naming her. She's not going to be mine," Emma admitted with strength far beyond her years.

Catching on, Sami apologised, "Sorry, I wasn't thinking."

"It's just how it is," Emma answered, smiling sweetly.

Placing a hand on her shoulder, Molly decreed, "You're doing a selfless thing. It's heroic."

Killian cave manned, from the backseat, "Unicorn girl, my cell is charging. Pass it back here." When there was no response, he went full Neanderthal, whistling and shouting, "Unicorn girl! Cellphone!"

Everyone looked at each other with wide eyes.

"Slam on the breaks. He's not wearing his seatbelt," Haley muttered, playing the game.

Driving, Astrid laughed, "Viking boy, let me save you some time. She's never going to respond to Unicorn Girl."

"You call me Viking boy. What's the difference?" Killian toyed, invading Haley's bubble by kicking the back of her seat.

Turning back, Haley said, "Seriously?"

"He's got me there," Astrid commented, as tires jumped a pothole, bouncing everyone in their seats.

Haley looked back and smiled while shaking her head.

Grinning, Killian baited, "Unicorn Girl likes me."

"I assure you, she does not," Haley bantered, pitching his phone at him.

"Don't you want to put your number in first?" The burly Adonis, baited. When there was no response, Killian nudged Zach, saying, "Do you have her number handy?"

"She'll kill me in my sleep, I can't," Zach whispered, grinning.

Glancing back, squinting, Haley enquired, "Why me?"

Peering up from his phone, Killian chuckled.

Her phone vibrated. Haley read the message, grinning. She tossed an empty coffee cup at Killian, demanding, "Who gave it to you?"

Arrianna and not really Markus left to get a room as the rest of Ankh sprung into motion searching for surveillance equipment. Shortly after calling to tell the others the coast was clear, the new Ankh, and their pack of immortal babysitters returned. Lexy and Grey were staying out of the way.

Haley swatted Grey's butt as she walked by. He leapt, laughing when he saw who smacked him and called after her, "Love you too, Haley!"

Shaking her head, Lexy scolded, "What did you do?"

With an arm around her waist, Grey kissed her cheek, saying, "It doesn't matter. She'll only have that number for five minutes."

Wandering up, Orin stripped off his shirt, saying, "Hope I get to stay with you guys."

Lexy gapped staring at his lean tanned abs. *Damn.*

Grinning, Grey whispered, "I forgot to put him on the list."

"I left you one," she teased, still watching.

Embracing her, he whispered, "Give me five minutes."

"You can have six," Lexy sparred, laughing as he put her in a headlock, messing up her hair.

Frost was moving seats out of the RV with Jenna and Lily. Kayn sauntered over, asking, "Is there a reason we're not all helping?"

Looking her way, Lexy explained, "We were getting in the way. There's a method to their madness."

"I'm too sexy, it's distracting," Grey chuckled, adding his two cents.

"Seems legit," Kayn teased, watching Frost's perspiration glistening in the sun.

"Why are we removing seats?" Killian enquired, watching the trio work.

Lexy answered, "They're checking for bugs and tracking devices. Markus has been switched out with a Third-Tier.

That's all we know. Arrianna and Bad Markus got a room. Jenna, Frost and Lily have the room next door."

"I've seen too much today," Grey said. "We can't leave until they're sure we're not being tracked. How's Emma?"

Kayn replied, "Ready to be done with pregnancy."

"Did you make sure she had orange juice?" Grey asked, watching Emma waddle after the others like an adorable downtrodden duck.

Astrid wandered past, saying, "She drank ten glasses of orange juice, Daddy Grey." Catching the unintended double meaning, Astrid glanced back, teasing, "That might stick."

Calling him Daddy Grey would definitely wreck their friend zone pact.

Frost jogged over. He gave her sister a sweaty bear hug. They flirted back and forth.

Jenna shouted, "Killian! Take over for Frost!" They took off like their Oracle's words were gunshots at a horse race.

"Wish we could shower," Grey huskily seduced in her ear.

Leaning back against him, Lexy provoked, "Keep it up and I'll take this friend zone out, Daddy Grey."

"Call me Daddy Grey again and I'll let you," he whispered, forcing himself to step away.

Exhaling as they parted, Lexy met his eyes and said, "We need distractions right now."

"I know," he agreed solemnly.

They had to get to work. She bent over to unlatch the storage.

Staring, Grey mumbled, "That's mean."

"Unintentional," Lexy replied, glancing back. Wide eyed, he backed away and took off. *The attraction would be mutual for longer if they didn't break the friend zone pact. That already felt impossible. They had to do what they planned and see other people.* Smiling, she went back to peeling something off the hot metal. It was just a sticker. Wiping perspiration off her brow as she stood up, Zach handed her a bottle of water. Smiling at her sister's Handler, she said, "Thanks. Have they found anything?"

"I don't think so," he answered. "They're putting everything back, getting ready to leave."

It was smoking hot out. Hair prickled on the back of her neck. *Uh, oh.*

Zach turned and ran away. She chased him on autopilot as did everyone else as Kayn's screaming echoed through the desert. Running over hills until they reached the source of the shrieking.

Angrily pacing as they approached, Frost said, "Relax, it's an Enlightening. I'm only angry at myself. I should have known something was wrong when she picked a fight and stormed off."

Glaring, Zach accused, "What did you say?"

"It's what I didn't say," Frost mumbled. Looking at her Handler, he explained, "I'm an idiot."

"Leave these two with her. It's evolution pain. Let's go, nothing to see here," Grey ushered everyone away.

As the others wandered off, Zach prompted, "You might as well tell me."

"I love her so much it hurts," Frost confessed, "Fear creeps in and stops me from saying it back sometimes. She took off. I didn't go after her."

Watching her writhing in agony, Zach whispered, "Your situation can't be easy, but hers isn't either. How do I fix it? Am I supposed to try?"

"It'll run its course. There's no way to skip past this, everyone goes through it," Frost responded. Guiltily watching her seizing in the sand, he caved, "If it goes on too long, you're immortal and her Handler. You can try."

Jenna walked up, urging, "We need to go. Zach will talk to

her. You can text her later. We shouldn't leave Arrianna alone."

Hesitating, Frost touched Zach's shoulder, and said, "Tell her I'm sorry. Make sure she knows I'll do better."

Understanding what he was saying, Zach answered, "Go, take care of Arrianna. I've got this." Wishing he had a lawn chair as they walked away, he watched her writhing in agony until his heart couldn't take it anymore.

15
The Things We Fear

*H*ours lapsed before Killian showed up. Zach got up to stretch his legs. The burly immortal passed a book. "This might help you pass the time. Hungry?"

"Starving. Thanks for this," Zach replied, waving the book. "I was about to do something stupid."

Grinning, Killian chuckled, "Do tell."

Watching her squirm, Zach said, "Instinct wants me to touch her."

Wincing, Killian cautioned, "Trust me, you don't want to do that." His phone buzzed, Big Sexy texted someone back.

Zach probed, "Frost?"

"You haven't been texting him back," Killian chuckled.

"My cell is in the RV," Zach sparred.

"Have you just been sitting here alone for hours?" Killian asked, "Why didn't you say anything?"

Grinning, Zach teased, "My telekinesis is choppy in these parts."

"You could have gone back to get your phone?" Killian countered.

"I didn't want her to wake up alone," Zach replied. "If you bring my cell and a snack, I'll text Frost. What's going on over there?"

The burly immortal answered, "They're having dinner at a restaurant pretending Markus is really Markus."

Her shrieking and squirming amped up a few octaves. A blast of energy knocked both men off their feet, rippling away under sand like an earthquake tremor. Thousands of snakes slithered out of the cracked desert floor. "I hope this is a hallucination," Zach stammered, scrambling backwards, kicking away swarming reptiles. Fangs sunk into his ankle, he shrieked, "Get it off! Help!"

Terrified, Killian yanked the snake off like a hero and whipped it away. Scurrying out of harm's way, Zach tripped over Kayn. He began screaming and thrashing with her. With the pair flailing, slithering reptiles slid between their limbs until they vanished beneath a slithering mass. Killian carefully backed away, "Hard no. I'll get help!"

ROASTING HOTDOGS OVER A CAMPFIRE A MASSIVE FRANTIC immortal bombarded them, losing his shit, "Snakes! Help me! Do something!"

Grey casually said, "This is new."

Twirling, tugging imaginary snakes off his body, Killian was panicking, "They're biting me! Eating us! No! Please!"

Grey calmly rationalised, "Buddy, calm down. It's okay, you're hallucinating. There's nothing on you, man."

Nope. Lexy snapped frantic immortal's neck and decreed, "Well, that was enough of that. Guess we'd better check on Kayn's Enlightening."

Grey sighed, "I hate snakes, take Orin."

Getting up, Orin laughed, "I'll go."

"Can I come?" Molly eagerly offered, taking her stick out of the fire.

Amused by Molly's infatuation, Lexy wandered away with Orin, saying, "You should stay. We don't know what that was."

Glancing back, Orin shouted, "You guys put Killian in the RV and protect Grey from imaginary snakes!"

"You suck!" Grey called out as they walked away. Getting up, he sighed, "Come on, kids. Grab a limb. Let's get the big guy inside. He'll be down until they come back to heal him."

Once they were out of earshot, Orin flirted, "Pulling the awkward, ex booty call Band-Aid off by volunteering to come with me?"

"Maybe a little," Lexy confessed, strolling away with her crimson hair shimmering in sunlight. "Are we good?"

Grinning, Orin replied, "We're good."

In comfortable silence, they followed heavy prints until they approached the area where they left Kayn. *They were gone.* "Do you feel that?" Lexy asked, with her lips moving, but not an insect's buzz or crackle of steps in gravelly sand registered in isolating silence. The hair on her arms rose as unnerving icy wind passed through her. A wave of nausea hit as ill-omened shadows snuffed out the sun and azure sky.

The temperature descended as rapid breaths pirouetted, Orin mouthed the words, "What is this?"

With not a star, nor a moon in darkness, turmoil ceased. Merging with dark places, the Dragon gazed into the onyx nothing with zen solidarity. Observing Orin yelling into his phone with the volume off, and then… nothing.

ORIN

Shadows extended until the desert was swallowed by darkness. Orin lost sight of Lexy in the vacuous muted void. Grasping the plausible scenarios, everything was in slow-mo. *Alone in the nefarious surroundings, it felt like a nightmare. Maybe it was? He was asleep on his bunk.* Something creepily caressed his hair. *No, no, he wasn't doing this.* Ducking, Orin tried bolting away with furry things pushing against his legs inhibiting movement. *These weren't snakes. Kittens? He needed to believe they were kittens.* Wading through the knee-high fuzzy herd with burning calves, his palm heated. *No, he didn't need a visual.* His Ankh symbol strobed, revealing enormous furry spiders as far as the eye could see. He talked himself down, *spider's sense fear. Be calm, be mellow. You are intelligent. You do not need to lose your shit.* The brand on his hand flashed another image as arachnid fangs sunk into his thigh. He tore spiders off with full body heebie geebies and nowhere to run. *He was bleeding.* The urge to shriek hysterically was overpowering logic. *He was going to have to fight. He wasn't ready.* His legs heated as they healed, but not fast enough to avoid riling up the writhing hoard, fangs sunk into his flesh, hairy legs crawled up his skin as the ravenous eight-legged monstrosities mercilessly attacked. Fending off spiders with spine-chilling visuals each time his symbol flashed, the herd of arachnids swapped eating him for saving him for later as sticky web bound his body. Struggling, Orin was rapidly spun into a cocoon. Once his legs were encased, they gave him a yank, and he toppled over. *They were going to stab him and liquefy his insides. He hated spiders. This was going to suck. He really didn't want to do this today.* Squirming, he froze. *He shouldn't make himself more appealing by being feisty. Lexy was down the Dragon of the night rabbit hole, she wasn't going to notice he was in trouble until he was killed, triggering longer strobes of her symbol. The Dragon's priority would be Grey. What if they were all encased by spiders? He might be furthest down the list. Grey, then newbies, Killian was already dead that lucky bastard. Damn it, he was an immortal.* Grasping his unfortunate predicament, Orin chuckled. *There was no purpose in awaiting impalement. Nobody was coming to save him.* Each time his symbol went off, spider shadows loomed ominously behind a white web veil. *He might lose it. He was going to have to bust out of this.* Opting to go out fighting, he punched through the cocoon and writhed his way out with relentless fangs punching into his flesh. Sweltering hot as his healing ability fought the good fight, it imploded, in the next strobe of his symbol, he saw a path. Releasing a battle cry, Orin ran through the herd waving his arms broiling hot until the lights went out.

GREYDON

Back at the campsite, they'd finished putting the massive immortal on a bottom bunk and were all standing there as the RV dimmed.

Reaching for the cord, Dean gave it a tug and said, "The light's burnt out."

A wave of nausea washed over Grey as the temperature rapidly dropped. *There was no time. He couldn't do it by himself.* Grabbing a bag of salt out of the closet, he tossed it to Dean, barking orders, "Get wet. Cover yourselves in salt, Emma first. Nobody leaves the bathroom." Armed with his own bag of salt and a knife, Grey leapt out of the RV into frigid darkness. Stabbing the bag, he encircled the RV giving the newbies spiritual protection and went back in. Standing on the other side of the bathroom door, Grey asserted, "Lock the door. Stay in here, no matter what anyone says, even me. They can imitate our voices. They will try to trick you. Your symbols will warm and flash as each of us goes down just like it did for Killian.

We have this. Ignore the urge to help. We're immortal, death is temporary. Protect the baby. Stay in here."

On the bunk across from Killian, Grey tried texting the others but there was no signal. *It didn't feel like they were safe with only him as the line of defence.* Clutching a knife in the darkness, with his heart palpitating, he went in the closet and dumped a barrier of salt in front of the bathroom door. Running to the kitchen sink, he turned on the water. It made a creaky noise as it started running. Planning to splash it on himself, he cupped his hands under the tap. His palms filled with a thick warm substance. He smelled pennies. *His hands were full of blood. He hadn't circled the RV with salt fast enough. They weren't protected. It wasn't safe inside.* Pacing in darkness, he took off the bracelet that stifled his Pyrokinesis and went outside.

IN A FLASH OF LIGHT, HE WAS BACK AT HIS MORTAL FAMILY'S rural home in Scotland. The six-year-old version of himself came out of the house with a toothless grin. *He barely recalled the time before they moved to Australia.*

His mother's voice hollered, "Greydon Zoa Riley, don't you dare leave the property!"

Momma. Mortal memories lured his consciousness away. *He needed to see his mom.* Smelling dinner as he went into his house, the beauty of a carefree childhood filled his senses. From the pictures of people he didn't recognise in the hall to the sensation of the rug beneath his feet, everything felt vaguely familiar. As he walked into the kitchen with yellow curtains and sunflower wallpaper, his mother carried on with dinner preparations. The rotary phone on the wall rang.

His mom turned and answered with her usual joke, "Riley summer home. Some are home and some are not."

Something about this place felt off. In the open cupboard were dishes with a pattern he didn't recognise. *Not much came to Australia. Including his mother's red hair. She'd always been blonde, hadn't she?* His heart reminisced as she chatted with easy humour until she looked out the window. He followed her line of sight to his six-year-old self, lighting the woodpile on fire with his mind. She dropped the phone, leaving the caller dangling as she ran out the backdoor.

His six-year-old self got up sobbing, "I'm sorry, Momma. I didn't mean to."

Kicking the smoking log away from the pile, she threw dirt on it. "Give me the matches," his mother commanded, frisking him for what he'd started the fire with.

Blubbering, he wept, "I don't got any."

Kneeling, compassionately looking into his eyes, his mom corrected, "I don't have any."

Looking up guiltily, he repeated, "I don't have any."

"Play inside where I can keep an eye on you until dinner is ready, I left Aunt Everly on the phone," his mom stated.

Following his younger self inside, he wanted to hear his mother's conversation. *He didn't remember Aunt Everly.*

Hanging up as he came in, his mom prompted, "Go play with your sisters. I'll call you when dinner's ready, sweetie. I'm nightshift tonight. Auntie will be watching you."

Sisters? He had an infant sister at sixteen when he joined Ankh. She'd survived his Correction. He'd been forced to finish the job when she was a teenager. This must be a dream. Confident it wasn't real, and curious about the rest of the house, Grey followed his childhood self upstairs to a room he didn't remember with bunk beds and a single bed. *This had to be a dream.*

A girl of eight or nine ran into the room giggling with a paper in her hand, chased by a teenage girl, scolding, "Give it back!" Snatching it off her, the older one stuck her head out the door, yelling, "I need my own room!"

What was this? It flashed forward to bedtime. His mother kissed the younger girl on the forehead, whispering, "Sweet dreams till sunbeams find you, Wendy Marie." She did the same to his younger self. Giving the girl on the top bunk a pat, his mom reminded, "No middle of the night phone calls Carol Ann, you're grounded."

"Whatever," the teenager answered, pulling covers over her head.

Time lapsed as he went downstairs. Aunt Everly was on the couch, engrossed in a book. Someone knocked on the door. She got up, mumbling, "Carol Ann, if that boy is here, your mother is going to kill you."

Shivers ran up his spine as Aunt Everly's hand reached for the doorknob. Shaking her head, she panicked, "No, no." A rifle boomed. His aunt looked down at the circle of red spreading on her nightgown and flopped in the doorway.

In a heartbeat, he was his six-year-old self, being picked up with dozy eyes and dangling legs, Carol Ann hid him in the closet, whispering, "Not a peep, Greydon."

The door in their room closed. It was eerily quiet. Carol Ann screamed. A shot rang out. Covering his mouth with her hand, Wendy Marie moved a plank and forced him into a small space. Concealing his hiding spot with the board, she whispered, "Not a peep, Greydon."

He recognised voices, but his sleepy mind couldn't grasp it. The closet creaked open.

Wendy Marie started crying, "Don't hurt me, don't."

"Well, hello little girl," a male voice said. "Where is your brother?"

With a shaky voice, Wendy Marie lied, "He's not here. He slept at a friend's house."

The gun clicked. *Momma.* Covering his ears as his sister pled for her life, Grey rocked, hugging his knees to his chest with eyes squeezed shut. A shot rang out. His eyes met with the shooters through the hole in the wall.

"There you are," the man taunted, reaching in.

He scrambled between boards. The stranger caught his

ankle and hauled him out. Clawing at wood, he was dragged by his sister, carried past the other in the hall squirming, and dropped at the top of the stairs. Fear-induced flames shot from his hands, engulfing his captors. He slid down a railing as a shot hit the wall. He ran down a country road until he stumbled, and everything went dark.

It flashed to the here and now. *He felt it in his bones. They were here. They'd come for the baby.* "I'm not a child anymore," he decreed as crimson flames shot from his hands, igniting his assailant. *There was no volume on the screaming.* Protecting the door, he ignited everything trying to gain entry until he was drained of energy. Lightheaded, Grey staggered back into the RV, felt pain in his back and went down.

16
As Dark Things Do

Moderately amused by the writhing mass of reptilian depravities, squirming between her thighs, menacing hollow eyes and the inability to hear, Lexy welcomed the scenario. Succumbing to fear was a choice. The Dragon smirked as snakes coiled around her limbs and she dropped backwards into a pool of serpents.

LUMINESCENCE RESET REALITY. *FIGHT TIME!* READY TO RUMBLE as dark entities attacked, she realised they were hallucinations. *She was impressed. Someone successfully drugged her. She might as well have fun with it.* As her darkest memories snuffed out her final flicker of humanity, primitive urges became her only concern. One with earth beneath her feet, menacing shadows rid her of visuals, isolating silence left scent as her only deviation. Deciding she was hungry she began chasing desert wildlife. Ravenous, she leapt on a coyote, and drained it's life force, leaving it incapacitated for scavengers. Wild Things had no use for empathy. Dragons didn't give any species of tortured souls a pass on a painful demise. Her palm warmed, flashed, and instinct led her over terrain with familiar urgency. Happening upon a smouldering corpse, she sniffed it and kicked sand on it. Movement caught her eye. Snarling, she pursued it into the void, and caught it. Squatting in desert sand, she ate her snack and cocked her head as she picked up an enticing fragrance. Sprinting to where instinct prompted, her routing nose hovered over an area of sand.

A hand burst out. Taken aback, she sniffed it. *It smelled delicious.* She bit it, and it glowed as fingers moved. Cowering in glare, as dark things do, she felt a pull to free it from the sand it was confined in when glow ceased, and the hand went limp. She licked it and started to dig, loosening sand. With a mission, time lapsed until she freed it. Tempted to sneak a taste, its eyes fluttered open, and it gasped. Ethereal glow shifted carnivorous impulse to curiosity. Its lips were moving, but with no volume she didn't understand. *She didn't want to.* Her peripheral vision picked up movement and she took off.

Pursuing prey through the desert hillside as more shiny things spotted landscape, drawing her eyes away from predatory tasks, the urge to remain in the freedom of shadows urged her further into the dark. This was where she stayed until glowing objects encircled her. Hissing, she swatted them away. Wrestling with each shiny thing that jumped her, inborn instinct to protect them wouldn't allow her to stop their irritating attack. Launching glowing things away, she took off into the shadows as fast as her Dragon limbs would carry her, but they were relentless. Eventually they gave up and left her in darkness where she belonged. Sensing their inevitable return, she opted to curl up and rest.

A soothing voice reached her through the nothing, the Dragon cracked an eye. As a sparkling being approached her lair, she froze. Contemplating digging to escape, she pressed her torso against the sand. Scurrying away as it grew closer, she pitched rocks at it, growling but it kept coming. *Instinct wouldn't let her hurt it.* Backing away as it inched closer shining like a beacon. She ran away as it chased her.

Waking up safe and warm beneath the covers on their bunk, Lexy overheard Grey scolding Kayn for dousing everyone with a nightmare inducing hallucinogenic toxin. *That was hilarious.* Grinning, her interest peaked when her sister asked if Killian was dead.

Grey explained, "That's why I came to get you. Sorry, I was sidetracked by pheromones. Emery is driving, Mel's exhausted and Lexy is post feral asleep. Can you do it?"

Post feral asleep. Funny.

Grey slurred, "I was never mad at choo."

Hearing a thud, Lexy mumbled, "Is Grey drunk?"

Looking up, Kayn answered, "He touched my shoulder while I was healing Killian."

Peering over the edge of her bunk, she saw Grey out cold in the hall, Lexy laughed, "He does things without thinking. I'll get him." She leapt down and gave Grey a jolt of energy. As he came to, she stroked his hair, saying, "You can't touch Healers when they're healing people, you goof."

"Hey Lex," Grey replied with adoration in his eyes.

They hit a pothole. The RV lurched. Lexy landed on him with their lips a breath apart. Sensing something weighing on his mind, she asked, "What's wrong?"

"Get off so I can think straight," he teased.

She got up and sprawled on their bunk, directing, "Spill."

Lying next to her, Grey whispered, "I remembered something too horrible to process. When I was in the in-between after I died, I had a chat with our Guardian. Azariah says you need to erase me."

Gazing into his eyes, she whispered, "What do you want?"

"If we don't move past our attraction, this scenario is never going to change," he whispered. Caressing her hair, he confessed, "I talk a good game, but being with you is all I can think of. It has to be your choice."

Smiling, Lexy embraced him, whispering, "Let's give our plan to move forward an honest try. You have to be able to let me date other people too without weeks of arguments and silent treatment."

"I can," he vowed, holding her closer.

No, you can't.

Killian laughed. Grey sighed, "His voice irritates me." Grazing her breast with a hand, he seduced, "Baby steps."

"Grey," she whispered as he toyed with her. "This isn't going to work."

"Probably not," Grey confirmed. "I need to hold you."

She needed to feel their connection too.

With his arms around her, he closed his eyes, whispering, "I love you."

She whispered, "Love you always," falling asleep in his arms.

In the wee hours of the morning, Kayn frantically shook everyone on the bunks awake. *Shit was obviously hitting the fan.* Half asleep, Lexy wandered into the kitchen and sat on the counter, swinging her legs. *What now? It was going to be hard to top being doused with psychedelic pheromones.*

Summoning authority, Kayn got everyone's attention, "We missed a tracking device when we searched the RV. The gas tank is empty, and we're being tailed." She grasped Grey's arm and froze like a deer in headlights.

Meeting her eyes, Grey touched her hand, prompting "If it's time-sensitive, spit it out."

Kayn whispered, "Emma's water broke. She's in the washroom." Grey raced to her aid as everyone lost their shit. From the driver's seat, Emery howled laughing.

Keeping well-intentioned newbies at bay by blocking the hall, Mel commanded, "Stay put. Act like adults. Kayn isn't finished."

On the counter, swaying her legs without a care in the world, Lexy chuckled, "This is awesome."

"No adults in here," Samid insolently mumbled.

Swatting the teen, Killian scolded, "Manners Sami. You're immortal now. I'm allowed to kick your ass for being a dick."

Her sister addressed the group, "Our closest backup is a few hours away. We need to take out the car two behind us and get gas while Emma delivers a baby, any ideas?"

No problem. Grinning, Lexy jumped off the counter. Looking at the roof, she clapped her hands, instructing, "Newbies to the closet for demon blades. Get on the left side of the RV." They took off. "Mel, circle the RV with salt as soon as we stop, you guard Emma with the newbies. Killian, thirty years ago, south of Montreal."

Chuckling, Killian unlatched an escape hatch on the roof, yelling, "Emery, we've got this! Lights off! Veer onto the first backroad you see with no turn signal! They'll drive by, it'll buy us a minute to get a few of us on the roof!"

Shaking her head, Emery sighed, "You guys are so much fun."

They were on speakerphone with the other car, and everyone was laughing. Killian repeated impressively insane instructions to the other vehicle. The car ahead gunned it and vanished as they turned off their lights.

"We'll have twenty seconds before the lights of the next car," Lexy explained, as she reappeared up front.

Emery's voice called out, "It's a straight turn off! Pray we don't tip this beast!"

Emma cried out in agony. *Eye on the ball. No time.* Lexy lured her sibling into the kitchen, tempting, "Want to do something crazy?"

"Do you have to ask?" Kayn sparred, grinning.

Lexy passed her a blade, instructing, "Up and out, when we make it around the corner."

Sticking his head out, Killian shouted, "Everyone on the left!"

Everything was pin drop silent, except for whirling tires as they stepped over to the left side.

Emery's voice loudly instructed, "Lights off!"

Everything went dark. Killian counted down, "Five, four, three, two, one… Now!"

They veered to the right, with the tires off the ground. Killian dove to the left with everyone else as they bounced back on all four tires and burned off the highway down a side road.

Dangling from the escape hatch, Lexy provoked, "Coming?" Kayn jumped up. Tugging her through onto the roof, Lexy asserted, "Flush with the RV, until we're out of sight." They laid there watching lights pass in the distance with the humming of tires on the road. The third set of headlights passed without slowing as they lost sight of the highway. Peering in, Lexy yelled, "Pass me that spiked strip."

Handing it up, Killian said, "We're only postponing the inevitable if we don't find out how they're tracking us."

"Get everyone to dig through their personal belongings, pockets, purses, wallets," Lexy suggested, getting up as they stopped. Haley and Astrid were parked taking jugs of gas out of their trunk. "There's more in our side compartment," Lexy yelled. They sprinted into action, refilling the RV. She leapt off and jogged down the road, hollering, "Give me a minute!" Positioning the strip, she sprinted back and climbed up the ladder. Joining her sister, gazing up at a spectacular starry night sky as they cruised down the road into nowhere. The fragrance of sulphur made her smile. *These assholes. If she hitched a ride, she could get a full view of the scenario they were facing.* She looked at her sister. *Kayn's inner dialogue was rolling full steam, but she couldn't hear it.* Her stomach flip-flopped as she watched the sky.

Her sister asked, "Why are we on top of the RV?"

"Sneak attack strategy," Lexy answered, rumbling down a road with Emma's labour as back noise and a full tank of gas.

Looking 'toss her cookies disturbed', Kayn repeated, "Kevin says, they've realised they lost us and turned around. Someone needs to take the baby and run."

Frigging Kevin. Snapping her neck for talking to him was going to wreck her plans for the night. "She's in labour, there's nothing to take anywhere," Lexy replied. *Take the baby.* Reading Kayn's disturbed expression, she clued in, "Does he want me to cut it out?"

Hesitating before relaying Kevin's response, Kayn said, "Grey has to do it."

No. He can't. Shaking her head, Lexy got up, decreeing, "No, I won't ask him to do that. I'll do it." *There was something she had to deal with first.* She stood up, balancing. With the wind and the warbling tires, she faintly heard Kayn warning her to get down. Roof surfing with wind blowing her crimson hair like flames, and a demon blade clutched in her hand, Lexy hollered, "I know! I'm trying to get a lift!" *There it was.* With a loud whoosh, a beastly pterodactyl with scales and talons snatched her off the roof. Laughing, Lexy yelled, "I've got this!" *She'd dealt with these Abaddon creatures. Their talons had venom. You turned into one. She didn't have to worry about it.* Once a Healer's ability was exposed, it found a work around. It was going to take her to a cave or watch her splat. It was circling where the RV stopped on a side road hiking in elevation. *Watch her splat. She had to kill it.* Emma's screaming reminded her of what had to be done. Too many headlights were coming in a line on the opposite side of the highway. They turned down the side road. *Ankh needed her for offence. She wasn't going to be able to help her Handler.* Distant whooshing summoned her eyes as the shadow of a larger lizard pterodactyl with curled clawed legs. *She forgot option three was tear her apart. Inconvenient.* Willing herself strength as talons snatched her legs, the beasts tugged her in opposite directions. Her torso strained. *Strength.* Her midriff and legs were on fire as healing ability fought the good fight. *Strength.* With no sense of up or down as she spun while being yanked from either end, she knew she had to kill both at once. Slicing one, it tuned to smoky ash. She dropped the blade. *Crap.* Concentrating, she drained the other of energy and it spiralled out of control, plummeting from the sky. Branches of trees slowed their descent and the beast cushioned her fall, exploding into ash. *Ouch.* Something glinted in moonlight. *It landed on the blade she dropped. What were the odds of that?*

Dusting herself off, a snake bit her. *Opportunist dick!* Enraged, she tore it off her calf and thwapped it on a tree. Cracking her neck, Emma screamed in agony. *They were right there.* Eavesdropping as she forced her way out of the brush, she smiled. *She was out of the loop. Zach was in a tomb to help him with his Enlightening. Emery was Kayn's proxy Handler this evening. Her sister needed Handler backup too. Maybe it was a Guardian offspring thing?* Walking towards the RV with twigs and flora in scarlet bedhead Lexy decreed, "Let's go, Dragons are offence. I'll take you out if your proxy Handler's a dud."

"No worries," Emery assured, patting Kayn's head like a puppy.

Reminding herself she liked Emery as Kayn leapt off the roof and walked over to her, extended pitchy shrieks froze her sibling's steps. They both looked at the RV. Grey *was doing it. They had Dragon shit to do. She couldn't let it in. Shut it off.* All unnecessary concerns dissipated into the void as the two Dragons sprinted away and separated, each taking a side of the road.

17
Emma's Childbirth

*P*sychic since childhood, Emma had been through plenty of dark shit. She'd almost made it through high school before fate pulled out the big guns, killing her family in a tragic accident. Couch surfing for a year, instinct told her she couldn't risk staying anywhere for longer than a few nights. As violent visions of her inevitable demise persisted, she distanced herself from everyone, continuing to go to school. Most nights, she found somewhere to hide so she could sleep. In time, the desire to survive fizzled and she decided to have fun with the time she had left. She partied with strangers and hung out with older guys, daring fate to finish her off. When she found out she was pregnant it was a laughable plot twist. Being knocked up was the first surprise in ages. Now, she had to survive. Avoiding freak accidents with visions, she spent most of her time in public places to protect the new life growing within her. Knowing the sand in her hourglass was trickling away, she planned to put the baby up for adoption. She held on to the idea of survival for the child as dreams fed her choppy imagery of how it was going to happen. Allowing instinct to lead the way until she was strangled by a stranger and resuscitated by Ankh moments later in a high school lavatory.

Watching a movie with nearly everyone else sound asleep on the backroom floor, she peed herself. Peaking under the blanket at her wet pants, Emma whispered, "Oh, no." She soaked it up with a sweater. Standing on it, she cramped. *Ouch. It might be demons.* Confusion over whether cramping was childbirth or demons was never in anyone's birth plan. She'd always known they couldn't take her to the hospital. Understanding pain was temporary was helpful but she really should have googled what happens during childbirth at least once. The only door with a lock was the bathroom so that's where she went to calm her mind. Clutching the sink, Emma cramped again. *That was fast.* Breathing through it, she knew it wasn't demons. *How was she going to do this?* Nearly toppling over as the RV went over a bump, tears flooded her eyes. She got down on the floor so she wouldn't fall. Kayn opened the door, as she doubled over crying. She told her she'd get help and closed it.

Someone knocked. Sitting by her on the floor, Grey was quiet for a minute before asking, "How long have you been able to see things?"

She couldn't chat. Breathing through contractions, Emma growled, "What things?"

"The future, ghosts, whatever it is you do?" He probed.

Agony surged within her. Releasing a tortured wail, she squeezed her eyes shut, hitting pause on her response. As agony tapered, Emma gasped, "For as long as I can remember."

Lexy popped her head into the washroom, tossed Grey a blade and said, "Thirty years ago south of Montreal."

As the door closed, Grey laughed. Shaking his head, he explained, "We're turning off with no warning to lose a tail. Worst-case scenario, we tip the motorhome."

Panting through a contraction, Emma mumbled, "What tail? Are we being chased while I'm in labour?"

"We have this. No worries," Grey soothed, sweetly taking her hand. "I'm here with you until the end."

Squashing his hand like a hazelnut in a nutcracker, as she spasmed, they simultaneously cried out. Someone yelled something neither one caught. The lights went out as the RV swerved. They were jostled to one side, driving on two wheels. Emma crushed his hand with no mercy as all four tires bounced on the road.

In momentary silence, Grey questioned, "If you knew what was coming, why didn't you avoid Correction?"

"How long do you rationally avoid what's inevitable?" Emma gasped, wincing as the next torturous wave surged, releasing a wail of anguish, squeezing his hand like a vice.

Randomly, Grey asked, "Why didn't you avoid getting pregnant?"

With perspiration damp hair, Emma confessed, "I was dying either way. Why wouldn't I have a one-night stand with a stranger? I didn't know the child in my visions was mine. It's like putting together a jigsaw puzzle if events play out figuratively. You can't fit the pieces together until you've seen the bigger picture."

Caressing her wet hair, Grey suggested, "Maybe it's time to take off your pants?"

"I've been told that will help move things along, but I'll pass," Emma teased, laughing as the next contraction began, squeezing his hand until he squirmed, relaxing as pain dulled.

Opting to keep her laughing, he pretended to be serious, "I'll take one for the team if it'll help."

Shoving him, she screamed as relentless excruciating waves surged.

In the middle of a hand squashing spasm, Grey asked, "Do you want orange juice?"

Asshole! Enraged, she lost it, "You son of a bitch, I don't want any fucking orange juice!" Tackling Grey like a savage beast, she maniacally strangled him.

Clawing at her hands, he croaked, "Joke, a joke."

Releasing his throat, she pointed, threatening, "If you ever even mention orange juice again, I'll kick your ass to next Tuesday," wailing as the next spasm hit.

Taking her hand so she could exact orange juice joke revenge, he cried with her as she squashed it. She released his throbbing hand, but the relief was short-lived. Her eyes rolled back, so only whites were visible.

Having seen their Oracle's ability, he knew he couldn't interrupt it. Waiting as her body spasmed with each contraction. About to shout for help, her eyes normalised.

Defeated, Emma looked up, and pled, "I can't do that. I can't." A swell passed without her trying to reach for his hand.

Wary, Grey assured, "You do whatever you need to do."

As a convulsion passed, she closed her eyes. Mustering up courage, Emma confessed, "You're going to need help."

Without clarification, Grey got up. He peered out the door and saw Killian. Waving the big guy over, he said, "We need help."

At the door, Killian rushed, "They need me out there."

Swallowing fear, Emma picked up the blade on the floor, and passed it to Grey, prompting, "There's no time. Pin me down and cut out the baby."

Freezing in place, Grey whispered, "You're almost done. We'll do this naturally."

"No time. Do it," Emma urged with tears in her eyes.

Panicking, Grey met Killian's eyes and pled, "You have to help. I can't do this."

Kneeling, Killian said, "First things first, why are your pants on?" Helping Emma get her pants off, he questioned, "How far apart are her contractions?" Roughly feeling her abdomen, he repeated, "How far?"

Brutally contracting, Emma cried out. *He had to do it.*

"I don't know," Grey replied.

Killian peered up, and said, "She's not dilated enough. It may take another day." Stroking Emma's hair, he gazed into her eyes, saying, "Are you sure there's no time?"

Doubling over in agony, Emma urged, "Do it!"

Passing her a rolled-up facecloth, Killian instructed, "Bite down on it, with any luck you'll pass out." He showed Grey where to cut, tracing his finger two inches above her pubic area, instructing, "A light incision with the pressure of slicing a banana. Don't think about it."

Blinded by tears, Grey repeated, "I'm sorry, I'm sorry."

As the blade sliced into her, Emma expelled a gut-wrenching wail. Pitchy shrieking with her eyes squeezed shut as the next layer was sliced. *She needed to die. Please. No more.*

Grey's voice soothed, "Pass out. I promise we'll make sure your baby's safe. Pass out."

As the infant released its first crackling cries, she went limp in his arms.

DEVASTATED BY THE PART HE PLAYED, GREY NUMBLY SAT there.

"Take off your shirt," Killian instructed. On autopilot, Grey did it. Passing the infant, Killian said, "Hold the baby against your heart, it's important. I'll be back in a minute."

Awestruck, Grey cradled the newborn. Even covered in goo, she was the most incredible thing he'd ever seen with pursed suckling lips searching for sustenance. *He'd spent his afterlife in search of beautiful things. This was the pinnacle. He'd never top it. New life squirming against his chest was impossible to beat.* Grinning with his heart ready to burst, Grey whispered, "I don't have what you're looking for wee one." His eyes drifted from the newborn to Emma's sacrifice. *This beauty felt stolen.* He held the infant suckling on its fist to Emma's face so the child could sense her and brought it back to his heart. Caressing a delicate cherub cheek, he pledged, "You're going to grow up to be brave and stubborn just like your Mom. I'll make sure you know her." *After your sixteenth year, when we meet again.* Grey kissed the newborn's head. Sensing a presence, he peered up. *It was time to let her go. He wasn't sure he could.*

Haley crouched, urging, "I need to take her. We have to go."

Holding her to his chest, Grey's vision blurred with tears as he gave her up and watched Haley walk away. His eyes returned to Emma on the floor with an open stomach. He didn't need to feel for a pulse, he'd sensed it as she slipped away. *She was gone.* Covering her with a towel, he moved her body into the shower and numbly cleaned up the blood. *For immortals, death was temporary but tending to her was his obligation. He'd experienced what she would always long for. She'd only hold her newborn daughter against her heart in dreams. His part in this would be forever etched in her nightmares. She'd never look at him the same, but she was more too. Before this night, she was just a girl who'd taken a few wrong turns, but he saw her now. She was brave and selfless. He'd believe her capable of anything. There had to be no hint of what took place when she healed. That much he could do.* Grey heard someone and looked up.

Solemnly, Killian explained, "This is the only road. We need to keep it blocked until Triad shows up."

"Thank you for what you did," Grey whispered, standing up with Emma's shell cradled in his arms.

Grabbing the bloody knife, Killian said, "Don't mention it. I'll bleach this so there's no breadcrumbs leading to the child's identity."

Placing Emma's body on pillows in the backroom, Grey peered out the window. *It was a new day.* He exhaled, walking down the hall to the kitchen. *He was grateful for the big guy's help but didn't want to be friends. Emery and Killian would go back to the other continent, and he'd be left with holes where bonds use to be.* Grey confessed, "I can't remember what happened at the end of the story?"

"Which one?" Killian taunted, rinsing off the blade.

Grey countered, "South of Montreal."

"Your girlfriend leapt off the roof of a moving RV onto the car tailing us," Killian regaled, with a knowing grin.

"It's not like that," Grey replied, noticing the lack of chaos. *The fight hadn't made it here, they were holding their ground.*

Waving the knife, Killian said, "I wouldn't advise going out there without a weapon."

Taking the blade, Grey asked, "What's the plan?"

"I'd know if I wasn't yanked from duty to cut a baby out," Killian sparred, opening the door. "The salt line hasn't been disturbed. Your baby momma is safe, kid."

"She's not my…" Grey paused his denial, seeing Killian's grin. *Ass. Kid? He wasn't a newb.*

The pair emerged into breathtaking crimson dawn as sun rose above a picturesque mountain with commotion of fighting down the road. Molly was motionless with her back to them. Grey called out, "Let's go!" She didn't move a muscle as they approached. Killian poked Molly's shoulder. Solid, she tipped, hitting the road with a thud. Looking into unblinking petrified eyes, Grey asked, "Any idea what did this?"

"A lizard pterodactyl snatched Lexy off the roof earlier," Killian disclosed, casually walking into battle.

Most of Abaddon's party favours were nocturnal. A carload of demon-possessed mortals. How bad could it be? "Try to keep up old man," Grey challenged, jogging away. Clutching his weapon, Viking guy, chased him, laughing. As they sprinted around a bend, their Clan was battling Abaddon shells. *This wasn't an even fight at all.* There were vehicles stopped on the road and bodies everywhere. Dean and Sami were still on their feet. Mel was fighting off a group and Emery was enjoying herself way too much. Joining the battle, Killian pitched a shell into the hoard with impressive airtime.

Fighting his way through the herd to back up Mel, Grey shouted, "This isn't one carload!"

Exhausted, Mel kicked one away and slashed another's throat, yelling, "They keep coming! I can't keep this up much longer! We need the Dragons out here not in the bushes!"

Scanning for Lexy's crimson hair in his peripheral vision, fending off assailants, his attention was split into too many directions. *The baby and Emma's unattended body weren't his job. Lexy was his sole duty. He had to focus.* A truck pulled over down the road. *It was Triad.* As Tiberius joined the battle jealousy tugged his heart home. *He hated that guy.* Fighting harder in his rival's presence, he gave it his all, hoping they'd leave before it was time to bring Lexy out of her emotionless abyss. *Knowing he was irrationally jealous, didn't stave off the desire to pummel Tiberius into a pile of mush.* A flash of red hair caught his attention. Distracted, a blade sunk into his back. *Damn it.* Choking, sputtering up blood, Grey staggered forward and went down. Struggling to lift himself up, he was kicked in the stomach. Someone stomped on his back as his head hummed. With seconds to live, he saw Lexy no holds barred slaying everyone. *Good, bad, Triad, Ankh. Oh, no. Shit.* His vision flickered and the lights went out.

18

Waking up in Mexico

Stirring in a moving vehicle, Lexy opened her eyes. *She was with Tiberius. What in the hell?* She panicked, "Where am I? Where's Grey?"

"Calm down. I can explain," her Triad nemesis replied.

"No! Stop! Pull over!" Lexy panicked. He swerved to the side of the road. She jumped out the car like it was on fire, leaving an open door dinging. *She couldn't do this.* Pacing by the side of the road, she vaguely recalled snippets of her Dragon state. Trying to figure out where they were, she heard the ocean. *Damn it. Grey was going to be pissed.*

Cautiously, Tiberius wandered over, explaining, "Grey died. I was sent after you because Ankh had to leave. Trinity was incapacitated, a newbie was stolen by Abaddon. I'm giving you a ride to meet up with Ankh with a quick Correction on the way. I have a lot to apologise for. Playing games with you was stupid. I wasn't thinking."

It didn't matter anymore. "My Handler bond can't take this. I promised Grey, I'd stop," Lexy whispered.

He tried to touch her, whispering her name, "Lexy."

She stepped away, ordering, "Take me back."

"Take you where? They're gone," Tiberius repeated.

Ceasing pacing, she implored, "I can't do this. I can't." Reigning in her reaction as he touched her shoulder, she closed her eyes. Reminding herself to breathe, Lexy faced him.

With a cut lip and shiner, he rationed, "You care about me too. You can't deny it. You're here."

Damn it. Touching his injured lip, every fibre wanted to kiss him. She whispered, "We can't keep doing this."

"I know," Tiberius confirmed with his sexy crooked smirk.

Fighting against it with their eyes locked, duelling libidos mounted intensity until restraint snapped. Mouths met in a passionate frenzy. Backing towards the car, tearing off clothes in a lusty blur, they tumbled onto the backseat to quench an intolerable ache, and bounced tires off gravel like heathens with a door dinging. Blinded by euphoria as their roadside hook up neared its explosive pinnacle, she animalistically cried out, raking nails down his back. Cursing, he pummelled her into the backseat finishing with a drawn out groan. A car drove by. With mouths hovering a breath apart, they started laughing.

Gazing into her eyes, grinning, he whispered, "Hi."

"Hi," she whispered with the will to fight against her self-destructive desires silenced. *She needed that so badly.*

"Is that my blood?" Tiberius chuckled, wiping off her lip with his thumb.

She whispered, "Your lip was cut."

"A Dragon kicked my ass for hours," he chuckled, licking his lip without getting off her.

"I guess we're even," Lexy teased. *She could heal him.* Tugging his mouth back to hers, she sensually kissed him as heat surged in her core and travelled into him, sealing wounds. He cursed, collapsing on top of her.

Whoops. Hoping she didn't kill him, Lexy whispered, "You alive?"

"That was mean," he gasped in her ear.

Staring at the ceiling, she realised what she'd done. *Awkward.*

Getting off her, Tiberius shimmed out of the car. Nearly falling, he grabbed onto the door, laughing, "Fantastic. You're capable of leaving me incapacitated and naked somewhere. How will you use this to your advantage?"

"I hadn't thought of it. Thanks for the battle advice," she baited, looking for her clothes. *Her panties had been torn off and her shirt was crusted with blood from the fight.* Naked beside the vehicle, Tiberius bowed, ass to the road, chuckling as a truck went by. *Freak!* Tossing shorts at his face, she accused, "You destroyed my panties."

Snatching her lacy underwear off the seat, he shoved them in his pocket, provoking, "Commando's a time saver."

"Fine, I'm taking your shirt," Lexy bantered, putting it on. "I need shorts."

Dashing around to pop the trunk, it didn't open. He sighed, "Shit."

"What?" She asked watching him run to the front.

Sitting in the driver's seat, he glanced back, suggesting, "Honey, if you fold down the middle seat, there might be a bag in the trunk."

Honey? Smiling, she felt around and found the bag. Digging through it, she discovered a sundress. *Much better.* Removing his shirt, she put on the stretchy dress, saying, "That was the last time. I promised Grey, I'd stop."

"If you say so," he flirted, turning the key in the ignition. *Leaving the door open burned out the battery. Awesome.*

"How long ago did the dinging stop?" He enquired, texting someone.

Smiling, Lexy teased, "Does it matter?"

"Did you see jumper cables?" He asked, texting away.

Climbing into the trunk in the short dress, she felt for them, responding, "It's too dark." Turning back, he was climbing over the seat to help, or so she thought.

Handing her his phone with the flashlight on, it was much better. She said, "No cables."

"Roll over and tell me what the year is. There should be a sticker on the top of the trunk," he instructed.

What does that have to do with anything? Humouring him, she turned over, looking. *Was he opening the doors?*

He toyed, "I'm not going to be able to focus until I do this," burying his face between her thighs.

Her eyes rolled back with delight. *She shouldn't let him but couldn't will the words from her mouth.*

"Admit you want this," Tiberius enticed, nipping her inner thigh, tortuously setting her aflame.

She pled, "Don't stop," clutching his hair. He picked up the pace until she was enraptured. Shivers of gratification coursed through her. Writhing she gasped his name. He persevered and bliss swelled again. Arching her back, moaning as another climax shivered. *She was so sensitive.* She tried squirming away.

"I'm not done," he reprimanded, relentlessly pleasuring her.

Succumbing, she imploded raspily crying out. *Was that tires on gravel?*

Sitting up, Tiberius chuckled, "We've got company. How's that for timing?" He tugged down her dress, reached for his drink in the centre console and left her there.

Sweating, blushing and pleasure frazzled, Lexy sat up, laughing. *He was insane.* She cleaned the blood off her arms, legs and face with wipes as he chatted with a stranger. They used their jumper cables to start the car.

When the truck drove away, she moved into the passenger seat. All cleaned up, she felt him watching as she twisted blood crunchy hair into a messy bun.

Pulling onto the road, Tiberius provoked, "You look ridiculously hot. Good thing you're a redhead."

Freshly satisfied with sun shining in the window, Lexy probed, "Are we behind schedule?"

"I'm taking out a serial killer on our way to meet up with Ankh. You'll be free to resume pretending you don't like me soon."

He switched personalities on her again. Idiot.

His ruggedly hot profile instructed, "Check the directions on my cell so we don't miss the turn off."

Picking up his phone, she scanned his messages. Kevin sent one asking if he was alive. *Hilarious.* Lexy shook her head, grinning. As they passed a sign, she replied, "The next right."

"See anything risqué?" He teased, as she snooped through texts.

Grinning, Lexy revealed, "Kevin's checking to see if you're alive."

"It's a legitimate concern. You slit my throat the last time we were alone together," he replied, watching her text. He chuckled, "What are you up too?"

She pressed send, laughing. **Peering up from his phone, Lexy read her response aloud,**

> "I'm naked in the trunk of the car. She's been singing Mack the Knife for hours."

Howling laughing, Tiberius nearly missed their turn.

The phone vibrated. Lexy shared Kevin's response, "Break a taillight. We'll come back for you. I told you she was going to bury you in the desert." She glanced at Tiberius, commenting, "I've always liked Kevin."

"He's warming up to me," her sexy nemesis revealed. **She texted back,**

> "Joking. It's Lexy. We're almost at the job. I haven't killed him, yet."

"I told him you were fine," she explained. A song came on that brought Grey to mind. She reached over to switch the station.

Swatting her hand, Tiberius complained, "I love this song."

"Fine, leave a song on that reminds me of someone else," she teased.

"Every song reminds you of someone if you're dwelling on it. Now, it'll remind you of me saying that," he sparred, sliding his hand onto her knee.

Smiling at his intimate gesture, she laughed, "If you say so."

"Don't make me pull over to prove a point," he taunted. "I have time sensitive shit to do."

Biting her lip, Lexy uncrossed her legs and inched up her dress, provoking, "Thanks for kidnapping me."

Watching her flirtation, he whispered, "You can't kidnap the willing."

He was full of shit. She taunted, "I just walked away from a fight?"

"You kicked my ass. I held my own. You were straddling me when…" He naughtily narrated.

"Go on," Lexy baited, leaning forward, crossing her legs.

Watching her, he chuckled, "I'm going to spank you."

"You can try," she provoked, enjoying their game.

Wide eyed frustrated, he abruptly turned into a dealership, scolding, "Stop that. We don't have time to pull over again." Tiberius got out. Dashing to her door, he leaned in, requesting, "Pass me the paperwork from the glove compartment. We're switching vehicles."

"Why?" Lexy questioned, handing it to him and getting out.

Opening the shop door for her, Tiberius provoked, "Triad obeys orders without asking questions."

"Seems legit. Questioning authority is a sign of intelligence." she bantered, strolling by. Walking up to the desk, Tiberius handed the paperwork over. Keys were passed back with not a syllable spoken. Trying to decide if this was high stakes espionage or stupidity, she followed him back into the parking lot, probing, "Did you know that guy?"

Pressing the key fob, flashed lights on a truck. He handed her the paperwork, politely saying, "Slip this in the glove compartment, honey."

Honey again. Getting in, she read the paperwork, laughing. *Barry Mckockiner. Funny.* Lexy laughed, "Tell me this name is on your driver's license."

"After I kill this guy, you can check anything you want," he bantered, smiling.

She put it away. Sliding into the middle of the bench seat, she dropped the backpack on the floor.

Shaking his head, he said, "If you behave, we might have time to pull over again before we meet up with the others."

Enjoying the effect she had on him, Lexy counter offered, "I'll do it."

Beaming, he replied, "Watching you in your element is fun for me but, you should wait in the truck."

"Why?" She not so innocently toyed, purposely brushing against him while recrossing her legs.

"Move over to the other seat, Lexy," he sighed, sliding his hand onto her thigh. Inching her dress up, he touched her. Tugging his hand away, he asserted, "Move into the other seat. Please. I can't have you this close without touching you."

"I can do it," she provoked.

"Don't you dare," he chuckled, smacking her hand.

Titillated by his naughty confession, Lexy slid a hand onto his lap, stroking him in retaliation. Groaning, he swerved to the side of the road. Clasping both of her arms, he bargained,

"When this job's done, I'll rail you into a sand dune until you're screaming if you stay over there."

Well, if he was going to put it like that. Shifting to the other seat, she grinned, enjoying their provocative playdate. Biting her lip, she glanced over at him.

Wide eyed turned on, he laughed, "You can't even look at me right now. I have never not accomplished what I've been sent to do."

"Never?" Lexy toyed, knowing that couldn't be true.

Shaking his head at her, Tiberius insisted, "This has to be done properly."

Opting to behave, she asked, "Where are we doing this?"

"There's a rest stop with a tavern on the beach. All I've been told is he needs to be marked first so there's no chance for an Abaddon side hustle. With an admitted kill toll of over sixty, it's twice that amount. He'd be an asset for them and a pain in the ass for us."

At least. "No description?" She enquired, trying to focus.

Putting the signal on, he pointed to the sign. "I usually walk around and brush against the people I suspect. It's easy for me to tell. I was planning to lure him into a bathroom, choke him out, mark him, and snap his neck."

She could tell easier. "Save your strength. I'll cut myself to freshen up the auras and point him out," she offered. Aware of the difference between replenishing healing ability and feeding the Guardian, as her stomach turned, she knew there was an edible immortal in the vicinity.

Turning down a side road, he said, "I'm sure there's a knife in the backpack."

Finding it as they pulled up, her stomach cramped. Seeing a sign with arrows leading to a tavern, she probed, "Are you queasy too?"

"No," he answered. "You'll see suspicious auras when we get inside, won't you?"

Maybe she wanted to eat him?

Concerned, he whispered, "Are you alright? You can tell me if you're not."

Refresh auras might tame her desire to eat her booty call. He smelled heavenly. Aware of heightened predatory senses, she shoved a shirt beneath her leg to avoid staining the rental, explaining, "We've had a few jobs recently where they were using illegal aura filters. I sensed it like this but talked myself out of it. You get the mortal. I'll take care of whatever shows up to defend him." Shivving her thigh, pleasurable heat instantly healed her. Wiping off blood, she looked his way.

"We have to destroy the filter before we leave," he decreed, meeting her eyes.

Cracking her neck as she got out, Lexy tossed him the knife. Walking down the path, fragrance of sweet flowers and salty ocean air was overpowered by sour flatulence. "Either your farts are heinous, or Abaddon is here," she teased.

"Inconvenience the demons while I take out the mark," he suggested. "We'll destroy the blocker together."

"Sounds like a plan," Lexy said, opening the door for him.

Standing there, he whispered, "Who is it?"

Smirking, she whispered back, "The man in the striped shirt has an impressively dark mortal aura. I feel like eating everyone else in here. They're all Abaddon."

"Expendable Abaddon violating a Treaty with an illegal aura filter. I wasn't going to have time to take you for dinner, will this do?" He flirted, cockily walking in.

All eyes turned to them. "Guess a sneak attack's out?" Lexy whispered, strolling up to the bar. Nobody moved a muscle. She sat beside the serial murderer.

Pretending he didn't know they'd been made, Tiberius asked, "What's good here?"

Leaned over the bar, their server said, "No shirt no service."

"But, I'm hot," Tiberius flirted with his sexy crooked smile.

"The chicken wings are good," the mortal offered. "Surely we can break the rules just this once. Where are you two from?"

"My brother and I are from Seattle. We're just passing through," Lexy responded. Everyone's interest peaked. *Maybe they hadn't been made?*

"I'm driving so I can't drink, but my sister would love a few shots of tequila, and hot wings. Is there a washroom in here?" Tiberius enquired.

"Public restrooms are on the trails to the beach," the mortal explained. "I'll take you there. I need to go."

Accepting his offer, Tiberius got up, cautioning, "No more than two. You know how you get."

"I'm not the one taking off with another hot guy," Lexy bantered.

Walking away, he set her up as the perfect victim, gossiping, "If she has more than two drinks, she'll sleep with everyone in there."

As the door shut behind him, she altered her order, "I'll take the entire bottle. My slutty brother won't be back for hours." As the server placed Tequila in front of her, she had the oddest sense of DeJa'Vu. Taking a swig from the bottle, as a guy sat beside her, she smiled.

"Why does it feel like I know you?" He flirted, sipping his drink.

She told the truth, 'My murder sprees blend together."

"Interesting perfume you're wearing," he baited like a cat sneaking up on a canary.

He could smell the blood in her hair. Opting to go with it, she said, "The cheating waste of oxygen had it coming." Chugging it, she slammed the empty bottle on the bar and asked for more. Everyone's jaws dropped as she met her drinking buddies' eyes, pretending to be inebriated, "I didn't have time to shower." Fascinated, the bartender opened another bottle, putting it in front of her. Wanting to be done killing everyone by the time Tiberius got back, she smiled as they brought her hot wings. *She could eat people food before Guardian snacks.* She ate a dozen hot wings like a maniac. With sauce all over her mouth, she wiped her face on a stranger's shirt, complimenting, "Nice."

"Almost time for the sexy crazy one to go," the dark eyed man with a sauce-stained shirt remarked.

He called her sexy. She'd eat him last. Unconcerned by the amount she was drinking because they hadn't been able to drug her on the plane, she finished it, slurring, "Does anyone have a shower I can use?" Everyone's hands raised. Excited, she clapped her hands and pretended to pass out.

Aware she was being carried to a second location, she heard someone say, "Find out why they're here." It crossed her mind that she might actually be drunk. *Oh, no. How did this happen? How long had Tiberius been gone? She'd forgotten about looking for the aura filter. Heck, she'd forgotten this was a job. Those were tasty hot wings. She really could use a shower.* He sat her in a chair and began restraining her. Unfazed, she teased, "This isn't the shower?"

Unfolding a black leather pouch of torture implements, the dark eyed man menaced, "We can do this the easy way, or the hard way."

"Hard way looks fun," Lexy provoked.

Smiling, he placed a bucket on the floor. Taking out the biggest knife, he sliced her arm. A line of blood seeped, healing before a drop fell into the bucket. *Oh, he thought he could steal her blood. That was adorable.* Turning back to look at what he'd collected, there was nothing.

Grimacing, he held a knife to her wrist and slit a larger vein. Watching it instantly heal, he interrogated, "What are you?"

"If I tell you then I have to eat you," Lexy provoked.

With the blade at her throat, he threatened, "Tell me.

Nobody stays on their feet with this artery severed. Last chance. Why are you here?"

Smiling, Lexy whispered, "I came for the tequila and stuck around for the kinky torture." He stormed out of the room. *She should check on Tiberius.* All of the Abaddon funnelled into the tiny room.

Without a word the guy slit her wrist again and it healed instantly. He said, "She seems unconcerned."

"What are you?" He questioned, stabbing her in the stomach.

Feeling the heat of her ability sealing wound, she baited, "That turns me on." Thinking of impermeable flesh as he slit her throat, it didn't break the skin. "I'm embarrassed for you. What shall we try next?"

Punching her, she didn't flinch. "I'll stop you before you piss me off." Snapping the cuffs off like nothing. Lexy got up, and waved an arm to shut the door before anyone could flee, announcing, "I'm Tri-Clan. I came for a drink, a snack and your aura filter."

Taking a gun out of his holster, she thought impermeable flesh as the leader shot her in the face. Plucking it out of her forehead, she said, "Ouch. That stung. Asshole."

Everyone backed against the wall. The head guy stammered, "Tri-Clan goes down with a headshot."

"I'm Lexy of Ankh, Guardian offspring. Star of old timey prophecies and shit," she revealed.

"We can work out an arrangement. The aura filter for your blood," her captor bartered.

Smirking, Lexy willed the door sealed. Touching his arm, she ingested his being and he flopped to the floor. "Follow my instructions and I'll leave without eating everyone."

"What do you want?" He conceded.

"We want all of your aura filters, the mortal serial killer and I'll require a snack. A drink of water would be nice. Stay out of trouble. No killing mortals. There's no point in trying to hide. We have Oracles. Tri-Clan will be checking on you to make sure there are no further violations. If you behave, and don't adopt mortal serial killer deviants, we won't have a reason to show up here."

"How do you know you still have back up? Our mortal is talented," he stood his ground.

Raising a hand, she ingested him from across the room. His body crumpled. *That was badass. She wasn't even sure that would work.* Everyone froze. "Does anyone else require a lesson on why a Guardian doesn't need backup?"

"I'll go get your glass of water and retrieve the filters if you don't eat anyone else," a demon in mortal disguise said.

She did not feel well. Yup, that was dumb. Standing there like she didn't desperately need to upchuck a demon soul, she decreed, "Everyone else will stay until you return."

Minutes later, Tiberius peered in, saying, "I've checked his mind. We've got them all. The mortal has been marked and disposed of."

With a straight face, Lexy held in the demonic energy, cautioning, "Don't give us a reason to return." Leaving without eating anyone else, they walked out.

As they left earshot, he whispered, "Something's wrong. I can see it."

"Shhh. I'll purge it as we drive away," she whispered. Reaching the vehicle, she rushed, "Start the car." Turning as the engine hummed, she wasn't sure how. Making the tossing motion, nothing happened. *Shit.* Black veins rose on her skin. She clasped her hands together. Parting them, a blue sparking orb with black spots appeared. *It wasn't yellow or white.* Semi confident she wasn't sending demons through the hall of souls, she pitched it at the building. Blue flames encased the place. *What did she do? Shit!* Slamming the door as flames rushed towards them, she smacked the dash, shouting, "Drive! Go!" They peeled away. Flames were sucked back in, leaving a black haze that dissipated to nothing. The building was gone.

In awe, he asked, "Did you just disappear a building?"

Looked out the window, Lexy confessed, "I have no idea."

Driving for a minute in silence, Tiberius said, "Guess there's no Aries Group clean up required?"

"I have to speak to Azariah. Maybe the building isn't gone? Logically, it can't be, right?" She asked, moderately concerned.

"A hallucination is more probable," he answered. "Whatever that was, it was awesome."

As they drove into an exquisite tangerine and fuchsia sunset, she whispered, "Our time is up."

"This day may be over, but this is only the beginning."

Smiling, she felt it. Meeting his gaze, she cautioned, "Don't fall in love with me."

Taking her hand, he pledged, "I won't."

"Good," she responded with him caressing her hand.

"Don't fall in love with me either," he teased.

She vowed, "Never."

He pulled over, prompting, "Quickly. Get out."

Watching the sun sink into endless sea, leaving a glimmering trail on the surface, he wrapped his arms around her from behind. Kissing her neck, Tiberius whispered, "We have a sacrifice to stop."

Relaxing against him, she sighed, "This is how people romanticise booty calls."

Walking backwards, he lured her back to the truck, teasing, "It's just a sunset."

Damn it, Tiberius. She had to get him out of her system. He set fire to resolve with witty repertoire and a crooked smirk. She used to think he was too much of an ass to be anything at all, but now, she knew better. He was lightning on a beach turning fragments of sand to glass, moulding aspirations and altering dynamics. Each time she felt their electric friction, she craved more. No good could come of admitting it. Lips sealed. No feelings.

They sped down a gravel road. Her stomach cramped as

they turned into the property. *This was the place.* In the lit barn area, a robust flamboyant man was giving dramatic speech to a mesmerized herd of mortals with torches.

"Frigging Leonard," Tiberius decreed. Revving the engine, they ploughed him down. Free of compulsion his herd of braindead followers crumpled to the ground.

They got out of the truck, cackling. Her eyes darted around. *Lily, Frost and Orin. This was the least judgey crew she could return too.*

"Guess we'll clean this up," Lily announced, flouncing away without a fancy feather ruffled.

There was a wild amount of sickles in this barn. Everyone sprang into action.

Catching her attention, Tiberius proposed, "Shall we chop this guy up and spread him out?"

"Sounds good. We'll take half, you bring half with you?" Lexy decreed, grabbing a sickle with a skip in her step. Out of the corner of her eye, she noticed Kevin ushering away a girl with her wrists bound. *Who was that?*

Wandering over to her bare-chested distraction swinging a weapon with red misted air while inconveniencing a demon, Lexy questioned, "Why are we dismembering Leonard?"

"He's a pain in the ass," Tiberius sparred, grinning with Dragon titillating spatter on his muscular torso.

Tiberius was Dragon porn. She couldn't be blamed for her depraved activities. Dicing him up, they were both covered in spatter as they shoved body parts into plastic bags and lugged him to the vehicles. The others were focused on torching the barn. Semi hidden from sight, they stared at each other.

"That was fun," Tiberius whispered, keeping his distance.

Concealed by shadows, Lexy confessed, "It was."

Clearing his throat, Kevin interrupted, "Time to go."

Fighting the impulse to glance back, Lexy wandered up to Ankh with a bag of minced demon, suggesting, "Let's get rid of this idiot."

Everyone's thoughts steered away from destroying evidence as a car pulled up with a window down. Leaning out, Orin instructed, "Toss that tool in the trunk. We'll scatter him on the way back."

Frost raced Lily to the vehicle, shouting, "Shotgun!"

"Guess I'll do it," Lexy said, smiling. As she reached the trunk, it unlocked. She chucked the bag in and got in the backseat.

Handing her wet wipes, Frost teased, "If we get pulled over with blood spatter on your face, they'll search the trunk."

"It's a bit of a red flag," Orin chuckled, keeping his eyes on the road.

Exhausted, Lexy cleaned her face and arms. Smiling as she looked down at her dark patterned sundress, she stuffed the moist towelettes in the trash. *Making that blue orb knocked the wind out of her.* Attempting to close her eyes, someone poked her. *Seriously?*

"How was your day?" Raven-haired Lily whispered, stoked for gossip.

Catching Orin's grin in the rearview, Lexy laughed.

Contestant two in this month's confusing harem of naughty gentlemen callers, teased, "She's not going to let you sleep."

Meeting Lily's eyes, Lexy bantered, "It was fun. I ate a bunch of demons. They made me sick." Stifling an inner commentary that wanted to keep adding dastardly deeds to the list, she closed her eyes, mumbling, "My battery is dead. I need a minute."

When they arrived, they left her at a gorgeous resort of beach cottages and took off because they had something to do before they were allowed to re-join the group.

Inhaling the sweet fragrance of flowers and salty air, Lexy strolled down a cobblestone path, seeing Mel.

All smiles, Mel said, "How does a few days at the beach sound?"

"Fantastic," Lexy confirmed, grateful for the break.

"Yours is the first bungalow on the left. Your bags are already in there," Mel explained. Catching sight of Zach, she asked, "Any chance I can sweet talk you into doubling back to give these to Kayn?"

"Sure," Lexy agreed, taking her sister's keys. Grinning, she wandered back and happened upon her sister smelling exotic flowers. Tossing her keys, she shouted, "Heads up, Brighton!" *They'd have time to chat later.* Jogging back to the line of picturesque cabanas with decks facing the sea. The scent of the flowers lingered as she walked in the open sliding door, expecting to find Grey. There was one bed, crisp white sheets and a fruit basket on the nightstand. *She didn't see his bags.* Walking across the room, she peeked into the ensuite with only a tile shower and vanity. *Grey wasn't staying here with her.* With a confusing mix of relief and apprehension, Lexy stripped down and showered away her diabolical deeds.

Emerging in a bikini with her hair done, makeup on and crimson red lipstick, she brought water and fruit out onto the deck and sprawled on the reclining lawn chair in the sunshine. Arguing with herself about going to find Grey, she resigned to let him come to her. Eating grapes, she slipped into a sordid replay of her titillating day. His squirm worthy grin and debauchery summoning eyes. *She'd had so much fun doing sketchy shit with him.* Opting for a nap in fresh salty air, she closed her eyes.

With chestnut hair glistening in sunshine, Mel reclined next to her, saying, "I ordered us lunch. Hope that's alright?"

Her eyes focused on Mel's dimpled smile. "Sounds perfect," Lexy replied, stretching. Before she had a chance to sit up, a server arrived with a tray of metal covered plates and fish bowl sized Pina Coladas. *This felt like bribery.* Checking out the beach, Lexy said, "I rarely have time for a Pina Colada in the in-between before I heal now." *What did she want?*

"Grey mentioned you never get time for one," Mel answered, checking out the food.

He was thinking about doing something sweet while she was bedding his nemesis. That didn't make her feel guilty at all.

While cutting her burger, Mel responded to her thought, "Don't feel guilty. By tonight he'll be coping with your altered dynamics by flirting with everyone."

Sounds about right. Dumping a disgusting amount of hot sauce on a delicious looking enchilada, Lexy admitted, "I'm sure my choices have been a lot to digest."

"I'd imagine his decisions over the years haven't been a party either," Mel answered. "I wish I knew you were together while we were hooking up."

Recalling it, Lexy said, "Ancient history." Eating in silence it was clear there was something on her mind. "What's this impromptu lunch about?"

"I need a friend with revenge experience. Help me murder my ex?" Mel tempted, pouring them each shots of tequila.

Fun. Clinking glasses with her, she drank it. *That arrow in the heart had to sting.* "I'm in," Lexy confirmed. Curious, she probed, "Timeline?"

"Soon," Mel decreed, getting up. "Coming to the beach?"

Slurping the bottom of her cocktail, she said, "I don't want to cramp my social butterflies style. Next time we bump into Trinity, it's on."

"Perfect" Mel replied walking away.

She liked her more now. With her scarlet hair tussled by the breeze, Lexy leaned on the wooden railing, watching Grey surf the waves. Everyone else was splashing in the ocean and tanning in sunshine, but she wasn't feeling social. Still exhausted from what she'd done to that pub full of demons, she went inside and snuggled under the covers for a siesta.

Blaring music made her smile as she awoke with cool sea breeze travelling in through open sliding doors. *It was dark out.* Her stomach complained loud enough to summon a whale at

sea. *She'd obviously slept through dinner.* Comfy in bed, she saw a light flashing on the nightstand. Someone left her a phone. She reached for it. *It was three AM. They must be the only ones in the resort.*
There was a text from Amar,

> "Have Fun?"

It was the middle of the afternoon there. **She messaged back,**

> "I took a nap in the afternoon and woke up at 3 am. I'm awake if you want to call."

There was another message from an unknown number.

> "You slept through dinner. I left cookies on the counter."

Swinging her legs out from under the sheets, she went to look. There was a bag. Assuming the cookies were from Mel, she wandered out onto the deck with her snack. Ankh was partying at a campfire on the beach. Listening to friends singing at the top of their lungs, Lexy lounged to avoid being seen. Enjoying the breeze while devouring cookies, her phone rang. *Shit. She left it inside.* Running back in, she dove onto the bed, and answered, "Hi."

Expecting Amar, Orin flirted, "Bring those cookies down to the fire. I saved you a seat."

For a creature whose needs were based on necessity, making sure she ate was sweet. Sprawled on her tummy, Lexy said, "I'm giving Grey space. Thanks for the snack."

"Grey's been chatting with Emma for hours. He's fine." Orin flirted, "Want company?"

Grinning, Lexy teased, "Let's not give Grey a coronary."

"Tomorrow?" He baited, chuckling.

"How drunk are you?" Lexy toyed. *She should save him the morning after humiliation and hang up.*

"Just sitting here thinking of our naked walk of shame," he seduced.

"Rain check on the naked walk of shame. I'm hanging up now," she chuckled. The phone rang. Assuming it was Orin, Lexy sighed, "Seriously?"

"You told me to call you," Amar teased.

Glad to hear his voice, Lexy replied, "Long story."

"I have ten minutes. Give me the short version," he prompted.

Getting up to shut the sliding door, she leapt on the bed, saying, "Where do I start?"

"I'll help. Did you make up with Grey?" Her side Handler asked.

Enjoying his attention, she admitted, "Right before they left me at a job and sent Tiberius to find me."

"Nooo," Amar gasped. "Did you have fun?"

"We did an Abaddon Correction and caught up with Ankh later that evening. I'm giving Grey space. He knows where I am," she responded, leaving parts out.

Amar toyed, "Why were you so feisty when you answered the phone?"

"I slept through dinner. Orin left cookies on my counter, then drunk dialled to see if I'd come to the bonfire on the beach," she confessed, enjoying their judgement free conversation.

"Look at you go!" Amar teased, loving it. "I told you Orin would be fine. You'll work it out with Grey tomorrow. I've been summoned back to the Third-Tier realm as Ankh's emissary, so I won't be around to answer messages for a few days."

She probed, "Are you concerned about going back?"

"Not when you're on my team" Amar confidently stated.

She'd go through the rift in a heartbeat to save him. Their connection was still there. She felt it. There was commotion in his room.

"I have to go. We'll chat when I get back," he said, hanging up.

She wandered back out onto the deck. Listening to everyone's laughter, she was torn between wanting Grey to show up, and basking in the aftermath. Leaning over the railing, her thoughts drifted to how fast she ended up naked. *However this played out, there was no denying it anymore.*

Lexy waited until morning before venturing out of her bungalow. 'Drunk Orin confident' and a little choked Grey left her twisting in the wind, she strutted towards the outdoor buffet. *They'd agreed to date other people. She woke up post feral in the backseat of Tiberius' car. Saucy banter turned her on.* Perusing the buffet, she bumped into Frost.

"You're here by yourself?" He asked, choosing pastries.

Pouring herself a coffee, Lexy said, "I'm letting Grey come to me."

"Have breakfast with us," Frost decreed.

If he'd worded it like a question, she might have opted out, but she sensed he had something to say.

As they walked back to their bungalow, Frost noted, "You have a glow about you."

Siren always caught onto naughty misdeeds. Her eyes darted his way as she sparred, "Weird."

"You have a hard job. Have fun. If you ditch the excuses with Grey, and own it, he'll get onboard."

With Tiberius. Not likely.

"There's no argument if you own it," he answered, stopping as they reached the bungalow. "Jenna knows who high-jacked Markus' body and how it plays out. You get wasted and train newbies on the beach. Don't try to stop anything. Only those with inner dialogue filters have details. Arrianna knows she may get tossed into another dimension, but everything is going to work out. It's all taken care of. The Third-Tier are onboard. It's going to be wild." He took a spelled bracelet off and gave it to her.

As she put it on, magic snuffed out concern. Apprehension receded until it was distant tide. Confused emotions slid into place. Frost placed the trays on the table, excused himself and took off. Waiting for her sister to come out of the washroom, Lexy stared at the pastries guessing flavours.

Her sister sat down, and reached for a delectable sugary treat, questioning, "Fruit or meat?"

Taking one for the team, Lexy picked one with red drizzle and bit into it. With a hand concealing her chewing, she said, "Fruit."

Kayn probed, "Are you okay?"

"I suntanned on the deck and went to sleep early," Lexy responded, selecting another as her sister's easy to read thoughts listed off reasons she was concerned about Grey, Lexy started laughing.

"What?" Her sister asked with a sugary morsel in hand.

That would be why Kayn wasn't allowed to know anything. She'd always had issues with hers too. Snatching a melon, Lexy teased, "Your inner commentary has no filter, you might as well just tell me now."

Tearing the Band-aid off, Kayn overshared, "He found out he had two older sisters and an aunt who died trying to save him when he was six. His life in Scotland was erased and the memories of his father were planted. He cut a baby out of Emma and died in the fight. Tiberius went after you. Instead of killing him, you took off together. Azariah helped him understand you needed these experiences. He's handling it."

Holy shit, her absence was badly timed. "He didn't light anything on fire?" Lexy asked with the weight of knowing she'd added to his stress.

Shaking her head, her sister replied, "Nothing. I'm curious though, how did you take off with Tiberius?"

Licking whipped cream off her finger, Lexy confessed, "It

doesn't matter. It can't go anywhere. It was a stupid rebellious move, but I don't regret it." *Frost was right. There was no argument if she owned it.*

With sisterly solidarity, Kayn handed her a shot. She raised her glass, saluting "No regrets."

"No regrets," Lexy repeated, downing hers. Sensing her Handler's presence, she didn't have to look. *Awkward timing.*

As she placed her glass on the table, Grey sighed, "Cute, parent trap move."

"Come on, Brighton. Let's grab food at the buffet," Frost suggested. "They need to talk it out. We have to be on the same page to keep up with Bad Markus."

Listening to footsteps rustling on sand, Lexy got up and faced her Handler. Not caring who was right, she embraced him, whispering, "You're my best friend." He caved, hugging her back. "I had no plans to leave you."

Hugging her tighter, Grey mumbled, "I know. We don't have to talk about it. I don't want to spend another day without you. I can't promise jealousy isn't going to rear it's head when we run into Triad, but I'll do my best to shut it down."

With joy surging in her heart, she held him tighter, saying, "Good enough."

Pulling away, he kissed her cheek and confessed, "Whoever you end up with has to understand, we hug daily."

Grinning, Lexy teased, "You can be my huggy wingman. I plan to be single."

"Good idea. It's better to work me into sharing you," Grey confessed. Stroking crimson locks shining in sunlight filtering through the curtains, he admitted, "You look happy."

"I heard about the memories," she changed the subject.

Gazing into her eyes, he said, "I don't even want to think about it. Let's have fun today."

Backing away, she dared, "Race you to the chairs?"

Pushing past, he ran down the stairs onto the beach.

Child. Vaulting over the railing, Lexy superhero landed in the sand, sprinted onto the beach and caught up. She shoved back. Grey face-planted and sand rained. With her arms raised like a champion, she stole the chair, shouting, "Eat my dust, Greydon!" With Ankh lounging on towels, Grey sat in front of her. Playing with his hair as he relaxed against her, everything was right in her world. She noticed, Kayn boiling a drink with her mind. *Wait, why was she this mad? Zach was here, dealing with it like he'd been her Handler forever. Frost wasn't here.* Following her sister's gaze, she saw Frost with the others. *They were here. She wanted to rip off that imposter's limbs and beat him with his dismembered leg.* With impeccable Handler timing, Grey squeezed her knee and her Grinch heart expanded ten sizes. *She was supposed to train the newbies.* Placing her hand over his, she squeezed it, saying, "Showtime."

"You only made it ten minutes," Grey played along.

"We can't have Kayn boiling drinks with her mind," she whispered.

Grinning, Grey said, "Finally, a Pyrokinesis buddy."

Her sister replicated Grey's ability. How could this go wrong? Brushing herself off, Lexy announced, "Brighton needs a distraction. Surprise training time." Motioning for them, she provoked, "Try to take me, newbies." They looked at her like she was crazy.

Leaping up like a badass, Molly put her hair up, declaring, "It's on!"

She might have a new favourite pony.

Laughing, Zach commented, "She's great."

Lexy cleared her throat as Molly put up her dukes. She tucked her thumbs, smiling.

Wandering up in a floral dress holding Markus' hand, Arrianna teased, "Some things never change." Void of polite pretence, the imposter sat and brutishly yanked her friend onto his lap.

Screaming like a maniac, Molly attacked. Using her

motion to launch her through the air. She landed with an explosion of sand. Leaving her lost in a cloud, Lexy laughed, "Next!"

Shrugging, Dean strolled over, asking, "Do I hit you first?"

"Try it," Lexy prompted. Dean swung as she manoeuvred out of the way like he wasn't trying, swept his leg and motioned like she was stabbing his heart. "Dean's dead. Who's next?"

"I'll go," Kayn declared, grinning.

Practically tackling her, Zach scolded, "Absolutely not!"

"I'll do it," Emma volunteered, crouching with fists raised.

She didn't want to trigger Grey. Lexy vetoed her, "You should give yourself more time."

"I'm a blackbelt. I won silver in my weight division last year boxing, and I was on the wrestling team. Don't wussy out," Emma challenged, smirking.

Did pixie cut girl just call her a wuss?

"We have a dark horse," Emery announced.

Intrigued, Lexy declared, "Bring it." Like a dance, they darted and weaved, avoiding leg sweeps. *Young Emma had skills. She loved it when newbies surprised her like this.*

Their Oracle's voice piped into her mind, '*Let her land one.*'

Seriously? Irritated, Lexy let her land a right hook.

As everyone cheered Emma on, their body napped leader's facade unravelled. Enraged, Markus tossed Arrianna off his lap and rifled a chair at her.

Lexy dodged out of the way. *Here we go.*

"Do you think me a fool?" Markus bellowed.

A Grinch grin curved upwards watching Markus storm over to the no longer pregnant girl, interrogating, "Where is it?"

"Where is what?" Emma with the flat tummy, baited.

This was fun.

Zeroing in on Frost, their body napped leader commanded, "Give me the location of the child!"

"She gave birth days ago. Did I forget to tell you?" Frost provoked wide-eyed.

"The LOCATION!" The imposter bellowed.

Casually, Frost answered, "Africa."

That was funny. "No, the last baby is there. This one went to Australia," Lexy corrected, sauntering over.

"I will have you all entombed for this," Markus menaced under his breath, pacing.

Arrianna needled, "Something wrong, Honey?"

Caressing her face, Bad Markus whispered, "As punishment for believing you could outsmart me, I'm keeping you as my pet." Tossing a coin, a spinning black portal opened mid-air. The imposter launched Arrianna into the swirling vortex, declaring, "Foolish Half breed spawn! Enjoy your last twenty-four hours!"

Waving, Frost grinned, and sang, "Enjoy yours."

Bad Markus stepped into the vortex. His body was spat out into the sand. *That was cool.* Orin and Grey picked up Markus' shell and carried it away.

"Carry on with your day," Lily announced, sprawling on her towel and closing her eyes.

Accustomed to not receiving plans past kill everyone, Lexy addressed the new Ankh, "Relax while you can. We're hardcore training soon." Meeting Emma's eyes, she praised, "Well done. I'll be at the bar." Picturing a drama free day, she wandered to the quaint hut surrounded by sand with wicker stools.

Leaving nothing to the imagination in a string bikini Emery seductively crossed her toned bronzed legs, doing her part to blur the mortal's recount of events.

Seeing a portal might be a tricky thing to erase. Shifting scarlet hair off her neck because it was damn hot, Lexy sat next to her. She recognized the agent posing as a bartender. *They'd preemptively switched out the staff. Good idea. Aries gag orders were handy when you had lots of Ankh in the same place. Alcohol affected them differently. It was related to mood. If they wanted to get drunk, they'd be wasted.* Fully aware it wasn't the agent's real name on the name tag, Lexy couldn't help herself, "How you doing, Paulo?"

Their sexy server with a crisp white shirt was focused on where the vortex vanished. "Refraining from asking about the body you carried away is more difficult than I thought it would be when I signed up for this babysitting job."

Reaching over the bar, Emery swiped banana liquor, saying, "It's above your pay grade hot babysitter."

Paulo snatched it back, reprimanding, "I know what you are."

"Really?" the bewitching immortal baited. "Do tell?"

Pouring liqueur into a blender, Paulo revealed, "We were warned you could control us. I've studied all of your files."

With a veil of lush lashes framing mesmerizing tools of seduction, Emery toyed, "I bet you have."

Grinding ice drowned out the flirtation. Lexy reprimanded, "Eating Aries Group is frowned upon."

"Come on, look at the guy. It's like they picked him out of a catalogue for me," Emery sparred, gawking at his nice ass in shorts.

Gazing at the ocean as a drink was placed in front of her, Lexy's thoughts flickered to Tiberius. *She'd stretched her scaly Dragon wings, and now, the wild thing in her yearned for the freedom to fly.*

Catching her thoughts, the worldly immortal teased, "Would you fly to him?"

Yearning to pick up where they left off, she nodded without thinking. "I don't need the you can't be together speech," Lexy clarified. *Sometimes knowing things didn't matter.*

Emery asked, "How are doing ability wise?"

"I could use a crash course with no witnesses," Lexy admitted. *This was nice.* Instinct tugged her gaze to a speck in the distance. Her Handler was hanging out with the newbies.

"I'll arrange it," Emery offered, sipping her drink.

She liked her. She didn't like a lot of people. Assuming she meant in the in-between, Lexy smiled, responding, "I'm in." *This was a perfect day. She'd made up with Grey. They had Markus' body. They'd slide his soul back in and everything would be back to normal.* With the fragrance of coconut oil, sand underfoot, and the toasty warmth of sunshine, tension drained as vacation mode set in.

With telepathy Emery gave her advice not for mortal ears, *'Freezing time leaves your healing energy well dry. We signed up as Sacrificial Lambs to die, whenever, and however often, the grand scheme requires. Don't hit pause to save Second-Tier. You can't let anything best a Guardian.* "I'll help when I can," Emery whispered like it was a secret.

"Sounds good," Lexy said, enjoying the vacay ambience. Noticing Zach across chatting with the bartender, she waved.

"Kayn's snack," Emery whispered.

Lexy rephrased it, "Kayn's Handler."

"Healer, Siren and Guardian offspring must have a feeding plan," Emery explained.

Always entertained by filterless logic, Lexy said, "I'd love to be there for that meeting."

"Pre-emptive measures," Emery said, stirring clumped ice in her drink.

"I've had higher energy requirements and lowered access to my Handler," Lexy revealed. "Everyone has their hands full with newbie drama. Why bother anyone with my issues? I'll figure it out."

Emery pointed out, "How's that going?"

"I was fine until you brought it up," Lexy laughed. *Was she trying to help or purposely pushing buttons? What was that delicious smell?* Her neck prickled.

"For heaven's sake, explain things before he drains a mortal," Emery warned with Zach standing right there.

"Hi Zach," Lexy chuckled.

Sitting with them, he said, "I know a thing or two about the needs of a predatory species being Kayn's Handler."

"Dibs," Emery proclaimed, pointing at the bartender.
"We don't eat Aries Group," Zach reminded, smiling.
"Don't sass me," Emery reprimanded.
Smirking, Zach said, "You left me for dead last night. Grey dragged me out of the water."
"Did you die?" Emery flirted, squeezing his shoulder.
Staring at her, Zach sighed, "Kayn didn't come running so I guess not."
She wasn't drunk enough for this conversation. Glancing over, Lexy offered, "Should I switch seats?"
"Yes," Emery directed. "We should chat."
Irritated, Zach countered, "No. We shouldn't."
"I was ordered to take you out of the equation," Emery explained, sipping her drink.
Entertained by the revelation, Zach asked, "Why?"
"You can't have sex right now. Grand scheme of things issue. Bad timing for you to trigger anything else," Emery answered, enjoying his reaction.
"Bullshit!" Looking at her, he said, "Have you ever been ordered to not have sex?"
Squinting, Lexy sparred, "It's not farfetched."
"No sex for you," Emery chuckled, enjoying herself.
She smelled sugar cookies. They must be making desert.
"Fill er up Paulo. I'm dry," Emery sang.
They all stared at his rear as he used the blender.
"Paulo does squats," Zach whispered.
"Paulo should follow me too the washroom," Emery flirted admiring his tush.
Refilling glasses, the agent taunted, "Paulo might."
Go Paulo. No holds barred sucking back her slushy, Lexy forgot the brain freeze rules. *Ahhh.* Wincing, she rubbed her tongue on the roof of her mouth.
Swaying her hips like a snake charmer, Emery left. *Paulo won't do it.*

"You're in charge of the bar until I get back," Paulo chuckled, pursuing her.

"Why would he go?" Lexy whispered, watching him jogging after her.

Grinning, Zach said, "Why wouldn't he?"

He had a point. They leapt up to snoop behind the bar. Checking out liquor by sniffing it, Lexy poured shots. Clinking glasses, she saluted, "Too a sexless week."

"Please. You just hooked up with someone," he laughed.

Dumping tequila into the blender, she stifled a grin while playing dumb, "No clue what you're talking about?"

"I was with Triad before Ankh. Tiberius was good to me," Zach volunteered, passing her a bottle.

Smiling, she shared, "It was fun."

"I bet it was," he flirted with a playful hip bump.

She hip-bumped him back, laughing. *Was Zach hotter?* His hand slid over hers. "How drunk are you?" Lexy teased, yanking her hand away.

"Oh... SHIT! Siren pheromones! Sorry, Lex! Um, I should go before I bust into that washroom like the Kool-Aid man." He ran away and left her there.

Ahhh. She smelled it now. One of their Siren had a malfunctioning bracelet. Grinning, she thought of Tiberius. *With her luck it would be months before their paths crossed. It's just sex. Insanely hot dirty sex.* Blending a drink, she caught a shadow. *Someone was sitting in on her X-rated thoughts.* Grinning, she glanced back at her sexy drunk dialler. *Of course, it was him.*

With his chin resting in his hand, Orin asked, "New job?"

"I'm chucking it all to follow my dream. Drink magician in paradise. What do you want?" Lexy played bartender.

"I'll have whatever you're having," Orin toyed, blatantly staring at her chest.

Awkward. High beams. Pretending the pheromones weren't affecting her, she placed a swirled slushie in front of him, daring, "Enjoy."

"What's in it?" He said, sniffing it.

She tempted, "What isn't?"

"Are the red chunks our missing bartender?" Orin teased. Fishing one out, he licked his finger.

Titillated, Lexy gapped, biting her lip.

In a teal one piece with damp hair, Jenna interrupted, "Everyone is getting antsy. Where's Emery?"

With a dry throat, Lexy revealed, "Eating the bartender in the washroom."

Finding the Siren's bracelet in the sand, Jenna sighed, "This vacation is about to get out of hand."

"I'll break it up," Lexy offered, getting up.

Blocking her, their Oracle insisted, "No! Never you. Is that clear?"

"I was going to snap her neck," Lexy mumbled, sipping the drink. *She didn't add mix. Whoops. This was just alcohol.* Reaching for Orin's glass, their fingers grazed like striking a match. She explained, "I forgot mix. I'll fix it."

Storming over, Lily accused, "He has to stop eye banging me!"

Eye banging?

Brushing past her to grab wine, Zach slammed, "Get over yourself. We hooked up twice last week. You've been ignoring me ever since. I couldn't be less interested."

Holy shit, Zach.

"Asshole!" Lily cursed, throwing sand.

Walking away, Zach provoked, "You want me bad."

Wild eyed, Lily took off after him, saying, "I'm going to kill him!"

"Please, stop that from happening," their Oracle pled.

Getting up, Orin sighed, "I've got it."

"I'll reunite my friend with her bracelet. Lexy, go to your room. Let's not complicate tomorrow," she instructed.

Let's not complicate tomorrow should be her new afterlife motto. Lexy stole banana liquor and left. *Run away from the Siren pheromones. Got it.* Wandering back with sand underfoot, and a flawless cobalt sky, she longed for fractured imperfection of the in-between. The multihued watercolour backsplash reminded her the fantasy world they were granted access too, wasn't reality. Climbing the stairs to her deck, she saw her Handler teaching newbies to surf. Leaning on the railing, she watched. *Grey was a great teacher. Pyrokinesis would have stopped that dream from coming to fruition in the mortal world.* Waiting for his return on a recliner, she sprawled like a cat in sunshine and tension went poof. *Emery put her bracelet on.* Watching Frigate birds soaring overhead, she was fed a short teaser of lavender stone and a tornado of furry pterodactyl. Blinking the image away, Frigate poop splatted on the deck nearly hitting her. Recalling Grey's speech about it being lucky, she didn't want to step in it so she went to grab a cloth. Standing in front of the bathroom window, she saw Zach plant a curl your toes kiss on Sami. *Holy shit.*

"Thanks for behaving yourself today," Zach flirted, walking away.

Kayn's Handler had all his bases covered. She wandered back, cleaned up and lounged on the deck.

Sensing a presence, she opened her eyes. *Grey.*

Grinning, Grey prompted, "Dinner is ready."

Already?

Opening the lid, he announced, "Fish with spicy sauce and rice with beans."

Stretching, Lexy grinned. *Her Handler had her back again.* She joined him at the table. Sitting in the chair facing the ocean, with a tangerine sunset as Grey's backdrop, she dug into her meal. "Thank you. I would have been bummed if I missed dinner."

Pouring shots of banana liquor, he shared, "Dean can surf as well as I can."

The new Ankh were full of surprises. She shared, "I heard Dean used to be a tech genius."

"I thought he was a stripper?" Grey asked, doing a shot.

"His startup went under after his mom died," she replied, following his lead. The sugary shot, meshed perfectly with her spicy meal. She questioned, "Is everything good with Emma?"

"Partying the pain away only postpones it," Grey answered, refilling their glasses.

"I remembered a tornado of furry pterodactyls," Lexy blurted out.

Chuckling, he passed her a napkin, teasing, "Sure it wasn't just a crazy dream?"

"I haven't been sure about much lately," she replied, wiping her face.

Grinning, he said, "You're missing it." Wiping the corner of her mouth, he pointed at her chest.

There was hot sauce on her boob. Trying to clean it up, she questioned, "Have you heard anything about Arrianna yet?"

"Jenna assured me she's fine. Wonder why Markus' body didn't go through and hers did?" Grey answered, glancing back at their friends on the beach as music cranked.

Snatching the bottle, Lexy teased, "If it's science chat time, I'm drinking."

"Bet it's a Healer thing?" Grey determined, focused on the party starting without him. "Hope it didn't hurt?"

Folding her napkin into a paper airplane, she sighed, "Why overthink it? Everything hurts."

"Just avoid reality. Why didn't I think of that?" He teased.

Her napkin airplane just dropped on the table, when she tried to fly it. *Of course.*

Slipping straws into the folds, Grey searched for flight worthy weighted material. "If we had paper umbrellas in our drinks, we could use toothpicks from straw to straw to weight the wings. Insert a few with paper included so it's a touch heavier into the main plane straw."

Clearly, he was willing to do anything to spend time with her. Light dimmed as sun vanished into sea and stars magically lit up the heavens. Touched, she altered subjects, "Did you avoid the Siren drama this afternoon?"

Taking the hint, he paused his project, replying, "We were far enough away. Mel mentioned Zach and Lily were arguing. I'm sure he's feeling the stress of being separated from Kayn."

"Frost and Kayn are right over there in a bungalow," she reminded.

Meeting her eyes, he said, "You know what I mean."

"I was only with him for four or five hours," Lexy sighed.

His face cracked into a smile. "You're single. Do whatever you want," he replied, fingering his Pyrokinesis stifling bracelet.

Appreciating the effort it took to pretend, Lexy tempted, "Let's go light shit on fire?"

Laughing, he said, "I'm in." Getting up, he held out a hand.

In near darkness with a flickering campfire on the beach summoning shenanigans, she revealed, "I may have vanished a pub full of Lampir yesterday."

"All of the Lampir in it?" He clarified, strolling barefoot on sand.

Pausing their walk to keep their chat private, she gave him the short version. "I tossed a blue orb. We were chased by blue fire. When I looked back, the building was gone."

Concerned, he whispered, "Have you told anyone?"

"I'm pretty sure I'm not supposed to mention vanishing a building," she whispered. "Logically, it can't be gone?"

"We'll check it out tomorrow," Grey assured, squeezing her hand.

Passing friends dancing by the bonfire, he put an arm around her, admitting, "I'm always going to want to dance with you."

Embracing, their bond secured it's hold. Swaying with her head on his shoulder, she whispered, "I never want to stop."

He was her first dance, and love. He was everything. Wanting to believe she could long for someone else without breaking their connection, she met his eyes. Time stopped as it always did, and she looked up at the stars.

"I haven't taken time to look at the stars in weeks," he said, staring up at twinkling light.

Was moving on possible without snuffing out his ability to find light in the darkness?

Cupping her face, Grey pledged, "You're my best friend, Lex. Give me time to evolve past wanting more and I'll be your wingman." He kissed her forehead. "Seeing you dating might be good for me."

"Anyone?" She teased. Playfully walking backwards, tide washed over her feet.

Narrowing his eyes, Grey followed, saying, "I reserve the right to set anyone I deem unworthy on fire."

Fair enough. "I reserve the right to murder anyone who irritates me," she provoked, splashing him. She sprinted into the waves, and he chased her. As water weighted legs slowed her, he caught her, rubbing sand paper stubble on her neck as she laughed.

Releasing her, he cautioned, "Pulling a string and running away would make Orin's night."

Impressed the hot sauce stain was gone with a dunk, she wandered into shallow water, revealing, "Orin drunk dialled last night."

"You don't know the half of it," he chuckled.

"What?" Lexy asked, wading.

Splashing her, he said, "I let the stray cat out."

He didn't come in. Maybe he did and she was having X-rated dreams?

He let go of her hand. Their eyes met. He exhaled and she could see it. Surprised he could meet her eyes at all if she was dreaming about the backseat antics, she defended herself, "It was fun."

Not expecting her to own it, Grey grinned. Shaking his head, he said, "Nobody evolves overnight."

Me or you?

"I lied. I'm planning to light him on fire," he chuckled.

Fair enough. Unsure of what to do, she hugged him. *Awkward. He was turned on. Greydon Riley you kinky guy.* Unable to resist pushing his buttons, she huskily whispered, "We've done dirtier things."

"You're making this friend zone harder," he scolded.

It's hard enough.

Submerging himself, he screamed underwater. Laughing as bubbles rose to the surface, she decided behaving was in her best interest. She bent to unwrap seaweed from her leg.

Taking care of the slimy weeds for her, he changed the subject. "You let Emma hit you."

"I did," she admitted. Sensing eyes, Lexy glanced towards the fire, saying, "Bet it looks like you're proposing."

"Would you still say yes," he taunted, looking up.

Always. That was the problem. "You've been extra annoying this month," Lexy sparred. A rogue wave mowed her down like divine Karma. Momentarily tumbling in the current, they found their footing.

Quickly wading closer to shore, he teased, "Next time I'm leaving the feral cat in your room."

Chuckling as she pictured Orin trying to catch a cat on the beach, she joked, "I feel bad about blowing him off after that level of romantic gesture."

"Right? Cookies, and a feral beach cat. The cardio alone," Grey bantered, laughing.

Wading in surf under a sparkling night sky with the moon's glow in a magical pathway out to sea, she professed, "If it was ever a choice…"

"It's not. I understand. We don't need to beat this conversation to death anymore," he affirmed.

Her spine crawled. Glancing back at the beach, music and

revelry added a lightness to ambiance of the waves. *Something was off.* With intuition nudging her, Lexy said, "Hope the Aries Group is somewhere safe."

"Why?" Grey questioned as rapid popping and flashing light lit up the parking area.

Everyone by the fire scattered into shadows. *Only mortals brought guns to an immortal fight.* Their palms heated and strobed giving away their location. Light flashed in the hills. *Snipers!* They dove into the ocean with bullets whizzing by. Staying underwater until their lungs demanded air, they surfaced in churning sea.

Treading water, Grey gasped, "What in the hell?"

Tugging him under as more bullets rained, Lexy motioned to swim out further. Fighting against current together until they burst up for air, she said, "Catch the riptide."

"That's a one way trip for me," he pointed out, swimming.

Treading water, Lexy vowed, "I've got you." Light flashed in their peripheral vision. Diving as projectiles riddled the sea, they swam into the murky depths. Holding onto each other, riptide swept them away in a blur of bubbles and rapid motion. Grey went limp as current calmed. Crimson hair billowed as they floated upwards with her mind whispering, *don't let go.* She bobbed up far from shore. *Inconvenient.* Each gasp of air was steam scalding her lungs. Something bumped her. *One of them was bleeding.* Bumped again, she kicked the demise party crasher, seething, *die insect.*

Emery's voice instructed, "Deep breath."

Water sucked them out. She clung to Grey's body as a massive wave deposited them in an alcove. *Convenient.* Tugging her deceased Handler to shore with her Ankh symbol strobing, and pop popping of bullets over crashing waves, there was no time to waste. She pressed her hands on his chest, willing him back.

His eyes opened. He felt his torso, gasping, "I got shot."

With a brutal headache, Lexy cut to the chase, "I healed you." *Sure she'd seen all of Grey's facial expressions, this one was new.*

"If you were missing a large chunk of your face, would you want to know?" Grey enquired.

She knew now. Thanks. Irritated, she responded, "For future reference... No."

Entranced, Grey overshared, "You're red meaty Terminator healing."

"Visuals aren't helpful," Lexy bantered as the need for sustenance prickled every hair on her body.

Inching closer, he gushed, "No, it's badass. How are you carrying on a conversation?"

She was hungry. Eating mortals was frowned upon.

Making it clear he caught her cannibalism dilemma, Grey sparred, "You look like a Zombie. Might as well own it."

Zombies aren't real.

'*Really? Why not? Everything else is.*' Grey taunted telepathically.

Good point. "Don't mess with me while I'm this hungry, Greydon." Using his full name triggered protective instinct. Focused on finding a snack elsewhere, a gigantic salt water alligator waddled out of the cave like an answer to a prayer.

Gingerly backing away, Grey whispered, "Great. You brought me back halfway through a B Horror Movie."

Instinct gave her a nudge. *Why not?* Cocking her head as predators do, she strode towards it.

"The Treaty!" Grey warned, coming after her.

She held up a hand to stop him. Maintaining eye contact with the Sea Gator, she cautioned, "It's an alternative." It didn't move. She touched it, draining life force until it's legs gave way. Feeling spectacular as veins tinted with her spine tingling, Lexy turned to her Handler.

"Please don't eat me," Grey bargained, keeping his distance.

"Why would I save you then eat you?" She rationed as

injuries sealed, leaving pristine flawless skin. Her scalp tickled as scarlet hair grew. Feeling the Gator energy, she decreed, "Let's take out the snipers."

"We're not sneaking up on anyone with strobing symbols in the dark," Grey explained, tying seaweed around his hand.

Unconcerned, she peered past rocks to scope out the fight. Each time snipers shot at targets light flashed in the hills giving away their location. "They are on the dock and hillside."

"The distance is an issue," Grey voiced the obvious.

Snipers opened fire into the jungle. They still had friends in the fight, she could feel it. *Healers could take a lot of bullets.* She shared her idea, "Let's take your Pyrokinesis for a spin. Take out the dock. Confusion and cover."

Yanking off his bracelet, he concentrated until it exploded. Engulfed in flames soldiers leapt into the sea.

Lexy pointed at men running to help. In a flash, they were ablaze screaming. *This was fun.* "Run!" They took off through the brush. Bursting out of the bushes behind a soldier. He turned and saw her. "Hi," Lexy toyed, just a girl in a bikini.

Walking out of the bushes, Grey lit him up, taunting, "It's not necessary to flirt with everyone, Lex."

"Look who's talking," she barbed. A man shouting their location into a radio ran at her. She stepped out of the way and sent the next assailant soaring into the jungle.

"Lexy," Grey whispered with his palms engulfed in flames. Soldiers burst out shooting, bullets whizzed from everywhere.

Shrieking with her hands out, she paused time, and shoved her flaming Handler against an RV. Contact reanimated Grey. Lexy rushed, "Behind the metal!" Holding countless hovering bullets with her mind. She tossed their guns and sprinted back to Grey. Bullets pinged off the RV as she drank in his excess energy. *Oh, that was just what she needed.* "Run!" With rather epic heat sensor night vision, she led the way through the jungle taking out those unfortunate enough to cross their path. With a view of the hillside, she sent rocks scattering through leaves with her mind. Bullets hazed the area. Pointing at flashes of light on the mountainside, she instructed, "That's the last of the snipers. Light it up."

"It's too far away," Grey rationed.

"It isn't," she motivated.

He concentrated on the area of light in the hills. The last snipers exploded in pitchy wails. Engulfed in flames, Grey dropped to his knees. *Shit. This was going to suck.* Embracing her Handler until his agony was silenced. She let go with smoke billowing from blistered flesh. "You did it," she praised.

"I hurt you," Grey whispered.

Lexy assured, "Just a flesh wound." Bubbled up skin smoothed. She swung an arm stirring up brush. *No cover fire. One on one combat now.*

Bushes rustled. Prepared to fight, Mel staggered out and collapsed. Checking her bullet riddled torso, Lexy pressed her hands on the Healer's chest. Energy travelled the extensions of her arms, rapidly mending her.

"It's a bloodbath." Mel got up, warning, "No time for chit chat. Thugs with automatic weapons rushed the beach. They're coming."

'Take out as many as you can,' their Oracle's voice instructed telepathically.

Grey released the Dragon, "No survivors, Lex."

She shut her emotions down and vanished into the jungle.

19
Murder Island Massacre

*L*istening to whirling tires, she smelled his cologne. *It couldn't be. There's no way.* Sitting up in a stranger's clothes, her pulse raced as their eyes met in the rearview mirror. *How did he have her? What happened?* Fighting the urge to leap over the seat, Lexy taunted, "Either I'm dreaming, or you've kidnapped me again."

"Short notice partner replacement," her sexy Triad nemesis sparred, tempting inhibitions away with a grin.

The second he pulled over it was on. "Explain," she prompted.

"Everyone died but you. Triad brought back your Healers and fuelled their recovery. That assassination was a parting gift from King Ricard. The Aries Group Agents are safe, but Emery and Kayn are in the back of a big rig in a magically reinforced lizard terrarium. Kevin's crew is in pursuit leaving me without shapeshifter backup for an Aries Group job."

He lost her at lizard terrarium.

He passed his phone back. "Grey wants you to call when you wake up."

Sure enough, his number was in the phone. *Maybe she was dreaming?* She pressed Grey's name.

Her Handler answered, "Hi Lex."

"You didn't light him on fire," she teased, smiling.

With the buzz of conversation back noise, Grey confessed, "He told me I could light him on fire for a decade if I let you come without a hassle. How could I pass that up?"

Recalling taking one for the team by lighting herself on fire, she questioned, "Are you okay?"

Taking his phone somewhere quieter, he answered, "I'm fine. I had an enlightening chat with our Guardian. We'll talk about everything when you get back."

Concerned she wasn't deciphering emotional context, she asked, "Who is going to put you out if it happens again?"

"It's taken care of. Tell Tiberius I'm holding him to our deal. I should go. Love you, Lex. Have fun," Grey said.

Maybe she woke up in an alternate dimension? "Love you more," she replied. Tiberius started laughing. Wide eyed, she hung up. "He was being sweet. You wrecked it."

"He's diabolical. Oh no. Everything is fine. Love you, Lex," he mocked, chuckling.

Denying her needs was reflex with Grey. Have fun? His acceptance threw her for a loop. She urged, "Pull over."

"Are we playing this game again?" He baited, obeying.

Getting out, she stood with her back to the car. Closing her eyes listening to gulls soaring over the beach. *Another hall pass for lusty escapades with a nemesis turned lover who shook her to her core.* The door closed. Listening to approaching footsteps, she faced him. *It felt too good to be true.* Her eyes softened, scolding, "You can't kidnap me every twenty-four hours."

Taking her in his arms, he seduced, "Thirty-six but who's counting?"

She playfully backed out of his embrace, toying, "I should wash this blood off." Stripping off her top, Lexy tossed it, luring him to a deserted beach with a trail of clothes. Slipping off panties, she sprinted to the water.

Tiberius picked up her top, shouting, "You're crazy! We're covered in blood! There may be sharks!"

In the water naked, she teased, "Afraid?"

Taking off his shirt, he said, "Not a fan of being eaten."

"If you want me. I'm right here," she baited, splashing his way.

"You're impressively crazy. I'm into it," Tiberius chuckled. Undoing his shorts, He chased her into the surf. Laughing as he caught her. Gazing into her green eyes, he whispered, "Hi."

"Hi," she whispered. Jostled by a wave as mouths met, their bodies slid against each other. Gasping as he caressed her until she was whimpering his name with sunshine glinting off water, lost in their lusty ocean encounter as it rose to an earth-shattering crescendo of rowdy curses.

Cupping her rear as rapture imploded, he raspily warned, "Fin."

She squashed interruptions with a burst of energy as ecstasy shivered, blinding her of everything but need for more.

"You may have only stunned it," he chuckled, trapped in her thigh's stranglehold.

She noticed something floating sideways in the water. *Oh, shit.* They dashed out of the surf.

Watching a shark revive and swim away, Tiberius wrapped his arms around her, chuckling, "It was worth it."

Lord help her, it was. She wanted to lock herself in a room with him and never leave. Lexy decreed, "Okay, I'm in. What's the job?"

"I didn't know it was still being decided," he flirted, kissing her neck. "I risked being eaten by a shark." He tugged up his underwear.

Putting on undergarments, she taunted, "I protected you."

"That was Guardian power Russian Roulette. I may wake up tomorrow with two heads," he teased, glancing her way.

"I could have lured you out here, had my way with you and let you get eaten," Lexy sparred, raking her hands through tousled crimson locks.

"I agreed to let your Handler light me on fire for a decade. Be as crazy as you want. I can match it," Tiberius admitted, in awe of her.

She believed it. They were going to get into trouble. Lexy sighed, "Good," chucking the rest of her clothes in the sea.

In solidarity, he tossed his too. Watching them vanish, he said, "Showing up at a job in our underwear is unprofessional. Hope there are clothes that fit us in that bag."

"Who cares?" Lexy provoked, walking back to the car. "Are you planning to tell me about the job, or do you want me to guess?"

Grinning, he revealed, "We're supposed to draw attention to ourselves today. We're staying on a yacht tonight. We get kidnapped by traffickers by late afternoon tomorrow."

Semi impressed, she revealed, "I've never been on a yacht." *Did he say late afternoon tomorrow? He needed a durable partner for the job. Don't overthink it.*

Opening the backdoor, Tiberius climbed in to dig through the bag of clothes. Holding up shorts that would fall off, he grinned, saying, "Guess it's baggy t-shirts. We'll stop and buy something. I bet you'd look amazing in one of those floral beach vender dresses."

Way too happy to see him, she got in and straddled his lap, saying, "We don't need clothes to make out in the backseat."

Grinning, Tiberius agreed, "We don't," as their lips met.

Making out like lusty teenage heathens in a frenzied blur of torturous kisses and intimate caresses, his hand slipped into her panties as hers slid under his waistband. With their union concealed by steamy windows, the rest of the world ceased to exist as they the bounced wheels off the road, reminiscent of the last time they crossed paths until they rowdily climaxed in unison. Gasping, they laughed as someone drove past honking.

Caressing her damp wavy hair, Tiberius confessed, "I'm so into you, Lexy Abrelle."

Smiling, she teased, "I'm impressed, you remembered my mortal last name."

"The hazards of being moderately obsessed with someone for decades," Tiberius admitted. Sweetly kissing her, he urged, "We should go. We're almost there."

Gazing into his eyes, Lexy sighed, "Fine." Clenching, she got off him, grinning.

Biting his lip, he chuckled, "You wicked thing."

Takes one to know one. Wearing baggy shirts over underwear, they rolled down the windows. Salty air drifted in as they pulled away from their beach. With scarlet hair blowing in the breeze and cerulean sky on the horizon, she glanced his way as music played sealing the moments' spot on her list of treasured excursions.

Touring picturesque shoreline with tourists cavorting in the sea, he pulled into a parking lot. They got out and jogged past sun worshippers to a stand with everything an unprepared tourist might need. The vendor was smiling as they perused. Placing a hat on Tiberius' head, Lexy teased, "I like it."

He took the woven hat off, saying, "I should show up in this sombrero."

Recalling his floral dress remark, she passed a short flower print sundress. "If you wear the sombrero, I'll wear this."

"Deal," he agreed, paying.

Darting back to the car, they fought tension changing into beach hut treasures. He opened the door for her and held out his hand. *The hat looked frigging ridiculous on him.* Loving the fact that he followed through with the dare, she took his hand. He didn't let go as they strolled onto the beach.

He confessed, "I have a recreational thing going on with our head agent. She knows I'm into you. It won't be an issue."

Of course, he did. Unconcerned, she teased, "You hope not."

Taking her in his arms, he gazed into her green eyes, vowing, "Nothing can wreck this."

"For at least twenty-four hours," Lexy taunted, barefoot in warm sand with her arms around his neck.

Crinkle eyed, smiling, he said, "At least."

Aries group witnesses. She flirted, "I can't be seen cuddling my enemy. I have a rep to protect." With a playful shove, she took off.

Chasing her to the water, he captured her, whispering, "They'll think we're acting. It's a job."

Feeling his breath on her neck, she flipped him. Pinning his shoulders to sand, Lexy taunted, "Why embarrass yourself? Your booty call might be watching."

"I won't have to explain," Tiberius toyed. "We're friends."

Rolling off, she sat on the beach, teasing, "You don't have friends."

"I don't get the chance to bond floating between groups of Triad," Tiberius reminded, sitting beside her.

"It must be lonely," Lexy replied, enjoying his company.

"With compulsion as my wingman, I rarely spend nights alone," he replied, watching waves wash on the shore.

Squinting in sunshine with her hand as a visor, Lexy baited, "Screw freewill."

"You know that's not what I meant," he sparred. "I just hate eating alone."

She did too. Water washed over their feet. "We're going to get wet," she laughed, standing up with ocean breeze tussling her hair.

He joined her, saying, "Let's go listen to their spiel about the job so the rest of the day is ours. Our yacht is at the boat launch."

Holding hands while strolling on a warm sandy beach

under endless blue Mexico sky it felt like they were normal people on vacation. They dodged a sandcastle. "There are no kids on this beach," Lexy noticed, looking back.

"You'll figure it out," he taunted, swinging their arms.

Topless sunbathers everywhere. A man in khakis was at a station with bottles of water and icy treats.

"I'm thirsty," Tiberius declared, taking a water.

She drank one too. They put her plastic bottle in the basket. Tiberius took the wrapper off and handed her a popsicle. Walking away, she tasted it, saying, "This has alcohol in it." There were tents all the way down the beach. As they walked by the huts naughty noises made her smile. *This was one of those resorts.* Squeezing his hand, Lexy clued in, "This is a couple's resort."

Grinning, Tiberius revealed, "I was going to do this job with Steph."

"Do you usually go to hedonism resorts with Steph?" Lexy probed, licking her melting popsicle.

Wiping her chin with his thumb, he disclosed, "Certain people do better with morally questionable jobs. If you're asking if I've slept with her. It was before we hooked up. She's in a booty call situation. He's in love with someone else. I relate to the scenario."

Aware he was watching her finish her popsicle, Lexy deep throated what was left and tossed her stick in the garbage as they walked up the ramp towards the rich people boats. *Ankh didn't get cool jobs like this.* Curious, she enquired, "Are you guys on the no-fly list too?"

"These are boats," he teased.

She knew that. Shoving him, she scolded, "Don't be an ass."

Chuckling, Tiberius revealed, "We weren't on the no-fly list until Frost and Lily joined the mile high club on a commercial airline."

Imagining the shit show, Lexy laughed, "Did it crash?"

"No, but everyone with spouses waiting at home wished it did," he replied. "Life paths were tanked."

"Divorcapalooza," she cackled, stopping at a yacht named Aries Group. "What's the Aries Group cover story?"

As they boarded, he said, "On the books they're a tech firm with assets in pharmaceuticals, robotics and technology."

"What kind of tech?" Lexy probed, messing with him.

"Science stuff," Tiberius sparred.

A woman she recognized from other jobs wandered over, teasing, "Science stuff. It almost sounded like you knew what you were talking about." They embraced.

As they parted, Tiberius introduced Lexy, "This gorgeous creature needs no introduction."

Grinning, the agent with a stunning smile, shook her hand, greeting her, "Agent Clarke. Ti has the biggest crush on you. Is he driving you crazy yet?"

"Hanging in there," Lexy replied, smiling at him. *Pet names. Cute.*

The sexy agent said, "Heard you ran into trouble?"

Glancing at Tiberius, Lexy joked, "Technically, I woke up in trouble's car."

"Resorting to kidnapping hot girls now, Ti?" She teased. "We were expecting Stephanie. Your dress for this evening needs to be altered. We'll fix it before dinner. There's only one shower. I'm sure you'll figure it out." She winked at Tiberius. "Everything you need is in the bathroom. I'll stall everyone talking about alterations. Twenty minutes. Your swimsuits are on the bed."

Following Tiberius down a hall, Lexy admitted, "She's kind of awesome." He opened the bathroom door. She wandered in, shocked at the size. Wincing at salt water matted hair in the mirror, she sighed, "You could have told me I looked like the missing link." Locking the door, he turned on the shower and backed her towards the counter. *They didn't have time.* "Twenty minutes," she rationed.

Putting her on the sink, he lifted her dress, seducing, "I'll satisfy you in three."

"They'll hear," she whispered. He tore off her panties, knelt and buried his face between her thighs. *He was crazy.* Clutching his hair, voyeuristically watching him stir up agonizing waves of bliss until every hair prickled as ecstasy imploded. Moaning, she tossed her head back revelling in hedonistic freedom.

Biting her inner thigh like a virile beast, he got up and said, "I'll shower and wait for you out there." He left her gasping on the counter.

That was impressive. They were going to get into so much trouble together. As her partner in debauchery lathered up, she pried her eyes away. Snooping through drawers to see what they had, she found wrapped toothbrushes and toiletries. Placing everything on the counter as the shower turned off, she smiled.

Kissing her neck, he whispered, "I'm going to screw you senseless in one of those beach huts."

Insanely turned on, she gapped, watching him brush his teeth. *She was going to rock his world.* Stripping behind him in the mirror, she got into the shower. Feeling him watching as she washed her hair and soaped up, when she turned to look, he was gone.

With towel dried conditioned curls, freshly brushed teeth and waterproof makeup, she felt like herself again. Wrapped in a towel, she peered out. *They had a swimsuit for her in the bedroom. He left without showing her where it was.* Checking the next room, she saw bags on the bed. There was a tiny white string bikini. *Stephanie's size. Too late to play coy.* Putting on the suit, she posed in the full-length mirror. *If they were supposed to be causing a scene, it was perfect.*

Someone knocked, asking, "Are you decent? Can we come in?"

"Rarely, you might as well," Lexy answered. Agents and a tailor wandered in.

Tiberius' agent friend said, "We need to adjust your dress for this evening. I thought we could multitask. What do you know about the job?"

"Not much," she admitted.

"You are newlyweds on your honeymoon," Agent Clarke explained as a tailor took her measurements.

Bet he didn't mention this part of the job to Grey. Shaking her head, laughing, Lexy asked, "Where's my husband?"

The sexy agent gave her a good once over, toying, "Hanging out at the bar by the pool waiting for his jaw dropping hot wife."

She was flirting with her.

Agent Clarke got back on track, "I worked with the bride for years. Brenda vanished on her honeymoon with her husband Theo. Anticipating a ransom demand, we were sent in. When we started digging, we found out a number of couples have gone missing while staying at hedonism resorts in the area. We've been gathering intel. Our agents posing as newlyweds, have gone missing. Their last transmission was a list of pirates suspected of human trafficking. Surveillance caught chatter of sacrifices, so I called in a favour with Triad." She handed her phone to Lexy.

Scrolling through honeymoon snapshots couples posted on social media. *All of them were attractive, wealthy, over affectionate and in their early to mid-twenties. Young to be getting married by today's standards.* When she reached the end, she scrolled back to see if she'd counted wrong. *How could this many couples go missing from four resorts without triggering public outcry? They were hedonism resorts. It was unfavourable publicity.*

Agent Clarke explained, "You'll notice similarities. The plan is to have you put on a show. Get kidnapped and let them take you to where they brought the others."

Sacrifices usually involved a lunar event. She wanted to ask her to google upcoming lunar events but decided not to open that can of worms. Mortals who know too much triggered Corrections. She wasn't sure where the line was for Aries Group employees.

"Tiberius will fill you in on the rest," Agent Clarke said, motioning for her.

"Okay," Lexy replied, following her out.

As they reached the deck, she showed her a picture of the first couple again, saying, "We're closer than family. Logic says she's gone, but recovering her body would help me deal with reality."

Bodies are just shells. She couldn't say that. Odds were something ate her. Not that either. What was she supposed to say? Flustered, she needed to flee. *Comfort her.* Lexy touched her arm. *What was she supposed to do?* She gave her a stiff pat. *Be friendly.* Relaxing her hand, she kept it there.

"I loved her," the Agent revealed. "Brenda was my first posting. I wasn't sure if Ti told you."

Recalling Grey's many lectures about it being insensitive to run away when people are sharing their feelings, Lexy squeezed her arm. Her Agent friend grinned. *Whatever works, I guess.*

"Your dress should be altered by six pm. Indecent public displays are a must. Push boundaries. Be inappropriate enough to get kidnapped," Agent Clarke instructed, winking.

This was her dream job. Waving, Lexy smiled, and said, "We've got this." She strolled down the dock watching jaws drop until her bare feet hit sand. *Wearing this small a string bikini with her curves, bordered on obscene.* Following signs, she strutted past men with no filters lounging on the beach. Her spine tingled. *There was something supernatural going on.* Wandering down a cobblestone path surrounded by flowering bushes, she saw her pretend hubby at the bar chatting with a suspicious group. *Let the games begin.* All eyes turned to her strutting over in a white string bikini skimpy enough to make the devil blush.

"There's my gorgeous wife," Tiberius announced as he

leapt up with a Pina Colada in each hand. He glanced back at his posse, teasing, "Thought I'd apologize in advance for the noise. Newlyweds." He jogged over and handed her a drink, explaining, "They have the spot next to ours."

"Awkward," Lexy laughed, waving.

Walking past suspects on the beach with his arm around her waist, Tiberius vowed, "I'm going to drill you into the mattress until you lose your voice screaming."

He revved her libido every time he opened his mouth. All she could think about was shoving him into their private hut to take the edge off. Walking on the stunning beach, their eyes met. *How was this happening?*

They were greeted by a concierge at their hut, "Welcome to paradise Mr. and Mrs. Aries. Your Honeymoon Hut is stocked with Enchanted Isle essentials. I'm your attendant Tony. Place this flag on the table when you need drinks. Shall I set a dinner reservation reminder?"

Leaving Tiberius to deal with everything, Lexy took in the honeymooner's paradise. There was a large tent with a covered area. Flowers in a vase on the table in the shade. A blanket on the sand with low tables on either side for drinks. The closest hut was far enough away for a semblance of privacy. With rolling teal surf, warm silky sand between her toes as sun caressed her skin, it was a romantic setup. She went into their hut to check it out. There was circular bed with crisp white sheets, tons of pillows and cool air blowing. A bowl of fruit and a basket of snacks were on the nightstand, beside it was a mini fridge with cheese, juice and bottled water. She crawled onto the rounded mattress and tore off a branch of grapes, waiting for him to fulfil his hedonistic promise.

Grinning as he saw her, Tiberius took off his swimsuit and crawled onto the bed, teasing, "Hi, Mrs. Aries." He bit a grape off her stem.

She caught herself wishing it was real. *She wasn't pretending.* Confused, her expression changed.

"What just happened?" He questioned, caressing her hair.

She tenderly kissed his lips. Her heart fluttered. *Damn it.* She whispered, "I'm glad you kidnapped me."

"I'm glad you saved me from sharks," he toyed, deepening their passionate kiss until they were alone in the universe. Time stood still as their lips parted. He whispered, "Don't let me wreck this."

She was one hundred percent going to wreck this. "You were saying something about making me scream until I lost my voice," Lexy baited. Laughing as they wrestled for dominance until she let him pin her. "We're supposed to be out there creating a scene," she reminded.

"Oh, they'll hear us," Tiberius huskily promised. Forcefully flipping her, he tugged the string on her bikini and smacked her ass so hard he left a red handprint.

Titillated, she glanced back. *Oh, she was going to tear him apart.*

"I know what you need," he whispered. Biting her ass so hard it buckled her knees, setting off her Healing ability. Clutching her hips, he mercilessly drilled her into the mattress, cursing. In a volatile haze of throaty moans and gratuitous synergy, he made good on his promise, repeatedly taking her to new heights with wicked prompts and teeth until limb trembling rapture overwhelmed her.

Destroying expectations, he taunted, "Good girl."

Even with her bliss stoned brain playing elevator music, she wanted to rally on. *Good girl.* Exhaling, she reigned it in, "We should get out there."

"I'm trying to break your record," he seduced with her beneath him. Nuzzling her neck, her nipped her ear.

Gasping as he moved, she provoked, "Good boy." Picking up the pace, he hammered her into the mattress. As a molten surge imploded, she raspily cried out, digging nails into his back, taking him with her.

Groaning, "Shhiiittt," he collapsed.

Holy shit.

Pleased with himself, he rolled off. Sprawling on his back, he sighed, "Mission accomplished."

She was in trouble. She'd never be able to stop daydreaming about this.

"What are you thinking?" He probed with a sheen of well-earned perspiration on his chest, tracing her abs with a finger.

"It's going to be hard to stop wanting you," she confessed with her senses humming.

"I plan to make it impossible," he seduced, nipping her breast. Trailing deviant kisses down her stomach, he tempted, "Bet I can get you off in under a minute?"

She was so sensitive. Laughing as he feathered kisses, her lips parted as he buried his face between her legs and pleasured her with his wicked tongue until her toes curled. Imploding with heat, she clutched his hair, whimpering. Feeling him get off the bed, she thought, *it's just a sexy adventure.* As she opened her eyes, he passed her a water and placed snacks in front of her. *Damn it.*

Pitching his empty bottle in the trash, he leapt back on the bed. Gazing into her eyes with soul stirring emotion, he said, "I can't believe you're here with me." Running a silky crimson ringlet between his fingers, he divulged, "I've wanted you in the worst way for so long."

She'd always felt this panicked urgency, she just didn't know what it meant. Chanting good time not a long time in her head didn't make it true. She teased, "Do that twenty more times, and I'll chuck it all to run away with you."

Nipping her ear, he flirted, "Baby, I plan to please you until you have a Pavlovian response orgasm whenever I walk into a room."

Grinning, Lexy teased, "Won't it be embarrassing when it happens to you?"

Kissing her freckled shoulder, he said, "Hold that thought. We should eat something. We were more than loud enough to get kidnapped before dinner." He opened the tray.

They were. He dangled a branch of grapes over her lips as the fan tussled her scarlet hair. She asked, "Are you like this with everyone?"

"Like what?" He replied, watching her eat a grape off the bottom with enamoured intensity.

Covering her mouth, she swallowed it, clarifying, "If it was Stephanie here instead of me would you be this sweet?"

"I wouldn't be feeding her grapes," he divulged, grinning.

They didn't need to have this conversation. Biting into a perfect apple, she offered it to him. He took an enormous bite, smiling as he ate it. Lexy said, "Ready to torment a psychopath?"

Getting up, he tugged on his swimsuit, toying, "Always." Helping her tie her top, he flirted, "This is the hottest bikini I've ever laid eyes on."

Grabbing coconut tanning oil from the basket, she tried to walk away, provoking, "Rub this all over me?"

Catching her in his embrace, he nuzzled her neck, flirting, "Everywhere?" Exhaling as he checked out her chest, he freed her, rushing, "Get out there before I toss you onto that bed and never let you leave."

She dashed out into the sunshine and stood watching waves crashing. Wrapping his arms around her, he kissed her ear, whispering, "Relax in the sun. I'll get drinks."

Sprawling on the blanket in sunshine, she closed her eyes, smiling. *She'd never had the time and freedom to enjoy a lusty encounter before.* She felt pressure beside her and turned his way. *It blew her mind that she didn't always see him.*

"We have no way of knowing the time," he pointed out.

Beaming, she sighed, "What time?"

A waiter appeared with a tray of drinks and placed four on a low beach table. She sipped a Pina Colada, listening to her enemy with benefits asking for a bottle of something tasty. *It was like he'd received a manual of everything she loved.*

Tiberius requested, "Can we have the bucket of ice?"

Grinning, the server passed the bucket of ice cubes, saying, "Shall I come by with a tray of deserts?"

"Please do," Lexy answered, glancing back.

They drank slushy drinks from curly straws enjoying the scenery, inconspicuously watching the neighbours. Their server brought a tray of deserts and left without a word.

Relaxing with luminous rays warming her skin, blissfully satisfied, she opened her eyes. *Yummy*.

Feeding her a chocolate strawberry, he declared, "Could this honeymoon be more perfect?"

Her eyes darted down the beach, Lexy whispered, "Our marks are captivated." Going with it, they fed each other bite sized chocolate cake.

Vanishing, he returned with tequila, announcing, "Guess this is the bottle I requested."

As he strengthened her slushy, her mind flashed an image of Amar, The King and his sister in an oddly familiar bar. She questioned, "Have you ever had your memory erased at one of those virtual reality Crypt events in the Third-Tier world?"

"It's way more fun with a licence for bad behaviour. Do what you want. Who you want. Nobody prepares you for the surprise memories six months down the road. By then, it's in the past. Well, unless you've made things awkward by hooking up with someone in your Clan," Tiberius divulged, trailing an ice cube down her spine.

Distracted as goosebumps rose on every inch of flesh, Lexy smiled, whispering, "That feels amazing."

Moving a melting cube down to the small of her back. Blocking the beaches' view with his body, he instructed, "Roll over."

Intrigued by the mischievous glint in his eye, she turned to her back. Tracing her lips with an ice cube, he seductively moved it down the pulse point of her neck, over each sparsely concealed aching breast bud. Arching her back, she gasped as he slid the melting cube into her bikini bottom and pleasured her until she was moaning his name. Enraptured by deviance, she forgot about witnesses, crying out.

Muffling her cries with his hand, he stared into her eyes. "We can get away with it," he dared, tugging the blanket over them.

Unable to wait long enough to tug the string, he shoved her bikini aside and entered her, groaning her name. Succumbing to reckless euphoria of each thrust as he took her in broad daylight. Gyrating her hips, she provoked, "Harder."

He lost it, violently pummelling her into the beach until she raked her nails down his back as release hit with such volatile limb trembling intensity, they simultaneously loudly finished, cursing. He collapsed on her. They were still, just breathing together, revelling in the satisfaction when he started shaking with laughter. *Awkward. They'd forgotten their rendezvous was public.* She provoked, "I'm so going to need you to do that at least a dozen more times."

Spent, he rolled off, toying, "Give me five minutes. I've got you." He winced, touching his back.

Sneaking a peek, her nails were bloody. *Whoops. Scratching over scratches had too hurt.* "My bad," she apologized. Shimmying closer to inspect the damage. *Holy shit.* Concealing her reaction to what she'd done to his back, she pressed her hands on his wounds. She felt the warmth of her Healing ability gather in her chest and travel down her arms, sealing his injuries. Tenderly kissing him, she whispered, "I scratched you."

"I know. I loved it," he baited with his sexy crooked smirk. Tucking a crimson ringlet behind her ear, he confessed, "I plan to do that at least twenty more times."

Birds squawked overhead. Her eyes followed as they soared out to sea. *She was thirsty.* Drinking iceless slushy was disappointing. Feeling his eyes on her, she turned as his lips met hers. Instinctually her mouth parted as he seduced her with his tongue. Their bodies melted together as their lusty connection brought her to the edge of ecstasy and took her over once again.

In the aftermath, she lay in his arms with sweet floral fragrance in the air as musical waves crashed. *She was happy. She rarely let herself admit it, pretending to be impervious to the need for more than the hand she was dealt. She wasn't naïve enough to pin happiness to a person. It was an inside job. Your soul found it in particles of dust floating in a ray of sunlight or the sensation of silky sand slipping between your fingers. She found joy today. Damn it. She was so into him.*

Kissing her hair, he whispered, "In a hundred years, I'll still be dreaming of you."

Her heart caught in her chest. *She wanted this day to go on forever.* With unconcealed depth of emotion in her eyes, she confessed, "Me too." Listening to his heartbeat, she realised they were covered in cake. "We need a new blanket."

Chuckling, he dove underneath, feathering kisses all over her as she laughed. Putting on his suit undercover, he asked, "Are our neighbours invested?"

Lexy glanced their way. *All they were missing was popcorn for the show.* "They'd buy season tickets," she replied as he put her suit on and tied it.

He intimately kissed her abdomen. Tossing the blanket off, he said, "Race you to the water."

She leapt up. They sprinted into the surf, embracing when they were submerged in salty water. Wrapping her legs around him, lost in each other they made out in the surf, frolicking for hours.

There was a clean blanket on the sand when they returned. Drying off in the sunshine, they gave each other coconut oil massages, tanned and slipped away for hedonistic adventures in their beach hut. Enjoying the day like they were really on their honeymoon, the line between reality and fantasy blurred. It was more than she'd hoped for. The sun, the company, the lusty escapades with a lover who went out of his way to satisfy her. When their server arrived with a message for Tiberius, he passed it to her. She read the note. *Come back to the yacht.*

Grabbing the tequila, he announced, "We're bringing this."

Looking around their memorable place, she didn't want to leave. "It can't be dinnertime," she bartered.

Holding her, moving to the music, her temporary spouse seduced, "New adventures await."

The yacht was far away. "Maybe they didn't see anything?" Lexy said as they trekked back.

Walking by marks with his arm around her, Tiberius flirted, "I have the hottest wife on the beach."

"You do," Lexy saucily bantered as onlookers laughed.

Approaching the dock, he clarified, "Are we saying we were acting?"

"Do you think they'll believe it?" She sparred, as reality peered into their fantasy jostling the facade.

"They signed a nondisclosure agreement," he assured giving her hand a squeeze. "Nobody has to know."

She might take flack for this, but she didn't care anymore. They were having the best time. They let go of each other's hands as they wandered aboard. Music was blaring like a party boat. Hanging out in casual attire the agents were drinking chardonnay while discussing plans.

Dressed every bit the part of a rich entrepreneur, Agent Clarke said, "Speak of the devil."

Grinning, Tiberius strolled over, saying, "You summoned?"

"We have a recording for you to listen to," Agent Clark said, pressing play. The voices mentioned a hunt and summoning the beast. *These mortals were in way over their heads.*

Agent Clarke explained, "We've contacted your Clans to let them know the job may take longer then discussed. If you're kidnapped by tomorrow afternoon, and taken to the next location, you'll need time to deal with whatever is going on. Forty-eight hours was our lowest guesstimate. We'll keep tabs on where they are for your return."

If she ended up hog tied and tortured, it was worth it. Even just the drive here was.

"You have time to shower and snoop before dinner. Your outfits are hanging in the closet. We're leaving to get ready. You have a few hours alone. We'll be at the restaurant for the evening." She winked at Tiberius and walked away.

They were friends.

Alone, he laced his fingers through hers, wandering down the hall. Gazing into her eyes, Tiberius caressed her face, disclosing, "I'd be the luckiest man in the universe to have you as my wife." Tugging the strings on her bikini, he backed her into the shower, and not so innocently reached past to turn on the water.

Ogling his squirm worthy everything, as he lathered up and washed his hair, she gapped, biting her lip. *He was ridiculously sexy.* As he rinsed off, she washed her hair. *This was nice. It felt like this was how they would be together.* Sharing a shower was a deeper level of intimacy. He stepped away from the spray and wiped his eyes. She took his place under it. Enjoying the hot water pummelling her skin, she smiled as hands began washing her back. Happy, she leaned against him as he soaped up her front sliding over peaked breasts. As his sudsy hands slid between her legs, she placed a hand on the wall, scolding, "Quit teasing me."

Kissing her freckled shoulder, he sped up, provoking, "Honey, I never do anything, I don't intend to follow through with. When this job is over, the mention of my name will soak your panties."

She believed it. He smacked her wet ass so hard it stung. She spun around, planning to give him shit when she saw his giant grin. Playing his game, she pressed her body against his. Stroking him, she whispered in his ear, "When someone says my name, you'll be painfully erect for hours."

Groaning, he cupped her face, confessing, "I've always..."

She'd deciphered their combustible chemistry as hatred for so long, but she saw him now. She silenced him with a kiss. As their mouths parted, she wasn't even fooling herself. *Damn it. This had to stay clear in her head. This was an adventure at a hedonistic resort. They were solving a mystery together. This was just forty-eight hours of kinky sex with her enemy.*

"You are so addictive," he sighed with the intensity of what they shouldn't say in his eyes.

With her lips, nearly touching his, she baited, "Your crazy turns me on too."

"We're insane. That's all this is," he whispered, playing with a damp lock of her hair.

Tugging him to her, everything was silenced as she darted her tongue against his. Stoking embers of desire, his hand slid between her thighs, she gasped. Grinning, he rubbed her into submission with titillating friction, prickling every hair on her body, working her into a leg trembling frenzy. Engulfed in a lusty inferno, pleasure imploded. Her knees buckled, moaning his name.

Nibbling on her ear, he whispered, "Good girl."

Oh, it was on. She kissed him, saying, "Your turn."

As she knelt in the shower, he groaned, "Baby, I've been fantasizing about you doing this for so long."

Meeting his eyes as she took his length in her mouth, he raked his fingers through her hair and rolled his eyes back, moaning. Making eye contact, she drove him over the edge. Cursing, "Shiiiiittttt. That's it." She went faster. "Yesss. Yes. Holy shit," he groaned, shivering.

That was fast. Pleased with herself, she grinned.

Helping her up, he chuckled, "I'm doing anything you want forever now."

"Anything?" she toyed, touching his hair.

Cupping her face, he swore, "Anything."

Making out like heathens in rising steam, he lifted her

against the stall and screwed her like it was his job until they raspily cursed in unison as euphoria detonated.

With her arms around his neck, she teased, "You've really been fantasizing about me doing that?"

"Ever since you straddled me, hung me upside down in the forest and bled me out in front of my men to humiliate me," he confessed, grinning.

"You've been my bitch for a while," she provoked, getting out of the shower. Drying off to his musical laughter, her heart twitched. *He was freaky and she loved it.* He walked by and she joined him at the sink. Brushing their teeth while sharing a mirror, it felt real. She dried her hair, leaving her crimson locks in flowing waves.

He vanished, returning with a bra, panties and a dress on a hanger. He flirted, "I can't wait to take these panties off with my teeth."

She hadn't planned on wearing any. Smiling in the mirror, she prompted, "Get dressed before they catch you strutting around naked." He kissed her shoulder. She watched his amazing ass go, hoping they didn't get kidnapped until tomorrow. *She wasn't even close to done with him.* She checked out the price tag on the red lacy panties. *Wow. That must be for the set. She'd never worn hundred and eighty dollar panties.* The red lace bra and panty set fit like it was made for her. Agent Clarke even correctly guessed her cup size. The bra didn't work with the backless dress, so it went back on the hanger. She felt like a rich newlywed putting on cherry red lipstick in the slinky red dress.

With kakis and a short sleeved patterned shirt unbuttoned just enough, he nuzzled her neck, toying, "That's going to be all over me."

She kissed the back of her hand and showed him, sharing "This brand stays put."

Embracing her, Tiberius flirted, "Is my stunning wife ready to go?"

"I am," she replied with her arms around his neck, lost in his alluring eyes. *This uninterrupted time with him was confusing her resolve for boundaries.* Lexy admitted, "Our Aries Group jobs are more demons, less ritzy places."

Gazing into her emerald eyes, Tiberius explained, "Ankh has a volatile mix of abilities. Triad is mostly shapeshifters with brute strength. Trinity gets their distance assassination jobs. I should give you a boat tour, so you know the layout."

She followed him as he opened doors. There was a master bedroom with luxurious red satin sheets on a king size bed across the hall. They walked down steps to a lower level with a large kitchen, closets and bunkbeds. He pressed a button. A wall slid aside to a secret room with weapons, scuba gear and a circular chamber. He explained, "This safe room is blast proof and watertight. Once they're in the hyperbolic chamber, they eject away. There's three days' worth of oxygen, food, water, medical equipment and a homing a beacon. When shit goes south, they'll seal themselves in here and we'll be on our own."

Why not be prepared for the inevitable? Snooping in the chamber, Lexy asked, "What defines shit going south?"

"There may be chainsaw torture involved. I figured you'd be down with it."

Fun. She asked, "How many agents?"

"Three or four, posing as our personal security," he answered.

"That's a lot of mortals to take care of," she replied.

Handing her earpieces, he said, "They have their minds set on planting trackers on our mark's boat."

Putting an earpiece in, she asserted, "Why risk it when we can just ask if they know of a secluded beach to anchor at tomorrow?"

He explained, "Mortals always make it harder than it needs to be. We'll filter our conversation and dispose of these the first chance we get. After we're done playing spy, I'm going to bring you back here, peel that dress off and do you all night. Tomorrow we'll fight chainsaw wielding psychopaths."

Best date ever. Tiberius understood her. They were motivated by the same things. "This is next level romantic," she teased, holding hands, strolling down the dock to bar music, breathing salty ocean air.

Walking into the fancy outdoor restaurant at dusk with torches and glowing white lanterns, they were seated at a table. Enjoying the atmosphere, Lexy perused the menu as wine was poured.

With adoration, he toasted, "To making fantasies reality."

They clinked glasses, staring into each other's eyes. Turning her attention back to the menu, she asked, "Have you eaten here before."

He chuckled, "A few times."

Catching the innuendo, as their server showed up to take their order, Lexy enquired, "What would you suggest?"

Pointing, their waiter said, "For spicy connoisseurs."

Grinning, she replied, "Perfect."

"Nothing is too hot for my wife. I'll have it too," Tiberius answered, playing footsies with her. By flickering candlelight, they sipped wine as he probed, "Has Orin used his naughty Healer trick on you?"

"That was random," she laughed. *She knew what he meant.*

He baited, "I'll answer every question you ask."

"Yes," she admitted. "Your turn. Heard Winnie was back in Triad. How's that going?"

Smirking, Tiberius confessed, "I'm taking orders from an ex who despises me."

"Awkward," she teased, sipping wine.

"I had her maimed a few years ago. It's fresh," he sparred.

"Sounds complicated," she flirted as a band played a cover of a popular song.

Grinning, he confessed, "You have no idea."

"I understand complicated relationships," Lexy divulged, watching his eyes sparkle in candlelight.

They bantered back and forth until their meals arrived. Devouring exquisitely garnished spicy culinary adventures while sneaking peeks at each other with palpable fascination, neither flinched. After finishing every morsel, they drank more wine, toasted to fake nuptials and chatted about their favourite places. With remnants of a tangerine and fuchsia sunset as their romantic backdrop, each lingering gaze was preserved for eternity in her treasured collection of beautiful, intoxicating things. Their perilous lust caused grief but granted amnesty from trivial emotion. They were a primal union of equally disturbed souls. Each time their eyes met, her libido spun off the hinges. With him, there was no need to apologize. No guilt and not a speck of ration involved. Sharing an assortment of delectable deserts, they'd all but forgotten about the job.

Agent Clarke's voice piped into their conversation, "Nod if you know which tables are theirs."

She hadn't even looked.

Nodding, Tiberius fed her a forkful of cake, saying, "It's delicious, isn't it?" She nodded, chewing with her hand covering her mouth aware they were being watched.

"We need you close to the guy with the goatee and red shirt. Brownie points if you can get away with leaving the phone on the table. We're cloning remotely. Lexy, meet me in the washroom."

The waiter came by to see if they needed drinks, Tiberius said, "I'd like to order a round for those tables as an apology for our public display this afternoon."

"I need to go to the washroom, sweetie." Getting up with legs for days, the crimson-haired warrior in a red dress strutted by the tables. All eyes followed her as she trekked down a path and went in.

Agent Clarke locked the door behind her, saying, "We're

alone." Wearing a short mint slip dress with dark smooth skin, she disclosed, "You can't stop anything until after they've taken you to where they're holding their captives. We want to plant a tracker onboard as an insurance policy. Keep everyone entertained and far away from the Yacht." She handed her a lipstick, explaining, "This is a sedative with a delayed reaction. The men at the table closest to the band need this in their system before their shift starts. Spraying it in the air has a higher witness risk but, you can do that by tugging the gold hinge. We've established, we can't sedate you. A kiss on the cheek while wearing it should work."

Lexy censored her response, "I'll do it my way."

"The idea turns my stomach too," she confessed, smiling.

"If something goes wrong, we'll improvise. I heal quickly. I'm flushing this before I leave the washroom. Do you want it back?" Lexy offered, handing her the earpiece.

"Thank you for not flushing it," she laughed, taking it.

Wanting to lecture her for pointlessly endangering herself, their hands touched. Lexy rationed, "There's no need for a tracker. I'll deal with everyone involved."

"I know you view us as helpless mortals, but I can handle myself," she countered, squeezing her shoulder. "Thanks for doing this." Someone hammered on the door. "We should go," the agent prompted.

Opening the door, it was one his men. Agent Clarke kissed her like she meant it. Wowed, as their mouths parted, Lexy slipped into character, "Too be continued."

"See you later, Mrs. Aries," she flirted, vanishing into a crowd.

That sexy badass. She saw why Tiberius was into her. She might be into her too but there was no way she was kissing a bunch of human traffickers. Enjoying the role as wealthy hedonism resort newlywed, she wandered back. Her hubby was at the table chatting with their target. *Well done. Time to figure out his trigger and bat it around like a ball of yarn.*

As she approached, Tiberius introduced her, "Honey, meet Laird Brock. Everyone calls him Brock."

"Hello Laird," Lexy provoked. *Why waste time with good behaviour?*

With a predatory glint in his eye, Brock taunted, "She's feisty."

"You have no idea," Tiberius confirmed as she straddled his lap. Clutching her hips, he toyed, "Hope this means we're about to have a wild night?"

"About to?" Lexy toyed. "How far do I have to take this to shock you?"

Raking a hand through silky scarlet waves, he tugged her in for a kiss so erotic, they lost track of where they were until friction from her gyrating had him straining against his khakis and her a hair from… Her lips parted as bliss shivered. She whispered in his ear, "My red lacy panties are soaked."

Uncomfortably turned on, Tiberius vowed, "I'm going to spank you so hard for that."

Catching sight of Laird, she smiled. *The ball of yarn was flying through the air. Time to drug pirates for a sexy agent.*

Dismounting her aroused co-conspirator, Lexy danced into writhing patrons on the dance floor, luring, "Come grind me, Mr. Aries." *She meant come find me. Still works.* She glanced back at her biting a knuckle turned on partner in debauchery. Laird's eyes were on her. Planning on pushing her luck much further, she danced to the table of men by the band. Taking an empty seat like she owned the place, all eyes turned to her. "Cool band," Lexy said, removing lipstick from her cleavage. She coloured her palms under the table and slipped it back in her bra, revealing, "I didn't want to carry a purse all night."

"What else have you got in there?" A guy flirted, leaning in.

Touching his muscular arm, she switched subjects, "You've been working out." Her eyes darted around the table as she questioned, "Which one of you is the strongest?"

A guy with a handlebar moustache on the other side of the table said, "Me."

"Arm wrestle me," Lexy insisted, scooting closer on a chair. They held hands, put their elbows on the table and began. She gave him a run for his money but let him win. After allowing the next one a victory, she sighed, "I owe you shots." She ordered a tray of vodka shots and did one with the guys, then dumped one in a napkin to clean her palms. *That was easy.* She wandered back to Tiberius and Brock, announcing, "I need to work out."

"Brock's yacht is three berths from ours. He told me about this secluded beach where the locals party. Feel like checking it out tomorrow?" Her pretend hubby asked.

Meeting Brock's intrigued gaze, she said, "Only if I can have a rematch."

"They outweigh you by 100 lbs," he laughed, entertained.

She revealed, "I wasn't trying."

Grinning, Brock toyed, "Try me."

"What do I win?" The crimson-haired Dragon of Ankh flirted, leaning in.

Fascinated by her, Brock chuckled, "What do you want?"

"I'd like to get wasted and fight all of you on the beach tomorrow," she persisted.

Chuckling, he looked at Tiberius, asking, "Is she crazy?"

Grinning, Tiberius replied, "Certifiable." Leaning closer to her, her pretend hubby whispered, "What are you doing?"

"If you want me to enjoy myself, play along," Lexy poked.

Scootching closer, Brock put his elbow on the table. He opened his hand, humouring her, "I'm ready."

"It's going to be embarrassing when I beat you," Lexy smack talked, taking his hand. The arm wrestling began. Barely trying, she slammed his down, provoking, "We have a date on the beach tomorrow, Laird."

Tiberius sighed, "I can't take her anywhere."

"Sexy and dangerous. I love it. You must tell me your love

story," the debonair stranger pressed, watching her every move as predator's do.

With no idea what she was up to, Tiberius dared, "Go ahead, Honey. Tell him."

"I tried to kill him. He was unexpectedly limber. We fell in lust," she regaled, maintaining eye contact.

Fascinated, Brock probed, "You believe you can take all my men?"

"With my hands tied behind my back," she provoked.

"We'll both anchor our yachts at the beach I told your other half about tomorrow. I'm thinking about investing in your husband's company. You can fight my men while we chat. Two birds, one stone."

And just like that, they'd planned their own abduction. She was having the best time. The Aries Group Agents were gone. They chatted and drank. *The lace was itchy.* She stealthily removed her panties and kicked them under the table. The band began a slow one. *She loved this song.*

Extending a hand, Tiberius tempted, "Dance with me, Mrs. Aries."

With the band singing a sexy rendition of 'No One,' they strolled onto the dance floor. As they embraced, she recalled swearing they'd never dance together. He'd responded, you will. Calling her bluff incited irrational lust, confusion, and now, the humility of knowing he was right. *In under a month, she'd gone from never in a million years to blowing up her afterlife for him. For this feeling. No rules, and no shame. They couldn't last but it didn't matter. They were beautiful, intoxicating, dangerous, and necessary.* Melting into each other with perfect lyrics, she whispered, "I may have done something bad."

He dipped her, teasing, "As expected."

Hovering, their eyes met with promise. Swooping her into his arms, they danced in the dreamlike ethereal glow of stars and lanterns, enraptured until their song ended. Neither could move, captivated by desire stronger than the gravitational pull of the moon drawing waves to shore.

Gazing into her eyes, he confessed, "I knew..."

She silenced sentiment with a kiss. As their lips parted, he understood. *They were lovers of chaos. An attempt at more than this sweet escape would be madness.* Music blared as the band took a break. Without missing a beat, he twirled her and reeled her back in as the night morphed into a hedonistic free for all.

Naughtily grinding, he whispered against her hair, "I'm going to bend you over the bow of our yacht and defile you."

He made her libido scream. She baited, "The beach is closer."

Feathering hot kisses on her neck, he chuckled, "Let's head back to the yacht before they speed up our timeline. Brock hasn't taken his eyes off you."

Glancing at the table, Lexy grinned. *He found her underwear. They should go. They couldn't fit a kidnapping into their illicit schedule until tomorrow evening.* Waving at her kidnapper, she wandered away with click, click, clicking of heels like clinking chains on a rollercoaster. Her reckless heart soared as they ran down the path onto the white sand beach.

Walking under a starry sky to music, he said, "Letting his guys win, then beating him was psychopath triggering genius."

"Hope he brings his chainsaw," she bantered.

"You get me," he sighed, dreamily smiling her way.

She was so into him. How did she let this happen? As they strolled on the wooden dock, he slipped his arm around her. Trusting he'd guide her footsteps, her traitorous heart peered over the mountain-sized wall that kept her eternally Grey's.

Grinning as they meandered towards their luxury booty call murder spree cruise, he teased, "I feel like a jerk for not mentioning it but I'm catching some of your inner dialogue. If kidnapping you twice this week hasn't made it clear, I'm into you too. Being into each other is an unfortunate side effect of spectacular sex. Reality will hit us. We'll be back to trying to murder each other in no time."

With electricity in the air as they reached the ramp, she turned back, admitting, "I should have given you the benefit of doubt after what you did for Kayn."

"What are we talking about?" He asked, flirtatiously walking her backwards onto the yacht.

"Slitting your throat was less about what you did and more about being caught with emotions," she confessed as he backed her against the door.

"I know," Tiberius answered, playing with a crimson strand of hair.

She whispered, "Are we alone?"

"Does it matter?" He dared, hiking up her dress.

Nothing mattered.

Caressing her, he groaned, "No underwear. Baby, we're doing this right here."

Wide-eyed as he rubbed her into submission, she didn't care who saw. Muffling whimpers of pleasure with a sensual kiss, he undid his shorts, picked her up and roughly took her against the door until she cried out with knee-trembling rapture. In a lusty hedonistic haze, they moved their illicit hookup to the bedroom. She tore off his shirt in a passionate frenzy. He shoved her on the bed. Sitting with her legs crossed awaiting his reaction, she provoked, "Heels on or off?"

Locking the door, Tiberius chuckled as he saw her, toying, "Leave those on." Without his eyes leaving hers, he dropped his shorts, seducing, "I've been dying to tear that dress off all night."

Shimmying up on red satin, he grabbed a blade off the dresser. She squirmed with anticipation.

"Shall we feed your Healing ability and whatever else shows up," he taunted. Straddling her, he sliced the material grazing her breast.

A thin line of red healed as he ripped her dress off, leaving her naked before him. He licked the blood off her chest as she gasped. *He was so crazy. She loved it.*

He tormented, "Did you like that?"

Aching for more, she directed, "Do it again."

"You're a Guardian. Tell me what you want," he whispered with the blade on her chest.

"Cut me deeper," she baited. He sliced with more pressure. Heat surged as he buried his face between her thighs mixing two intense deviances like an artist as she writhed on satin. He cut her again as his tongue simultaneously detonated a sheet clutching climax. As her breathing slowed, their eyes met.

Climbing up, he kissed her lips, chuckling, "I'm getting off so fast after watching that."

"We have all night," she said, touching his hair, looking into his eyes. "How come you didn't use your ability to see into our Brock's past?"

"I didn't want to wreck the time we have," he disclosed. "I suspect his memory is all violent visuals. I bring it with me."

"You read mine at the Summit," she reminded.

Caressing her hair with the depth of his emotions in his eyes, he confessed, "I wanted to know you."

"Why?" She asked, genuinely curious.

Kissing her cheek, he whispered, "I coveted you. I wanted to know why you went with Grey instead of me the day we met."

She whispered, "Did you find what you were looking for?"

"Information is fed to me over time. I've been dreaming of you and Grey for months from your point of view. As much as I want to hate the guy, I can't now," he whispered, gazing into her eyes.

Revealing weakness was laying your soul bare. Enamoured by his confession, she said, "Promise you'll never hurt him again."

"I'll never personally hurt him," he vowed, kissing her head.

Snuggling against his chest, she whispered, "I'll know you still care if you don't."

Stroking her hair, he whispered, "That's not fair. How am I supposed to know you still care?"

"I'll think of something," she pledged, kissing his chest.

"We're enemies, fighting isn't optional," Tiberius whispered caressing her hair.

Tilting her face, she offered, "I'll kill you quickly."

Laughing, he rolled her on top of him, teasing, "I'll kill you quickly."

Straddling him with crimson locks cascading over freckled ivory shoulders, she said, "You can try."

Gazing up, he touched her breast, sighing, "This would have been so much easier if you came with me the first time."

"You won't have to kidnap me next time," she whispered.

"I didn't have to this time," he revealed.

Fascinated, she whispered, "What did you mean by that?"

With knowing eyes, Tiberius disclosed, "The Dragon wants me too."

Pinning him to the mattress, she stated, "The Dragon doesn't want anything."

"You beat the snot out of me like last time until I tapped out, and said, I give up. Fuck me or kill me, Lexy."

Shaking her head, she decreed, "The Dragon wouldn't give a shit."

"I'll show you," he said, touching her arm.

In a blink, she was on the receiving end of a Dragon asskicking from his perspective, trying to get through to her until he was pinned. As the beast who cared for no one raised her blade, his dirty flirtation lured emotion out. He severed their connection, but she caught the gist of it. *The Dragon backed down. She'd let him live twice.* Shaking her head, she whispered, "This isn't good."

"We won't last past this adventure," he affirmed.

With their eyes locked in a game of chicken, she knew it was bullshit. "If you tell Grey I went willingly, I'll kick your ass."

Ticklishly sketching something on her abdomen, he toyed, "What if I need my ass kicked? I'm a bit of an asshole."

He was. She loved it. She sighed, "I'm serious."

"I have to lull you into a sense of complacency before I use my Dragon seduction skills for nefarious things. I'm the villain of this story," he teased drawing a heart with his finger.

"I'm not sure you're the villain anymore," she sparred, pretending she didn't know he'd written the word love.

Done pushing her limits, he chuckled, "Good to know my bedroom skills can still blind a lady of reason."

A lady. She hadn't been called that in a while. Nobody had ever accused her of using reason. Enjoying being with him, she said, "I don't remember getting into your car."

"Turning you on was easy. Getting you into the car was not. Orin helped me wrangle you. Jenna gave you a time out. Does that help?"

That had to be fun for Orin.

"I'd feel special if I didn't know the Dragon also has a soft spot for Orin," he toyed, lounging beside her.

Leaving out the drunk dial, she decided his gifts were endearing enough to mention, "How can you compete with someone who gifts a sleeping girl cookies and a feral beach cat?"

"I have to step it up if my competition for your affection is taking this full backwoods romance," he chuckled.

"He doesn't have a yacht," she countered. Shutting down the game with a sensual kiss, they picked up where they left off in a lusty blur of kisses and caresses for rapturous hours.

Stirring in his arms, she cracked her eyes open. *He was looking at her.*

Tiberius enquired, "Hungry?"

"Starving," she confessed.

"Let's grab a snack from the kitchen and go up on the deck to look at the stars," he suggested.

She leapt up and checked out the closet. Her agent friend

bought out a beach vender. She put on a long baggy t-shirt. and followed him out barefoot. Wandering down the stairs into the kitchen with faint music from someone else's boat. *What was this song again?*

He turned on the light and opened the fridge, asking, "What are you craving?"

"You," she provoked, cupping his ass.

Glancing back, he chuckled, "They're in the next room."

"Dangerous," she whispered, biting his shoulder.

Grinning, as he checked out a cupboard, he put a jar of peanut butter on the counter. They made sandwiches, grabbed drinks and went upstairs.

Opening the door to blaring music, Lexy said, "Laird didn't invite us to his party."

"It's a mystery," he laughed, leaning on the railing under a magical ceiling of stars.

Enjoying a peanut butter sandwich, listening to the ruckus a few berths away, they moved to the music.

With breath on her skin, he taunted, "I sent a thank you to Grey. Enjoying the hedonism resort. Thanks for being cool with it."

Bullshit. "Must you always provoke me?" She sighed, gazing at the moon.

Leaning on the railing, Tiberius said, "Acting like you hate someone is easier than wanting what you can't have."

This intimacy might leave a mark.

Chuckling, he massaged her hand.

"You're good at that," Lexy complimented, meeting his eyes.

He toyed, "I'm good at a lot of things."

"You are," she confirmed.

Kissing her hand, he said, "No one gets a pass but Grey. I'll still tear your friends arms off for being lippy."

"Venting happens," she replied.

"You fascinate me. I tell you I want to rip off a friend's arm, and you say, venting happens," he chuckled.

Grinning, Lexy sparred, "I'm not judgey. I've ripped off a few arms in my time."

"They're always so surprised," he bantered, smiling.

She replied, "Right?"

A chainsaw revved. *It was a small boat.*

Embracing her, Tiberius chuckled, "Thought the shit show was starting early."

"I'll volunteer tomorrow," she offered. "I'm a Healer."

"If we skip grand gestures, I might get out of this with my ego intact," he whispered with choppy water sloshing against the yacht.

Gazing into his magnetic eyes swaying to music with arms laced around his neck, she wanted to tell him, he'd changed her forever.

Sentiment squashing, he picked her up, declaring, "I haven't bent you over the bow yet." Carrying her there, cat calls and outdated slurs prompted him to turn around, sighting, "Too many leering eyes, Mrs. Aries."

Yearning for him, she seduced, "Take me too bed, Mr Aries."

"I'm calling you Mrs. Aries forever," he whispered.

"I'm kicking your ass either way," she toyed, laughing as he struggled to open the door.

With passion so intense clothes were shed in a frantic blur, they naughtily instructed each other. Free of modesty in a gasp, they were lost in unspeakable acts, fulfilling darkest desires. Vigorous thrusts heightened squeals of delight as clutches and claw marks intensified moans. Giving themselves to each other with no boundaries, they were deviants, triggering climaxes so mind blowing neither silenced their screams until they exhausted themselves and heavy eyelids flickered shut.

Awakening on top of him with sunlight flowing through

sheer curtains, his chest rose and fell with their bodies fused. *She'd never woken up like this before.* He was out cold beneath her, but ready to go so she picked up where they left off.

"You're insatiable Mrs. Aries," he gasped, moving with her. Squinting in sunlight, he raspily instructed, "Harder."

She could wake up like this every day. She cried out as euphoria shivered through her.

Clutching her hips, he urged, "Don't stop. This is my best wakeup call ever."

Someone knocked on the door. *Shit.*

With the widest smile, he shouted, "Ten more minutes!"

"It's past eleven, you've slept away half of your day. Brunch is ready. Put on your swimsuits. It's time to work. Their boat just left. We're going for a cruise," one of the agent's explained.

"My wife made arrangements to kick everyone's asses later this afternoon," Tiberius called back.

Lexy swatted him. *Asshole.*

He chuckled, "We'll be right out."

Lexy slipped on her dress and grabbed her bikini.

He scolded, "Don't you dare leave me like this."

Laughing, she peered out the door. *The hall was empty.*

"No, come back," he groaned.

Glancing back, Lexy provoked, "We should shower," darting to the washroom.

Grabbing his suit, he chased her in there. Melting into each other, passionately making out, he backed her into the shower and took her against the wall without games.

Holding her captive in the aftermath, he gasped, "Reality was bound to show up to wreck the fantasy."

She was too wrapped up in him. This was a job. Ridding her mind of craziness, as he put her down. Her feet contacted solid tile. She joked, "It was fun while it lasted."

Caressing her jawline, he implored, "Don't leave me yet. I need this like air. Be my wife until the job is over. I've been floating through half a century alone in every way that counts."

He was asking her to leave herself exposed.

He kissed her cheek, prompting, "Breakfast is getting cold."

They quickly showered and got ready. He walked out of the washroom, revealing, "I may have suggested a breakfast based on your memories."

He held the door open. She walked out. They strolled over to the table. Grinning as he pulled out her seat, she lifted a silver lid. *Eggs Benny.* She teased, "What happened to skipping the grand gestures?"

"That guy realised he was an idiot," he replied, pouring her a coffee. He slid the creamer closer.

He had to stop being wonderful.

Breathing salty ocean air with the sun shining, they ate and drank coffee enjoying the ride. A phone started ringing. They glanced at the pile of towels. Rifling through them, Lexy answered, "Hello."

"We need your itinerary. Please text it back so the captain has directions," the agent answered.

She passed the phone to Tiberius, instructing, "He wants us to text our itinerary." *She was more a fly by the seat of her pants, less premeditation.*

An agent came out with a carafe of coffee. Silently refilling their cups, he left a note on the table and promptly walked away.

It read. *Deck may be bugged, stay in character.* Other boats were specks in the distance. Someone turned on club music.

Grinning, Tiberius got up, and said, "Dance with me, Mrs. Aries."

Taking his hand, he tugged her into his arms. Romantically swaying, he playfully nibbled her ear, confessing, "Bending you over the bow is all I can think of."

Now, it was all she could think of. "What's stopping you," she provoked. Her traitorous heart fluttered as they erotically kissed, vaguely aware of witnesses as their titillating game heated with each heartbeat.

Someone returned with champagne. Hitting pause, Tiberius hugged her tightly, whispering, "I always knew we'd be like this."

With her arms laced around his neck, she met his eyes, probing, "Always? You've spent decades provoking me."

"I wanted you. You couldn't see it. I understand that now. When I caressed your thigh before the Summit, it turned you on. I've never been on the receiving end of a miracle. You were all I could think about after that," he confessed in her ear.

She couldn't deny it. She didn't fall into his arms, she leapt. It was worth it. His hand on her spine, nudged her to misbehave as waves jostled the boat. *She was going to hit repeat on the song that was playing until it drove her mad reminiscing this.* Teal sea sloshed as the yacht sped up. Lost in each other, they danced barefoot with breeze tussling hair under a sapphire sky. Resting her head on his shoulder, Lexy closed her eyes.

He caressed her hair, whispering, "Our fantasy is coming to an end a tad early. That's our friend's yacht."

Regaining control, Lexy stepped away, suggesting, "Let's have champagne." Feeling his eyes on her, she saucily swayed her hips strutting away. "That's the cove we're supposed to meet at," she said, stretching out on a lounge chair.

"It certainly looks like it," her partner in crime responded. Grinning, Tiberius popped the bubbly.

Squinting in sunshine, as he passed her a flute of golden champagne, she sighed, "I could get used to this."

"Every vacation from reality has to end," he said, laying on his lounge chair.

He was right. They couldn't want each other after this.

Their eyes met as he bartered, "Maybe we'll find our way back here someday?"

Pretending it was possible, she whispered, "Stranger things have happened."

Squirting coconut oil in his hand, he went through mortal motions of oiling her up as an excuse to keep touching her as one of the agents placed a tray of meat, cheese and fruit between them with a note. *They caught our agents last night. We opted to carry on with the plan versus intervening. It's what they would have wanted. We have no way of knowing what you're walking into. They may not know who you are.* Neither reacted as they read it. She hadn't seen their mutual agent friend today.

Tiberius got up, saying, "I need to use the washroom, Sweetheart."

Thinking about the woman they admired, she watched him go. *That's why they were here at lunchtime instead of late afternoon. Being here didn't mean the game would be played differently, it just meant they had to reign their emotions in until it was time to reveal who they were. She was a weapon. A tornado released to vanquish the damned. She wanted to turn off her emotions. Why did they have to get in the way? Damn it. They had to save her now.* Lexy got up and followed him inside. *He wasn't in their room.* She peered into each one searching for the rest until she entered the galley. They were in the safe room. She pressed the button. A screen lit up and she saw her reflection. The door opened. She slipped into a heated conversation. The door shut. Tiberius continued reprimanding them for not telling him immediately. There were only two agents. She interrupted, "What do we know?"

One of the Aries Group Agents explained, "They went aboard to plant tracking devices. Scanton set off his, Agent Clarke hasn't set off hers."

Recalling their kiss outside of the washroom, Lexy decreed, "She wanted them to take her. She's saving it for the second location. We'll play out this newlywed adventure like we have no clue. I'll fight his men. Tiberius will have his fake business meeting. Shut yourselves in the safe room so we don't have to worry about anyone sneaking aboard to take you out."

Unable to tell him what she was capable of in front of mortal ears, she met Tiberius' concern, assuring, "I have this." *What were mortals going to do to her? Being dismembered was just going to piss her off.*

Looking at the agents, Tiberius directed, "When the shit hits the fan, eject. If we get in over our head, Tri-Clan will show up. We'll call for clean-up."

"We've gathered intel. This island was purchased for thirty-five million two years ago by Iris Basilisk. We have no record of that name. We have the satellite feed from this morning. There's a bay on the other side with five yachts, a gated mansion, and approximately eight luxury cabins scattered throughout the jungle."

She'd assumed it was a deserted island. Lexy commented, "Guess they aren't concerned about witnesses?"

Pointing at a still shot, the agent explained, "There's miles of jungle between this cove and everything else. Let them take you. If they sedate you, please pretend."

Smiling, Lexy clarified, "I've done sketchier things on a Wednesday out of boredom."

"What is that?" Tiberius enquired, pointing at a hint of colour in the jungle.

"Flowers, a flock of birds maybe?" The agent replied. "Find out after the job is finished."

These mortals thought they had control over how they did things. Cute. "We'll find your people and make sure the punishment fits the crime," Lexy affirmed, smiling.

"Take the cooler with you. Nobody leaves for an afternoon without drinks and snacks. Don't forget towels and we left bags on your bed with a change of clothes," the mortal instructed.

True.

20
Hunting Party

*A*bruptly leaving the agents to plan their strategy, Lexy said, "I should change." Wandering back, she whispered, "They aren't going to save themselves and leave, are they?"

"Not a chance," Tiberius confirmed. "They should have told us they were taken last night."

Entering their room in silence, she wanted to say something to settle his nerves but couldn't. *If she knew too much, surviving this job wouldn't alter her lifespan.* Putting on fight worthy attire over her swimsuit, Lexy clarified, "Are we allowing the scourge of humanity to torture us?"

"I'd rather avoid it. If I can get close enough to deep dive into their leader's head, I'll know what they're planning. We can play it by ear once we know where they hold their captives," Tiberius answered. "Either way, every witness has to be Corrected."

He heard her thoughts. "Where does Triad draw the line with the Aries Group?" Lexy probed, plucking fluff off his shirt.

Grinning, he admitted, "Killing them is frowned upon, not out of the question."

"I'm sure they'll be stoked when they watch this recording later," Lexy sparred, as her eyes wandered to the luxurious bed they'd destroyed.

"She wouldn't let them record us," he decreed, trusting his friend.

"Are you sure? They may replay our greatest hits at their Christmas Party" Lexy enticed, trying to distract him. When he didn't bite, empathy surfaced, "She has plenty of espionage tricks up her sleeve. She's capable of taking care of herself until we bust her out."

"She's emotionally involved and that's when you make mistakes," he countered.

Unable to help it, Lexy took her distraction tactic down another lane, "She was my first mortal kiss."

Shoving clothes into a bag, he chuckled, "She's going to love that."

Watching him pack, she knew his faith was wavering.

"No point in leaving anything on a boat destined to sink," he replied. "We'll hide our bags on the island." Picking up her crumpled dress, he whispered, "I'm going to have so many fantasies about dancing with you in this dress."

"How could anyone top a murder vacation at a hedonism resort?" Lexy teased, stretching. Cracking her neck, she did a few lunges.

"Limbering up before your murder spree. Smart," Tiberius chuckled. "Hate to pull a hamstring, dismembering someone."

"Heard I grew a limb back in minutes. I'm not sure pulling hamstrings will be an issue anymore. Better safe than sorry," Lexy revealed, smiling.

"That's why you volunteered for chainsaw duty," he teased, walking out.

"I don't know how to switch abilities yet," she confessed, following him.

Strolling onto the deck, Tiberius explained, "It's the same as your Healing ability. You want to heal someone, so you can. Chainsaw torture sucks." Bending over in front of her to lower the small boat, he added, "Make it bounce off me, and I'll owe you one."

He had a sexy ass. "One what?" She teased as he turned to face her.

"We'll figure out a repayment plan," he toyed. "I'll shove you into a closet and bury my face between your legs while our Clans fight until you purr like a kitten."

Flushed with parted lips, she forgot what they were doing. *He turned her on in a crazy way.*

"Keep looking at me like that and I'm peeling your shorts off with my teeth right now," he seduced. Snatching her bag, he tossed it into the boat below.

They had good people to save and bad ones to kill. She had to get her shit together. As their eyes met, she vowed, "After this job is done, I'm going to wreck you."

Shaking his head, he climbed over the railing, confessing, "You already have."

Following him down the ladder, she noted they were on the other side of the boat hidden from prying island eyes but knew they had to hit pause on their rendezvous. Helping her into the boat, waves jostled them against each other. *This time together was going to be difficult to see past.*

Grinning, Tiberius bantered, "Sit before we fall overboard."

Waterlogged wasn't a sexy look for anyone. Taking a seat as the engine started, their small rumbling boat approached the white sand beach of what might be the most beautiful place on Earth. Surrounding the white sand mecca was a lush emerald jungle bursting with sweet flora. Intoxicating perfume on warm inviting ocean breeze, luring in those arriving by sea.

Leaping out, he towed them to shore. Colourful starfish were strewn in the shallows. *She could bring the beauty of this place with her to the in-between. Think about him with the perfect backdrop. Nothing evil could happen in the most beautiful destination, she'd ever seen.* Getting out to help, they towed the tiny boat up into the bushes past the driftwood markers for high tide. They set up a romantic picnic on towels.

With her toes in warm sand, she peeled seaweed off her thighs, and tossed it by a rock. Crabs scurried away. Their kidnappers were anchored just offshore down the beach.

Taking her hands, he towed her to him, flirting, "Strip down to your bikini and lay on that towel. I'll oil you up and give you the best massage you've ever had."

With a saucy smirk, Lexy took off her top. Crimson locks trickled over her shoulders concealing her chest as she stepped out of her shorts. Coyly peering up, he was watching every move she made. Turning away from him, she sprawled on her stomach in the sunshine. He placed fruit in front of her and filled her glass with wine. "The Aries Group is spoiling us," she commented, smiling.

Straddling her, he flirted, "What's a little dismemberment if they have good snacks?"

"Exactly," she replied, serious.

Chuckling, he saucily tugged the strings on the back of her bikini and squirted oil all over her lower back, saying, "Play along, my love."

Love, obsession, wicked deviance, destroyer of afterlife peace. Biting her bottom lip as he kneaded her into submission, hardening against her. She sighed his name. His finger shifted her bottoms aside and slid into her. Clutching her glass, she gasped. Ration dissipated as he pleasured her.

"Let's fix this tension so we can focus," Tiberius raspily suggested.

Teetering on the edge, there was no need to agree. She'd follow him into a volcano to finish this.

Abruptly stopping, he tied her top, saying, "There's privacy where we left our bags." He leapt up and took off.

Scrambling up, she chased her partner in debauchery across warm silken sand into the bushes. He snatched her into his arms. Laughing as he nuzzled her neck and kissed her throat, her heart surged with joy. With the overwhelming desire to spill her guts, she kissed him, seducing him with her tongue. Sliding a hand into his shorts, he was rigid. *He was a hedonistic rollercoaster on pleasure island. She wanted to go again even if there was no seatbelt. They were destined to veer off the tracks and go up in flames, but it didn't matter. Nothing did. Just this unfiltered lusty free for all. She was enjoying him... Too much.* Succumbing to the whirlwind of kisses and caresses, as he whispered his desires, made her want more. With an undeniable urge to make afterlife tanking declarations, she pulled away. *He felt it too. This time together didn't tie up loose ends, it over stoked the fire. Their worlds would go up in flames if they didn't leave this fling here.* Panicked, they gazed into each other's eyes. For a breath, they were star-crossed lovers.

Smiling, Tiberius cautioned, "Don't. We can't say it."

She didn't. They couldn't. Shoving her feelings down into the muck where they belonged, she said, "Do me before they show up to murder us." Eyes crinkled as they both cracked up.

He tugged her bikini string, confessing, "I'm so into you." Taking off his shorts with a squirm worthy visual, he sat on the ground and leaned back. Enraptured as she mounted his lap, he groaned, "Lexy."

Blinded by euphoria, they succumbed to what couldn't be denied. As entangled thrusting bodies broiled into a molten implosion, she whimpered his name.

"Lexy," he gasped. "Coming," he groaned.

"Twenty seconds," she whispered, quickening the pace.

"They're coming," he rushed, laughing.

Glancing back, *they were coming. Shit. She was so close.* He bit her neck, thrusting into her. Splintering into icy hot tingling shivers of ecstasy, she cried out. Their worshiping gazes locked in awe.

His wicked eyes glinted in the sun as he boldly licked her blood off his lips, whispering, "Duty calls. Pause this bump and grind until half time."

They scrambled into their swimsuits. Putting on her shirt, she tugged on her shorts, and kissed his lips, saying, "Thanks hubby."

"I'd never leave my wife wanting," he vowed, picking up the cooler. They strolled back to their towels. "Thirsty honey?" Tiberius enquired, offering to top up her wine.

She snatched the bottle out of his hand and drank from it. Aware he was watching, her thoughts travelled to just killing everyone and staying on this island until the need for him subsided. *How did she get swept away in a torrid affair with Tiberius? This was insane. It was the most fun she'd ever had.*

Grinning, he suggested, "Brush the sand off before they get here."

She peered down at the sand spackled to coconut oil. *Crap.* Realising wiping it off was pointless, she snatched the oil, saying, "It's only fair." Spraying him as he laughed fending her off. Wrestling in sand until he pinned her, their eyes darted to the hum of approaching conversation. She sighed, "We have company."

Shifting a crimson wave off her face, he went in for a kiss, enticing her with his deviant tongue until shadows loomed. Tiberius teased, "Honeymoon pause, it's business time. Play nice. Don't kill anyone."

Resisting the urge to smile, she bantered, "No promises."

"Funny," their host decreed, overhearing their exchange.

Grinning, Lexy bid them adieu, "Have fun chatting about boring shit." Neither one turned back as they walked away, leaving her with too many rough weathered men. Repressed emotions from the dark vault, hollowed her throat, tickling her lungs. *These are mortals. You're Guardian. Get your shit together. She needed to kick someone's ass.* Standing up, her gaze travelled the dim-witted herd of muscle-bound henchmen, as she tempted, "Which one of you wants your ass kicked first?"

"I'll go," a burly guy with the swagger of someone who went down on the first punch offered as the others surrounded the pair.

With the agility of a goddess, Lexy mirrored his every move, baiting, "You must be the stupid one?"

"I'm confident I can take you," he sparred cockily jogging in a circle.

Grinning, she ceased moving. "Come at me," the crimson-haired warrior provoked. Each time he swung, she ducked. Manoeuvring out of the way of every leg swipe and uncoordinated kick. He went down on the first punch. They came at her in a steady stream of ineptitude, as she paid extra close attention to who watched and who fought. Gaging skill level, she wore out his posse, announcing, "I could use a drink."

Grabbing what they wanted from their coolers, she opted for her own, knowing drugging was the go-to method. Being impervious to it was a red flag. Uncorking wine, she drank the bottle, provoking, "Are you professional muscle?"

"We work for a cut of our take," a man with a silky floral print shirt, confessed. "You have skills. Asking to fight us was a strange request."

She shrugged, surveying the crowd of men with dancing eyes clutching blades. *Even a mortal would be suspicious. She was going to erect a severed penis Stonehenge on this beach if any of these assholes got handsy.* "Practice," she replied. Everyone pointed guns at her. *Guess they weren't pretending to be friends anymore?* Taking a swig of wine, Lexy sighed, "You're only going to piss me off with those."

Intrigued by her lack of fear, floral shirt guy said, "We've been instructed to bring you back to the compound to take part in the festivities. Our boss wants a rematch."

With a hint of mockery, she under reacted, "Oh, no. Can I bring the wine?"

"Fill your boots," he quipped. Knitting his brow.

Roughly clutching her arm, another guy ordered, "Walk!"

Fine. Rolling her eyes, Lexy sighed, "If I must." A revving chainsaw and pitchy shrieks drew her eyes to the yacht. *Shitty deal.* She chuckled.

"No concern for your husband?" The man holding her arm baited.

"Que Sera Sera," she toyed, smiling.

"I like you. Hope we keep you as a pet," he chuckled.

"I'm too bitey to be domesticated," she bantered. Someone shoved her. She stumbled forward livid. *Eyes on the prize. She couldn't pluck anyone's toenails out yet, but she was going to start with that asshole.* Harnessing Guru Grey, she used her inner dialogue to talk the Dragon down, *be calm. Be chill. What do you smell? Flowers with sweet nectar. Now, she needed to find something beautiful.* Watching parrot's wings flapping as they fled their jungle trail intrusion, she smiled. *Those flowers really did smell incredible. What were they called again? They were at lots of resorts. Her mind was drawing a blank. Didn't they find it weird that she just let them kidnap her after kicking their asses? They were impressively dumb.*

Towing her through the jungle with wine sloshing in the bottle and a trail of men following her, one probed, "Why aren't you scared?"

"Of what?" Lexy baited.

"It'll be entertaining to watch you give seasoned pros a run for their money," he commented with his footsteps crunching on the path.

Had they stumbled into a heathen's fight club? Won't they be in for a treat?

One interrogated, "What are you?"

Sketchy.

He demanded, "Speak!"

"You're all sand fleas in comparison," Lexy taunted. *She*

was enjoying this conversation. He yanked her. She dropped the wine. *Damn it. She was going to drink that.*

"You want to be sober," one of her kidnapper's advised.

Wanna bet? Frustrated, she glanced back at her wine bottle on the trail. Listening for chainsaws and screams, there was silence. A tarp was concealing something on the trail. A man tugged it off. *Nice, a Jeep.* She provoked, "Are we going on a safari adventure?"

"Get in," he prompted, opening the door. He placed a hood over her head, explaining, "Not seeing anything helps your survival odds."

She didn't need help. The engine purred as they pulled away. Listening to tires on uneven terrain, she recalled the satellite images of a compound on the other side of the island and scattered cabins in the jungle. *There was no point in counting the minutes, she'd always been shitty at gaging time.* When the tires hit a smooth surface, her stomach cramped. *Demons.* The cover was pulled off her head as they coasted up to a fantasy mansion. *She could eat.*

The door was opened. Stepping out onto broiling cement barefoot, pain tapered her murdery vibe. *She was supposed to play nice until she knew what they were up against.* Walking through double doors into a wide hallway it looked like a hotel, she was ushered into an enclosed exotic courtyard. There was a small bridge over an interwoven creek with koi and hanging floral masterpieces. Laird Brock was sitting at a table. *How did he beat her here?*

Standing, her captor greeted her, "You're confused. My twin is at the boat. I'm Ivan. Sit. Let's get to know each other."

Smiling, Lexy sat across the metal table, toying, "So, this was a planned kidnapping?"

"I prefer surprise visit," Ivan sparred.

That was almost witty. Lexy probed, "Is my husband safe?"

"For now," the duplicate of Laird baited. Inquisitively

cocking his head, Ivan enquired, "I'd imagine you have questions."

"There's something sketchy happening later," she revealed. "You want me to take part or join you?" *She was queasy.*

"Close enough," he toyed. "You're hot and you can fight. Sexy badasses are my type."

"I'm married," she sparred. "Do I get points for coming willingly?"

"I appreciate you not killing my men. I'll need them later," he replied, motioning to a fancy plate of cookies.

Only a complete dumbness takes food from a kidnapper. Crossing her legs, she interrogated, "Are you Abaddon?"

Without a twitch of concern, he revealed, "They're our largest contributor."

Plot twist. She asked, "Do they know I'm here?"

He probed, "Should they?"

Grinning, Lexy decreed, "You're going to get so many brownie points for bringing me to this party."

Casually eating Marzipan, Ivan enquired, "What breed of Second-Tier are you?"

He knew the lingo. She smiled.

Fascinated, he questioned, "What ability do you have?"

"It's complicated," she baited. *Oh, she was going to kill everyone.*

He cut the pretence, "We need Second-Tier blood to bind our entertainment to this island."

Shrugging, Lexy agreed, "You can have my blood if I get what I want."

"Agreed. Sign this," he said, passing a paper.

Signing a contract when demons were involved was always a horrible idea. She teased, "I don't have a pen."

"With your blood," Ivan clarified.

"No," she decreed.

"I don't need your permission," he bantered with a smirk.

"Yes, you do," Lexy cautioned. "Give me more details, then ask nicely."

"I'll show you. Come with me," he stood up. "I'll allow you to purchase your husband's freedom."

Allow. That was hilarious. "With what," she baited.

"We could use a sacrifice who can survive long enough to put on a show," he answered.

"Nefarious," she bantered, grinning. "So, you're kidnapping tourists for blood sacrifices?"

"It's complicated," he sparred.

"Try me," she mocked.

He enquired, "You spanked me arm wrestling last night. What gives you superhuman strength?"

Finding it humorous he thought a woman would need superhuman strength to beat him, she responded, "Kale."

"Sure, kale." He sighed, "Shall I cut to the chase?"

"Please do," she bantered.

"We have plans for an exclusive resort catering to a specific clientele. Do you want to have a torrid affair with an enemy? Is murder your secret thrill? Torture for others or maybe yourself? A room of men, pleasuring you, succumbing to your every whim. Women? Both? Anything your heart desires, I can make a reality," Ivan revealed like he was promoting a theme park.

Yes, yes, yes, maybe. "A resort where you can torture, murder or seduce people," she deduced, intrigued. *Sounds lovely.*

"Much more. You can book a murder spree like this event. We've captured high demand product. The bidding war should be exciting," he preened.

So many people to kill. She suggested, "I'd love to see this bidding war."

"That can be arranged," he replied, smiling.

She stopped walking as she saw a familiar apple tree. With her spine prickling, she stated, "That's not supposed to be here."

"Why?" he pressed, intently watching her reaction.

The garden morphed into a mirror image of an orchard. *Well played. The night she was kidnapped. These assholes had a powerful witch if they were able to tug a mortal memory from the night before that five-year long cesspool of depravity.* Her mind flitted back to languishing in stall 11. *Captives came and went, but a pliable runaway with no will or place to flee, did whatever she had to do to survive. Her priorities were food and water.* She got thirty minutes of sunlight when she left her stall to be fed on. It worked as a sunshine deterrent. *Understanding they purposely rid her of humanity to create a Dragon capable of surviving Immortal Testing, didn't stop the dark farm from being what summoned it. Idiots.* Unshakable, Lexy plucked an apple off a low hanging branch, saying, "I'd like to meet your talented witch." *To kill her.* Ice water pumped through her heart as she met his gaze.

His eyes narrowed, questioning, "Are you not seeing a treasured memory?"

If they were searching for a treasured mortal memory, they'd have nothing to work with. Happiness didn't enter her life until she met Grey. Recalling her Handler's smile softened her demeanour. "In theory," Lexy answered. As she wandered away the garden switched back to the fragrant display that lured her in.

Going inside, they entered a wide ivory stone hallway lined with hotel rooms. *The captives didn't appear to see them. One way glass. Soundproof rooms. Locked from the outside. Most locks could be disarmed with a surge of energy. Depleting her healing ability was risky. She had a sneaky suspicion this game she'd volunteered for was going to be next level.*

He gave her the tour, explaining, "Write down the numbers of who you want to save before my clients go shopping. Make me an offer. I'll decide if you're worth it."

An apex predator couldn't be coerced by sentiment but may play along if it amused her. "Alright." Looking into each room counting captives, she recognized the girl her agent crush was desperate to find. "I want the blonde in that room."

"Agreed," he answered.

Strolled past suites with unconscious people and a corpse in each, she asked, "What did you give them?"

As she passed rooms with numbered doors, Tiberius was sitting on the bed. Their agent friend was unconscious on the floor and the other one was body parts in a see thru plastic bag. Lexy said, "I want to speak to my husband."

Ivan questioned, "Is the girl your plaything too, or just his?"

"Ours," she fibbed without flinching.

"I'd appreciate those three being saved. I'll take whatever you need from me in return," she offered.

"Five minutes." He opened the door.

Playing the role to a tee, Lexy walked into her fake husband's embrace, whispering, "That mirrored wall is one way glass. Two alive and one dead in every room. They're about to take clients through to purchase captives for a macabre hunting game. Abaddon is involved. They know I'm not mortal. I've volunteered to be hunted in return for you two and Brenda. Get them out of here before it starts."

Tiberius whispered, "I'm not leaving this island without you."

"Why not? This might be therapeutic," she sparred, smiling.

"What if something eats you before I get back?" He countered, smiling.

"You'll gut monsters and look for my body parts while I have a slushy in the in-between," she answered.

Grinning, he flirted, "It's close to the perfect ending to our getaway. I don't want to miss the murder spree."

She asked, "Will our agent friend stay put if you hide them?"

"Not a chance," he whispered.

Lexy whispered, "Brenda isn't Aries Group. If Demons

show up, and she's involved, we're bound to put her down. No witnesses. Those are the rules."

"I can erase a slot of time. They may get off on a technicality. Did you see Brenda's husband, Theo?" He questioned.

"Three hostages for me was a stretch," Lexy said, meeting his gaze.

Cupping her face, Tiberius whispered, "If intimacy is his price, your answer is no. We'll find another way."

As the door to Tiberius' room opened, someone called out, "Stall 11!"

Funny. She would have her vengeance later. Smiling, Lexy left without responding. They ushered her out and the blonde she'd chosen in. A guard walked her back to the botanical fantasy. *She could shut it off once they were gone. Until then, she had to play along.* Strolling over to her host at the ornate metal table, she smiled.

"What do I get in return for taking three out of the game?" Her Captor enquired.

"Anything you want," she bartered, reaching out to touch a flowing vine.

"You'd remain here as my plaything?" He questioned, watching her.

"Yes," she confirmed, dead eyed.

"Deal." Picking up a CB, Ivan barked orders and left it on the table. Getting up, he prompted, "Follow."

This was too easy. Walking with him out of the garden into a narrow hall, she asked, "You're just going to let them leave?"

"Drugs will wipe out the last twenty-four hours. My men will drive your yacht back to the resort. We'll leave him with his plaything and a dear john letter. She'll mend his wounded heart," he wrapped up their goodbye with a bow.

"Perfect." She declared, "If there isn't a decent financial kickback, I'll be pissed. Show me the beast you're trying to bind to the island."

Intrigued by her dismissal of her old life, he probed, "How much of a beating can you withstand?"

"Why? Am I fighting monsters too? Hope there's a cage match involved, I have energy to burn off," she nonchalantly decreed.

His eyes narrowed. Gaging her reaction, he baited, "What if I said, you're fighting everything?"

Shrugging, she replied, "I'm not concerned."

"What are you?" He probed, touching her scarlet hair.

Recoiling inside, she shut it down. "You'll figure it out."

He held a door open. Overcome by nausea as pungent sulphur wafted out, Lexy entered the room where onyx smoke hovered over emissaries of evil seated at a massive circular table. *She might be willing to trade her life for an air freshener.* Predatory impulse snuffed out concern as her eyes darted to each bidder. *She was hungry.* Her stomach growled. *If her Guardian requirements snuffed out ration and she ate everyone, the jig was up.*

Pulling out a seat, her new boss instructed, "Sit. We're about to begin."

No one cared who she was.

Their host turned on a large screen, announcing, "Stall one. The opening bid is 50,000."

A life was worth 50,000. They raised signs as the bids grew until the occupants of stall one were bought by one man for 300,000. The screen switched to stall two. Bidding continued as she imprinted faces funding this depravity into her mind. As each stall flashed up, bidding began. When he finished stall 10, her hand tightened. *Had her trio been evacuated?* He skipped to stall twelve and carried on to 24. The screen flashed to cages in an open space with an assortment of creatures, gnashing teeth and tugging on bars, howling. *What was this?*

As paddles raised, she realised they were bidding on obstacles for their opponents to up the level of difficulty. *They needed her blood to magically bind these beasts to the island. It made sense now. They would need more blood than she had to spare. This was going to be so much fun.* Remaining silent as they rose and shook hands, patting each other's shoulders like they were hunting deer. The patrons looked through her.

Following as they left, the man in charge announced, "The hunt begins at sundown. There are no rules. See you at first light for the breakfast buffet."

When the room was empty, Ivan said, "Those caged beasts need to be bound to the island. We'll stop them short of killing contributors with shock collars."

"You had a witch summon a bunch of demons to add to the game?" Lexy clarified, moderately impressed.

A man came in with a tray, offering, "Hot chocolate?"

Cute. She was drugged with hot chocolate and kidnapped at eleven on a country road by an apple orchard. Too many coincidences. Squinting, Lexy refused, "No thanks." *It was possible the orchard was linked to the kidnapping incident in her memory. What else did they know?* Watching as he took one, she probed, "I'm curious. What do you think I am?"

Smiling, Ivan revealed, "You are strong with sketchy inhibitions. You fantasize about apple orchards and opt out of hot chocolate. You're a newlywed, pretending she doesn't care about her husband. Past trauma is weighing you down. How did I do?"

"You should moonlight as a roadside fortune teller," Lexy sparred, walking away with him.

"Secrets are currency," he teased. "We laced their champagne with psychedelic drugs to enhance their experience." They strolled into an open area of empty cages.

Impressed, she chuckled, "You got them to pay for hallucinations?"

"Pre-recorded holograms. You know cages can't hold real ones. We want them to maintain their sense of mastery."

Curious, she asked, "How does this work?"

"We bring the captives to the cabins. They have weapons

to defend themselves. Food, water and about a half hour to live," he disclosed.

This was dark even for her. "So, if they survive the night, they go back into the game?"

Ivan flirted, "No rules. No survivors. It's simpler that way. Are we going to have sex?"

That came out of left field. She laughed. He pressed a button. The floor slid away. Lexy plummeted into darkness, landing with a bone snapping thud. *Asshole!* She looked up.

He shouted, "I'm a shitty person! I lied! Your fake hubby and that sexy Aries Group agent are in a cabin in the jungle! Pretty sure, the blonde is possessed! If the serial killers don't catch them, they'll be slaughtered by monsters or her! You've got half an hour, Guardian spawn!"

As the floor above slid shut, light vanished. *Shit. Ego walked her right into this. Abaddon knew everything.* Snapped limbs broiled as her Healing ability worked magic. *The all-access pass threw her off. Leave your billionaire husband to come do sketchy shit for us. Will you be my bitch? Sure. Can I come watch you bid on people? No problem. A hick pirate trapped her in a cave under a mansion on a jungle island full of serial killers. Her afterlife was bullshit. Dethroning a King a few weeks ago was cool. This, was just embarrassing.* She got up. *She needed to see.* Night vision turned on. No details just black and white silhouettes. *Okay. She could find her way out of this. She was a Guardian.* Shaking her head at herself, she stopped walking as something tickled her hair. *No. She wasn't doing this.* Shivers crawled up her spine as she leapt away, looking back. Gigantic furry spiders were scurrying down webbing from the ceiling. *Nope.* Sprinting away, she ran off a ledge and splashed into water, submerging into murky depths. Something bumped into her. *For Fuck's Sake.* She fought her way to the surface as gigantic spiders soared on webbing towards her. *Nope.* Inhaling a deep breath, she dove under and swam against the currant praying instinct was right. Clutching the ledge, she forced her way through and surfaced as daylight ebbed in the jungle with vibrant tangerine and scarlet slashed across the sky. *She should get out of the water.* Something grabbed her leg. *Of course.* It tugged her under. With every speck of rage in her being, she willed it dead. It released its hold. Water whirled as she surfaced, inhaling fragrant jungle oxygen. *Much better.* She swam until she could touch and crawled onto a rock. *Awesome. She was going to be cold and wet all night. She was going to kick that inbred pirate's ass. Bet he didn't even have a twin. He fed her a line of bullshit and told her she could play.* She took off her top and wrung it out as she noticed creatures floating on the water. *Guess this was a thing.* Cracking her neck as she squeezed water from her hair, she noticed light through the foliage. *Was that a cabin? What were the chances?* She staggered as she began walking. *She'd used too much energy healing and killing whatever the hell those were. She had to eat something.* Branches cracked behind her. She stepped out of the way as a middle-aged mortal killer lunged at her with a machete.

With a cringe worthy grin, he said, "I've always had a soft spot for redheads."

She wasn't supposed to eat mortals. A freak with a rumbling chainsaw burst through the bushes, bounding their way. Lexy dove out of the way as her murder buddy got his arm lopped off, shrieking. *Handy.* Lexy cackled, sprinting away. Pushing through brush, she sensed she was being watched. The path was right there but the easy route was always a free ticket to the morgue. *There were at least nine murder loving psychopaths in this jungle, not counting herself and Tiberius. He wouldn't be waiting at a cabin to die but there was nothing wrong with luring killers to her.* Sensing evil as she opened the door and went in, she grinned as she saw who was waiting at the table.

Doing the slow clap, her host praised, "Under thirty minutes. I'm impressed."

"The spiders were a nice touch," Lexy remarked, curious as to why he'd be sitting there. *This felt too easy.*

"Impressive healing ability," he toyed.

"Bold of you to double cross me," she stated, lunging at him. He vanished. *A hologram. Cute.* A chainsaw rumbled outside. Strolling to the drawer, she selected a butcher knife. Pocketing a fork, she snooped through the rustic kitchen full of mortal distractions. Snacks, alcohol, a cell on a port. *No service of course. Shocking. There was music. Fun. Let's speed this up.* She turned it on. Eighties rock piped out through speakers. *Nice.* She took a swig of tequila. *She didn't have spelled demon blades. Any demons she put down would rise in minutes. So much cardio.* The door opened. Without looking, she smiled. *When her predatory nature was triggered, she feared nothing.* Lexy casually turned. A killer wearing an oozing flesh mask was standing in the doorway holding a machete. *Creepy.* Her eyes darted to the window. *She was surrounded. The music worked. Convenient.* They ran at each other, she ducked and weaved. Stabbing upwards through his ribcage, she punctured his heart. With vacant eyes, he flopped to the floor as a macabre hoard of murderous foe burst through the open door. Taking them on with a smirk, she booted one in the chest, slit the other's throat and shivved the next in the gut. They just kept coming so she took out the human trash until there was a heap on the floor and the wise fled into the jungle.

Taking a breather, the pile shifted. *Someone was alive.* Tossing bodies away until she found the culprit, she peeled off its mask. *Mortal. None of these were the bidding Abaddon she'd seared into her memory. Her count of serial killers in the jungle was way off.* Lexy sliced her palm and pressed her glowing Ankh brand to his forehead as she spoke the words assuring his destination with the damned, "From this life unto the next." Light faded from his eyes. She brushed herself off and got up. *Not a snackable demon in the bunch.* She heard rumbling and screaming. Opting to leave out the window, she leapt into the jungle and sprinted towards the action.

Under cover of darkness, she moved through the jungle like a panther, unceremoniously slitting masked mortal throats until her stomach cramped. Anticipating an all she could eat demon buffet, she gingerly stalked prey without even snapping a twig, until she was able to get a clear view of a ravenous long fanged beast devouring the entrails of someone who'd suffered a notably grotesque demise. There was a hint of mortal in its movement suggesting it was a Changeling. *She'd never fought one of these. She didn't know what it did, but it smelled like swass.* Erring on the side of caution, she summoned her get out of having your innards devoured free card. *Come on, impermeable flesh.* She made her presence known, "You are a messy eater." Lightning fast, it had her pinned to soil, slashing with razor sharp claws but not getting anywhere because she'd had the foresight to prepare. When clawing failed, it chomped on her stomach, accomplishing nothing. Grabbing the swass scented drooling depravity as it gnawed to no avail, she inhaled its essence. Rapturous warmth blurred everything. Veins darkened as the beast went limp. Euphoria amped her emotions until the speaker blew and the Ankh symbol on her palm lit up lush greenery like a beacon. With her eyes locked on the brand prohibiting her from passing through the hall of souls, tepid emotions succumbed to fiend energy as her dark heart sunk into nothing. Power presented as rage. Lexy balled her fist. Light dimmed as her eyes narrowed. *She was Guardian. No Demon attacks her and walks away.* In a breath, she was cross-legged on dirt, creatively inconveniencing a Demon by cutting off its fingers. *Come at me now, stank asshole.* Lexy pitched long clawed digits into the emerald utopia of ferns spackled with gladiolas. Going 'can't find my demon blade medieval', she lopped off its hands. Apathetic as thick burgundy currant gushed, she provoked, "Try tugging out intestines with meat nubs." It moved. Scrunching her nose, she got up. It swung a nub. She stomped on its groin, using it as leverage to yank off a leg. Blood fountained from the severed limb. Mesmerized by the rhythmic swell and spray, she watched until it slowed to a trickle. *It shifted.* Doing the same to the other leg, she pitched it into the jungle. Its eyes opened. *This thing had the IQ of a spool of thread.* "Die until I walk away, dumbass," Lexy said. "Now, I have to make this permanent." She shoved the blade down with her full weight, it shifted only making it halfway. Choked, she got up, stomped on its neck, then leapt on the blade. Irritated, she got on the ground. Anchoring her feet on its shoulders, she yanked until the head popped off. Satisfied, she booted the severed head into the jungle like a crimson spattered soccer ball. Sensing she wasn't alone, she saw mortals. *Damn it.*

Standing with terrified people clutching weapons, Tiberius questioned, "Did everyone see her behead a demon?" Mortal's heads swung side to side.

"I didn't see shit," Agent Clarke teased, unfazed.

Unprepared to people, Lexy squinted at nearly transparent orange hued mortal auras. *It would be humane to snap their necks now. No muss. No fuss. Getting complications out of the way like a champ.*

Her frenemy with benefits, huskily seduced, "You still look sexy in red."

Risqué flirtations from the Summit, resurrected libido as Lexy bantered, "I look sexy in everything."

"You do. Quit flirting with me," Tiberius chuckled.

Narrowing her eyes, Lexy hissed, "I hate you."

He called her bluff, "Liar."

She was supposed to remember something.

"While you were playing with your food, we saved five people," Tiberius sparred.

A mortal ran away. "Four," Agent Clarke changed the tally.

After the crackling of escapee's footsteps into darkness, it was eerily silent. Smirking, Lexy whispered, "It was nice of you to gather everyone who saw too much in one place."

"No chance they survive," Tiberius whispered.

Bushes rustled. Panicking, another human tried to flee and

was intercepted by Swamp Thing's inbred cousin. A baptismal mist of blood speckled leaves. *He was right. The mortals were pegging themselves off.* An army of damned shoved through bushes in every direction. *Time out was over.* Heavy metal began. *Perfect.* Spinning to face an assailant, the fight commenced like they'd hit pause on a slasher movie.

Kicking jaws away while fighting incoming monsters, her eyes kept darting to the mortal Tiberius cared about, holding her own. Agent Clarke had skills but the demons were regenerating faster than they could put them down. It felt like an endless stream coming out of the jungle as they persevered.

Clarke shouted, "Above you!"

Trees crackled as more leapt from tree to tree. *The mortals were toast. If she saved herself, she'd kill everyone.*

"Lexy!" Tiberius shouted, fending off a herd.

A massive demon launched her into the bushes. Hitting the ground with such force it knocked the wind out of her and the knife from her hand. Leaves rustled as it leapt on her. Holding away snapping jaws while struggling to breathe, Lexy switched her role from hunted to hunter, absorbing the demon's energy. It slumped on top of her. Shoving it off, she was trampled. Tumbling out of bushes with crushed ribs and a punctured lung under flawless flesh, her healing ability broiled repairing damage. *She couldn't breathe.*

Slashing demons away with the agent fighting what came at his back and mortals between them, Tiberius shouted, "Get up!"

With her brain screaming for oxygen, she altered intention to survival. *Heal, damn it! Heal!* Grabbing a scaly ankle, she siphoned energy and scrambled up outmanoeuvring snapping jaws and swinging blades, patting herself down for a weapon. *It's in the bushes. Shit.* Ducking to avoid a tail, she snatched a piece of wood as dagger like nails raked her back. Releasing a war cry, she grabbed the arm of her assailant and thwapped it on the dirt. A blade ran across her throat. Warm blood gushed from the slice. *Heal! Heal!* Healing energy sealed the wound as she spun to face who cut her. Her immortal battle partner had already taken it out.

"We're not winning!" Tiberius yelled, tossing a knife.

The mortals had to go. With a swing of her arm, Lexy froze time, and touched Tiberius.

In awe, he took in the paused battle, muttering, "What did you do?"

Waking the mortals, she urged, "Get as far away as you can!"

Irritated she'd forced his hand, Tiberius accepted his roll, ordering, "Go! Run!" He chased them into the jungle.

She slit motionless monsters' throats, thinning the herd. Granting precious time they needed to escape, she noticed long clawed demons frozen in mid-air, descending from trees above her. Stumbling out of their landing zone with her brain about to explode, she needed energy. *With demons everywhere, there was only one thing she could do to take everything out at once. With her. Sacrificial Lamb time.* Moonlight filtered through shadows of palm trees. *The full moon was enormous. Grey would love this.* Images of her Handler's smiling face confused her intended narrative.

Time commenced with thudding of depravities landing. Skewered from behind, she sputtered up blood. Dangling in the air, she looked down at her stomach. *Oh, no.* She'd been impaled by a giant smooth horn. *Sneaky. What was this attached too?* Healing energy broiled. *They needed more time.* Perspiring, Lexy gurgled, "Is that all you've got?" *She couldn't die first.* Fighting to remain conscious, the crimson-haired Dragon of Ankh clutched the beast's horn, draining it's life force. It lowered its head as it slumped. She slid off the appendage. Landing on all fours, her intestines spilled out onto dirt. *Shit.* All she could smell was sulphur. Bushes moved as the jungle flickered. *Turn it off.* Vaguely aware of a tugging sensation, her vision focused. Demons were gnawing on her intestines. *This was embarrassing.* Everything went black.

TWITCHING HER FINGERS IN WARM SAND, LEXY SMILED. *She was safe in the in-between. Maybe she had time for a Pina Colada?* Blinded by glare, she peered up.

In a beam of heavenly light with flaxen hair and a flowing ivory gown, Ankh's Guardian Azariah scolded, "Get your ass back there! Nothing gets off that island! NOTHING!"

LIGHT FLASHED AS HER CONSCIOUSNESS RETURNED TO A supremely screwed up scenario. Something walked by with her leg in its mouth. *This was excessive.* Tuning out the knowledge that she was in pieces, fury seethed as Lexy hissed, "Die!" Dark mist and meat rained down on what was left of her. Struggling, she couldn't move. *Wouldn't it be ironic if she was viewing this macabre bullshit from a severed head?* Her eyes focused. She was alone in a sea of sulphur and copper scented meat. *She'd experienced many fucked up scenarios, but this was impressively brutal.* Her eyelids were heavy, so she closed them.

Sensing someone, her foggy vision cleared. *Perfect.*

Crouching, stroking her hair, Tiberius asked, "You okay?"

Seriously? Lexy mumbled, "Why do you ask?"

"I left our friends in a cave and came back for you," Tiberius explained. Holding up the bottom half of her leg, he confessed, "I put you back together. I found your final piece in the bushes over there."

Perfect. Her booty call put her back together like a jigsaw puzzle. He positioned the limb at the socket. Snakelike veins reattached it.

Bones calcified extending as muscle stretched and solidified. Her neck was steaming as everything fused and insides filled in her gaping torso.

"Tell me you weren't alive the whole time," he probed.

"Azariah gave me shit and sent me back," Lexy replied. She sat up in her underwear, crossing her arms over her chest.

Taking off his shirt, Tiberius offered, "Here."

She put on his top. Looking at her hands, she wiggled her fingers, confessing, "That sucked."

"I bet it did," he commented. Gazing into her eyes utterly amazed, he said, "You healed from dismemberment in minutes." He held out his hand.

As she got up, she remembered, "The blonde is possessed. Go back if you need too. I have to find the compound and shut this down."

"Clarke can deal with it. Lead the way," he prompted.

With the moon's rays as their only light, she mumbled, "I overshot my healing ability giving you time to get away. When I resurrected, it was carnage. My brain is all bird tweets and elevator music."

"Leading the way is the least I can do after you sacrificed yourself for us," he taunted, taking the lead.

Sort of. She sparred, "Allowing island hicks to kill me is bad for my Guardian Street cred. Azariah was pissed. No witnesses. Nothing gets off this island."

Ankle deep in innards, Tiberius flirted, "Still enjoying our romantic getaway?"

Taking in macabre Dragon friendly ambiance while trying to figure out where they were, she sparred, "Ask me on the drive home." The moon granted mediocre light through the veil of palm trees. *If she turned it off predatory instinct would take the wheel.* Lexy stumbled.

Tiberius caught her, toying, "Admit you need a minute."

"No time," Lexy decreed. *If their host saw her regenerate and rise from the dead like a phoenix, he'd send an army.*

He offered, "Feed from me."

Tempted, she sped up, saying, "Stay alive. The Aries Group can't tranq me anymore."

Catching up, he probed, "Are you sure?"

She wasn't sure about anything. "Hey Grey, I need backup at the hedonism resort," she provoked.

He chuckled, "I see your point."

Time to turn it off. He caught her arm, stopping her emotionless descent. *Damn it.* Libido fluttered. Her eyes were drawn to where he was caressing. Shaking her head, Lexy whispered, "That's not going to help me shut it off." He let go.

Tiberius clutched his weapon, prompting, "Do whatever you need to do. I'm in."

Inhaling musky copper and sulphur with sentiment idling, she returned to the dark farm trigger. Her eyes emptied as shots echoed in her heart. Tossed into the well, her mortal shell sunk under the surface until she was gone. As her soul settled in isolating darkness, metaphorical scales prickled with vengeance. Predatory certainty awoke the entity that feared nothing and no one. Pain was amusing and death wasn't optional as senses elevated to an adrenaline inducing pinnacle, and then nothing but the echoing beat of her heart. Viewing terrain as a nocturnal creature with tribal thudding in her ears, pa pum, pa pum. A twig cracked. A Tri-Clan aura showed allegiance by kneeling. She picked up vibration beneath the soles of her feet. *Snack time.* Planning to pursue foe who fled her wrath to the gates of the compound, she sprinted at the edible damned.

In a pa pum, blades clashed. Vaguely aware of the aura fighting alongside her, they fended off Lampir with martial arts in blurred shadows and slivers of moonlight. Anticipating searing heat and blood loss, there was nothing. Protected by a golden sheen, she slayed everything in sight.

Tiberius held his own thinning the herd like the warrior he was created to be. She embraced the higher demise setting by ditching her blade and ripping out hearts with her bare hands. Breath in, clutch heart, breath out, tear it out and pitch it into the jungle. As Lampir solidified, they kicked forms scattering ashes over innards. Doing what Dragons do best until they reached the gates, humming helicopter blades focused the time sensitive scenario. Foiling their escape, by heaving a statue, metal crunched, it sputtered, slowing blades to a half assed spin and stall. The destructive duo sprinted around the side of the compound down a slope to the dock to stop the boats with *'kill everyone'* on replay in their brains.

A boat pulled away. Tiberius leapt after it. Hanging from the ladder, he shouted, "Stop the others!"

As a depraved yacht club scurried around decks preparing to flee, she shoved over a pole. It teetered, and men leapt overboard as it pinned a boat. They launched projectiles until every craft was sinking, then snapped necks as mortals climbed onto the dock.

"Jump!" Tiberius yelled to back noise of rapid clicks.

In a pa pum, Lexy leapt without looking. Bubbles rose as she submerged watching squirming leggy masses hit the water sinking after her. He towed her under the dock. They surfaced gasping for air in the foot of space between wood and water. Back enough for witty repartee, she gasped, "Fucking spiders."

Treading water, Tiberius grinned, teasing, "Mental note, the Dragon doesn't do spiders."

"You said jump," she bantered, swimming.

"You listened," he pointed out proudly.

Deciding his ego didn't need to be stroked, she opted out of admitting it, concentrating on staying afloat.

Spitting out salty ocean, he confessed, "I have hard limits too."

Treading water, gazing at each other, they momentarily forgot they were mid-flight. Grinning, Lexy flirtatiously pushed away, disappearing underwater. Swimming far enough away to avoid being jumped on by a spider, she bobbed to the surface. There were spiders on the dock. *Guess she was swimming to shore.*

Surfacing closer to dry land, Lexy breast stroked until she could stand. *Where was he?* Echoing legs were scurrying on the dock, dragging a squirming cocoon. *Damn it, Tiberius.* Knowing he'd used precious seconds before leaping to save her, she begrudgingly trudged to shore. *His presence pulled her out too early.* Counting five, she flinched. *What kind of asshole brings giant arachnids to a fight? This was a dickish move even for that tool. His witch was going to die.* Ringing ocean out of her hair, Lexy caught their attention, "Over here!" Leaving their spoils on the dock, the spiders came for her. Cockily, she picked up driftwood and swung at sand, disorienting arachnids with projectiles. She removed two more from the equation with the sharp end of her weapon, sending another soaring through the air pitchy shrieking. They came at her with a vengeance. Kicking eight legged freaks away barefoot, she persevered. In her peripheral vision the rest were towing her cocooned booty call up the hill. On all fours she sunk her hands into the sand narrowing her eyes. Sensing a shift in dynamics, the spider froze. Launching herself forward, she chased it. Allowing it to flee, she turned her attention to spearing the spider towing her booty call burrito up the hill and raised the shrieking arachnid kabob prompting the rest to scurry away, leaving her battle buddy wriggling in silk. Kneeling, she tore open the webbing, mimicking his earlier words, "You okay?"

Relieved, Tiberius gasped, "Touché."

Helping him up, she said, "You'd do the same for me."

"I would," he responded, squirming with heebie jeebies. "Having your insides liquified sucks."

It wasn't the worst way to go.

Looking around, he enquired, "Did you kill all of them?"

"Some got away," she admitted, walking up the hill.

"Fantastic," he sighed, jogging to catch up as they entered a pool area with statues and a bar beneath a waterfall.

Sensing something off, she said, "Either a five-year-old made these sculptures or …"

Smirking, Tiberius shoved a statue. It shattered and a dried-up corpse flopped out.

"Pterodactyl demons?" She questioned.

The bodies eyes twitched. "There are lots of ways to be turned to stone," Tiberius confirmed. Slitting a wrist over puckered lips, he said, "Just a guess." Miraculously fast, the body filled out. Recognition lit up Tiberius' face. Smiling, he said, "Hi Conrad from Lucien's Crew. How did you end up here?"

As he helped him up, Conrad recounted, "We ran into a Coven of witches while checking on a missing hive."

Tiberius trusted Conrad. That was good enough for her. Hearing more than enough, Lexy commenced tipping stone to free the rest, rushing, "Demon fight. No time for chit chat."

After giving each Lampir enough blood to revive, they rose leaving behind only withered witches on the cobblestone. Tiberius staggered, slurring, "Problem, Lexy."

With her back to hungry Lampir, she healed their donor, hoping they'd attack, so she'd have an excuse.

Winking at her, Tiberius turned to the Lampir, explaining, "You've risen in the eye of a storm. We've been fighting demons and serial killers since dusk. Lexy saved you instead of curbing her hunger. We need the same from you. You cover ground faster. Heal any injured Aries Group Agents with your blood and compel them to forget. Bring everyone to us. We'll sort souls, give you evil mortals to feed on and leave this forsaken place together."

Conrad rallied his troops, "You heard the leader of Triad. Clear this island." Lampir vanished in darkness.

21

Witches & Botanical Gardens

Entering the compound into a lit ivory hallway, Tiberius whispered, "Inconspicuously give me another hit of healing energy."

They were being watched. She felt it too. Placing her hand on his back, energy filled her torso, travelling down her arm. As her palm warmed, her spine tingled. Recalling the warning, she let go. Lexy whispered, "Think they're hiding?"

"We just woke Lampir they encased in stone, I'd hide," he quietly confirmed. Nudging open a door, Tiberius peered in and gave her a thumbs up.

Clearing five or six rooms without a hint of activity, she heard a click with faint conversation. Grinning, she whispered, "I've got it," booting open the door. Greeted by a rat tat tatting machine gun, she barely flinched. Peering down at her shredded top, Lexy sighed, "I borrowed this shirt." Bullets dropped out as she healed tinkling in the hall. *Frigging mortals.* Yelling orders into a radio the pirate vanished into an adjoining room. "Okay, I'll be it," Lexy taunted. Grinning, she pursued him. A grenade came sailing at her. With lightening reflexes, she pitched it back. A deafening blast sent her soaring backwards in a hail of people meat.

Leaning on the doorframe, Tiberius teased, "Having fun?"

Flat on her back, Lexy chuckled, "It's on." Leaping up, she apologised, "Sorry about the shirt." They kissed. As their lips parted, she directed, "Cut the power. I'll keep them occupied."

"Don't do anything I wouldn't do," he flirted, jumping out a window.

Smiling, she collected daggers amidst slimy hunks of mortal and strutted out into the hall. Noticing a hallowed red dot on her chest, she sighed, "Seriously?"

With his machine gun aimed, the pirate shouted, "Drop your weapon!"

"No," she decreed with a sassy smirk.

As she took a step, he yelled, "Last chance!"

"Oh, no. It's my last chance already? Don't you have a list of demands?" She provoked, taking another step forward.

"Don't make me shoot you!" He warned, white knuckling his gun.

Smiling, Lexy explained, "Attempting to assert non-existent dominance over an immortal is pointless. Put the gun down."

He dropped his gun. Confused, he gasped, "How did you make me do that?"

Intrigued by what she'd done, Lexy ordered, "Hop on one foot." The mortal hopped. *This was fun. Where did the compulsion come from?* With no time to play games, she directed, "Stand still." The mortal stopped jumping. She handed him a blade dripping with innards, commanding, "Slit your own throat, I have shit to do." Hearing gurgling as she walked away, she kicked open double doors and strode into a conference room with a heap of executed mortals who didn't live long enough to fight for their lives. Fuelled by thirst for retribution, she stormed the ground floor slitting throats and snapping necks until ivory halls were spattered red. Slick with the blood of her enemies, she burst through a door into the botanical garden. *Better not.* She turned to go. It was all apple orchard for as far as the eye could see with fruit dangling from branches. Wiggling her toes in silky grass, she smiled. *It's not real. You're a Guardian. See past the magic.* Plucking one off a branch, a smear of blood on the golden delicious apple tainted the witches grift. *Good try.*

Rustling grass drew her attention. Wandering towards her, Grey's endearing grin and enrapturing ice blue eyes wooed away animosity. Soothing her soul with an embrace, he asked, "Why are you here, Lex?"

What was she doing? In his arms, she whispered, "You aren't real." As he held her tighter, it felt like it was.

"I miss you. Come home," he enticed, his voice a soothing ballad to her heart.

Searing heat plunged into her. Staggering away with a sword in her chest, sputtering blood, the mirage flickered revealing her evil host. She yanked a sword glowing with white light out of her heart.

Shielding his eyes from the glare, he shouted, "It works!"

As light subsided, three men and a young girl with a unique swirling aura joined her host. Meeting the witch's eyes, Lexy siphoned the stolen energy back into her, declaring, "This useless hunk of metal can't hold my magic." She tossed it to the witch, taunting, "Go ahead. Try to save yourself."

The witch started casting a spell, "Darkness rising flowing tides in…"

Lexy cut her off. Waving a hand, she trapped her in an orb, saying, "Shh." Water washed over her feet. Watching the four panicked mortals trying to find a way out with water filling the fantasy garden, she laughed. *Powerful enough to recreate a sword capable of absorbing Guardian light to send dark beings through the hall of souls undetected but didn't understand she couldn't kill one with water. It was funny.* Catching her smug expression in the watertight orb, Lexy provoked, "Your air is going to run out."

"What?" The witch mouthed from the soundproof bubble, bobbing on the surface.

Waist high in water, Lexy clarified, "You're going to run out of oxygen."

"I can't hear you," the enchantress mimed, steadying the orb by evenly distributing her weight.

Wanting the teenager to have a taste of her own medicine, Lexy slowly mouthed, "I, control, your, oxygen. You're, going, to, die."

Losing her cool in the face of certain demise the teen sent the orb into a flat spin panicking as Lexy's feet left the ground. Treading water by the teenager's muted pleas for salvation, she felt a speck of guilt. *She'd taken a few wrong turns on this job due to her power expanded ego. Maybe this was the lesson?* Caving, she willed her oxygen. Taking a last breath as space closed between stucco ceiling and watery demise, she submerged into a liquid wonderland with flowing crimson hair and swam over to the dying mortals. *In comparison to other methods of disembarking this world, drowning was peaceful.* The henchmens' struggle ceased as light left their eyes. Maintaining eye contact with their host, he smiled as his soul vacated his shell. As the oxygen deprivation migraine subsided, warm shivers lulled her into complacency. *Sleep. It's time to go to sleep.* She let go drifting lifelessly in the botanical garden.

Embraced in warmth, a flash of light returned her to the in-between. Her palms twitched in warm sand.

"Get your ass back to the fight," Ankh's Guardian Azariah reprimanded.

Before Lexy had the strength to raise her head to meet her disapproval, she disintegrated into the endless desert.

22

The Many Demises Of Lexy Abrelle

Motion of water whooshing into halls and receding startled her awake. On her belly in a wet hallway, Lexy gasped oxygen into deprived lungs. Sensing someone, she peered up as bulbs flickered. *Hello naughty distraction.*

Standing above her, Tiberius teased, "Taking a break?"

Getting up sopping wet, Lexy announced, "Good news. I caught the witch."

Laughing, her partner in debauchery revealed, "I found a surveillance room. Everyone on this island has red, white, or green tracker implants. You snuffed out an impressive number of white ones while I used my ability to dive into the tech guy's memories to disable the live feed. We need to find two more remotes before five AM." He waved a gadget. "There's a timer set to sedate everything in the game."

"What time is it?" She probed with no clue.

"I didn't check. I'm more efficient when I'm not under pressure," he revealed.

Fair enough. Walking down the hall searching for the orb

where she'd stored her magical pain in the ass, Lexy peered down an open stairwell, enquiring, "You didn't happen to see a witch in an orb?"

"I caught the end of your game of murder suicide chicken, but wasn't certain which button opened the garden doors, so I opened the stairwells with this handy gadget, broke the picture window, and shut myself in a room," he revealed, entertained by her animated search.

"I expect my booty calls to leap in front of a tsunami for me," she bantered.

Naughtily backing her against the wall, he pressed his body against hers, seductively whispering, "Is that what I am? Shall we clear this place and discuss terms?"

Held by electric tension, goosebumps prickled as he tucked damp hair behind her ear, provocatively trailing fingers over her pulse point. With a dry throat, she swallowed trying to summon ration. Hall lighting remained on, as she suggested, "I should check you for a tracker. Mine would have fallen out by now."

"If you start touching me Lexy, I'm taking you right here," Tiberius cautioned. "I'll let you look for it, after we're done."

Pulling away from his distracting games, she said, "Only I can free the witch. We'll find her later." She walked away from temptation, smiling.

As they entered the stairwell, he sprinted past her upstairs, explaining, "There are seven to ten white dots in a room on this floor."

Chasing him, she sparred, "Fun."

Trying to figure out his vantage point, he turned from side to side, admitting, "I have no idea what side the surveillance room was on. Let's do this the easy way." Tiberius grabbed a vase off a table. Stepping back into the stairwell, he pitched it at the wall. Fractured glass rained on carpet as guards rushed out.

Running at the men, Lexy slid beneath a hail of rapid fire.

They spun in a haze of bullets as Tiberius snuck up and slit their throats. Assailants crumpled onto the burgundy carpet. *Brilliant flooring choice.* Heat surged as her healing ability rid her of projectiles, spitting bullets out. Seamlessly working together as mortals booked it into an adjoining suite, Tiberius took out who fled into the hall as she ducked to avoid flying objects, laughing. Enjoying every second, she launched a burly guy over the bed onto the floor, kicking the next in the groin, and then flipped one over her back as they came at her in a blur of punches and manoeuvres until the last mortal was down.

Holding his side, Tiberius limped in, prompting, "Heal me fast if you need back up."

"Does it look like I need back up?" Lexy taunted, touching his chiselled chest. *She wanted him. It was a subtle distinction but there was no denying it anymore.* Their eyes locked as ability warmed her core, travelling the length of her arm healing his injury. His heart thudded beneath her palm. *Nobody was watching the door.*

With his mouth a breath from hers, he vowed, "I'm doing shockingly inappropriate things to you after this job, Mrs. Aries." Walking away, he went to keep watch.

"You're going to wreck my Ankh cred," Lexy sighed, ogling his ass as he peered out into the hall.

Glancing back, he flirted, "We'll talk about the terms of our service agreement later."

Service agreement. Freak. Biting her lip, she snapped necks and checked pockets while he watched the door. Finding a pack of gum, she got up and said, "No remotes. Just gum." She gave him a piece.

Smiling, he took it, whispering, "Thanks, hun."

Her Healer tank was running low. With jangling nerves, cheap men's cologne stung each time she inhaled, Lexy questioned, "Was that everyone on this floor?"

"Adrenaline clouded memory issues. It'll come back in a minute," he admitted. Sauntering after a guard crawling away in the hall, he slit his throat, wiped the bloody blade on his shorts and checked his pockets. He returned, saying "You'd think one of these assholes would have a candy bar."

Her skin was crawling. Jonesing for immortal energy, she ate a stick of gum. Her eyes watered. Sinuses tickled. *Shit. Peppermint.* Squinting at squealing florescent lighting to deter a sneeze, she couldn't stop it, "Harumpfffhhhh, harumpfffhhhh!"

Wide eyed, Tiberius gasped, "What in the hell was that?"

"Harumpfffhhhh," Lexy honked like a moose summoning a mate.

He tugged her into an alcove by a suite with his hand over her mouth. Shaking laughing, he sighed, "Baby, that was crazy hot. I'm so marrying you for real now."

Asshole. She bit his hand.

He tugged it away, teasing, "Quit flirting."

"Dick," she mumbled, grinning.

Embracing her, he toyed, "You love it," groping her butt.

She did. Two could play at this game. She nibbled on his ear.

"Fighting with a woody will destroy my Leader of Triad cred," he seduced, pressing against her.

Hearing a thump, they peered up. *Someone was upstairs.* "No rest for the wicked," she sighed.

"Rarely," he sparred, heading for the stairs.

Swatting his ass as she caught up, she noticed raised veins on her arm. *Guess this was a thing now. She was going to freak out the mortals.* Catching his concern, she explained, "Guardian issue."

He offered, "Can I help?"

Healing ability energy needs were sketchy enough without bringing a Guardian paternity into play. "I want you alive, Ti." She used Agent Clarke's pet name.

"I knew you were jealous," Tiberius chuckled, going up the stairs.

She changed the subject, "How many were up there?"

"None," he responded, as they reached a closed metal door with a security panel. "Wonder what they're keeping up here?"

She reached for the panel. He swatted her hand. Narrowing her eyes, Lexy warned, "Do you have a death wish?"

Exploding into a grin, he flirted, "If I had to choose a way to go."

They had a job to do. Dead eyed, she swatted him back.

"I'm just pointing out there's usually a reason for excessive security," he explained.

"I'm at the top of the food chain," she decreed, pulling out her Guardian card.

Grinning, he caved, "Go ahead. Press a button."

She pressed a long narrow one. A digital timer started a countdown. *Thirty minutes. That might have been dumb.* She suggested, "Let's check the basement."

Frustrated, Tiberius rationed, "What if the compound is blowing up in thirty minutes? Lucien's crew will be back soon with survivors."

Taking off, she sparred, "Healing from a splat on cement is taxing. I'd better find a snack."

"Cute," he taunted, descending the stairs behind her. "We have too many scenarios in play to Ankh wing it. You do that. I'll check the surveillance room for paperwork about what happens when that timer goes off."

Smiling, she provoked, "Bet the timer releases something?" Continuing, Lexy passed the last open door to a lit hallway on slippery cement. *Water drained out this way. Maybe the witch ended up in the basement?*

The descent into darkness wasn't a chore for creatures who thrived where sun didn't shine. Musky stairs and unknown foe were par for the course. Sacrificial Lambs were never meant to make the closing credits. A healing ability only gave her more time in the game. Electricity flickered as she

SACRIFICIAL LAMB CLUB

purposely walked into an onyx cloud. It tingled as euphoric power pulsed through her, fine-tuning senses, and fuelling abilities. The light burnt out a few stairs before the basement door. Glancing back at darkness, she couldn't help but smile. *This was always the case. Damned if you do, damned if you don't, but saved either way.* Hearing a noise, she selected impermeable flesh. *Not being injured was a time saver.*

Lexy walked past a row of washing machines affirming, "I'll make it quick." A whoosh in darkness drew her attention. Her stomach growled. A giant snake with dagger fangs unhinged its jaw as it shot out of the shadows, chomping into her stomach. *Shit.* Frustrated by not puncturing flesh, the beast beat her like a dusty blanket on cement. *Not cool.* Scrambled thoughts fused into Ankh's afterlife mantra. *Stand up, Lexy. Stand back up and fight.* Clutching rigid reptilian jaws, she turned the tables, ingesting essence until it untangled and flopped at her feet. *She didn't care about snakes.* She got up and felt the wall until she turned on a light. *Gross.* It was an oozing wet blob of snot with snake arms. *Glad she didn't see that before she ate it.* Opening a panel on the wall, there was a timer. *Seventeen minutes. Why not try to turn it off?* She pressed a button. A wall slid away revealing the cave system. *That thing was guarding the escape route. Smart.* She pressed another button. Mist sprayed on her. *What was that?* Hearing scampering legs, she sighed, "Come on." Pressing another button, trying to close the wall backfired as the timer sped up. *Crap.* She smashed the panel and spun to face creepy crawlies clutching her blade. *Fine.* A sea of spiders parted. *This scenario never went well.* A hideous, gigantic black leg curved the opening. *One large thing versus countless small ones was a fair trade.*

"Why are you waiting for it to come in?" Tiberius enquired, from behind her.

Grinning, Lexy confessed, "I accidentally sped up the timer, so I broke it. I've got this."

Taking his place at her side, he sparred, "If this place blows up at least we'll be trapped together."

Wielding their weapons, they ran at the monstrous creature, each slicing legs until it teetered. Spinning, Lexy gouged its eye as a mass of smaller arachnids climbed over it, coating her face with sticky webbing. Tearing at silk encasing her nose and mouth. *She couldn't breathe.* It tugged her off her feet. She landed on her side. *She couldn't free herself without taking out Tiberius.* In the haze of faint shadows through white silk, it was torn open.

Gifting her sweet oxygen, her battle partner grinned. With a mutual distain for spiders, he revealed, "Back up arrived."

A massive animatronic spider was sparking with electricity as she got up. *Cool.* Noticing they'd been joined by Lampir, Lexy confessed, "I bought it as real." *The other spiders were gone.*

The Lampir touched it, saying, "It's a theme park attraction with motion sensors set off by those genetically enhanced clones. One of you was dosed with pheromone."

"Ah, that's what the spray was," Lexy said, glancing back at the busted panel.

Conrad bit his wrist, offering, "They loath our scent. My blood will counteract it."

That was a horrible idea. Dabbing some on her wrist and neck like perfume, Lexy said, "Thanks."

"That might work," he replied, staring at her chest.

She had a titty in the wind. She glanced down. *Yup.* Tying torn material to conceal herself, she caught his grin.

"They won't bother us. We'll check the tunnel system and bring you anyone we find," Conrad announced, waving at his men, they took off into darkness.

The timer was flashing zeros when they reached the top floor, "Shall we find out why this area was locked?" Tiberius said, opening the door with no issue.

Wandering down the empty hall, they heard conversation, and stopped by a door. *They didn't know the door was unlocked.*

Lexy mouthed the words, "Play along." Musically knocking, she covered the peephole with her thumb.

"Is that you, Ben?" A baritone voice answered.

"Room service," Lexy sang.

Tiberius shook his head as a masculine voice replied, "We didn't order anything."

Wow. "Pizza," Lexy responded.

Someone asked, "Who ordered a pizza?"

Holy shit. She persisted, "Four large pizzas for Rick." *There was always a Rick.* Listening to their search for money, she squinted. *Nobody was this dumb.* The door opened. Wearing a machine gun shredded mid-thigh length men's shirt, with no pizza, she commented, "Wow."

Mortals froze like deer in headlights. "The jig is up. Don't bother reaching for your guns," Tiberius cautioned, as they strolled in.

Recognizing a guy who shoved her earlier, Lexy said, "I remember you."

"I saw you die," the pirate in a floral shirt stammered, fingering his holster.

"We're immortal," Tiberius clarified, enjoying the game.

A man with a tattooed face whipped out a gun, threatening, "Everything goes down with a bullet to the head."

"You don't want to piss me off," Lexy decreed, shifting her hand. His weapon flew across the room. Staring down the man she'd magically rid of his gun, she probed, "Why was this floor locked down?" They refused to speak.

"Restraining captives is much easier when they provide zip ties," Tiberius chuckled, binding mortals' hands behind backs.

The masked pirate, asserted, "I have to enforce the end of the game."

Waving his remote, Tiberius baited, "I showed you mine. Now, you show me yours."

"My what?" He toyed with a smize.

Binding his wrists, Tiberius explained, "I've seen your surveillance room. We know about the implants."

"We should cut your tracker out," Lexy suggested.

Turning so they could watch, Tiberius whispered, "I prefer private knife play."

Ignoring his flirtation, she pressed his lower back until she found the tiny mass. She sliced into his flesh, dug it out, and tossed it. "I'll make it up to you," Lexy said, healing him.

"That was fun," Tiberius bantered, winking her way.

The masked guy sighed, "Just kill me now."

Unmasking the lippy captive, it was Laird. Lexy exclaimed, "Best holiday ever. Five star macabre. Is there a site where I can leave a review? Oh, wait. You won't be around to see it."

"I like my odds," Laird countered, smiling.

Meeting Lexy's gaze, Tiberius asked, "Is there anyone in the room worth saving?"

"Nobody," Lexy revealed. "We freed the Lampir encased in stone by the pool and promised they could eat the worthless captives if they helped us search the island for our friends."

"They have implants," Laird countered, unfazed.

Lexy revealed, "The trackers fell out. Decomposing bodies. What can you do? It's been a slice, Laird. Say hi to your brother for me."

Squirming, Laird shouted, "I'll gut you like a fish bitch!"

"Can you believe Laird Brock was hiding in here the whole time?" Tiberius casually bantered.

Pretending they couldn't hear his rage fuelled hissy fit, Lexy slammed, "Pussy," as they left.

In the hall, Tiberius suggested, "If we don't want it to get around, we should keep our fling a secret from the Lampir."

Meeting his gaze, she whispered, "How did we end up here alone? What should we say?"

Backing her into an alcove by a suite, Tiberius seduced, "They kidnapped me to dive into your memories." Caressing her shoulder, he slid his fingers along shredded material to where she tied it. Hovering his lips a breath away, he played with her top, enticing, "I'm going to pull over our rental car and kiss every inch of you."

Hearing someone coming up the stairs, she sighed, "Game face on, the Lampir are back." As they stepped out of the alcove, grenades were pitched down the hall, rolling to a stop in front of them. *Shit.* She shielded him with her body as multiple sweltering blasts buckled her knees. He scooped her into his arms, kicked open a door and ran through connecting rooms. *All she could smell was pennies and burnt hair.*

Laying her in a closet, he closed the door behind them, whispering, "Your battery must be dead. Feed from me. Take what you need to heal. I'll find you when I wake up."

She couldn't see. Touching crunchy hair with meaty spots on the back of her head, Lexy whispered, "Is it bad?"

"No, no. It's fine," Tiberius assured, bullshit pitchy.

"Liar," she answered. "Lead them away. I'll heal. Go!"

Tugging her onto his lap, he quietly teased, "I'll stay."

"Date night was a blast," she mumbled, chuckling in her mind.

He quietly affirmed, "Unforgettable."

Voices grew closer. *He had to go.*

Tiberius whispered, "Play dead."

The closet door squeaked. "Found them," a voice shouted. A weapon clicked as the man commanded, "Out of the closet. Leave your dead."

Shifting her off his lap, he covered her with something soft and closed the door. Footsteps faded as she succumbed to her injuries.

23

Snacks

Certain she was dreaming, her eyes focused on the Agent's gorgeous smile. *Holy shit. She made it.*

"I brought snacks," Agent Clarke slurred, drunk on Lampir venom.

Snacks? Tiberius had her back.

Lampir knelt by her, offering, "If you drain us. Bring us back so we can feed. I can't do another day on this island."

Ravenous, she clutched their arms drawing energy in until they crumpled in the closet. Feeling like she'd chugged five cases of Red bull, Lexy shoved off limp shells and got up. *Her scalp was itchy.*

"I thought Ti was pulling my leg. You really did jump in front of grenades for him," Clarke teased.

Touching the back of her head, there was stubble. Healing abilities repaired bodies in order of importance. *Hair grew back last.* Flashing back to her last demise, Lexy answered, "I heal faster."

"The Lampir have your witch. Lucien's crew will cross this line if she's not punished. Ti is guarding the orb."

Referring to Tiberius as Ti enticed a grin as the agent led her downstairs to her partner. A crowd was gathered by vending machines.

"Where are our people?" A Lampir grilled, scowling.

Walking through the angry fanged mob, Lexy revealed, "I ate them." The crowd closed in. She froze everyone by waving. Holding them in place, she tugged down everyone's pants and motioned to set them free. Everyone mid attack lurch fell with their pants around their ankles. Loudly, Lexy declared, "Shut down the testosterone show. When I'm finished with the witch, I'll heal them."

Covering his mouth to stifle laughter, Tiberius defended Lucien's men, "They're starving. They aren't thinking straight."

Puffing up her chest, a female Lampir got in Lexy's face demanding, "We want the witch."

Without contacting her skin, Lexy declared, "It will be a cold day in hell before Tri-Clan hands over a youth Correction to a pack of hungry Lampir. Know your place in the food chain." Sucking back energy like a Capri Sun, her shell dropped in the hall. "Does anyone else want to go? I can do this until morning," she dared, eyeballing the herd.

"She held us captive in stone. We starved in agony," their leader explained.

Scowling, Lexy scolded, "If you kill someone tagged by Abaddon, she's going to stand back up and melt your asses. How old are you?"

With an enormous grin Conrad replied, "Over two centuries old."

"Act like it," Lexy quipped.

Meeting Tiberius' eyes, she enquired, "Did Laird escape?"

Her partner filled her in. "Lampir were helping injured agents while men posing as Aries Group escaped. Tossing those grenades, alerted the Lampir. The men who escorted me away had the shared IQ of a spool of thread. They're tied up with the others."

Lexy addressed the group, "Go upstairs. Do whatever you want to the guy who runs this place. The young witch was following his orders."

Their leader turned to his hive and gave up, "I'm hungry. Let's go kill the asshole who created this place."

"You can't just let her eat Wendy?" A Lampir complained.

Meeting Lexy's eyes, their leader reminded, "Lucien has a Treaty with Tri-Clan."

"Give your hive a refresher course on immortal hierarchy or I will," Lexy suggested, dead eyed.

He bowed and ushered his group away. One tried to stay. Grabbing him by the scruff of his shirt, Conrad commanded, "Go!"

As footsteps echoed upstairs, Tiberius whispered, "Have I mentioned how much my badass wife turns me on?"

Grinning, she whispered, "We should deal with the witch." Placing her hand on the orb, it splatted.

Peeling gooey film off the teen, Tiberius remarked, "This is impressively gross. Did you catch her name?"

"We skipped introductions. She tried to steal my power with a spelled sword and drown me, so I put her in a sound-proof orb," Lexy answered. Noticing the witch was seething with rage, she cautioned, "Before you try uttering a spell, next time, I won't put oxygen in your orb."

"Do you have a name?" Tiberius enquired, watching.

Covered in slime, the furious witch hissed "Where are my friends?"

"You filled the garden with water. They drowned," Lexy said, intrigued by her chosen emotion.

Grasping her arm, Tiberius dove into her memory, and said, "Her name is Caydence."

"Enter without permission again and I'll trap you in there!" The teenager threatened, struggling.

Not a hint of yellow in her aura meant she couldn't be granted amnesty. Altering an outcome after the coin was tossed wasn't impossible. All mortals had to do was ask for forgiveness. Lexy rationed, "Do you know what we are?"

"Angels are supposed to save people," the teen decreed, saucily fixing her ponytail.

He lost it laughing. "I can't breathe," Tiberius cackled.

Locking eyes with Caydence, Lexy explained, "We're Tri-Clan. We correct mistakes, and more often than not, end up sacrificing ourselves while doing it. Mortals helping evil human trafficking pirates operate an island where serial murderer's hunt innocent people, funded by Abaddon falls into the just kill everything category."

"My Coven was trying to kill me. I didn't have anywhere to go," she defended her actions.

Tiberius questioned, "What did they want in return?"

"I opened a door for Leonard," she replied, gaging their response.

"How in the hell did shifty pirates on a tropical island pull off this calibre of a resurrection? His pieces were distributed to Covens and sealed in artifacts," he countered. The teen smirked. Not messing around, Tiberius clutched the witch's face and shut his eyes, scouring memories. Checking behind her left ear for the mark of Abaddon before releasing her, he revealed, "Laird has a witch from each Coven." Narrowing his eyes, he compelled, "Where are they?"

Resisting compulsion, Caydence taunted, "I haven't heard a peep from your friends who went upstairs. Have you?"

Smart at distraction, dumb at reading a room.

Tiberius pushed, "Kill her. We're wasting time."

Caydence mimicked, "Kill her. We're wasting time."

"I'll cut out your tongue so you can't summon shit and hand you over to the Lampir," Tiberius decreed.

"Ohhh, I'm so scared," the teen mocked.

"You don't feel guilty?" Lexy clarified, enjoying the sassy brat.

"I'm doing well all things considered," she decreed.

"You summoned a demon," Lexy reminded.

Caydence said, "I don't care."

Lexy questioned, "You knew what they were doing on this island?"

"It's all murderers and whores," Caydence decreed.

Tiberius gasped, "Everyone?"

"Everyone," the teen confirmed.

"How did we get kidnapped?" He feigned shock.

"It's a mystery," Caydence provoked.

"Clearly, she doesn't want to make the end credit scene of whore island," Tiberius chuckled.

"None of us will," Caydence decreed.

No noise besides them. Nothing.

"Kill her," Tiberius repeated.

"Have you checked the time?" The teen toyed.

An Aries Group battle ending pitch contraption went off. As they dropped to their knees in agony, Tiberius tossed his knife with scrambled senses and missed.

Casting at will, the witch shouted, "With this sacrifice I bring forth Jezebeth. Jezebeth…Jez …"

With force of will Lexy drained her essence until her mortal encasement emptied of animation. Tainted by evil, rage surged, rigid veins black as the spirit she ingested, pulsated, growing thicker. Willing silence didn't cease the agony. *This was not the time for a brain expansion.* Shrieking to release pressure, she cast out the soul. The dull orb pinged off surfaces like it was in a pinball machine and soared out the window. Hovering for a heartbeat, it shot into the dirt without shifting a grain. Tiberius was languishing, bleeding from his eyes and ears. Focused enough for a hail Mary, Lexy stumbled past writhing Lampir, and dove for the silver contraption. Sliding on her stomach down the hall, she closed it. *Holy shit.*

Peering up with her ears ringing as Lampir regained their senses, she gasped, "You're welcome."

Laughing, Wendy groaned, "What in the hell was that?"

She really was new. As they all got up, Lexy confirmed, "Did you enjoy Laird?"

"Not sure which one he was, but they were delicious," Conrad responded with a grin. "Did you kill the witch?"

"I hulked out and purged her," Lexy volunteered.

He questioned, "Where did she go?"

"A spirit vanishing into dirt isn't headed anywhere fun." Lexy commented, grinning.

"Wouldn't it be hilarious if her spirit was bound to whore island for eternity," Tiberius said joining them.

That was funny.

"Whore island?" Conrad asked, smiling.

"She was spouting off shit. We should check on the Aries Group," Tiberius explained.

They made their way to the front doors. Watching venom tipsy agents staggering while trying to load the jeeps, it was clear they hadn't set off the device. *Someone got away. Being Guardian weakened her with ego. She'd died far too many times today, trying out gifts instead of sticking with what made her legendary. Maybe that was the lesson? I guess not many survived to tell the tale. This was her training ground.* Radiance lit the horizon with their hands nearly touching. Resisting the urge to lace her fingers with his, Lexy whispered, "The Lampir can't leave until I feed them."

He whispered, "Are you stable enough?"

"Unlikely," Lexy whispered, fake smiling for the high agents.

"Give me five minutes. I'll find a creative way to explain why they'll be unconscious and join you," Tiberius affirmed. "You need a change of clothes for the drive back."

"Something wrong with what I'm wearing?" She provoked with matted scarlet hair and a bullet shredded blood-spattered shirt.

As their eyes met, he whispered, "I'm far from done with you, Mrs. Aries."

Denying the urge to kiss his smirk off, Lexy strutted away. Glancing back while opening the door, he smooched his middle finger and blew her a kiss with it. She returned the gesture, forfeiting the match by laughing as she went inside. Wanting to run back and leap into his arms as she reached the stairs, she stood there willing ration. *She'd been granted ability practice and enough give on her leash to lose herself in an illicit affair. They were going their separate ways after this job. How did she get involved with someone else she couldn't be with? What was she thinking? It's just sex. Stop romanticising this. They were free to move on.*

Descending stairs to the Lampir's reprieve from sunlight, Lexy walked into the laundry area. They were waiting for their 'free to walk in sunshine' Healer feast, perched on machines and standing around having an animated chat about what they were going to do once they made it back to civilization. All eyes turned as her stomach rumbled. *Having Healer cravings amped by Guardian's requirements, wasn't helping her slide under anyone's radar.*

Conrad wandered over asking, "Did the Aries Group set off the noise?"

"They were packing Jeeps like nothing happened. Someone got away." Offering the leader her wrist, Lexy cautioned, "I'd advise the younger Lampir to wait for Tiberius. He'll only be a minute. Healers siphon energy back."

"I can handle it," Conrad vowed as fangs emerged. Taking her hand, he bit into her wrist.

Pleasurable toxin released. *Her immune system hadn't built a resistance to this strain of Lampir venom. Had she mentioned she was Guardian? It didn't matter. Nothing did.* As Tiberius came in, the venom squashed her desire for secrecy.

Witnessing the erotic scenario, Tiberius exhaled. He spread out a blanket, saying, "Lucien sent a private boat. We have to speed this up. The Aries Group wants the hive in storage to avoid complications on the ride back to the mainland." Sitting with his back against a washing machine, he motioned for her to join him.

Fangs released from her wrist. The head Lampir said, "Only those over two hundred can feed on the Healer."

Sitting, she leaned back against the dryer next to Tiberius. His arm brushed hers. *She wanted him even more now if that was possible.*

"They're waiting. Everyone at once," Tiberius rushed.

Ravenous Lampir fed from their arms and legs as they voyeuristically watched each other endure the illicit exchange. *There wasn't a word for the pleasure one received from feeding Lampir.* As soon as her Tri-Clan partner slumped, she drained the hoard, and everyone collapsed. Revelling in satiating energy, it felt different. *She'd always been able to reverse a current to take what she needed to heal but her requirements had risen tenfold.* Mischievously peering up, Lexy whispered, "I want more."

"Please don't eat me. I have things to do," Conrad bartered, smiling.

"I'll wake you up," she enticed. With sultry eyes, Lexy got up and wandered over. Tilting her head to expose her throat, she offered, "I'll give you more." The neck was a coveted honour only bestowed during backdoor deals and a dangerous suggestion when you were so turned on your nerves were jangling.

"We'll get in trouble," Conrad rationed, breathing heavily.

She seduced, "I get in trouble with everyone."

"Your friend is waking up," he taunted, darting his eyes to Tiberius.

Good. Shifting crimson locks aside to expose a fluttering pulse, Lexy tempted, "I can handle myself."

Without debate, fangs sunk into her artery as a ribbon of crimson trickled down ivory flesh. Stroking his hair as he fed, Tiberius got up and tension thickened as reckless eyes locked in a pact of mutual self-destruction. With her libido shrieking, and emotions dulled to a hum, she reversed the current. Before the Lampir's shell hit the floor, they were making out with such volatile intensity nerve endings lit like sparklers.

With senses reeling as their mouths parted, he checked to see if he had enough pull to idle the Dragon, seducing, "Still want to kill me?" He tugged down her shorts.

Titillated, she scathingly dared, "Yes."

Wild eyed turned on, he taunted, "Good."

Dying mid orgasm in the clutches of a praying mantis didn't faze him. Tearing off clothing in a frenzy, they were on the floor. Lust blurred everything, but the wicked euphoria of him angrily grinding her into cement until they were whimpering and gasping through limb trembling spasms. Laying there with entangled limbs and unconscious Lampir everywhere, reality trickled in. They started laughing.

Rolling her on top, he teased, "I screwed the Dragon out of you."

Seekers of unfiltered deviances were loyal, dangerous addictions. She didn't have to say it. He was enraptured by the same parts of her. Straddling him with matted crimson locks, Lexy changed the subject, "Rain check on your murder." Dismounting, she put her shorts on. "Best to not get caught by the Aries Group."

He pulled up his shorts, offering, "I'll tell the Aries Group to come get them."

Waking the head guy by stroking his angular jaw, she observed his return, saying, "As promised."

Grinning as his eyes opened, Conrad said, "Thanks."

"We'll bump into each other," she whispered. "It's a long afterlife."

The Aries Group's arrival ceased their exchange. A new agent motioned for the head Lampir as others entered with black UV filtered bags.

Everyone was chatting about a final drone sweep of the island as they left. His eyes kept darting her way, doing a sexy squint. *Doing it in a room of unconscious Lampir just got checked off her unbucket list. She was going to have to wear a thought blocking bracelet for years to stop these X-rated daydreams.*

An agent directed, "Shower and change your clothes. First door to your right on the main floor. We're waiting in a Jeep out front, keep that in mind. The boats are anchored on the other side of the island."

Playing it cool, they normally climbed the first flight of stairs. Once out of sight, they no holds barred raced upstairs to the privacy of the room. He clicked the lock as she rid herself of clothes. Leaving them in a heap on the floor, Lexy went into the washroom and turned on the shower. Stepping under the spray, it pummelled away remnants of battle as red water pooled at her feet. Curtains shifted as he joined her. Smiling as he wrapped muscular arms around her, she teased, "How will you ever top this date?"

Nuzzling her neck, Tiberius whispered, "We still have a yacht ride and day's drive to meet up with our Clans."

Good. She wasn't ready to let go. Relaxing against him as sudsy hands toured her curves, she reached for him.

Capturing her wrist, he vowed, "I'm pulling over our rental car, and railing you until you lose your voice screaming." Sliding a free hand between her thighs, he rubbed her into delirium, whispering dirty intentions until a wave of bliss swelled. Biting her shoulder, heightened the intensity as it crashed and swept her away. Gasping in the aftermath of pleasure so intense, it left her shook. *She wasn't sure if she wanted to smack him or kiss him. His control issues did it for her in a crazy way.* Exposed by a rush of emotion as their eyes met, she rationed, "We can't... This can't be..."

Shampooing her hair, he responded, "We do, and it is, but I get what you're trying to say." He rinsed the blood out of her hair and rung it out, teasing, "Why wreck our marriage with reality?"

He had a point. She got out, tossed a towel at him and

wandered to the sink. Opening a toothbrush and paste, she brushed beside him in the mirror and spat in the sink. They dug through bags of clothes on the bed. He got dressed in the washroom. When he came back in, she was wearing a short halter sundress, putting on makeup.

"No bra?" He probed, kissing the shoulder he bit.

Meeting his eyes in the mirror, she provoked, "No panties either."

"That's it," he said. Tossing her over his shoulder, laughing. He smacked her bare ass carrying her to bed, flipped her onto it and as she bounced laughing, he climbed up and kissed her. Undoing his shorts, someone knocked. They quietly laughed.

"Reminding you we're waiting outside," a voice said.

"Be right out!" Lexy shouted.

They shoved everything back in the bags. Tiberius tempted, "Two minutes in the bathroom?"

"We'd hate to keep your special agent friend waiting," Lexy bantered. Zipping a bag, she tossed it, rushing, "Tick Tock Player."

Lugging the bags out of the room, he defended himself, "I haven't been a player for centuries."

"I can still count my dalliances on one hand," Lexy sparred jogging downstairs. *Wait a minute. Could she? Grey, Tomas, Orin, Tiberius... Amar, was a maybe. If she did it in an alternate reality, did it count? Either way, she intended to have fun. This was the end of that joke.*

24
Guardian Taboo

Watching the compound vanish into jungle as the Jeep's tires took on uneven terrain, passing meat spatter. *She wasn't usually where a massacre happened the next day. The Aries Group hadn't even begun the cover-up.* Listening to colourful conversation on the drive to the beach between Tiberius, and Agent Clarke, the driver tried to call ahead. The phone rang, one time, two, three times… four. Speeding up, their driver hung up, concerned.

"Something wrong?" Lexy asked, watching the driver fidget.

Tightening his grasp on the steering wheel, he replied, "It's fine."

They looked at each other. *Clearly, it wasn't.*

Pulling up at the beach, he jumped out, sprinting to the sand.

A man in a suit jogged over, explaining, "We were forced to put down a Lampir and restrain the others. We're on the next boat." He pointed at a speck in the distance.

"We haven't met. I'm Agent Phillips," he greeted, shaking

hands with Agent Clarke. They wandered off talking. Watching the other boat leave, something wasn't right. Glancing over at the agent who drove, Lexy enquired, "You haven't met that guy either?" Catching a hint of copper mixed with salty breeze, hair rose. As the imposter marched out of the bushes firing a gun, she stepped in front of the driver and took three in the chest as her thoughts darted to Clarke leaving with the shooter. Blood sputtered from her mouth, saturating her top. With no alternative, Lexy paused time, reanimating Tiberius with a kick. He sprinted at the shooter and snapped his neck. Unable to heal while holding the fight, Lexy succumbed to injuries, dropping in the sand.

Kneeling, the driver yelled, "Tiberius!"

That was dumb. Waves faded to nothing, drifting off into a sweet sleep.

Mid death gurgle, Tiberius clutched her arms, shaking her, shouting, "Feed! Take what you need."

Instinct siphoned energy luring her consciousness back as her booty call slumped. Squinting in sunlight with her hands in warm sand, it wasn't as soft as it should be. As her vision focused to the here and now, she recognized the driver's wide blue eyes. *Guess she wasn't dead.* She saw Tiberius unconscious and it didn't take a brain surgeon to know what happened.

Panicking, the agent stammered, "You took three in the chest. How are you alive? Tiberius snapped his neck. He fainted. We need to find Agent Clarke."

This guy saw way too much. Nighty night. Lexy touched him and he passed out. She laid her hands on Tiberius. As he woke, she said, "Chat later. Let's find our sexy agent friend."

Getting up, he saw the comatose agent, accusing, "What did you do?"

"He's fine," Lexy assured.

Agent Clarke staggered out of the jungle waving.

Running to her side, Tiberius teased, "You have nine lives."

Clarke sparred, "Just another day at the office."

Shutting down her reaction to the hue of her aura as they reached her, Lexy didn't have the heart to say it. *After all this insanity, she couldn't die. It wasn't fair.*

He scolded, "Move your hand so I can see."

"Can't. I'm pinching off an artery," Clarke replied, meeting his eyes.

She'd lost too much blood. She wasn't going to make it.

As he twisted his ring around, Tiberius said, "If you don't want to be a part of this, leave."

What was he doing? Lexy rationed, "You can't. You'll be entombed."

"Freeze time. I need to tell you something," he whispered.

She had to explain how much this took out of her. Waving her hand, the world stopped. She released him from pause with a touch.

"She was healed by Lampir. If we let her die, she'll turn. Her daughter has Pyrokinesis. That's how we met," Tiberius explained. "The Aries Group has her. She'll tier up. I can feel it."

"It might have been her father's genetics," Lexy pressed.

"You healed Freya's daughter and triggered my grandson," Tiberius called her out.

How did he know about that? "Yes, giving Second-Tier a bump of healing energy is cheating but I'm Guardian now. I have no idea what I'm doing."

"Please," he pled with teary eyes.

Shit Tiberius. Time commenced. Sputtering blood, her aura vanished. Shoving him out of the way, Lexy laid her hands on her chest, giving her everything she had left.

Trading places, Lexy woke with her hands in sand. Opening her eyes, she rolled onto her back. Laying on the white sand of the in-between she gazed at endless cerulean sky. *Oh, she was in so much trouble.*

A voice boomed, "Stop handing out immortality like it's a supernatural STD!"

Who was that?

"You know where you are!" The voice decreed.

Oh no. Awkwardly, she whispered, "Is that you, God?"

"He wouldn't show up for you," the voice boomed.

Fair enough

"I knew I'd be forced to deal with his spawn," the voice decreed.

She'd heard Trinity's Guardian an omniscient being. How does that work? "Show yourself," Lexy insisted, getting up.

"Wow. You're not known for your intellect but come on," the unseen Guardian mocked.

"Oh, goody. Another relative who left me languishing on a demon farm for five years," Lexy bantered.

The voice provoked, "We're not supposed to breed with lower beings."

Rolling her eyes, she slammed, "I thought your brother was the biggest cunt."

The voice scolded, "Language!"

"Why? What's a voice in the air going to do?" She taunted, slowly turning with arms outstretched. Suddenly she was in a white cube with walls. *Angel jail. Well played.*

The voice mocked, "You were saying?"

"Fine. You made your point," Lexy backed down.

"Did I? Four immortals. You've made four," a baritone voice reprimanded.

How did he get four?

The voice decreed, "You must be punished."

This ought to be good.

A huge furry black spider was in the cube with her. *Holy*

hell. Squirming away from the arachnid with nowhere to go, furry beachball sized spiders covered the walls. *It's not real.* The cell started shrinking. *It's just a hallucination.* As walls closed in, the lights went out. Furry bodies brushed against her. *Nope. No. She wasn't doing this. Die!* She splatted everything in the box.

Azariah strolled up, scolding, "That was cruel, Emmanuel."

"You said her Handler was the overdramatic one. She blew herself up," the voice chuckled.

"You put a Dragon in a box," Ankh's Guardian countered.

"That one needs to understand our hierarchy," the voice piped in from everywhere.

"What hierarchy?" Azariah pointed out, "There were three Guardian, and now there are five. Get used to it. I understand why she did it. She cares for Tiberius and the mortal."

He toyed, "Which one do you think she did it for?"

With patience, Azariah used wisdom for lesser souls, "She's stretching her wings. In time, she'll understand how fate works. If it's meant to happen, it will. Choosing the hard road still gets you there. We've all done sketchy things."

He sparred, "Like what?"

"You sunk a city," the golden haired glorious being with a heavenly glow in a flowing white gown reminded.

"I forgot about that," he confessed.

She warned, "You have one more minute to play before I take your toy away."

"She was rude," Emmanuel sighed. "What happened to be polite to your elders?"

"You always take unnecessarily graphic liberties." Smiling,

she stated, "If she has no abilities, it won't trigger a Correction. No harm no foul."

The voice echoed, "What if she tiers up a mortal?"

Smiling, Azariah warned, "That's a titillating wild card. I'm waking her up. Stay quiet."

Sprawled in the desert, Lexy gasped. Blinking in sunshine, she leapt up ready to rumble, cursing, "Asshole!"

Ankh's Guardian laughed, "Agreed."

Lexy spun around, saying, "My bad for the alien but the agent deserves to survive."

"If you've gifted an ability without the genetics to endure the brain expansion, she won't survive her first Enlightening. You've sentenced her to death," Ankh's Guardian clarified as they strolled on silken sand.

"She was sentenced to death either way. She'd been healed by Lampir," Lexy answered, by her relation's side.

"If you healed her on Oracle live stream, she'll be on a watchlist. If she gains an ability, it will trigger a Correction." Ankh's Guardian reminded, with wavy tresses shifting in desert breeze.

"I'm friendly with Third-Tier," Lexy answered.

"Making out with a few royals doesn't give you enough pull to stop anything. Let's hope they were so preoccupied, nobody saw," she sparred, smiling like she had a secret.

A few royals? She might need details of that erased time.

"Nobody brands her until she's earned her place in Tri-Clan. Deter Tiberius from doing something he'll be entombed for," she cautioned, stopping in endless desert.

Before Lexy had a chance to speak, she disintegrated into sand and blew away on a breeze.

Awakening in someone's arms with auditory rushing of the tide, Lexy opened her eyes.

In a sublime halo of sunshine, Agent Clarke tenderly kissed her. With teary auburn eyes, she said, "Thank you."

Confused by unsolicited intimacy, she wasn't this time. *She felt it too.*

Neither moved until Tiberius teased, "I can leave you two alone."

Lexy summoned him, "Join us."

He wandered over reprimanding, "I'm spanking both of you so hard if I have to cover my junk when they come to shore."

Her radio went off. Clarke sighed, "Duty calls." They got up as Agent Clarke wandered away talking.

Once their mutual friend was out of earshot, Tiberius questioned, "What happened?"

Details flooded back. "If I triggered abilities, she'll have to earn her place in Tri-Clan. If you brand her before Correction, you'll be entombed. It's possible I didn't set off anything."

Cupping her face, Tiberius stared into her eyes, affirming, "If you didn't do this, she'd be Lampir. You gave her a chance to fight another day. What happens after this is up to fate."

Dying peacefully in his arms was far from the worst way to go. "What are you going to do if this was caught on Oracle live stream and her Correction falls on your lap?" Lexy asked with their gazes locked.

Sombrely, Tiberius whispered, "I'd hand it over to someone else in Triad. She can't earn her way in fighting me." Watching a boat approaching, he probed, "Did you get in trouble?"

"My uncle locked me in a box with spiders," she responded as Clarke ran out to meet her fellow agent.

"Dick," Tiberius commented, empathetically wincing.

"I blew myself up," she said, as they towed the boat to shore.

Standing next to her, he whispered, "I already miss you."

"That's a shame. I have no feelings for you at all," Lexy toyed, strutting away. When she glanced back, he was grinning and shaking his head. *She already missed him too.*

25
Back To The Mainland

*E*ating a sandwich with her hair blowing in humid ocean breeze as the island grew smaller in the distance, Lexy knew she was going to replay this glorious escape for decades. *For forty-eight hours, she'd been free to be every version of herself. What she kept hidden in hotel rooms got a chance to thrive in the sunshine of a new day. She wasn't going to fit back into the box she arrived in. Perhaps, that's what all great adventures were for. She needed to continue this progression.* Guilt tightened her chest. She swallowed it. *She spent a day at a hedonism resort with Tiberius, and a night slaying serial murderers on a tropical island. It was just what she needed. She had fun. She didn't want to apologize or feel remorse. Tiberius was overthinking something too.*

Bumping open the door with her hip, Agent Clarke wandered out with drinks, saying, "Thank you for having my back."

Taking a glass of champagne, Lexy wondered what would trigger her thoughts to return to this. *Would it be the hum of an engine or warm ocean air with a hint of coconut scented sunblock?* Golden bubbles bounced as they clinked flute glasses.

Tiberius saluted, "To erasable shenanigans."

Hoping he wasn't erasing everything, Lexy sipped her drink.

Lowering her glass, flecks of amber in her chestnut eyes sparkled in sunlight as Clarke bargained, "Come on, Ti."

"Don't worry, I'm not erasing much," he affirmed.

The rules of this immortal game were clear. She couldn't remember being healed by her.

Kissing her cheek, Tiberius tweaked his friend's recollection of events, "You'll remember everything from the beginning of this job, including our naughty deeds playing a married couple, and the flirtation with Lexy leading to a steamy distraction kiss by the washrooms. They must have drugged you. You came to held captive in a secure room with a deceased Aries Group agent at their compound on the island. I was tossed into your room, later that day we escaped. While freeing hostages, we found Brenda, but not her husband Theo. This job was more nefarious than expected. Wealthy people were paying to hunt hostages. Each cabin was central to a purchased hunting area. There were automatic weapons and chainsaws. When supernatural aspects came into the fight, lots of innocent people died but Lexy held them off while I helped you and Brenda get away. I left you in a cave. There was an explosion. You were unconscious again. Your friend died in the blast. Lampir healed you. Everything else is a blur." Smiling, he resumed his reconfiguration with cheat notes. "Trust instinct. Never brush an uneasy feeling off." Stroking her face, Tiberius whispered, "Earth to Clarke. Was there something you needed to say?"

Squinting, Agent Clarke admitted, "I gapped." Looking back at the tiny speck in the distance, she confessed, "I don't remember the drive to the boat."

"Lampir venom packs a punch," Lexy responded, smiling.

"It does," she flirted, eyeing her up.

Maintaining a straight face, Tiberius announced, "Let's go find out our itinerary."

They left as Lexy leaned over the railing watching white-caps dance on teal sea. *She'd never contemplated a threesome, but she was now. Itemized in order of titillation, she had a list of deviant deeds to check off. She wasn't going to apologize for this, hide from it, or play it down. Adoring deviancies as much as strengths was the goal for any friendship. What were the chances Grey would hop onboard to her new way of thinking without a weeklong pout fest? Being overly attached was a side-effect of their bond. He needed a minute to let change sink in. Knowing what happened when he was a child, it made sense. When she returned, she'd let him come to her when he was ready again.* With a plan of action, she went inside to find out what was in store for the final leg of their adventure. Bumping into Tiberius, she said, "I was coming to find you."

With a devious grin, he towed her into the washroom, shut the door, backed her up against the wall and tenderly kissed her. With their eyes locked as he pulled away, he whispered, "If you want to keep this job a secret to make your life easier, I'll play along. The Aries Group has a non-disclosure agreement. They can't say a word."

Adjusting her footing to move with motion beneath her, she embraced him, confessing, "Grey knows the truth even when I don't tell him."

"The truth about what?" He toyed, nuzzling her neck.

With arms laced around his neck, she reminded, "Stroking your junk before I slit your throat set off cataclysmic drama."

"It was innocent in comparison," he teased with a crooked grin.

With an inconvenient fluttering heart, she said, "I might have to kill you the next time we bump into each other."

Swaying with the ocean, he affirmed, "I know."

Unspoken emotion hovered in a cloud of uncertainty as he toyed with her hair, confessing, "I panic and do stupid things to regain my control when I care."

"Same," she admitted. "I'm not telling everyone about this, but if Grey asks…"

With twinkling eyes, a tilted brow and mischievous grin, he whispered, "Surely you're not going to tell him everything?"

"Giving an immortal a coronary isn't on my unbucket list," Lexy toyed, groping him.

"I know we're supposed to be enemies again, but if they stumble upon a murder island sequel, I told them I'd resume our unorthodox partnership," he confessed.

Her heart skipped a beat with their eyes locked in longing. *It was wrong to hope there was another murder island.*

"Would you join me again?" He taunted, tucking a loose tendril behind her ear.

She loved the way he looked at her. The awe in his eyes, made her feel like he'd do anything to be with her. There weren't many lines she wouldn't cross for a night with him after this risqué adventure. The boat lurched. Losing her footing, she ended up in his arms. *She should stop hugging him.*

Nibbling her ear, he naughtily seduced, "Maybe our agent friend will join us next time?"

Her inner dialogue was going to be off the hook.

Clutching her ass while feathering hot sensual kisses on her throat, he hiked up her dress, saying, "Let's cross something off your list."

There wasn't enough time. They were docking. She cautioned, "I heard your wife is mean when provoked."

He put her on the sink. Caressing between her thighs, he toyed, "I heard I can have her purring like a kitten in under two minutes."

With intention clear, he knelt. Arching her back as his wicked tongue drove her to the edge of sanity, she went with it. Teetering on climax, someone called his name. Clutching his hair, she gasped, "I will kill you." Finishing her off in seconds, tension released in a surge of pleasure so intense, she had to bite her fist to stop herself from crying out.

"Shimmy over, gorgeous maniac," he prompted, reaching past her to turn on the sink.

Gorgeous maniac. Fair enough. Shaking her head at her lack of filter, she slid off the counter, mumbling, "Thanks. Sorry about the murder threat."

He brushed by, teasing, "I'm aware death threats are part of our booty call deal."

He left her standing there. *Holy shit.* Exhaling, Lexy saw her reflection. Hiding the fact that he just rocked her world, she reached for the door. *Game face.*

Accustomed to surprise destinations, not being back at the resort didn't faze either one. Disembarking, they were handed the backpacks they'd left on the beach. They strolled down a dock without the bells and whistles of the last one. Their fingers brushed. They walked further apart so they wouldn't be tempted to hold hands.

Walking with them, Agent Clarke explained, "Your meet up location for this evening is punched into the GPS. You have time to kill."

"Do we have phones?" Tiberius questioned, peering inside.

"Throwaways," she confirmed as they wandered into a dusty parking lot. Grinning while unlocking a truck, their friend announced, "It's not sexy but there's air conditioning."

Embracing the agent, Tiberius said, "Text me tomorrow."

"Everyone from the island job is sequestered for forty-eight hours," Clarke disclosed. "I'll have plenty of time to kill too."

Best to keep their agents safe until the Lampir blood was out of their system.

Shaking Lexy's hand, Clarke flirted, "Until we meet again."

She felt it too. Like the shit disturber she was destined to be, Lexy reciprocated, "Feel free to text me tomorrow."

Her eyes darted from Tiberius to Lexy. Shaking her head, Clarke teased, "Don't do anything I wouldn't do."

"We're going to do everything you'd do. All of it," Tiberius baited with a Cheshire cat grin.

Walking away, she said, "Be at the rendezvous point, Ti."

Opening the passenger door for her, Tiberius toyed, "Mrs. Aries."

Sliding into her seat, she said, "Mr. Aries." He closed the door and walked around to get in.

Driving away, Lexy tinkered with the radio until she found a station, she enjoyed. Listening to music as they pulled out onto the main road, Tiberius reminisced, "You dove in front of grenades for me."

"I did. Didn't I?" Lexy confirmed. Passing teal ocean and flowering bushes, she confessed, "I'm glad you made me come."

"Which time?" He provoked, grinning.

Laughing, she clarified, "To the resort."

"Even after you were blown up," he countered, darting his eyes her way.

She confessed, "Even after I was dismembered."

Watching her, he mumbled, "Wish we had a backseat."

"This works," she teased. He veered down a dusty side road with her laughing.

With smouldering eyes, he dropped his shorts and turned up the music. Hiking her dress, she straddled him with parted lips and no pretence. With hands clutching her hips, she rode him harder and faster until her eyes rolled back with pleasure. Whimpering with the wheel jabbed into her back, she gyrated her hips through each lusty wave, crying out. He brutishly tugged her mouth to his, taunting her with his tongue until he was bucking, huskily gasping her name.

"Now," she demanded, biting his neck.

He dug his nails into her hips, cursing and shivering beneath her. Savouring euphoria with his head on the rest, he confessed, "I'd marry you for real."

"I barely like you," she fibbed, straight-faced.

Caressing her scarlet locks, he baited, "Liar."

Enjoying every second, she reminded, "Booty call rules strictly prohibit feelings."

Gazing into her eyes, he said, "I'm putting another Aries Group work vacation on the letting my baby mama take Seth's place without bitching wish list."

Someone knocked on the window. *Shit.*

Wiping his blood off her lips, he whispered, "Play along."

A male voice cautioned, "The congregation is about to come out."

Caught in a compromising position with her on his lap and only her dress concealing frisky exploits, Tiberius apologized, "Newlyweds. Sorry. Leaving!" The well-dressed man walked away. She scrambled into the passenger seat. He tugged up his shorts chuckling, "Check off sex in a chapel parking lot." He drove away.

He looked proud of himself. She swatted him, accusing, "You purposely pulled over there!" He lost it laughing.

Shock switched to awe. Impressed with how far he was willing to go to make their time together so epic it couldn't be outdone, she shook her head smiling as they slowed to a crawl.

A crowd was gathered in the road. Her neck prickled. "Let's find out what this is about," Lexy suggested, getting out before he'd stopped. Walking through the mass of locals, she caught enough pieces of conversation to see the big picture. Tiberius joined her. She shared, "Two missing children aged six and three. Their father ran into the store for five minutes. He left them outside with the dog who always comes when called." *That is the red flag for her.* "Do we have time to find a few kids?"

Checking out bystanders, Tiberius probed, "Five minutes to silently kidnap a dog and two people in a busy town square. How would Ankh do it?"

A corner store, restaurant, hairdresser and gas station surrounded by sparse bush and ocean. Scanning auras as everyone separated to begin searching, Lexy whispered, "Lure the pet, the children would follow. You can't hear a dog barking in a restaurant freezer."

"Nope, it doesn't fit the five-minute timeline," he answered, heading into the narrow space between buildings.

Following, she teased, "What would Tiberius do?"

Pointing at a wrapper and scattered candy on the ground, he shared a theory, "Lure the dog with beef jerky. Give kids drugged candy and toss everyone in the trunk of a car."

"It doesn't fit the timeline. Candy has to be digested." Gesturing to a cloth in the alley, she said, "Smell that rag."

He picked it up and sniffed it without thinking. Shaking his head at himself as he staggered. He chuckled, "You got me."

"It works every time," she laughed, counteracting woozy effects of chloroform with a touch of healing energy. *She needed an aura refresher.* Impaling her hand on an exposed nail without flinching, her flesh warmed, solidifying. They stepped out behind the restaurant. Seeing tire tracks in the sand, a hint of sulphur lingered. *Shit.* They sprinted back to the truck, leapt in, and drove around back following the tracks until they hit pavement.

With the engine running, Tiberius prompted, "Which way sweetheart?"

"I'd go the opposite direction and loop back to the road out of town," Lexy directed.

He turned back the way they came, saying, "I saved her number on your phone."

They didn't have time to mess around. Grinning, Lexy taunted, "Pedal to the metal, Ti. They're getting away."

Bouncing on uneven backroad terrain, they spat up gravel peeling out onto the main route. Scanning cars while weaving by with the pedal to the floor, he questioned, "Planning to read auras in cars ahead?"

"Seeing who I have the urge to eat," she disclosed, knowing he wasn't one to judge.

With a devilish glint in his eyes, Tiberius exhaled, proving her assumptions by flirting, "Lexy, Lexy, Lexy." Gunning it, he swerved vehicles.

Driving for a half hour at full speed with the thrill of the hunt, a predatory tug shifted her eyes to the right. *There was a turn off.* Catching the tail end of a vehicle as it vanished behind trees, she pointed out, "There they are."

Turning, he taunted, "We'll lose them if it's not."

With her stomach growling as they pursued, she confirmed, "Pretty sure."

He unrolled her window, prompting, "Blow the tire."

She leaned out and swiped an arm, sending gravel projectiles at the tires, metal tinged. *Shit, she missed.* They sped up. About to try again, trees cleared and on one side of the road there was a cliff with ocean below. Getting back in, Lexy decreed, "They won't survive the drop."

Tiberius bantered, "What now, Superhero?"

"Get as close as you can," she ordered, climbing out the window of the speeding vehicle onto the roof. On all fours, she shouted, "Closer!"

Unrolling his window further, Tiberius yelled, "This crazy shit is why other Clans have to bail Ankh out!"

Crazy shit. That was funny. "They refused my tea party invite!" She screamed back, launching herself onto the roof of the other car. It swerved before she had time to grip the window lip. Cackling as her nails scraped metal, it didn't shake her off. Peering in the window, she threatened, "Don't make me come in there!" Manoeuvring out of sight as the lone driver pulled out a gun, she grinned.

Recklessly shooting through the roof, the middle-aged guy screamed, "Psychotic bitch!"

Aware she'd been hit as her stomach and arm heated, he swerved to shake her off. *Dick.* Punching through the roof, Lexy clutched a handful of his hair, commanding, "Pull the fuck over!" He dropped the gun and stomped on the brakes. Skidding to a stop inches from plummeting over the ledge, he struggled free and ran away. Sliding off the roof as Tiberius sprinted over, she said, "Check on the kids while I eat this guy." She took off after him. Screaming as he saw her on his tail, he opted for death. He ran for the cliff and leapt. Catching his shirt, she tugged him back. Grinning at his dusky aura, she didn't care what its intentions were. *Scavengers were of no concern to lions.* Draining his energy, Lexy tossed his husk off the cliff into the sea and wandered back.

Having already moved the unconscious children and their loyal companion to the backseat of the car, Tiberius filled her in, "They're overheated but they'll make it. The Aries Group is twenty minutes out. They were still at the boat launch. There are wipes in the console. You might have time to clean up and change."

Wet wipes were so handy. Peering down at her dress, she strolled to the truck and rifled through the bags. Finding a strapless stretchy tube top sundress, she stripped and began cleaning off blood.

"I'll get what you can't see," Tiberius offered. Wiping her face, he enquired, "Find out anything?"

Naked, she stated, "We didn't chat."

Watching her dress, he asked, "Where's his body?"

"I ate him and tossed his corpse off a cliff," Lexy revealed, adjusting the tube top. *The breeze was nice.*

Patting down wild crimson hair while gazing into her eyes, he declared, "You are impressively crazy."

"Back atcha," she teased, as a black sedan came into sight.

Getting out, Agent Clarke laughed, "How did you already find those children? We just found out about it."

"Let's not worry about the details," Tiberius responded. "The kidnapper is fish food. He jumped off a cliff."

"Ahh, I see. You didn't happen to find out why?" Their agent friend pressed, grinning.

"It was a Tri-Clan thing," he confirmed.

Clarke probed, "So, he just leapt to his demise?"

"Sure," Lexy replied, watching limp children being carried to the sedan.

The dog woke up, as Tiberius placed him on the backseat in the sedan. Scratching is neck, he praised, "You're a good boy. I know you won't tell anyone about us." The scruffy dog leapt up overzealously licking his face. Carefree laughter thawed her resolve. *She needed to derail this train of thought before it evoked more than she wanted during the final leg of their steamy road trip.*

Interrupting her thoughts, Agent Clarke observed, "One of you punched in the roof. Shove that car off the cliff into the water before you go."

Shooing her away, Tiberius scolded, "Don't crash on your way back. You're supposed to be sequestered. I'll message you after we do your job."

"Don't get involved in more local drama," Agent Clarke bantered, laughing as she got in. Unrolling a window as they drove away, she called out, "Don't be late!"

Pushing the car to the ledge, they listened as it splashed into the ocean. Aware of the sun's placement in the sky as rays glittered white caps with their fingers nearly touching, taunting desire, Lexy summoned reality, "I should have questioned that guy before eating him."

"You should have but, as per usual, the scenario was more than anticipated." Removing a phone from his pocket, Tiberius handed it to her, baiting, "Found fish bait's phone in the car. Shall we stop by?"

Fantastic. Messages referring to the children as a meat delivery. This shit was eating away their day. Lexy sighed, "Guess it was too much to hope for an afternoon off? We can't not deal with this."

With arms around her waist, he tempted, "Quick murder spree and then we'll stop for a Pina Colada?"

"I'm onto you. Spoiling me with romantic gestures so when we're back to being enemies, I kill you quickly?" Lexy taunted. Dying to tow him to the truck and have her way with him, she playfully shoved him away. Strutting over there, she shouted, "Let's go player!"

As he searched for a radio station, she leaned back. Closing her eyes as cool salty air tussled her hair, every part of her was alive in a way she'd never experienced. *The woman and beast were one entity. There was nothing to hide or tone down for comfort.*

Watching her instead of the road ahead, he turned away as they arrived at a busy tavern with a full parking lot. Glancing at the address, he confirmed, "We're here."

How was he delivering children to a bar? Snatching his cell, Lexy reminded, "Sitting here with the engine running is a red flag."

Coasting so the truck was hidden, he took out the keys, and toyed, "Are we pretending I don't have a thousand years of experience?"

Quietly getting out, they met at the rear of the truck. Wiping perspiration from her hairline, she suggested, "We'd position ourselves at various vantage points, text the number to see who picks up and send in Siren distractions to lure those involved out. We'd put them down elsewhere."

"Or we could do this in five minutes," Tiberius teased.

"Fine. What would Triad do?" Lexy humoured him.

Watching her reaction, he provoked, "Silent Cannibals in a remote location with UV-tinted windows. Gee… I wonder what they are?"

"I thought I wasn't dealing with dick you until after we parted ways tonight?" She taunted, smiling. "Lampir wouldn't refer to children as meat."

Laying it on thick, he said, "Sweetheart, we've all been clearing out genetically enhanced hives north of the border. Why wouldn't the same thing be going on down here?"

Wanting to throat punch him, she cautioned, "It's like you don't think I'll snap your neck in this parking lot and leave you frying in the sun?"

"Quit flirting. I'll screw the frown off your face after we're done," he taunted, walking away.

Asshole! Broiling with rage, she pitched a nice sized rock at him.

Without turning to look, he rubbed his back, chuckling, "It doesn't take much to set you off. Good idea, though. Let's take out the windows so we're not covered in spittle."

Not relishing the idea of hybrid Lampir and Lycanthrope saliva, she scooped up another handful. Grinning, the problem-solving duo smashed every window, revelling in pitchy shrieks of flaming crossbreeds as they raced around lighting everything inside on fire.

By his side, watching evil vanquish itself, she appreciated the simplicity of how Triad dealt with things. When the building was fully engulfed, they strolled back to the truck having barely lifted a finger. Realising she had the phone, Lexy waved it, saying, "I forgot to toss this in fire." On a whim, she called the number the kidnapper was texting. As he got into the truck, she heard a faint ringtone. Waving, she followed the tune to the back of the rig they were parked behind.

Curious, he got out, asking, "What are you up to?"

"It's ringing in the back of the rig," she answered, trying to open the door. *There was a keypad with a light.* "Have you ever disabled one of these?"

Tiberius remarked, "Pimped out security. We rented one a while back for our Crypts. Bet the Lampir playing genetic roulette with local Lycanthrope has his coffin in here."

"Bet the only person who knew the code died in that fire?" Lexy teased, knowing Ankh would have called the phone first.

That was the purpose of research before action.

Using brute force Triad thinking, Tiberius suggested, "We'll burn this too and wait until it blows up before leaving."

Something felt off. Her spine shivered. Wracking her mind, to decipher why she was triggered. Tiberius took off his shirt, distracting her. *Maybe she was overthinking this? She could let him set it on fire and have her way with him in the truck while it burned.*

Wrapping a stick with his shirt, he stuck it in and was posed to strike metal with a rock to create a spark.

What was that sound? "Wait," Lexy insisted. With her ear against hot metal, she willed herself to hear inside. *Was that a child?* "Put that down. We have to get in there," she rushed, prepared to punch the side.

"It's not the roof of a car, you can't bust through that," he warned, smiling.

Not listening, she shattered her hand without even making a dent. Storming back to the door fuming as fragmented bones mended, she placed her hand against the keypad, willing, *let me in!* In a flash, she was somewhere dark and cold. *Whoops.* Tiberius' muffled voice was shouting her name. *She didn't. She couldn't?* Bumping into solid frozen things, stinging her arms, her nose ran into icicles. *It was freezer cold with demon stank and a telltale hint of copper.* "Hello?" Lexy gasped. *She wasn't usually this gullible.*

"Hello," a child's voice sang.

Her throat tightened with each excruciating breath. She indulged it, "What's your name, sweetie?"

"Name for you, no," a childlike voice misworded.

Wearing a sundress with no panties while being freeze-dried was not a good time. Her hypothermia scattered brain didn't have enough function left to beat around the bush, "You smell like Satan's asshole after a five-mile jog."

Chains jangled, as it tugged against them, cackling, "Flesh sweet."

Wonderful. She'd willed herself into a freezer truck full of people meat with a child of nefarious demonic pedigree. The disorganised speech of a flesh-eating Demon was a frequent flyer scenario. Things with a low centre of gravity were hard to fight. How much slack did it have on those chains? Inching closer shivering, she played along, "Hope you have a jacket."

"Colder, I make it," the childlike voice granted.

No, no. The humming grew louder. *Crap.* "You shouldn't have," Lexy whispered as muscles knotted. *Capture a demon that eats flesh to skin your victims for you. Diabolical. The atrophy was concerning. At this rate of icy descent, she'd be a Dragonsicle in half an hour.* Heading back the way she came with scrambled senses, she was vaguely aware of banging. *Tiberius knew she was in here. That's good. Being skinned alive was unpleasant. She could eat it if she could catch it.* She laid her cards on the table, "I'm Ankh. Nobody is coming to feed you."

"No care. Care not, skinny skin, skin you raw," the depravity sang. Cackling maniacally, it knocked into things, grunting and yowling.

Which way was she facing? Moving away from the ruckus with joints stiffening, she found the back door. Pressing hands against the wall, she willed herself out. *Nothing. It was too cold to summon shit.* She sat down. *She'd drained too much energy counteracting the temperature. She couldn't will her way out of this.* Hoping she wouldn't slump forward when her healing ability petered out, she closed her eyes. *This was the choose your demise portion of the job.* Willing Tiberius to hear, Lexy croaked, "Burn it! Blow it up!" Chains jangled. Outlines shifted. Immobilised with eyeballs too stiff to move, she called it. *If the chain had too much slack this thing was winning the flesh-eating monster lottery with a healing continuous skin source.* Blood in her veins turned to slush, slowing her heart. Pa pum, pa... pum... pa... pum... pa... Enveloped in warmth, her consciousness floated away absolving her of torture.

A voice pulled her from the precipice, *'Get your ass up!'*

Her last flicker of brain function recognized it. *You've got to be fucking kidding me.*

'Language!' The angelic entity reprimanded.

This idiot. Enraged, heat surged in her core travelling down her limbs. Blood warmed, and her heart started beating.

"Good, good. Rage is your trigger. Now, find a conductor," Emmanuel instructed.

What?

'Didn't you go to school?' The Guardian provoked.

Held captive on a demon farm, you dick.

'This again. You made it through Testing with a Dragon ability. Suck it up,' he bantered.

Livid, she digested the ignorance. *Suck it up?* Heat surged again focusing her brain. *Atrophy was still an issue.*

His voice instructed, *'That wasn't that hard, was it? Now, tip forward. It will trigger healing ability as it skins you. You'll amp up fast, then eat it, and use it.'*

Voluntarily be skinned alive. No big deal. Son of a... Lexy lunged into ravenous gleefully giggling clutches. *This was unpleasant.* As it reached the third chorus of its catchy happy skin eating song, she reversed the current, draining it limp. With a full battery, cold barely fazed her. She got up, demanding, "I want out." *Nothing happened.*

'Need vengeance? I'm outside. Focal point and intention,' Emmanuel provoked.

He was toast. Furious, she jumped out.

BLINKING BACK INTO EXISTENCE IN SWELTERING SUNSHINE WITH aftereffects of spinning in a circle, and Tiberius repeating her name, *she had to purge it. It was too much.* Dropping to her knees with hands in the gravel, Lexy shrieked a seismic tremor. Splitting the parking lot like an earthquake with underground explosions leading away from the pub, down the mountainside it created a massive fountain of water once her wrath made it too sea. *That wasn't good.* She leapt to her feet like a superhero.

"What was that?" Tiberius muttered, awestruck.

No idea.

As smoke billowed, he rushed, "Run!"

Scrambling into the truck, they sped away, he warned, "We have to involve the Aries Group."

"You can't tell them I did this," she countered.

Glancing her way, he vowed, "I won't." With near missing rocks tumbling down the mountainside, there was a large crevasse in the narrow lane and nowhere to go. He put his foot to the floor. Jumping it, he swerved as tires bounced, regaining control as they sped down the road.

"Mad action hero driving skills," she commented, looking back.

He pulled over on the highway, saying, "Call the Aries Group, they have to cover this up."

She trusted him. About to call, his cell rang. Wincing, Lexy pressed speakerphone. In unison, the frenemies with benefits answered, "Hello."

Agent Clarke scolded, "You ignored me and went on a side trip. Which one of you blew up a mountain?"

Taking his silence as a hint, Lexy explained, "We found a cellphone with an address for a meat delivery in the car before pushing it into the ocean. It was a bar full of rabid Lampir Hybrid. We broke the windows. They burned. Don't let locals sift through the ashes. There's a freezer truck full of human meat in the parking lot. We're guessing they had explosives stored in underground tunnels from the bar to the water. The fire set it off and the road was damaged by a slide. You'll need another route in."

"Is that all?" Agent Clarke sighed.

Shrugging, Tiberius confirmed, "Predators exterminated. No more side excursions unless it's for fun, I swear."

She had fun.

"Tell everyone it will take a few days for toxins to clear. Triad will come back to do a sweep," Tiberius offered.

"Alright. We'll keep local authorities away," she replied.

"Do not go in there," he cautioned.

"Guarantees are above my pay range. If you're not back fast, a dumbass with no self-preservation skills will arrange a team," she clarified.

"Not you," Lexy insisted, driving the point home.

She laughed, "I'm locked down for two days."

"Text me a contact number for Lucien," Tiberius bartered. "They can deal with this mess. He owes me a favour."

"Duty calls," Clarke curtly responded, hanging up.

Their eyes met as they started laughing. They saw the time. *It was three thirty. They'd wasted most of the day.* Longingly staring at each other, as cars sped by, Lexy suggested, "Let's eat something and find a deserted beach."

"That's the best idea I've heard all day," Tiberius agreed, smiling as they pulled out. "What is my gorgeous wife in the mood for?" He asked, still playing the game while fiddling with the station.

She flirted, "Maybe you should pull over first?"

With mischievous eyes glinting in the sunshine streaming through the window, and a sexy uneven grin, he toyed, "Mrs. Aries, needs to tell me what she wants to eat before I service her for the hundredth time."

Biting her lip, she crept her sundress up her thigh, sparring, "Mrs. Aries might not be able to wait."

"Ohhh, Mrs. Aries wants to be drilled into a sand dune," he bantered.

"Mrs. Aries would love it," she dared.

With a pained expression as she inched it up even further, he cautioned, "If I bury my face between Mrs. Aries thighs right here, we'll get arrested."

"We've been through worse," she provoked, flashing him.

Veering, Tiberius chuckled. Regaining composure, he dared "Keep it up and you'll be bent over the hood clawing the paint when Ankh shows up."

With her luck it would be Grey. "I'll behave," she gave in, fixing her dress.

Sneaking glances at each other with the tension so thick, they were hangry by the time they reached the next town, he pulled over at a gas station with a fruit stand and food trucks. He handed her an Aries Group card, suggesting, "Figure out what you want. Surprise me. I'll fill up the tank and grab drinks."

Figure out what you want. Guilt turned a suggestion into a quandary. Everything looked delicious. Ordering enchiladas, churros and frozen fruit on a stick dipped in chocolate, she turned to see where he was. He was sitting at a picnic table with slushies and bottled water. She wandered over wishing there was alcohol in it.

Jangling keys, Tiberius said, "We're close to where you need to be later. I got a room so we can clean up."

Relishing the idea of privacy, she placed their food on the table, asking, "What's in the bag?"

Passing her a bottle of tequila, he replied, "Thought you might want to spike yours."

"Are you sure you can't read people's minds?" Lexy teased, grinning.

Digging into the assortment, his eyes met hers, admitting, "I've been cheating. You've allowed me into your thoughts a few times. I've been gaging your needs by what you've enjoyed in the past."

"How does it work?" She questioned, wanting to know more.

Swallowing his mouthful, Tiberius reached for her hand, revealing, "I make a connection like this." Tenderly caressing her fingers, he said, "I aim it to what I want to find out with intention. Ever since you made a deal with me to see what created the Dragon when they tricked us into fighting together against Abaddon at the Summit, I've had a crash course on you in my dreams."

Staring into his eyes, Lexy probed, "Even intimate things?"

"All from your perspective. I experience what you felt," he revealed, grinning.

Having every secret exposed, she didn't have anything left to lose. "Promise you won't tell anyone?"

"You know secrets that would get me entombed," he teased, playing with her hand.

Watching their connection, she whispered, "I haven't even told Grey."

"I know," he confirmed. "I bet it was hard to not say the one thing that would explain how you went from despising me, to this."

She circled back to his confession of perspective, "So, you're me in these dreams sleeping with Grey?"

"I knew you weren't going to let that slide," he chuckled, biting a churro.

"That's why you were so quick to agree to promise you'd never hurt him," she provoked, sipping her tequila spiked slushie. Innocently baiting him under the table with her foot, she teased, "Have you seen Orin too?"

"You're having far too much fun with this information," he countered, reciprocating her under the table games. "Probably why drunk me picked a fight with Orin at that banquet in Vegas."

Thinking on it for a second, she decided there was no reason not to tell him. "Mel, told me you confessed to having feelings for me."

"That should be obvious by now," he bantered, grinning in sunshine. "Orin's talents in bed were messing with my head."

Trying to not react, she sparred, "It's a Healer thing."

"I'm going to avoid fighting Grey. Promise me one thing," he whispered.

"Why are we being so quiet?" She whispered, shaking with laughter.

"I'm not sure I could take the visual of sleeping with either one of my brothers," he whispered.

Seeing the perspective trauma, she baited, "I'm immediately sleeping with Thorne if you hurt Grey."

"Hilarious," he sparred. He sucked up slushy and blew it out the straw at her.

What in the hell? If he saw her sex life, he also knew her pet peeves. With sticky slushie on her chest, Lexy reprimanded, "I'm spanking you for that when we get to our room."

"I'll lick it off, Mrs. Aries. Let's go," he provoked, gathering up their garbage.

With sunshine flashing through the window as they drove away, she closed her eyes wanting to pretend the relationship was real until reality showed up to smack it out of her hands. *This was an afterlife altering stint away. She'd flexed her scaley Dragon wings with a co-conspirator who got her. There was so much going on. Arrianna was sucked into a vortex on the beach. Her sister was in a lizard terrarium in the back of a big rig. She didn't even know how everything played out. If she called to check, she knew the delicate film of soap encasing her fantasy bubble would burst.* Selfishly needing to let her heart float freely, she glanced at her illicit addiction. *She was going to be back with Ankh soon. For now, she needed this.*

"You're overthinking something, Mrs. Aries," Tiberius said, pulling down a driveway towards the beach.

Smiling as their eyes met with salty ocean breeze moving through her crimson hair, she sighed, "It feels like we've been alone together for weeks, Mr. Aries. Thanks for showing me a good time."

"Back atcha, Mrs. Aries," he replied. Parking, he fiddled with his cellphone, saying, "This one is ours."

Grabbing her bag, so she could fix herself up afterwards to hide the evidence of her torrid hedonism resort murder island affair, she couldn't look at the time. *A part of her wanted to get left behind so it didn't have to end. The fantasy of having this.*

He snatched her bag off her, threw it inside and picked her up. With her legs wrapped around his waist, he carried her over the threshold, kicked the door shut and tossed her on the bed.

Peeling off his shirt, Tiberius said, "We have a few hours to break this bed before we have to come up for air."

Ridding himself of his shorts, he pitched them across the room and crawled onto the bed after her. He rolled down her dress, roughly yanked it over her hips and tossed it. Before she could think, he buried his face between her thighs. Laughter turned to gasps. Clutching sheets moaning, he flipped her whispering dirty intentions as he smacked her ass hard. Making damn good and sure she'd never forget their exploits, he drilled her into the mattress with such angry force, and speed, it triggered an implosion so intense, her knees gave way as she raspily screamed into a pillow. *Oh, it was on!* She gyrated her hips.

"Wait, wait," he bartered, pulling out. "One minute. I'm too close."

She turned his way, teasing, "I'm not done."

"My point exactly. It's now my mission to make you scream like that again," he seduced, smiling.

Straddling him, she shoved him onto his back, saying, "My mission takes priority."

"Does it?" He flirted, caressing crimson hair concealing a breast.

Kissing his neck, she scolded, "You'll do as you're told."

Watching, he cautioned, "I'm already obsessed with you. Going off too fast will stunt my ego."

"For the good of mankind." Kissing his abs, she provoked, "I'd grab a pillow."

"Destroy me if it'll gives you a thrill. I'm here for it. Anything you want is yours," he submitted. Watching as her mouth slid down his length, he groaned, "This is dark even for you." Clutching her hair as she hit the rhythm that would finish him off in a flash like she'd read his mind, his eyes rolled back, cursing. With his eyes closed, he whispered, "That might be the meanest thing ever done to me."

"You're welcome," she teased. Getting up, she tossed him a bottled water, suggesting, "Drink up." Downing what was left of the tequila, Lexy chased it with a water. Placing hers on the nightstand, she straddled him, nibbling on his ear.

"I'm going to let you wreck me," he sighed.

Same. She enticed, "What do you want?"

"Everything. All of you," Tiberius whispered, caressing her hair.

She'd given him too much already. She kissed him, enticing, "My offer expires in, 3… 2… 1…"

Grinning, he clarified, "Anything?"

"Anything," she confirmed, knowing this was all they had.

"Sit on my face," he baited with devious crinkled eyes.

That request came out of left field. Shifting up until she felt his breath, she hovered, asking, "This is fun for you?"

Breath seduced with a whisper, "You have no idea," tugging her thighs so she was flush with his face.

Clutching the headboard as he stirred up ripples in her sensual sea, his current took her away from duty and concern. Coasting over waves, their differences meant nothing. As he gained momentum, she fought the urge to tell him she'd never forget their adventure, and if the world ended tomorrow, this was worth it. Moaning as a ten-point tsunami crashed with limb trembling rapture, she cursed her way through it. Glancing down, at his smug grin, she smiled. Floating in a mindless haze, she exhaled, attempting a dismount.

Holding her there, he reprimanded, "I'm not done."

She was going to be horny all the time after these sexcapades. Gripping the headboard, she lost herself until the lusty libido rollercoaster plunged downhill with her reckless heart thudding like a kick drum. She moaned as her toes curled. With shock parted lips, she flopped next to him, tingling.

"Okay, I'm ready," he announced.

Funny. He was making a point. "One minute," she reused his excuse. Pleasure frazzled, her eyes softened as he kissed the arch of her foot, then her ankle, carrying on up her leg. *They couldn't make love.* Feathering tender kisses up her abdomen to her chest, she arched her back. *She shouldn't close her eyes.* His lips came towards hers. She melted into his embrace as he seduced away inhibitions. Kissing her like it was the last time, he made her forget her reservations. Wrapped in his arms, she felt adored. *Damn it, Tiberius.* Grabbing a handful of his hair to part their lips, her eyes softened, as he grinned. *He was a kinky guy. He was messing with her.*

Gazing into her eyes, he whispered, "Every time we meet up, I'm saying it."

"What?" She asked, loving the way he looked at her.

"Fuck me or kill me," he flirted with the Dragon and their final hours were lost in an unfiltered hedonistic blur.

26
Unfortunate Liaisons

Waiting for Ankh, Tiberius reminded, "Tell Ankh, there was another attempt to force you to put your ability into a blade."

"I forgot about it," she replied lost in satisfied peace.

Unrolling the windows, he reminisced, "That job is forever engrained in my memory. You lit yourselves on fire like badasses, taking Guardian Spawn out of Abaddon's game."

"I woke up in your trunk," she added as he took her hand.

"We stayed at the same hotel and hooked up for the first time," he regaled their adventure, caressing her fingers.

"Grey lit you on fire," she reminded, staring at their joined hands. *She was going to climb onto his lap if he kept doing that.*

"Let's avoid bringing him to future booty calls. I gave him permission to light me on fire. I enjoy having skin," he teased, gazing into her eyes.

Future booty calls. "There's no need for labels," Lexy clarified.

"My thoughts exactly," he replied, letting go of her hand as a car approached. "We'll part single and keep our emotions in stasis. If you're seeing someone when we bump into each other, I'll respect it. If not, maybe we'll kick each other's asses for show and hook up."

Lovely long winded let's hook up speech. She taunted, "It's over the second we go back to our respective Clans."

He called her out, "Lexy Abrelle, you don't want to end our affair with a boldface lie."

Wanting to kiss him, a door opened. *They had company.* She grabbed her bag and got out.

Frost wandered over, teasing, "I'm alone. No need to leap away from each other."

"How's your girlfriend?" Tiberius greeted his brother.

Peering in the window, Frost revealed, "They crashed. Aries Group divers recovered their shells. We don't have all the information yet."

"If she's with Emery, she's fine," Tiberius assured.

Giving the roof a pat, Frost walked away, saying, "Kill you later, brother."

They got into the truck. As the engine purred, she sighed, "Was that necessary?"

"Damn straight it was," Frost chuckled, pulling out.

Looking back until Tiberius was a speck in the distance, Lexy exhaled. *Back to her regularly scheduled afterlife.* Adjusting her mindset as the skyline darkened, she deterred thoughts of the adventure she'd left in the rear-view by concentrating on the tire's mesmerizing hum. When Frost didn't speak, she teased, "What? No hooking up with the enemy is bad speech?"

"From me? I'm the reason it exists," Frost chuckled with eyes on the road.

He wasn't wrong.

"Snacks are in the console," Frost offered.

Smart guy. Lead with snacks. "How's Grey? Did we find Markus? Is Arrianna back yet?" She asked while unwrapping a chocolate bar.

"When I left, Grey and Orin were in a passive aggressive

standoff. No clue where Markus is. Jenna says Arrianna will be back soon."

Sensing the tiff had something to do with her, she asked, "Why are Grey and Orin fighting?"

"Remember these symbols on our hands. We get triggered when one of us is in danger. We can ignore injury, but your repeated demise set off Grey."

Oh, shit. She'd selfishly wanted to be a separate entity, but she wasn't. She was in a marriage of souls with everyone in Ankh. The side effects of her dying repeatedly hadn't crossed her mind.

"Last night must have been the death Olympics," Frost replied, looking her way. "We haven't slept. Orin put Grey down. We resurrected your Handler when the Aries Group assured us the job was over. Earlier today our Oracle went into a screaming trance. Everyone's ears were bleeding. I suffocated Jenna with a pillow. Orin took out Grey again. They woke them up after I left."

"Guess a warm welcome is out?" Lexy remarked, staring out the window.

"We have roughly an hour to get the story straight. I'll be your explanation trial run," he offered.

Deciding nobody needed to know the personal aspects, she filtered day one, "We were human trafficker bait at a resort. We were supposed to get kidnapped by the following afternoon and taken to the second location. Aries Group Agents were caught planting tracking devices on a yacht and the timeline sped up. The pirates were affiliated with Abaddon. They have a murder island for wealthy serial killers and immortals. They drop everyone off at cabins, bid on areas, and go on a murder spree. We were taken separately and brought to a compound full of hostages. They knew I wasn't mortal. I bartered myself to free Tiberius, so he could save an agent and a benefactor's daughter. Witches wanted my blood to bind monsters to the island. These were the idiots who resurrected Leonard. They needed a lunar event and enamoured newlywed sacrifices to resurrect his girlfriend."

"Frigging Leonard. I hate that guy," Frost mumbled.

She continued, "He didn't need my blood. I was played. The guy tossed me into a cave full of giant spiders and told me I had thirty minutes to escape to save my friends."

"That's funny," he commented.

"I made it to a cabin where I killed psychopaths and caught up with Tiberius, the agent, and pack of mortals who died horrifically while we were fending off chainsaw wielding psychopaths and supernatural creatures."

"So, you had fun?" Frost deduced, smiling.

"Yeah, but it was a shit show. This job was supposed to help me learn how to use my Guardian abilities. If mortals didn't get involved, I could have cleared the island. I sacrificed myself in the fight so Tiberius could get away with two mortals. Azariah sent me back. You know, waking up mid dismemberment is unpleasant, so I blew up everything with my mind. I was in pieces so, whatever."

"I see what happened," Frost commented.

"Tiberius assembled me. I tried to turn it off, but I think I hit a dimmer switch," Lexy regaled. "We went back to the compound, smashed a helicopter, sunk yachts, and freed some of Lucien's Lampir encased in stone. They were sent after survivors. We separated clearing the compound. I got stabbed with one of those swords by a hallucination of my Handler. I trapped a witch in a bubble and drowned with pirates in a botanical garden. I've also been disembowelled, dismembered, shot and blown up. I lost count of how many times I died. Every time I was shoved back to reality by a Guardian and told to suck it up. Basically, my training went horribly."

Listening intently, Frost said, "It sounds like this job was about choosing when to use a dimmer switch. Did any mortals survive?"

"A few Aries Group Agents were healed by Lampir. They

had a slot of time wiped by Tiberius and were sequestered by the Aries Group until the venom is out of their system." *She'd better leave the sexy agent she brought back from the dead out of it.*

Turning into a campground, Frost enquired, "How many mortals did they have?"

"Twelve rooms with three in each room," Lexy answered. "There could have been more. I didn't even look in the rooms across the hall. It was a no chance scenario."

"I bet you haven't slept. I'll explain everything," Frost said, as they pulled up to her Clan sitting by flickering campfire.

She'd barely slept. Pondering the idea of skipping pleasantries, she said, "I should talk to Grey."

"What happened before murder island doesn't matter," her Siren friend whispered, meeting her gaze.

Whore island.

Catching inner commentary, he rationed, "Has Grey ever given you a blow by blow of a booty call?"

Never. Smiling, Lexy said, "No."

"I'll tell everyone what happened. Go to sleep," Frost prompted.

With no will to argue, she got out of the truck. Walking past, all eyes turned to her.

"Look what the cat dragged in," Sami slammed.

Insect. With a swipe of her hand, the lippy teen soared into the fire, landing with an explosion of floating embers. *That was fun.* Going inside his pitchy shrieks put a skip in her step.

The group playing scrabble at the table froze instead of running for the door when their symbols flashed. Grinning, Zach greeted her, "Hi Lex."

"Hi Zach," she played nice.

"Problem?" Her sister's Handler probed, sipping whatever was in his plastic pink flamingo wine glass.

Grinning, Lexy toyed, "Not anymore. I'm exhausted. Do try to keep it down."

"We'll go outside," Zach offered, getting up.

Climbing onto her bunk, Lexy snuggled under the covers, rolled over, and closed her eyes.

Grey tried to follow Lexy inside. Blocking his friend's path, Frost said, "She won't have to repeat herself if you stay for five minutes."

After sending the untested Ankh for a walk, Frost relayed the existence of murder island and the mayhem of having the Aries Group and mortals in the mix when all hell broke loose.

With chairs encircling a crackling fire, the seasoned Ankh listened, and when he paused the story, their Oracle said, "How many mortals did she have to put down?"

"Only a few agents survived," Frost replied.

Jenna whipped her stick, sending a flaming marshmallow soaring his way.

It landed on his crotch. Panicking, Frost whapped himself in the nards, putting out flames.

"That's for snapping my neck," Jenna decreed.

Dumping hot chocolate on Frost's lap, Grey said, "You're welcome."

Smoke pirouetted from singed material. Scowling, Frost complained, "These were my favourite shorts."

"I decide who gets taken out," Jenna reprimanded.

"You were shrieking like an Oracle does to subdue powers after Testing," Frost explained.

"Have I done it before?" Jenna questioned, staring at Orin.

"That was new," Orin answered.

"I'm close enough to link to Lexy's memories." Closing her eyes, Jenna concentrated. Her eyes opened with only a slit of white. Blinking as she came out of it, their Oracle sighed, "If that actually happened, I'm in deep shit."

"What?" Grey pressed, concerned.

"Did you dispose of your burner phone with his number?" Jenna asked, staring at Lexy's Handler.

"It's in my pocket." Grey tossed it to her.

Assuming the leader of Triad's name was the one saved as Dip Shit in Grey's contacts, Jenna explained, "Let's hope Tiberius covered her ass with the Aries Group."

She texted,

> "Jenna here. I wasn't able to intervene in that coastline alteration issue. How big was the rift?"

The phone buzzed with his response.

> "Tiberius here. A seismic event took a portion of the mountainside, but a cave system channelled most of the blast into the ocean. We've intercepted the local authorities. Lucien's crew is here to help with clean up. Dealing with it right now."

Relieved, Jenna texted,

> "Is there anything else I should know?"

Less than a minute later the phone vibrated with his response.

> "Witches from every Coven were taken to resurrect Leonard. Artifacts are missing. Tri-Clan wasn't informed. I'm concerned about lack of Treaty follow through. Setting up a joint effort with Lucien's crew and Trinity to gage the threat. Are you in?"

> "We'll check the status of the west coast Covens on our way,"

Jenna texted.
The phone vibrated and she read it.

> "You should know, they used imagery of Lexy's Handler to take another run at her with one of those swords. Duty calls. The Dragon was heroic. Fry that phone."

Pressing a sticky patch on the back, Jenna tossed it into the fire, announcing, "It's my job to stop one of you from altering a coastline. If I have to answer for this during training, I'll be choked. Was she agitated on the drive back?"

"Have we shifted Lexy's sanity margin so far tossing a lippy newbie in a fire pit isn't a red flag?" Frost answered, grinning.

With a handful of marshmallows, Grey passed the bag to Jenna, saying, "Ammo?" They commenced pitching uncooked marshmallows at Frost, laughing.

Grey got up to go inside. Grinning, Jenna urged, "Don't wake her. She's tuckered out from the murder spree."

"That's the best time to wake a Healer," Orin whispered.

Under his breath Grey mumbled, "Danger whore."

"Takes one to know one," Orin taunted, as he went inside.

"Guess Sami learned a lesson about pissing off Dragons," Zach whispered.

Shoving him, Mel teased, "You ran her over with a truck."

"I was Triad. I would have dropped a house on her to get away," Zach defended his actions. "Why bring up traumatising shit? She threatened me for a year."

27

Happy Endings

Lexy woke in her Handler's arms. Remaining still, she smiled.

Hugging her tighter, Grey teased, "I know you're awake."

Shifting to face him, their eyes met. Words vanished as happy domestication shoved the feral beast into the muck. Mesmerised by his angelic pale blue orbs in near darkness, she whispered, "Sorry I made you freak out. Heard you got your neck snapped."

Tucking crimson tresses behind her ear, he whispered, "No need to apologize for being repeatedly killed. How are you feeling?"

"Peaceful," she confessed, soothed by his presence.

He tenderly kissed her forehead, saying, "Glad you're back."

"Me too," she answered.

With their friend zone securely in place, Grey quietly teased, "Just so you know. I'll be throwing myself into a slew of slutty hook-ups while you have your enemy romance."

"I'd expect nothing less," Lexy said as her afterlife aligned. *Maybe they really could find a way to stay where hearts don't get broken at the crack of dawn and he didn't have the urge to light her booty calls on fire?*

"Your inner dialogue is coming in loud and clear," he teased. "That's the plan. After the beach slaughter, our Guardian helped me understand what you need right now, and why."

Caressing his face, she smiled. *It was like they'd never parted.*

"Everyone's eating breakfast," Grey sang, whipping the blanket off. "I'll meet you out there."

So perky this morning. Unenthused, Lexy stretched and went to the washroom to get ready.

Wandering outside, she didn't recognize the campsite. *She'd resurrected way too many times in the last forty-eight hours. Her memory was overkill sketchy.* Everyone was slightly out of focus. She chose a muffin while Grey poured her coffee. Biting into an apple cinnamon muffin while taking in the aroma of blossoming trees, her eyes drifted towards her sister's Handler.

"Morning Lex," Zach said, snatching a muffin.

Grinning, she responded, "Morning Zach."

Grey whispered, "He's a Healer now."

"I know," Lexy answered, sipping coffee. *A Siren too. That was going to cause a shitload of drama.*

A breath of fresh air floated by with silky midnight tresses glistening in sunlight. Ankh's magical distraction, Lily poured herself a coffee, saying, "It's a beautiful day."

Ugh. Morning people. Seeing empty seats by Frost, she nudged Grey, and they wandered over.

Sitting down, Grey started a conversation, "What's going on with Kayn and Emery?"

"Following a trail of assassins," Frost replied, drinking his coffee.

That made sense. She glanced at Grey, watching their jaded Snow White feeding a sparrow.

Even after a lusty excursion to whore island, her Handler's fascination with Lily still irked her. Concentrating on the bird, Lexy thought, *want some muffin?* Its head bobbed up. They stared each other down. *Have some, birdie.* It didn't budge from the raven-haired Siren's palm. *Maybe it sensed her predatory nature?*

Frost made a kissing noise. The coveted sparrow flitted over and landed on his palm. He whispered, "Everything in nature wants to eat or mate with you. Birds appreciate the simplicity of our beautiful feathers. Siren require specific energy. Birds aren't on our menu. In a pinch, a Healer can feed from any lifeform." He pointed and his fair weather feathered friend flew back to Lily's waiting hand.

She vaguely recalled eating a Sea Gator. Her spine tingled. *Shit. What now?* "Heads up!" Lexy shouted, standing.

Everyone leapt up. Glancing back at the new Ankh, Jenna instructed, "Grab a weapon."

Greenery rustled as rabid salivating Lampir burst out of the bushes. One shook and spittle rained on her. *Nooooo! She didn't like it! Ahhhhh!*

Tuned into her distress, Grey whispered, "All good, Lex?"

Gross. Catching the blade Astrid pitched her way, Lexy sighed.

"Are they rabid?" Dean asked, clutching a knife.

"Excessive salivation is what happens when a Lampir with a God complex try to make Lycanthrope hybrid," Grey whispered.

Like he'd been introduced, a pretentious Lampir in dated brown velvet pants and an ivory puffy wristed shirt strode out of the jungle, announcing, "It is I, Eugene of Imporia!"

Imporia?

Relaxing his stance, Frost asked, "Why are you interrupting our breakfast, Eugene?"

"A heathen has defiled my mate's purity," he accused.

Everyone looked at Frost. Fighting to keep a straight face, he said, "I have a girlfriend."

That was adorable.

"Who fed a Lampir?" Their Oracle questioned, eyeballing the Ankh. Her gaze landed on Orin.

Busted by his grin, Orin confessed, "My bad. I hooked up with a Lampir in a gas station bathroom when I filled up the rig."

"She fed her friends," Jenna reprimanded, swatting him.

"I can see that," Orin chuckled, rubbing his arm.

"Dude," Zach whispered, shaking his head.

"What? She was hot," their free-spirited friend bantered.

She could eat. Moving a hand in shimmering light, Lexy siphoned swirling Aura particles. Sensing her Handler inching closer, she dodged contact, warning Grey with narrow eyes. *I'm hungry.*

Her Handler piped into her thoughts, *'You can't eat every immortal who has a dispute.'*

Why not? Tuning into the rant about heathens, she squinted as it spewed nonsense. *She needed it to shut up.*

It stormed at her, demanding, "Kneel before me foul depravity!"

Nope. Lexy ripped off Eugene's head and tossed it into the bushes. The rest of him flamed. Hybrid attacked. In a blur of yelps, the inconvenience was resolved. As ash rained, Lexy said, "I was done listening."

"Caught that," Grey chuckled, calming feral rage by putting his arm around her.

She couldn't be mad now. Smiling, Lexy commented, "Sneaky."

"I do my best," Grey teased, side-hugging her.

With murdery vibes vanquished, he kissed her cheek and her Handler pliable heart turned to squishy goo. She mumbled, "You suck, Greydon Riley."

Grinning, he playfully shoved her, saying, "You love me."

Always and forever. Damn his endearing smile.

"Set up the tombs in the back of the rig," Jenna instructed, picking up garbage.

Walking past, Grey mumbled, "Danger whore." Orin chuckled.

Jenna tossed a garbage bag at him, directing, "You can take out the trash for interrupting breakfast." Grinning, at his ex's disdain, Orin wandered away.

Unruly behaviour turned her crank. Watching Grey cleaning up garbage, she faintly recalled being told to kiss her Handler's ass because he had the patience of a saint. Sensations flickered through her mind of darkness, soft feathers beneath her, and sightless hedonism. *She was used to having missing time and Dragon state deviances returning in glimmers of thought, but the feathers threw her off. Was this missing time in the other world? She hoped it was. She needed distractions to vent unsustainable libido requirements that even passing thoughts of her two-day lusty murder island free for all summoned. She wanted to see him. It had only been one day. She had to focus this into something else.* Experiencing a twinge, she swatted a wasp and plucked a stinger from her thigh. Aroused by watching the wasp squirm, her eyes darted to Grey. *Oh, no. Everything made her hungry or horny now. She had shit to do. This was inconvenient. Ahh. She had to take herself down a notch. She had a knife in her hand five seconds ago. Where was it?*

Frost complained, "Eugene got ash on the muffins."

Searching for a weapon, Lexy slammed, "Nobody gives a fuck about your muffins Frost!" *Whoops, she said that out loud.*

"Problem?" He baited, entertained by her frazzled state.

As pain triggered libido shifted to murderous intent, Lexy cautioned, "Don't come any closer."

"If you need to feed your ability," Frost offered his hand.

"You can't," she backed away.

"Why not?" He provoked, following her.

"You know why," she hissed, swatting him. He smacked her back. *Oh, you did not!*

Frost scolded, "Talons down, Dragon. Go have a shower."

What? He pointed at her blood-spattered shirt. *Ohhh. That made sense.* "I need a knife," Lexy stated.

"Why does it feel like I'm going to regret this?" Frost said, passing her his.

She sliced her hand. Blood seeped but it healed instantly. Sawing her wrist accomplished nothing.

Leaning in, Frost whispered, "What do you need?"

Since he asked. She shanked him. *That felt good.*

Staggering, Frost shouted, "Handler Boy! Your Dragon!"

Both Zach and Grey looked. *That was funny. Her sister wasn't even here.* Her eyes darted to the morbidly fascinated newbies. Willing injury she gripped the blade so hard blood trickled through her fingers.

Coming towards her, Grey soothed, "Having an issue, Hun?"

Wandering off to find a Healer with pressure on his wound, Frost bantered, "No shit, Sherlock!"

That was hilarious. Her Handler captured her in a hug. *She was going to be getting a lot of unsolicited cuddles if she didn't figure out how to pat down her horns.*

"Now, I need to change too," Grey whispered, hugging her tighter.

Tossing a wet cloth, Zach called out, "Heads up!"

Catching it, Grey wiped blood off her face, shouting, "Grab us clean shirts?"

This was one of the ten million reasons why she adored him.

Catching her inner dialogue, Grey smiled and said, "If it isn't clear, I adore you back. I'm curious though."

"About what?" She asked as he cleaned around her ears.

Her Handler probed, "When I walked away you were fine. Five minutes later, you stabbed Frost. Why?"

Opting for honesty, she revealed, "A wasp stung me. I was turned on, and hungry. I cut myself, but it didn't work. Frost offered to help so I stabbed him. I was going to heal him, but he tattled."

Latching onto her confession, Grey whispered, "Stings turn you on?"

"Pain does," Lexy confirmed with palpable tension. "It's a Healer thing."

"Ahhh," Grey responded, visibly turned on.

Zach interrupted, "Here's your shirts."

She took hers off wearing a lacy bra. Grinning, Zach turned away.

Watching her put on the shirt, Grey toyed, "Are you wearing matching panties?"

Their Oracle shouted, "Get your asses in the rig!"

Chuckling, her Handler jogged away. *She really didn't want to obey orders anymore.* Casually following her Handler, Lexy played along.

Feeding birds muffins, Big Sexy teased, "Do you usually rip a guy's head off to end a conversation?"

"Long winded speeches aren't my thing," Lexy sparred, marching up the ramp to where Frost, Lily, Jenna and Grey were waiting. *Guess this was the murder crew. Where were the newbies?*

Clasping her shoulder, Grey responded to her thought, "I'd imagine they're hesitant to go anywhere with us after watching you rip a guy's head off."

If she'd lost any Dragon cred for hooking up with an enemy, she'd regained it. She tossed the Ankh stone in her palm as the newbies came up the ramp. A hologram of her tomb appeared and solidified. *That never got old.*

Everyone else threw rose quartz stones. As they morphed into engraved Ankh tombs, Grey asked, "Are we each taking a newbie?"

"Who do you want?" Their Oracle questioned.

Unable to resist messing with Amar's spawn, Lexy offered, "I'll take Sami." He didn't budge.

"Baby steps. You tossed him into a fire last night," Grey whispered.

Smiling, Lexy instigated, "What's your point?"

Stepping forward like the dark horse Lexy suspected she was, Molly volunteered, "I'll go with you."

Lexy pressed her hand on the grooves. Scraping of stone on stone, as her tomb opened, revealing a rose quartz interior. Wishing they were going in the same tomb, she smiled at Grey.

Sandy blonde hair appeared at the top of the ramp. Orin shouted, "Don't kill me five minutes into training, Lex!"

Climbing in, Lexy bantered, "No promises." She shimmied over to give Molly room, smiling.

The lid ground shut, sealing them in. As the tomb jolted to the side, she smiled as it hummed. Closing her eyes shut as it began to strobe, Lexy shouted, "Don't barf on me!"

"No promises!" Molly yelled over the warbling echo.

Funny. Eighties rock blared from Grey's tomb. Excited to have an extended trip to the in-between without being forced back to the land of the living by her rapid Healing ability, she grinned as Grey hooted. Others joined in as the strobing humming grew brighter and louder until it was deafening. Shrieks of glee echoed as the sensation of being catapulted suctioned them to rose quartz. Spinning upwards without the slightest semblance of control, Lexy laughed like they were on a carnival ride. *She loved this.* It carried on just a smidge too long then paused with her equilibrium in a blur. *Here we go.* Her stomach turned as the stone encasing them vanished.

Plummeting through clouds, wind whipped her skin until light flashed as the white sand desert came into focus. Catching sight of the new Ankh falling, she grinned. Dean and Emma were calmly descending. Sami was trying to stop himself to soon, and Molly passed out. *Unfortunate.* Warm air rushed. Forcing energy away, Lexy landed like a goddess, crouching in silken sand next to Ankh as two newbies created sandy explosions in the desert. A Pina Colada appeared in her hand. *A curly straw. Nice.*

Grey wandered over, saying, "I told him to get you one."

"Who?" Lexy pretended she didn't know.

"Well played," Grey whispered, looking up.

Molly was out cold during her next re-entry. Shitty.

"She can't stop. She's unconscious!" Dean panicked, moving beneath her with raised hands. He tried to slow her descent by forcing his energy up. Molly squashed him in the desert.

Scenery flashed. "Where is Dean?" Emma asked, walking over to where his body was. He materialized. She tripped over him and looked up. All she had time to say was, "Shit."

Chuckling, Frost sat down, saying, "Get comfortable. This may take a while." Everyone sat on the sand as the scenario played out again.

As Emma and Dean materialized with no time to get out of the way, and Molly's body took them out like an airplane toilet seat, Sami commented, "Fun training."

Attaching this kid was going to be hard.

"Bet Orin is choked," Grey whispered.

Raking fingers through the sand like the in-between was her macabre Zen Garden, Lexy snickered. *This was funny.*

"How many demises are we at?" Frost chuckled, crossing his legs, thinking up a cocktail.

She hadn't laid a finger on anyone.

Their Oracle hinted, "Nothing you can do, Sami?"

Watching the bizarre scenario, Sami said, "We've established stepping in won't help."

Molly thudded again. Lexy shook her head. *Holy shit, kid.*

A new form flickered. Twitching his fingers in the sand, Orin gasped, "What in the hell?" His eyes narrowed on Lexy.

The Dragon of Ankh cackled, "I'm going to pee."

Getting up, Orin accused, "You killed me in under five minutes."

Their Oracle laughed, "Check it out."

Standing there, Orin watched the bizarre scenario unfold and reset. "How did this happen?" He questioned, amazed.

"Molly passed out in the tomb. The landing redo is happening too fast for her to regain consciousness. Dean got squashed trying to stop her descent. Emma went to help. She tripped over Dean when he materialized with no time to get out of the way and was squashed by Molly."

Impressed, Orin said, "Diabolical." Noticing Samid hanging out, he prompted, "Do something. This is time sensitive kid."

"Lack of action based on intelligence isn't a bad thing," Sami answered, watching.

Identifying with detachment, Lexy reminded, "If all our Healers die while you're twiddling your thumbs, our Guardian will be pissed."

Blinding light flashed to reset the scene. As they materialized, Sami shouted, "Roll out of the way!"

This wasn't about survival. The purpose of training was to imprint their Sacrificial Lamb duties as instinct. All for one and one for all. You can't escape any version of death in Immortal Testing. If you avoid a demise, it keeps happening.

Disintegrating into sand, Orin complained, "I wanted to see how it plays..." Silenced mid-sentence, he blew away on the breeze.

Light flashed as the next drained Healer materialized in the in-between. Twitching her fingers in warm sand, Mel looked up as Molly limply dropped from the sky, squashing her friends.

Sami nervously looked her way, saying, "Give me a minute."

"Oh, take your sweet ass time. It's not like we're dying or anything," Mel bantered. "I didn't get to use the washroom before Orin died. I'm slitting my throat and coming back to kick his ass if I peed myself."

Loudly slurping the last of her slushie drink, everyone turned. Lexy offered, "I'll snap his neck to reset it."

Mel disintegrated into ivory granules, as she healed in the land in the of the living becoming one with clean slate desert.

With the scenario relentlessly playing out, they watched Sami do nothing until the next immortal killed by indecision materialized. Astrid got up, explaining, "The Healers used me as a battery."

Frost chuckled, "Ohhh, you're in trouble."

Raking a hand through her short hair, Astrid wandered over to Sami, asking, "What's the issue?"

"I'll die," Sami replied, gathering the nerve to be irrational.

"Is he serious?" Astrid questioned, glancing at their Oracle.

With resolve, Jenna sighed, "I've been spread thin with new Guardian and childbirth drama. We knew attaching this one would be a lot of work."

In a flicker of white light, their oldest Healer reappeared. Beyond irritated, he brushed off sand. Orin got up and decreed, "Haley and Zach aren't a year out of Testing. They won't be able to sub in for much longer. Kill him and call it."

She'd never felt more attracted to him. With crimson hair rippling in breeze, Lexy threatened, "Get your ass over there and help or I'll rip your arm off and beat you to death with it. One… two…"

"Lex," Grey cautioned, getting between her and the newbie.

"She won't do it," Sami said, backing away.

Not addressing her directly was a mistake. "Three… four…" Lexy continued, dead eyed.

Down with her countdown, Orin wandered over, taunting, "It wouldn't be the first time she beat someone with their own dismembered limb."

"Not even the first time this week," Lexy revealed. "Five… six."

Killian materialized in the sand. Pushing himself up, Big Sexy took in the warped scenario.

Leaping and waving, Sami tattled, "She's threatening me!"

"I've got this," Killian said, situating himself between her and Sami.

She wasn't done counting.

Disappointed in the teen listing off excuses to avoid heroism, Killian confessed, "This is my fault. I've got it."

"What are you doing? You wouldn't!" Sami shouted, flailing as Killian launched him into the path of Molly's descending body. Landing by Emma and Dean, Sami looked up, saying, "Shit," as they all vanished into an ivory cloud.

As the air cleared, everyone gathered at the crater, peering in. *It was empty. Nobody was descending from the sky, and no one materialized on the sand. Guess, that was fixed.*

A shadow passed over Killian's demeanour. "I branded and snapped his neck myself. The kid's never had to prove himself worthy of anything."

Caressing his shoulder, Jenna teased, "It took you weeks to admit that."

Confused, Killian said, "Why would you let me come here to train a kid I destroyed?"

Gazing into his eyes, their Oracle said, "You don't need to apologize. I know your backstory."

"Ahhh. Those infamous missing decades, I pretend I haven't caught onto," Killian sparred, looking away.

Their Oracle assured, "All of us have erased time."

"That's why I haven't bitched about it," Killian said, smiling.

"It's best to not air complaints to the person taking your Karma hit," their Oracle whispered, smiling.

Wincing, Killian whispered, "Sorry."

"What does that mean?" Astrid questioned.

Leaning closer, Orin whispered, "Our Oracle pays for our sins."

"That job must suck. We never behave," Astrid whispered. *Shitty deal. She'd just blown up a mountain.*

Eavesdropping on their chat, Jenna grinned.

"I've admitted to spoiling a child and destroying his afterlife. Now what?" Killian said with his arm around their Oracle.

She'd heard Sami's I didn't get to make a choice rant. She hadn't caught the severity of that confession.

"It's too late for a one-way trip through the hall of souls." Jenna addressed the Ankh, "This is why we aren't allowed to brand anyone who hasn't passed through their Correction."

Shit. About that.

Jenna responded to Lexy's inner dialogue, "You get off on a technicality."

Grey chuckled. Lexy swatted him. *He was his regular carefree vibe. He wasn't fixated on her hooking up with Tiberius.* Her pulse raced. *Damn it.* Steamy images of their escapades flooded her thoughts. *Even thinking his name revved her libido. Shit. She needed to shut this down.* Abruptly walking away, Lexy didn't even exhale until there was plenty of space between her thoughts and everyone else.

The sky darkened as smears of auburn, lilac and scarlet lured her back to a passion so intense it blurred reality. *She'd never had a chance to lose herself in that way. She wanted more.* Wiggling her toes, granules of ivory sand slipped between them. *Could she find him?* Urgency, blurred duty. *No, no. What was she thinking? This was a training exercise.* Sensing Grey, she stifled her thoughts, *chicken noodle, potato soup, french onion, beef barley.*

Her Handler approached, teasing, "When you start listing varieties of soup, I know you're trying to block me."

Facing him, Lexy confessed, "It was yesterday. I'm trying."

Cupping her face, he affirmed, "I know you are." He

tenderly kissed her forehead. As his warm lips parted with her skin, Grey whispered, "It's best if you don't give everyone a blow by blow of your jobs with Tiberius."

Right... Jobs. Whore island.

"What?" Grey questioned, walking away with her.

"Murder island," Lexy corrected, straight-faced.

Putting his arm around her, he suggested, "Adjust your focus and you won't obsess about it."

"You are being way too calm about this," she said, enjoying their conversation.

Steering her back towards the others, Grey confessed, "I'm still jealous. Just at peace with it, I guess."

They felt like they used to. All unconditional love, no games.

As they re-joined everyone, their Oracle taunted, "Sticking around for the lecture?"

Aware it was sarcasm, Lexy provoked, "My attention span is sketchy. Can we speed it up?"

"Sure, I'll rush through it for you," Jenna toyed, smiling.

Good. She had shit to do. Lexy questioned, "Is there a decision about Amar's punishment?"

"He's being erased from Sami's memory, limited contact for twenty years," Jenna revealed.

"Perfect. Let's compel attachment to a family and redo his Correction," Lexy suggested. *Problem solved.*

"I'm sure Azariah will grant us permission to murder a family of mortals to fix our mistake," Jenna bantered.

She was saucy today. Lexy reworded it, "Tiberius erases a slot of time and gives them a backstory."

"Triad's Guardian doesn't have a moral compass. Emery lets Tiberius do whatever he wants," Jenna countered.

Emery?

Clicking in that everyone heard her misspeak, Jenna cursed. Raising her hands, white light strobed. Everyone crumpled on the sand but Lexy. Scowling at the disobedient

Dragon, their Oracle decreed, "I can't maintain order if you override my will." She raised her hands.

Amused, Lexy cautioned, "Try it. I'll freeze time and leave you naked with Orin in a naughty pool."

"You wouldn't," Jenna called her bluff with light breeze shifting her chestnut locks.

"Try me," Lexy challenged, getting in her face.

Stubbornly puffing her chest, Jenna provoked, "Submit or I'll screw your Handler and erase him."

This was getting hot. No question. She was into girls too.

"Stop flirting," Jenna scolded, maintaining their eye contact standoff.

"I didn't say anything out loud, but if you're into it," Lexy sparred, entertained by her new ability to throw off her Oracle's game.

Shaking her head, Jenna pointed at her then back at herself, saying, "Huge conflict of interest." As everyone stirred, she warned, "Not a peep."

Flat on his back, clutching his head, Frost complained, "Stop doing that."

Wait... Was Emery, Seth? Holy shit. Noooo. Emery slept with Grey, Orin, and Frost for sure. Gross. Her mind was going to explode.

"Damn it, Lexy! Filter!" Jenna waved her hand again and everyone collapsed in the sand.

This was messed up. Lexy backed down, "I don't want to know this. Erase it."

Their Oracle sighed, "Do you see where everyone else is? I don't think I can."

Holding his head, Frost hissed, "Holy shit. Stop doing that." Everyone got up, confused.

"Killian and Grey can stay. Everyone else, go find the newbies," Jenna directed. With a clap of her hands, they vanished in a flash of light.

At Lexy's side, Grey asked, "Why am I staying?"

"Killian needs memories altered and I'm way too exhausted to deal with this one's attitude," Jenna explained.

They had company. Scowling, Lexy mumbled, "Shitty ambiance is lurking."

Wide-eyed, their Oracle reprimanded, "Omniscient beings don't play games with disrespectful half breeds."

She knew who shitty ambiance was. That was funny.

"Uncle Emmanuel does," Lexy decreed. With an insolent smirk, Ankh's crimson-haired Dragon slammed, "That stealth cunt is enjoying this." Boisterous laughter boomed. Lexy shouted, "I knew you were revelling in the shit show!"

Absolutely livid, Jenna hissed, "What are you doing?"

Lexy asked, "Why would I play nice with a see-through dickhead who locked me in a box of spiders like he was scolding a newb?"

"You're forgetting your place again," baritone boomed from everywhere.

Giving the air the bird, Lexy provoked, "I'm a frigging Guardian, you flaccid dick! You can't do shit to me! We're equals!"

The omniscient relation pressed her trigger, "You are an insolent thing whose sole purpose is to be fed on and defiled."

Right in the childhood.

Without saying a word, Grey laced his fingers through hers, whispering, "Hope you know what you're doing."

Their connection worked its magic, broiling rage simmered, leaving only a whisper of steam. Calmly, Lexy offered, "Show yourself and I'll give you a do over."

Granules rose swirling into an ivory sand cloud, solidifying into Emmanuel's physical representation wearing gossamer Greek attire. Coming towards the four, the Guardian toyed, "You'll find, you get more with sugar than salt."

"In my line of work salt is favourable to sugar," Lexy replied, strolling towards him.

Grinning, Emmanuel teased, "If you argue with everything I say, you won't have a chance to ask questions."

"You've been eavesdropping. You know what we want," Lexy sparred with a smile.

"Ahh, you want permission to erase the memory of an Ankh causing problems. Is laughing about the irony allowed?" Her uncle toyed as they started walking.

"If you must," Lexy bantered with Grey at her side.

"I was the one who sent Amar's spawn through without a speech after the big guy snapped his neck," Emmanuel revealed. "When I wipe this spawn, I get to play with him to determine his worth." He addressed their Oracle, "No toll leniency."

"Do your worst," Jenna responded.

The Being's face crinkled into a wide smile. "Paying their tolls for over a millennium without flinching. How noble."

Jenna responded, "I do the spells, I pay the price."

"You have to do spells because Ankh is full of feral horny train wrecks," he bantered.

It wasn't a lie.

"Azariah wouldn't be pleased you were insulting us," Jenna reminded.

"Even Steven for calling me shitty ambiance. Don't even get me started on stealth cunt." Giggles erupted as Emmanuel addressed Killian, "Amar negotiated with the Third-Tier on your behalf. You keep your memories. They're letting you off easy to make amends for the shit Ricard pulled. You can go now." He clapped his hand and Killian vanished.

"We effectively blocked Third-Tier from your training exercise, but you stopped a fated Lampir turn. Azariah says, you did it, you make up the story. I'll feed the information to your Oracle."

"I'd appreciate you using my name," Jenna clarified.

"I'd appreciate you not screwing my brother while I was

into you, but here we are," Trinity's Guardian sparred, touching her shoulder.

Holding hands with Grey, they disintegrated into the breeze.

Once again encased in rose quartz, Lexy asked, "How are you doing, Molly?"

"That was pointless," Molly sighed.

It sure was. She didn't even get to kill anybody. Her stomach turned as they plummeted. In a nausea-inducing high-speed flat spin, glaring strobes kept their eyes shut until they stopped. *The ride back to reality was always shitty.*

Their rose quartz tombs ground open in unison. Covering her mouth, Molly gagged as she leapt out and ran.

Grinning, Lexy climbed out. *She liked this song.* Moving to the music, she touched her tomb. It became a translucent hologram, then nothing. She retrieved her rose quartz stone and it vanished into her palm. Moving past everyone, she stood at the top of the ramp and closed her eyes. Yearning for more lovers on beaches and less cramped spaces, someone honked. She opened her eyes, laughing.

Leaning out the window of an idling van, Orin rushed, "No rest for the wicked. Your bags are in the van. Let's go."

No rest for the wicked. Fair enough.

The Beginning.

Biography

Kim Cormack is the dark comedy-loving author of the Children Of Ankh Universe. She worked for over 16 years as an Early Childhood educator in preschool, daycare, and as an aid. She's lived most of her life on Vancouver Island in beautiful British Columbia, Canada in the gorgeous town of Port Alberni. She's a single mom with two awesome offspring, an MS fairy fight club participant, and a lover of cats. If you bump into this author, slowly back away and toss packages of hot sauce at her until you escape.

A Note From The Author

I began writing this series shortly after my M.S diagnosis. I had many reasons to fight. I had incredible children, family and friends, but this series gave me purpose. Whenever things become dark, I use my imagination to find the light within myself. No matter what life throws your way, you are stronger than you believe. I hope the character's strength becomes an inner voice for the readers who need it. Stand back up, and if you can't stand, rise within yourself. We are all beautiful as we are. We are all immortal.

Chapter one of Sweet Sleep came from a nightmare that started at a slightly open door and ended with a creepy lullaby. I wrote it down in the middle of the night, and from that dream came a universe that gave me an outlet to thrive. I made a deal with myself to stay true to my imagination and never alter ages or scenarios. Adversity makes you stronger. I vowed to have the guts to let my warped sense of humour ride, and it became a thing. Come with me on this journey. We're going to have so much fun together.

The Children Of Ankh Series Universe

There are many books in this universe to keep you occupied while you await the next one. Read on Dragon lovers.

Children of Ankh Series
Sweet Sleep
Enlightenment
Let There Be Dragons
Handlers Of Dragons
Tragic Fools

Coa Series (Full length books in the same universe)
Wild Thing
Wicked Thing
Deplorable Me
Sacrificial Lamb Club

Coa Novella Series
Bring Out Your Dead (A short novella)

THE CHILDREN OF ANKH SERIES UNIVERSE

Subscribe to The Children of Ankh Universe website and be the first to get updates, contests, and series release info. Hope to hear from you on social media. *"She's a batshit feral hitwoman for a Clan of immortals, and sometimes just a girl in love with a boy destined to be her Handler. The only thing standing in their way is cannibalism and intimacy induced amnesia.*

Jump into Lexy's part of the universe. BUY IT HERE:
www.childrenofankh.com

Manufactured by Amazon.ca
Acheson, AB